ALL
THAT
Really
MATTERS

ALL THAT Really MATTERS

NICOLE DEESE

BETHANYHOUSE
a division of Baker Publishing Group
Minneapolis, Minnesota

Published by Bethany House Publishers
11400 Hampshire Avenue South
Minneapolis, Minnesota 55438
www.bethanyhouse.com

Bethany House Publishers is a division of
Baker Publishing Group, Grand Rapids, Michigan

Printed in the United States of America

Library of Congress Cataloging-in-Publication Data
Names: Deese, Nicole, author.
Title: All that really matters / Nicole Deese.
Description: Minneapolis, Minnesota: Bethany House, [2021]
Identifiers: LCCN 2020046780 | ISBN 9780764234965 (paperback) | ISBN
    9780764238130 (casebound) | ISBN 9781493429929 (ebook)
Subjects: GSAFD: Christian fiction. | Love stories.
Classification: LCC PS3604.E299 A78 2021 | DDC 813/.6—dc23
LC record available at https://lccn.loc.gov/2020046780

Cover design by Jennifer Parker

Represented by Kirkland Media Management

For Mandy

Your unapologetic love for *all things beautiful*
is as inspiring as your unwavering support
for your chosen tribe.
I'm blessed to be counted among them.

I adore you.

◇◇◇

Do nothing out of selfish ambition or vain conceit.
Rather, in humility value others above yourselves,
not looking to your own interests
but each of you to the interests of the others.

PHILIPPIANS 2:3–4

◇◇◇

◆ 1 ◆

Molly

I used to marvel at the way my Great Mimi's arthritic fingers would pinch her eyeliner pencil and trace a perfect stroke of midnight black along her upper lash line. The way her tired, nearly translucent skin would transform into a picture of regal elegance with only a few pats and swipes of color. For an eleven-year-old girl whose mother had never owned a single tube of mascara, it was a magical experience.

I'd watch my Mimi's routine with my elbows propped onto a gold-leaf vanity and eyebrows disappearing behind poorly cut bangs. My mouth would form an opera-worthy O as she became a living, breathing masterpiece, her best features showcased and enhanced, her flaws minimized and concealed.

And in those final few seconds before she closed her makeup drawer and blotted her ruby red lips, she'd hand me her blush brush and say with a wink, "Molly, when you feel good in your own skin, it's easy to help someone else feel good in theirs."

I'd tap the remaining rouge onto the apples of my pale cheeks and smile at the stringy-haired girl in the mirror, promising myself that one day I would do just that: I would help someone else feel the way my Mimi had always made me feel. And now, sixteen years and 606,000 Instagram followers later, I'd kept my promise to that often misunderstood little girl, one emboldened cat-eye and sheer lip tutorial at a time.

Beep! Beep! Beep!

I snapped the compact of my recently reviewed translucent face powder closed—four-out-of-five lip smacks, dinged for a shorter wear life than advertised—and primped my hair one last time in the mirror before following the sound of my oven's cry.

"See, Ethan? I told you I could finish getting ready before the oven preheated. That took what, five minutes? Hey, maybe that could be an idea for a future post series. 'How to Get Date-Ready in Five Minutes or Less.' Or wait—'How to Get Date-Ready in Five Minutes *and* Five Products or Less' is even better. Then I can feature that new Hollywood Nights collection that just came in. I'll have Val add it to the schedule." I rounded the corner into the kitchen, expecting to see my boyfriend on the recliner in my living room. Only he wasn't there.

"Ethan?" I slid the glass pan of chicken marsala into the oven and lifted the charcuterie board I'd spent nearly an hour preparing. There was something strangely satisfying about arranging cheeses, meats, nuts, figs, and olives.

"The chicken will take about forty minutes to bake, but our appetizers will go great with that wine you bought last month. I've been saving it." I wove around the island, gathering the glasses and balancing the cheese board on my palm like the trained wait-ress I was not. If my twin brother were here, this would be his cue to crack a joke about my propensity to drop plates of food, even though that had only happened *one time*. Granted, it had been on Thanksgiving Day, and granted, I had been carrying our twenty-five-pound stuffed turkey, but still, there should be a statute of limitations on bad family jokes.

I continued my balancing act into the living room. "I'm sure your appetite is still on East Coast time, but—" I stopped abruptly at the sight of my boyfriend stretched out on my sofa, eyes closed.

"Ethan?" I set both the appetizers and stemware on the coffee table and tiptoed over to him—quite a feat in four-inch cork-wedge heels. I approached him as if he were a wind-up toy ready to spring into action at any moment, which was perhaps the most fitting description of Ethan Carrington.

But there was no springing.

Apparently it didn't matter how much time a woman spent creating the perfect cat-eye if the man she wanted to impress was unconscious. I crouched low and waved a hand over his face before he released a snore that had me cupping a hand over my own mouth to stifle a laugh. This had to be the most anticlimactic start to a date ever.

I covered him with a vegan angora throw from a boutique in Canada I'd promoted last autumn, then decided to capitalize on the rare moment. After all, Ethan's favorite marketing motto was *Never miss an opportunity to relate to your audience.*

I whipped out my phone and proceeded to take a ten-second story, featuring my adorable sleeping boyfriend, a tray of untouched appetizers, and one pouty-lipped me. I captioned a post with *Jet lag is the thief of romance.*

Not even eight seconds later, my phone began to vibrate with notifications—likes, comments, emojis. An immediate endorphin boost. The temptation to scroll through them proved too much. After all, my manager-turned-boyfriend showed no signs of waking any time soon, and truth was, even if he had woken up, he'd tell me to reply to at least the first twenty or so commenters. Something to do with increased visibility and reach.

> You're so cute, Molly! And so is your boy toy! Hubba hubba . . .

> Ah, sorry girl! But at least that maxi dress is ADORBS on you! Link please???

> Good hair days like that should never be wasted tho. Wake him up already!

I liked a few dozen comments, replying in kind to their emoji strings and creative hashtags, then scrolled through the rest of my feed, hovering over the latest post by Felicity Fashion Fix, the snotty diva and ex-client of Ethan's who once stole an entire vlog series idea from me two days before mine went live. I breathed out my nose the way Val always encouraged me to and tried to let go of the negative static in my chest . . . but not before glancing at Felicity's latest follower count. 415,687. *What?* How on earth did she get such a big jump in followers so quickly? *What is she doing?* Besides stealing other people's ideas, of course.

When Ethan finally began to stir, it took a hefty force of will to silence my phone and shove it in the crack of the chair cushion. Yet I did it with a smile, because that was what committed couples did for each other. At least, that was what I'd read from a popular blogger I followed: *"Healthy couples ignore the pressures of social media to be socially present in their relationship."* I'd saved the pretty graphic to my photo reel just two days ago. Ethan and I didn't get much face-to-face time since he traveled for business roughly three weeks out of the month, but perhaps the strain of a long-distance relationship would dissipate if we practiced being more *socially present* with the time we did have together.

"Hey there, sleepyhead," I crooned from the recliner, where I'd kicked off my shoes and tucked my frozen feet under the skirt of my dress. Most days, springtime in northeast Washington was just a less snowy version of winter. "Welcome back."

He jolted at the sound of my voice and blinked. "Molly?"

"Happy date night."

Ethan rubbed at his eyes again. "What time is it?"

I glanced at the wall clock, surprised at how much time had passed while I'd been scrolling my feed. "A little after six."

He pushed himself up to a seated position. "You should have woken me. I don't even remember dozing off."

"No way, you looked way too peaceful to disturb." And it was nice to see him without a screen on his lap or in his hand. Ethan wasn't the greatest at leaving his work behind. Then again, neither was I. "Besides, you've been up since two in the morning Pacific time. Dozing off for a few minutes seems perfectly acceptable—even for someone as immune to naps as you are."

He ran a hand through his thick butterscotch-colored locks, and my breath actually hitched in my chest at the sight. In no way did he look like a man who'd spent his entire day traveling on an airplane. He smiled at me with those same midnight blue eyes that had won him many a client—myself included.

"Well, I hope you don't hold it against me, because I've been looking forward to tonight. To being with you." His expression cleared, then sharpened on my face. "There's actually something big we need to discuss. I wanted to tell you in person."

The professional tone made my palms grow damp. "Something to do with the agency?" There'd been a lot of changes happening within the Cobalt Group recently. Most had been great—bigger sponsors to partner with their contracted influencers, which, of course, meant bigger paychecks, bigger referrals, and a bigger bottom line. But nobody was immune to the volatile nature of our industry. There was always somebody waiting to rise to the top. Somebody willing to do more at whatever cost.

"Wait," I said, remembering the chicken. "Before you answer that, I need to check on our dinner first."

As if on cue, the oven timer buzzed as I scrambled to my feet to make for the kitchen. But Ethan's hand reached out for mine, and he tugged me toward him. He held out my arm to turn me this way and that. "You look really good, babe. That dress is on point. Did your fans choose it?"

"You'd know if you stopped by my pages more than every couple of weeks," I teased as I swiveled my hips to show the flare of the skirt as it swept over my bare toes. Once again, my online poll had proven itself accurate. This particular maxi dress had won over three other options categorized under "Best Home Date Dress" by nearly seven thousand votes.

I pecked his cheek and unhooked my hand from his. "I've got to get that chicken out or we'll be eating charcoal for dinner." I made my way from the sofa to the kitchen. "Oh, and don't think

I forgot about your promise to take pictures for me while you were at Fashion Week."

He chuckled and slid out his phone from his back pocket. "I managed to take a few, but I doubt they'll meet your queenly standards. Not all of us can be top-trending influencers."

Ethan's hyperspeed mode usually left little time for snapping quality pictures of anything. Over the last nine months of our dating life, I'd received many a blurred selfie—Ethan in front of the Golden Gate Bridge for a triathlon, Ethan wearing his scuba gear on the coast of Fiji, Ethan jumping out of an airplane. There was never much context to his photos, other than his signature cheekbones and jewel-toned eyes, but even in the chaos of his shots, his zest for taking all that life could give him was palpable.

Ethan's all-gas-little-brake personality had found me at the perfect time.

After so many years of playing the role of outsider in a family who strived after intangible things, someone finally understood me—believed in me, even.

Allowing the pan of chicken to cool on top of the stove, I made him up a plate of smoked gouda and dry salami from the charcuterie board, arranging several crackers around the edges, and then poured him a glass of red wine. I placed both on the table and sat next to him. He didn't touch either offering.

Instead, he perched on the edge of my couch as if ready to sprint. "Babe, I had a meeting with Mr. Greggorio yesterday. About you."

About me? Mr. Greggorio was Ethan's partner at Cobalt, only he had about thirty years on Ethan in life and in running a successful marketing agency. His name always sparked a flurry of nerves. Maybe because Ethan had never once referred to him by a name other than Mr. Greggorio. Then again, perhaps wealthy, yacht-owning Italian men who agented all kinds of entertainment, talent, and business professionals didn't have first names? "But my numbers are on the rise. I just passed the six hundred thousand mark."

Ethan turned on the magnetism he was known for. "Oh, he

knows. He's been keeping tabs on you himself. In fact, he's been doing a lot more than that."

I had no response for this. None. Mr. Greggorio didn't deal with influencer riffraff like me. He handled Cobalt's VIP clientele only—partnering with product lines associated with sponsors and companies that ranked in the top brands and corporations worldwide. I wasn't even certain he'd remembered me after our first meeting last year when I signed on as an influencer with them—a low-level one at that. My numbers had barely brushed the one hundred thousand mark, and my brand had been anything but focused. But Ethan had believed in my talent, in what I could do for the fashion and beauty industry as a whole, and he'd signed me on the spot.

We went on our first date just two months later. He'd flown me to dinner at the Space Needle—just under an hour flight from Spokane, Washington.

He stood now and paced my living room floor, his new flat-front chinos flexing with each step without a single winkle in sight—a fashion miracle considering his earlier state of hibernation. He stopped without warning and turned on the heel of his loafer. "He says you have the *It Factor*. The special quality that separates the fakes from the real thing." His grin revealed freshly whitened teeth. "Do you have any idea how many clients Mr. Greggorio has worked with in his lifetime?"

If I was stunned before, then I was practically catatonic now. I gave the tiniest shake of my head.

"Thousands." He laughed. "*Thousands*, Molly!" A wild spark ignited his gaze. "And I'm not the only one he told that to, either. He pitched you to the media moguls at Netflix. They're looking to recruit fresh talent for a new feel-good series slated for next year. And their response to him was, '*Molly McKenzie is already on our radar.*'"

"*What?*" I leapt off the sofa, unsure of what to do with my body other than gawk and flail my arms like a flightless bird. "No. No way. You're lying to me. This can't be real. Tell me you're lying." A scratchy, unrecognizable whisper escaped my throat. "Are you lying?"

He laughed. "Not even I could tell a lie that good."

I flung myself at him, and he caught my waist and spun me around. "Oh my goodness! I know you said it would happen someday, that you'd take my brand places I couldn't even begin to imagine, but I . . . I just can't believe it's actually happening!"

Ethan lowered me to the ground and cupped my face in his hands. "As long as you stay focused on the goals ahead, I will work to make your wildest dreams come true." He smiled as if to let his words soak in. "But before I can submit your official audition to the producers this summer, we need to eliminate every potential weak spot in your résumé to edge out your competitors."

"Sure, of course." Whatever cloud-like euphoria had inflated my entire being only moments ago had sprung a leak. Ethan reached for his briefcase, and just like that, Manager Ethan had shown Boyfriend Ethan to the door.

"I wrote some key targets down for you on my last flight. I know how much you like to visualize your goals."

"Right. Thanks." My gaze dropped to his briefcase as he popped open the lock. "Whatever I need to do, I'll do it."

A slight curve lifted the corner of Ethan's mouth. "That's exactly what I told Mr. Greggorio you'd say."

He scooted the appetizer board and wine glasses to a separate side table.

"So you're wanting to go over all this right now, then?" I asked, glancing back at our cooling dinner.

"Waiting time is wasted time." An Ethan quotable if ever there was one. Ethan was not someone who believed patience was a virtue.

"Right." I took the bullet point list from his hand, and my gaze immediately snagged on the first objective listed.

1 million subscribers

"A million subscribers? By the end of August?"

"Gaining the edge is never easy."

I raised my questioning gaze to his confident one. "But that's . . ." On principle, I didn't say the word *impossible*, but gosh, if there ever was a time for that word, it was right now. "That's almost four hundred thousand subscribers in just three months."

"Yes, it is. And I have a strategy for how to get us there."

"Does it include praying for a miracle?" My joke fell flat with a quick shake of Ethan's head.

"You know I don't believe in miracles. I believe in hard work, dedication, and plenty of grit. All things you have in spades. And all things that make us such great partners." He grabbed another document from his briefcase and laid it out flat. Pie graphs and algorithm reports I didn't have the first clue how to read stared back at me. "Between your campaign photo shoot next week with Hollywood Nights Cosmetics and the endorsement quotes Fashion Emporium is adding to their stores, I estimate your boost will be around twelve to thirteen percent." He traced a line with his finger, indicating the growth he'd already mapped out. "But that leaves a large gap to fill while I work on getting you some more widespread campaigns. We also need to find the right celebrity collaboration, someone who will take your hand and pull you up to their level—I have a few ideas already in the works. But there's something else as well." When he looked up at me, I got that strange woozy feeling I had whenever I glanced down in a glass elevator.

"What?"

"We need to show a different side of you to the public eye, work to expand the reach of the woman behind Makeup Matters with Molly. Which is why item two is so important."

I slid my focus down the page as his second point assaulted me in an entirely new way.

Partner with a human-interest cause

A burning sensation flared in my lower gut, a premonition I knew all too well. "What kind of human-interest cause?"

"It actually needs to be something quite specific." Ethan

leaned in, as if the discovery he was about to share was too confidential for my living room. "After calling in a lot of favors and piecing together several off-the-record conversations, I was able to figure out the producer's hook for the show you'd be in the running to host." He held his breath for a full three seconds. "It's called *Project New You*, highlighting America's underprivileged youth. It will be a more holistic approach to the usual makeover show—not only focused on the physical side of things. The older teens who are featured will be chosen by a nomination system— teachers, mentors, foster parents, etc. The kind of show that leaves you reaching for a tissue and a tub of ice cream by the end of it."

The buoy keeping my hopes afloat sank inch by inch.

I opened my mouth to say something—anything—but then closed it tight again. So many thoughts spun inside my head at once, pinging against memories better left undisturbed. Though I "helped and supported" women on the other side of a digital screen several times a week via makeup tutorials and comparables and as-honest-as-I'm-allowed-to-be product reviews, helping people in the outside world was a different beast entirely. A much scarier, much more exposing beast. One I was quite familiar with, considering both my parents and my brother had given their souls to serve in full-time ministry.

Sometimes I wondered just how many prayer teams around the nation—perhaps the world, even—were committed to praying for the McKenzies' prodigal daughter, the girl who made a living profiting from one of the seven deadly sins: vanity.

Seeing as Ethan and I didn't share much about our pasts, he didn't take my silence for the fear that it was, the fear that stepping too close to the humanitarian line would only end in failure and disappointment for everybody involved. There was only one person in my life who would have believed otherwise, but Mimi had died nearly four years ago. Before I'd even hit five thousand subscribers on the channel she'd encouraged me to start. Had she known this day would come? Had she envisioned me hosting an on-demand show? I could almost feel her fingers rake through my hair as she said, *"Share your spark with the world, Molly. Stop trying to hide what God created to be seen."* Was this the big break she'd been hoping I'd find?

"The producers are going to need to see more of your empathetic side. More heart. More compassion. More generosity and selflessness. They're impressed by your charm and wit, and no one would ever question your natural charisma on screen, but for this to move forward, we need to see the host of Makeup Matters with Molly get her hands a bit dirtier in the muck of real life. Because as it is right now, you're just a pretty face with an addictive personality."

The sting of his words throbbed in the back of my throat, and I swallowed against the ache. I'd never cried in front of Ethan, and I wasn't planning to start now. "I'm more than that."

He glanced up from the paperwork, brows crimped in confusion. "What?"

"I'm more than a pretty face."

"Oh, babe. I know that. Of course I know that." He touched my knee, squeezed, smiled. "But it's my job to assess how you might be perceived by the public eye, even though I know you have the potential to be so much more."

Only, his use of *potential* didn't quite pluck out the insult dart he'd thrown.

"You don't need to look so worried. I've got all this covered for you. It's not like I'm suggesting you go live in a homeless shelter for a month and serve rice and beans with the kitchen staff." He chuckled. "We'll find a good match for you somewhere. Something with older kids that you can pop in to see once a week. Hear some hard stories you can retell, take some heart-jerker pics, and then be done with it. Simple."

He paused, and I could almost feel the way he redirected the energy buzzing around us. "My assistant is already compiling a list of local charities and nonprofits for us to go through. The closest we can get to the premise of the show, the better. Plus, we'll need to steer clear from what other influencers in your space have going on right now. Felicity is—"

"Felicity?" Just the sound of her name made my hackles rise. "What does she have to do with this?"

"Have you seen her latest numbers?" he asked, as if I'd missed a presidential election.

"I may have glanced at them once or twice in the last few weeks."

"Well, since she added the no-kill shelters as a cause she supports, her numbers have skyrocketed. And it's no wonder why. People care *more* about successful people who pay it forward. Partnering with a cause will grow your influence, *and* it will give you a giant leg up in your audition submission."

I huffed a sigh. "I have a hard time believing that any self-respecting animal would choose to be in the same room as Felicity. She's basically the platinum blond version of Cruella de Vil."

"While that may be true," Ethan said, all managerial-like, "the numbers speak for themselves. She's grown nearly eighteen percent across all her platforms in the last four months."

"Eighteen percent?" I slumped back in my chair. "Wow."

"Yep. And," he said, tapping my knee, "I have no doubt you can do even better. You have more personality and charisma in your left earlobe than Felicity Fakes It."

"Felicity Fashion Fix," I corrected on a chuckle, my mood slowly on the rise again.

He curled a long piece of my hair around his finger and tugged gently. "I don't really care what her brand name is because she's not my client anymore, you are." He edged closer to me, taking my hands in his and rubbing his thumb over the inside of my wrists. "You've proven you know how to hook your viewers' loyalty, Molly. Now you need to hook them in the heart. If you can do that, then I can get you a makeover show in front of millions that will make everything you've done to build your brand to this point seem trivial in comparison."

I tried the phrase on for size—*hook them in the heart*—imagining how my twin brother would respond to such a statement.

"Oh!" I sat up straight and flattened my feet to the floor. "I've got it."

"What? A nonprofit we can contact?"

I shook my head. "Not exactly, but I do know the person who can lead me to one. Miles. My brother has a connection to every nonprofit organization within a hundred-mile radius of here." And beyond.

"Ah, yes. The preacher," Ethan said, finally reaching for his glass of wine and reclining back on the sofa. "Weren't the two of you supposed to do an interview together for your channels? I thought I suggested that a few months back—show your viewers the whole twin bonding thing you two have going. Did Val forget to put that on the schedule?"

I tried to ignore the raw way his tone rubbed against me whenever he spoke of my brother. Though he and Miles had only interacted twice, it was abundantly clear that neither of them was going to take up calling each other *bro* any time soon. Truth was, I often felt like a goalie between them, blocking any potential insult and negative jab.

I stood up, slipped between him and the chair, and made my way back to the kitchen. "He's not interested in doing an interview for Makeup Matters, and I'm totally okay with that. It's not his thing."

Ethan laughed. "Why not? Are preachers banned from social media? Is that one of the twelve commandments?"

"Ten."

"Ten what?"

"There are only ten commandments, not twelve."

He pulled out his phone and tapped on the screen, either not hearing me or not caring to respond. "You should really change his mind on that. It's a missed opportunity."

It probably was, and yet I knew my brother. The same way I

knew my parents. Though at least Miles understood some of the benefits to social media and what my career as an influencer actually entailed. My parents, however, shared one flip phone between the two of them with no fancy apps or internet service—all in the name of frugality and stewardship.

As I pulled our plates down from the cupboard, I said nothing more on the topic of my family to Ethan. It was one of the clear boundary lines I'd drawn when we started dating. He hadn't known me as a child or as a lonely teenager searching for her place in a household she'd never quite measured up to. And I liked it that way. The two of us had come from two totally different lifestyles, two totally different histories, two totally different worlds, and perhaps that was what I enjoyed most about being with him. Our pasts didn't have to matter, because all we focused on was the future dreams we chased together. And in that aspect, we were very much the same. Ethan and I were a goal-making, goal-crushing machine. And signing on with his agency had been one of the best decisions I'd ever made.

He believed in me. And perhaps that was the only encouragement I needed to push toward my next goal.

"Hey." He came up behind me and put his hands on my shoulders while I reached for a spatula. "What do you think about skipping the chicken tonight and going out to eat instead? I'm craving that little Italian place downtown, the one with the breaded artichokes and fresh caprese salad." He brushed my hair off my back and planted a kiss to my neck. "We can continue this conversation over a nice plate of veal parmesan. And, bonus, there'll be no dishes needing to be washed."

I glanced down at the chicken I'd been marinating all day, based on a recipe I'd chosen a week ago when he told me he'd be flying into town tonight. "I do love that place, but I've been looking forward to trying this chicken out all week, and—"

He spun me around and touched my chin. "Babe, once this deal goes through, the only meals you'll ever want to try will be cooked by professional chefs. Come on, let me treat you tonight.

I'm proud of you." He went to the door and shrugged on his jacket before removing my blush cardigan from the rustic wall hook and holding it open. "After all, it's not every day I get to celebrate the accomplishments of my best client, who also happens to be my beautiful girlfriend."

• 2 •

Molly

"I need a cause." The words reverberated off the gymnasium walls as if I'd spoken them through a megaphone.

My brother wiped the sweat off his brow with the hem of his shirt—*why are guys so gross?*—and twisted to find me blazing a trail on the polished floor in my taupe booties. Though Miles worked to school his surprise at seeing me here, of all places, I could have spotted the humored twitch of his upper lip from across the Pacific Ocean. He was a terrible actor—truly the worst. He once got cut from our fifth-grade Christmas pageant only three days before curtain call because he couldn't stop his nervous chuckle every time Mary's donkey lumbered on stage, heaving a pillow-stuffed virgin mother. His debut theater career ended abruptly after a fed-up Mrs. Martin told him to bite the inside of his cheeks because there was no such thing as a laughing wise man. To which Miles had smartly replied, *"There was no such thing as a wise man at the nativity scene, either. They came later."*

"Morning, sis. It's nice to see you, too. My trip to Guatemala was great, by the way. Thanks for asking." He chucked the ball at the wall, retrieving it on the bounce back. "You come to play doubles with me?" At this he cracked a full smile. Prior to Miles taking up wall ball on Tuesday mornings at his church gymnasium, I truly believed wall ball was a pretend sport, like the kind playground teachers made up for the athletically challenged to pass recess. Like hopscotch. Or tetherball. But nope, for some unknown reason, my twenty-seven-year-old brother was all about it.

I enunciated my words a second time. "I. Need. A. Cause."

He bounced the red rubber ball twice at his feet. "I heard you the first time, and yet I still have no clue what you're talking about."

After lying awake half the night, strategizing and typing out nonsensical notes for my assistant Val to find in her inbox this morning, I'd convinced myself that Miles was my best hope for finding the right connection to a cause that would offer both experience—for the Netflix producers—and minimal commitment in light of my sixty-hour workweek. The thing was, Miles couldn't know about the possibility of a makeover show. Or even the possibility of an audition for one. Because Miles was . . . well, Miles was a saint among humans. If I was gonna ask for help in his area of expertise, then he'd expect my motives to be pure. Which they were. Sort of.

As he looked to me for an explanation, I worked to recall the heartfelt speech I'd written in my head on the way over regarding the importance of serving others. I hoped my stall seemed genuine enough, and not like I was trying to call up empathy from the depths of my being. "It's come to my attention that I have the platform I have for a reason. Not just to grow a profitable business in the beauty industry but also for a greater vision and purpose."

His expression bordered on intrigue and suspicion, a look I'd seen a few dozen times in our lives, and one I could mimic perfectly. Though we were fraternal twins by birth, our faces were identically expressive. Growing up, I'd envied Miles's unique eye color—a bottomless amber with ribbons of ivy swirling throughout his iris. But his hair color he could keep. It registered three shades darker than my chemically engineered blond highlights, placing him firmly in the same brownish-blond category I was happy to escape by my eighteenth birthday. "What kind of greater vision?"

"To better serve my local community." I paused the adequate amount of time for self-reflection. "Specifically, I'm feeling drawn to the area of hurting, underprivileged young adults." I stopped myself from adding that if those young adults could live within a fifteen-mile driving radius and were available on a time frame of once a week, that would be best.

He blinked, as if not quite sure how to interpret this strange turn of events during his sacred wall ball hour. "And what brought about this *realization*, do you think? Because I specifically remember calling you two weekends ago when I was down three volunteers at our annual job fair for adults in transition. That would have been a great opportunity for you to serve your local community."

"I was in the middle of shooting a two-part series on flat irons, Miles. Val was waiting on me to send her the raw footage so she could edit."

He blinked. "Right."

"Just because I work from home doesn't mean I don't have daily responsibilities to tend to or people waiting on me. Plus, isn't that one of the charities I donate to each month?"

He sighed. "Yes, it is. But as I've said before, we don't call them charities anymore. This isn't 1945. We call them *ministries*."

"Sure, but still—it's not like you can say I don't help you or your *ministries*."

"You're right, Molly," he said in that slow, pastorly way of his. "Your generosity has been a huge blessing to the church over the last couple years. Thank you."

I had the distinct feeling that he had more to say on that topic. "But?"

"I'm still trying to understand where this is coming from—especially in regards to serving *underprivileged young adults*, as you called them."

"Those are formative years, Miles. I've always cared for that age group."

"Oh? Like when you wrote that check for the van repairs last spring break so that I didn't have to cancel the youth group's mission trip to Mexico . . ." He quirked an eyebrow at me.

"Yes, exactly. See?" Huge points to me. I'd forgotten all about that van repair bill. "I've been concerned about the safety and welfare of our teenagers for a long time."

"Molly, you wouldn't hand me the check until I promised never to ask you to chaperone for such a trip. You said your lifetime quota for stinky armpits and bad road trip sing-alongs had been filled by age fifteen."

"Don't even act like that's not true. You know how we suffered at the hand of Dad's off-key Gaither hymns in the back seat of that old Corolla. Plus, you greatly lacked in the area of deodorant until you were a legal adult." I stared him down. "Shouldn't you be more encouraging about this? Aren't pastors supposed to help people . . . *help* people?"

"I'm not your pastor; I'm your brother."

I swiped the ball out from under his arm. "Oh, so now you want to get technical?"

He sighed. "How about you cut the drama and just tell me the truth." He crossed his arms over his chest, his face unflinchingly sincere. "Does this have something to do with Mom and Dad? With your endless quest for their approval? Because if so, then I think we should talk about—"

"*Reverend.*" In saying that single word, I'd just called a truce, one that pledged our highest level of honesty to each other. "This has nothing to do with them." Reverend Carmichael was the most devout believer we'd ever known—a man who could quote Scripture the way my brother could recall every lyric from every Christian rock band of the early 2000s. Reverend Carmichael's skin had been as brown as his beard had been silver, and the animated way he'd moved his hands had been a special kind of mesmerizing. Those same hands had baptized us in the Spokane River just two days after our seventh-grade summer began, and neither my twin nor I would have dared breathe a lie to him for fear of instant smiting.

"Okay," Miles said on a deep breath. "I believe you."

"Good." Satisfied that I'd finally captured his complete attention, I added, "Because I do want to make a difference in my industry—to do something more with the following I have." A declaration that sounded as right as it felt.

"What about taking a short-term trip to Mongolia with our missions team next month? You can post all about it."

A quick recall of the many slideshows Miles had made me watch of dirt floors, thatched roofs, threadbare clothing, and soups made of literally any scrap of food flooded my mind. My skin instantly grew hot and clammy and prickly all over.

Miles burst out laughing. "I'm joking, Molly. Relax. I wouldn't do that to you."

My cheeks warmed. "Oh, ha. Right."

I searched for a positive deflection, something that would throw Miles off the scent of an alternate motivation. And then I knew exactly how to plead my case. "But aren't you always saying that we're all supposed to live as missionaries? At our jobs and in our homes?"

"Yes." A questioning look crossed his features then, and I was fairly positive where his thought trail had led him. Sure, I was the only person living in my home, but hey, not everyone in the Bible was married with children. And sure, my work was almost exclusively online, but I did interact with my virtual assistant multiple times a day through live video chats. Oh, and last week I gave Val a paid day off so she could go on a field trip with her son. That should definitely count for something, but . . . *Hmm.* I crimped my brow and tried to think of a single instance of when I'd helped my community in the last . . . ever.

"Why do you look like you're trying to divide fractions without scratch paper?"

"I'm not, I'm just . . ."

"You're just what?" Miles probed.

"Do you think I'm selfish?" I blurted out.

"What? Uh . . ." He swallowed, his attention shifting uncomfortably. "Where's that coming from?"

I shook my head. "It doesn't matter where it's coming from. I'm asking you as my brother. Do you think I'm selfish? It should be a simple question to answer."

He actually laughed. "Nothing with you is ever simple."

I crossed my arms, unwilling to let it go.

He gripped the back of his neck, tugged. "All of us are prone to selfishness. It's our sin nature."

I waved a hand at him dismissively. "Don't 'sin nature' me, *Pastor Miles*. Just tell it to me straight."

He exhaled for longer than a human lung should be able to hold air. "On occasion, you have a tendency to be a bit . . . self-focused."

Self-focused. I tried on the hyphenated word like a fitted jacket, instantly annoyed by the confinement of the material. *Self-made*—now that was an adjective I'd wear proudly. But self-focused? That certainly wasn't how I wanted to be described by the people who knew me outside of Makeup Matters with Molly.

"It's an understandable struggle," Miles continued. "Given your profession. You have a million followers vying for your attention and your approval at all hours of the day. You've worked hard to build a career brand, and you've been generous with your—"

"Six hundred thousand."

"What?"

"I don't have a million followers." But I needed to by the end of summer, according to Ethan.

He chuckled. "Still, six hundred thousand in just a few years is an astounding number."

"It's not enough," I said absently at first, and then more strongly as something warm lined my lower stomach. "It's not enough, Miles. I want to be more than a pretty face with an addictive personality. I want to be seen as the real deal. Someone who uses their influence to pay it forward. For good."

"Wait a minute, I never said you were a pretty face with a—"

I shook off his confusion. "I know you didn't. And that doesn't even matter. What matters is finding a cause I can partner with inside our community." After all, I'd built a nearly seven-figure business from the ground up. What was stopping me? I didn't have to pledge my life to the call of full-time church planting like my parents to do something right in the world. Nor did I have to go to seminary. I could be fully me and still be seen as a good person—couldn't I?

"A cause," he echoed, narrowing his eyes once again.

"Yes, a cause." Why was that such a hard concept for him to understand? "You work at a church, Miles. You must have contact with tons of needy people. I'm simply asking for you to give me everything you have in the underprivileged youth category."

"Everything I have in the underprivileged youth category," he repeated slowly, unhelpfully. "You'd like me to just hand over a list to you."

"That would be great, yes." I held out my hand as if he had some sort of Santa-size scroll of needs tucked inside his jersey shorts ready for the taking.

"I'm afraid it doesn't work like that."

"Why not?"

"Because there are protocols for this kind of thing. It's not like I have some sort of Santa-size scroll ready to hand over to you." He laughed at the face I pulled. "Wait, that's literally what you thought, isn't it? Oh wow. Okay."

"Shut up." I rolled my eyes.

"Usually when there's a need in our community, an organization or an individual will call the church and then Susan will take down their information. I follow up with a phone call first, and then schedule a visit to get more information—"

"I've aged twenty years in the time it's taken you to talk about your protocol."

He snapped his attention back to me. "Silas Whittaker."

"*Who?*"

"I met with him a couple years ago during an outreach down-town. He's a good guy, sharp and ethical. He manages a house for young adults who've aged out of the foster system and are now transitioning to independent living. They're looking for some volunteers for their summer program to help the residents learn life skills like budgeting, cooking, cleaning, job interviewing skills. That kind of stuff. I guess he's short on female mentors. But he runs a super tight ship—"

"A summer mentor?" I smiled, already imagining picnics and trips to the lake while talking about goals and dreams. "I can *so* do that. Consider it done." I could see it now as a clickbait article: *Makeup Matters with Molly becomes a mentor to young women transitioning from the foster system, saves them from a life of crime and sadness.*

It couldn't be more ideal if I'd planned it myself.

Again, Miles studied me, this time seeming to reconsider his offer. "On second thought, I'll call you when I'm back in my office, see what else I can find. Maybe something a little less . . . involved."

Hands on my hips, I glared back at him. "Less involved? Why? This sounds perfect for me. Val has most of my video posts edited and scheduled out through the middle of July, so I have a bit more time and flexibility right now. Plus, life skills are totally my thing."

Miles seemed less than sure about this, but that was just Miles.

"Silas Whittaker." I cemented the contact name in my brain. "Text me his contact info, and I'll call him this afternoon, okay?"

"Molly, listen, the residents there . . . a lot of them have had hard lives—some harder than others. If you go out there for the summer, it needs to be because you feel called there specifically. Not for any other reason."

"Of course, I know that." I stared him down, daring him to come at me again with an accusation of trying to please our parents, parents I hadn't even seen face-to-face in nearly two years. They were in Panama. Or maybe it was the Philippines. Since they took their church-planting ministry abroad, it had become increasingly difficult to keep track of their whereabouts.

Without hesitation, he hooked an arm around my back and pulled me in for a hug, squishing my cheek against his sweat-damp T-shirt. "I'm proud of you for taking this step, sis."

I wiggled out of his hold, working to leave behind the twinge of guilt his words caused as I retreated several steps. "Thanks." I smiled. "And don't forget to text me that info, okay?"

"As if you'd ever let me forget."

No truer words. With that, I pushed out the gymnasium doors and breathed in the fresh May air. I would do this. I would partner with a worthy cause like Ethan suggested, and I would become the best volunteer Miles and his church had ever commissioned into the real world . . . and perhaps, I might also inspire a following of 600,000-plus to go and do the same.

· 3 ·

Molly

I glided into a parking space and searched for my notebook to double-check the address once more. Silas Whittaker's receptionist had rattled it off so quickly I wasn't entirely sure I'd written it down correctly. Then again, I wasn't entirely sure about several things regarding The Bridge Youth Home.

After completing their fourteen-page *Become A Mentor!* application online, I no longer wondered why volunteers weren't flocking to this establishment in droves. The process was ninety-five percent interrogation, five percent request for unpaid help. I hoped to address this catastrophic marketing mistake with Mr. Whittaker once I passed the initial volunteer interview set for eleven this morning.

I'd already warned Miles that if any staff members came at me with syringes or a urine sample collection cup, I'd be looking for a new community service venue STAT.

His only reply was *#dramaqueen*.

I slid my Coach sunglasses down the bridge of my nose and scanned the oversized locked mailbox at the edge of the road. The address stenciled along the side matched the one I'd written down: 589 Fir Crest Lane. Much like the majority of my expectations thus far, the building ahead of me was not at all what I'd been antici-pating. The setting was as fairy-tale as you could get in this part of town, with its rolling hills and farm-like landscape. Nobody would guess that the industrial blue-collar districts of Spokane were only a few miles away. Yet it was the massive craftsman-style home parked in front of me that was beyond anything I could have imagined. It certainly was not the typical Band-Aid–beige government institution with barred windows and a cement slab for a yard. No, The Bridge Youth Home was a gorgeous display of crimson and buttercream brick laid between tapered columns, sweeping balconies, and exposed rafter tails, framed by turrets worthy of a Disney princess collection.

I knew this architect's work well. My Mimi had taken me on a tour of all the mansions in this area when I was seventeen years old. All built by the same man. Only I'd never been to this one. Of that I was certain.

As I locked my car and crunched over the gravel in my nude peep-toe sandals, my phone buzzed against my palm. *Ethan.* I shot him a quick text stating I'd call him when I got back home to my office. I had a mission to check off my list today.

The sun warmed my back as a stiff breeze caught the underside of my midi chambray wrap dress. I pinched the light linen fabric closed and climbed the porch steps. Taking in the solemnity of my surroundings, I reached for the buzzer on the side of the front door, noticing the gold lettering above the doorjamb: *Fir Crest Manor.* A tiny, rectangular wooden sign to the side caused me to hesitate for only a moment: *No soliciting.*

I pressed the shiny black button, and an instant later, a female voice crackled over a speaker I couldn't locate.

"May I help you?"

"Uh, yes. Hello, I'm Molly McKenzie. I have an interview at eleven with Mr. Whit—"

A pleasant two-note chime sounded from overhead, and the front door unlocked. "Come on in, Miss McKenzie. I'll be out to meet you in the lobby shortly."

"Oh, okay. Thank you."

The heel of my sandal caught in the tight weave of the welcome mat, and it took me three hard yanks before I could free myself and open the door. I hoped whoever was on the other side of that hidden camera had missed that little faux pas. But the instant I was inside the lobby, all thoughts of shoe shenanigans disappeared. This place had the kind of grand entrance that should require a butler named Jeeves, someone who'd offer to take my coat and handbag and then quickly show me to the drawing room for crumpets and mid-morning tea. A mansion like this could make a person question which Clue character they were supposed to represent upon entry. *Was it Colonel Mustard in the library with the candlestick?*

The space before me was vast yet sparse, first drawing my gaze upward to an elaborate chandelier surrounded by an ornate stained glass skylight, then to the mahogany spiral staircase that led to many doors and windows I could only catch a glimpse of from the first floor. I spun in a slow circle, continuing to marvel at the details of the home's architecture.

"Welcome to The Bridge."

I shifted my attention from the minimally furnished room to search out the owner of the same voice I'd heard on the porch speaker. A middle-aged woman with long silvering hair tied loosely at the base of her neck entered the room. Her coppery complexion was so dehydrated by the sun I wanted to dive into my handbag to offer her an SPF moisturizer sample. Black Birkenstocks slapped against the hardwoods unapologetically as her open flannel revealed a faded ribbed tank top and a pair of worn mid-rise jeans.

"I'm Gloria Harvey, the house manager at The Bridge." She stuck out her hand, and I quickly obliged. "Though most folks around here just call me Glo."

"It's great to meet you," I said. "This house is beautiful."

There was a beat of silence as Glo scanned the length of my dress and bottomed out on my shoes. "You wear shoes like those often?"

I glanced down at my feet, confused. "Like what? Sandals?"

"You call those sandals?" She chuckled and tapped her own sandaled foot. "I own plenty of sandals, but none of mine have a heel that could knock me flat on my face if I lost my balance."

So, it would appear my little issue at the doorstep had not gone unnoticed. "Believe it or not, I'm actually more comfortable wearing heels than I am flats." I shrugged sweetly, and Glo's eyebrows twitched. "That is, aside from an occasional confrontation with a welcome mat."

"You know," she said with a puckered side smile, "I'm not sure I've ever worn a pair of heels in my life, and I'll be fifty-eight in September." A warm, raspy sound sputtered out of her, followed by a hacking cough she tried to mute with her elbow. "I haven't had too many occasions to wear something that fancy, I guess."

"Oh," I said, my mind sparking to life at her comment. "But not all heels require a fancy setting. Take kitten heels, for example. They pair lovelily with a casual denim blend or even a flexible knit pant." I pinched my thumb and forefinger to show her the heel measurement I referred to. "Most are only about a half inch high or so, but they can add so much pizzazz to almost any outfit." I stopped myself from adding *"like the one you're wearing today"* because something about Glo's expression told me she didn't discuss fashion trends on the regular.

"Kitten heels, huh?"

I nodded encouragingly, and again she smiled so wide that the skin around her eyes forked into four distinct lines. Most women I knew her age had already Botoxed those wrinkles out upon first sighting—with the exception of my mother, who was far too pragmatic for anything anti-aging related. And maybe it was that same sensible quality in Glo that I found so inviting now.

She tilted her head, her face softening as she took me in. "How much do you know about our mission here at The Bridge, Miss McKenzie?"

"A fair amount," I said confidently, hiking my purse higher up my shoulder. "I've read through all the online materials, and I share a mutual acquaintance with Mr. Whittaker." I wasn't exactly sure how well Miles and Mr. Whittaker knew each other, or the full extent of their relationship, but whatever I'd learned about The Bridge was a drop in the bucket compared to the information they'd obtained about me.

"Ah, well good." She nodded, though her curiosity seemed to climb. "We've been needing some fresh faces for mentoring around here for a while now."

"How many are there? Mentors, I mean."

"We try to keep a rotation of three to five, since not every girl bonds with the same mentor. But for various reasons, we're down to only two ladies this summer. And one is getting fairly close to delivering her first baby."

"Oh . . . well, I can see how that might pose an issue." I was just about to ask how many young adults called The Bridge their home when an alarm on her digital watch beeped.

"Ah, that's my meeting reminder. We have a new community college rep headed here in a minute, an advisor to help the kids get squared away with summer credit options. I need to get a few things set up for her arrival." She slowly began her retreat down a corridor I couldn't see the end of. "You have about fifteen minutes to kill before your interview time, but Silas will take you to his office for the interview as soon as he wraps up the morning session. Feel free to help yourself to the water cooler over there, or we have some drip coffee on the table in the back corner . . . but between you and me, I'd stick to the filtered water."

"Thanks for the tip," I said. "And I'm perfectly fine to wait for him while you see to your other tasks. It was good to meet you."

"You too." And then Glo stopped and twisted back, a huge grin on her face. "Kitten heels, huh?"

"You should really give them a try," I called out after her. "You just might love them."

Her wheezy laugh echoed down the corridor, then faded quickly, leaving me with nothing but the sound of my own breathing for company. I scrunched my lips together. Fifteen minutes until the interview—the perfect amount of time to do a little exploring to better acquaint myself with this place and its inhabitants. Though I typically used any wait time in my day to check in with Val or compare my last live video stats with other trending fashion videos on Instagram and YouTube, this gigantic house was much too fascinating for me to ignore.

It made me miss my Mimi something fierce. She would have loved this place.

With quiet footsteps, I trailed past a set of worn fabric couches and a twin pair of built-in bookshelves—but apart from a handful of plaques featuring businesses and organizations around town, most of the shelves were empty. A shame, really. They were practically begging for books.

Though the custom carpentry of the manor was stunning, the chosen furnishings fell short of its grandeur by a mile. How had The Bridge purchased such a magnificent property?

My intrigue soared as I reached a cork board hanging on a back wall, displaying an open brochure of colorful pictures mounted by a thumbtack. Something tugged in my chest as I skimmed over some of the faces I'd seen on the internet. All young adults varying in size and shape, skin color and gender. An older man with a Santa-type beard and a plaid shirt posed in the bottom left corner, his arm slung around an African-American boy. Oddly enough, the jolly-looking lumberjack was exactly who I'd pictured Mr. Whittaker to be. A gentle soul with friendly eyes and a relaxed demeanor, as if there wasn't an issue in the world that a few corny jokes couldn't solve. No wonder Miles liked the guy so much. Nobody disliked Santa.

I scanned the rest of the candid shots, wondering about the stories of each. The mission statement on the website for The Bridge said, *"We are a program dedicated to co-partnering with youth ages 18–21 as they make a successful transition into independent living through life skills classes, mentorship, and spiritual guidance."* Did these young people have families they were still connected to? From what I'd read online and gathered from my brief conversations with Miles, many of the residents here had lived through difficult life situations, growing up in foster care or group home environments as teenagers.

Something pinged against the large window beside me, pulling me out of my spinning thoughts. I shifted the curtains back and split the blinds apart, catching a glimpse of a group of people wearing sweatshirts, goggles, and multicolored beanies, all of them darting in and out of the forest beyond my vantage point. I moved down the hallway, glancing out each window, until I reached a set of French doors. Stepping onto a patio that led to a cobblestone path, I quickened my steps toward the lush lawn area and then farther still to the edge of a thick forest of pine trees.

I strained to hear something other than the whistle of wind through pine needles or a random bird call. Strangely, there was nothing. No sound and no people scurrying about like I'd seen from inside. Disappointed I'd missed all the excitement, I turned back to the Clue Mansion.

"There they are! Go! Go! Go! Attack!"

A rush of voices paired with pounding footsteps charged at me from every direction. I didn't have time to distinguish the type of projectiles that two groups on either side of me were shooting, but it was clear the instant a round of neon darts pelted my upper back that I'd stumbled into a wrong-time-wrong-place scenario. I threw my purse to the ground and crouched low, covering my head and yelping each time a rubber-tipped dart peppered my torso, backside, and legs. Holy heavens, how was it possible for foam to hurt this badly? Wasn't foam used in pillows and mattresses and other comfort items? Certainly not this brand of foam. *Ouch!* I flinched as one death missile after another pinged off my limbs.

"Cease fire! Cease fire!" A masculine voice cut through the chaos, followed by a quick succession of footsteps.

I had the strangest desire to raise my hands above my head and plead not guilty as the attack finally halted. Instead, I remained in the duck-and-cover position, peeking out through my curtain of blond beach waves in time to see a man standing over me, his arms spread wide like a human shield.

In the silence that followed the command, I assessed the pile of orange shafts pooled around my heels and handbag. As I lifted my head, a lone one swung from the curled end of my hair like a fashion accessory gone horribly awry.

"Ma'am? Are you all right? I'm afraid you were caught in the crossfire of our final showdown. I apologize we didn't detect you sooner—the nightshade goggles are a part of today's challenge, a lesson in team building and communication."

He reached a hand down for me.

Half blinded by my hair, I involuntarily accepted the same challenge as the residents to view my surroundings with obstructed vision. My gaze settled first on a bronzed wrist and climbed up a scarred forearm to land on a corded bicep tucked under the sleeve of a slate gray T-shirt. And then, finally, I saw him. My rescuer.

"Um . . ." I swallowed, blinked, and stared straight into the eyes of a much younger, much sexier version of Antonio Banderas. He was Zorro, but unmasked. If this man were an Instagram influencer, his dark eyes alone could sell any number of products. Ethan called this rare trait *marketable presence.* Zorro's naturally toasted skin and raven hair glistened in a way that could put even my most reliable photo editing filter to shame.

"Ma'am?" Concern pinched his brow. "Are you . . . hurt?"

I took a breath and demanded all my brain cells back to order. "No, no, I'm okay."

I straightened my dress on my hips, and his eyes followed the movement.

"I'm not sure your knees would say the same."

I glanced at the thick smear of dirt and grass on my kneecaps and dusted them off, aware of the heavy scrutiny from the tree line. "Perhaps next time I take a walk outside the house, I'll remember to grab my bulletproof vest."

"Might not be a bad idea." His eyes lingered on mine for a few beats more, before a muffled catcall and cough sailed through the air, causing our attention to shift from each other to the gathering crowd around us. Unsure of my role, I waved and offered a hearty, "Hello there, it's so nice to meet you all."

With weapons lowered to their sides and shaded goggles lifted, the mix of males and females met my greeting with mumbled hellos and perplexed expressions. By the locked-down stoicism shared by this group of barely adults, it was plain to see that this crowd was not the same smiling, joking, kumbaya-singing-around-a-campfire bunch I'd seen advertised on the lobby's cork board. Not possible. Though The Bridge advertised themselves as a reputable program to aid young adults in their successful transition to adulthood, a few of these individuals looked to be a step closer to incarceration than independence.

"Again," Zorro said, clearing his throat as if to cover up their obvious lack of enthusiasm and warmth, "we apologize for the mix-up. It's not common we host many guests at the house during group time." He reached down and lifted my nine-hundred-dollar purse off the damp grass and handed it to me. "I'm guessing you're the new representative sent from SCC? Our house manager, Glo, usually holds our student advisory meetings in the joint office just past the dining hall. I can have one of our residents escort you if—"

"Oh no. I'm not from the community college. I'm here for the mentor interview with Mr. Whittaker. At eleven. I arrived a little early." I smiled and shrugged. "Thus my detour outside."

"You're . . . Miles McKenzie's sister?"

"Yes, that's right. I'm Molly. You know my brother?"

"I do." A hint of confusion crossed his features before he glanced down at his watch. "Would you please excuse me a moment?"

"Of course."

He rotated to address the group. "Let's take five, everyone. Diego, you can lead our wrap-up in the Plaid Room. Also, Wren, would you hang back a minute and kindly walk Ms. McKenzie to the lobby?"

"Oh, I'm sure that's not necessary. It wasn't a far—"

But before I could finish the statement, his eyes were focused on me once again, or rather on my hair, as he gently removed a neon missile from my now tangled tresses. "It's a safety protocol—for our guests, as well as for our residents."

"Oh, of course. Sure." But seriously, it wasn't like they didn't have security cameras lining every hall and doorway.

The residents moved like a swarm of bees across the grass, all except for a young woman with waist-length hair the color of wet pennies in sunlight, braided into an elaborate double Dutch plait. She slipped away from the mob and focused intently on the ground as she walked. Her voice was the faintest whisper as she passed me. "It's this way."

I felt obligated to follow the poor girl, even though I could literally see the French doors from where I stood.

"I'll meet you in the lobby, Ms. McKenzie. At our scheduled appointment time," the man at my side said with a distinct air of professionalism that snapped my earlier assumption wide open: Mr. Whittaker wasn't a bearded Santa look-alike with a jolly grin and a rounded belly. Mr. Whittaker was Zorro.

"You're the director?" I clarified, my voice a bit weaker than I'd intended.

"I am." He held out his hand, and this time I shook it with a much different understanding. If I took this position, this man would be my supervisor. Which would be fine, of course, just not at all what I'd been expecting. An ongoing theme with this place, it seemed.

"Miles speaks highly of you," I said.

"Your brother's a respectable man."

"He is." A good sign of commonalities to come, I hoped. "I appreciate you taking the time to meet with me today."

He responded with a simple nod.

Not everybody made the instant connection between my twin brother and me, but then again, if Mr. Whittaker had been expecting the female version of Pastor Miles, then he would be sorely disappointed.

As we reached the French doors, Wren moved aside to let me go in first. She might be a bit unsociable, but her manners were intact.

"The color of your hair is gorgeous. It's natural, isn't it?" I asked as she stepped over the threshold into the house.

Her eyes flicked up to mine, and her porcelain skin flushed pink within a few blinks of her lightly mascaraed eyes. "Yes." She touched the twin ends of her braids.

Unlike the majority of the girls I'd seen on the lawn, Wren's face was almost makeup free. She could benefit from some coral rouge, an auburn eyebrow pencil, and some tinted lip gloss to highlight her best features, but even with a nearly naked face, the girl was uniquely pretty. Her body was curveless, no hips or chest to speak of, but she had the kind of svelte frame most people could only duplicate with Photoshop.

"If I had natural color like yours, I'd never dye it," I said. "It's siren hair."

"My mother used to call it that," Wren said in a voice so low it was barely audible.

"Did she?"

Wren nodded. "She was Irish, but her hair was a lot more . . . carrot color. And a bit frizzier than mine. She used to complain about it a lot. Wished she could be a blonde—like you."

The past tense of her mother's description chilled me. Where was Wren's mother now?

"Well, don't tell anybody, but I'm not a natural blonde. I'm a brunette." I smiled. "Actually, that makes it sound prettier than it is. My natural color is more like . . . hmm." How did I describe such a shade of boring brown? "It's more like the color of mud when it dries on the bottom of rain boots."

Wren cracked a smile and gave a lift of her shoulders. It almost could have been classified a chuckle . . . if there'd been any sound to it. "I can't imagine that."

"Good. Because I've paid way too much money to a hair wizard named Charise so that nobody can imagine it."

This time Wren did more than shrug. She laughed. It was only a tiny squeak of a sound, but it definitely qualified. Yet as quickly as the humor had lit up her eyes, her face downshifted to an expression that looked as if she wanted to become one with the wall plaster. "Silas should be out here to meet with you soon."

"Is that what you call him?"

"What?" she asked nervously.

"Silas."

"Yeah . . ." She drew out the word as if searching for the hidden meaning in my question. "All of us here call him Silas. Only guests call him Mr. Whittaker."

I found it interesting that a man with so much authority would approve of being addressed so casually. Then again, that had little to do with the timid girl still waiting for some sort of explanation for my curiosity. I smiled extra big to put her at ease. "Sounds perfectly reasonable to me," I said. "Thanks for walking me back to the lobby, Wren. I appreciate it. Maybe we can chat a bit longer the next time I'm here."

Something opened in her expression. "Will you be teaching a class here?"

"I think so, yes."

"What will you teach?"

Honestly, I hadn't narrowed it down to a single topic yet. I always had more ideas than time to plan. "I have a few thoughts, actually, so maybe you can tell me what you'd like to learn."

She rubbed her lips together for a few seconds, her eyes flashing with a hope I understood so well. "I dunno . . . like maybe something to do with how to talk to people or whatever."

How to talk to people? That's what this girl wanted to learn?

"Okay," I said, trying to sound like her suggestion was totally normal. "Well, I'll do my best to work that into my curriculum."

Another faint smile. "Okay. Cool."

She looked behind her down the hallway. "I should get going. I have chores to complete after our group session, so . . ."

"Oh, sure. I won't keep you, then."

Slowly, she retreated a few steps, her eyes lowering to my hand. "You probably shouldn't put that down while you're here."

"What?" I followed her gaze and lifted my left arm. "You mean, my purse?"

She nodded. "Not if you like everything inside it."

"*Wren!* Are you coming? We have chores." A female voice hollered from some unknown location.

"Sounds like your friend needs you."

She glanced up at me, her eyes saying so much more than her words. "She's not my friend."

With a quick wave, she turned and jogged down the hallway.

"Bye, Wren," I murmured after she'd gone.

I squeezed the handle of my purse in my hand and wondered at the world of secrets a girl like Wren must know about The Bridge and its inhabitants. Because chances were high that a house as large and as lofty as this one could put Nancy Drew and all her detective work to shame.

I took out my phone to do an Insta story with the remaining moments I had left before the interview. Searching for the best lighting, I did a quick scan of the lobby and had just begun to tease my upcoming partnership with this lovely establishment when Silas cleared his throat behind me.

4

Molly

With minimal fanfare, Silas ushered me from the lobby at eleven o'clock sharp. I followed him up a spindly staircase and down at least three hallways, though I lost track of how many turns we made in total. I hoped the conclusion of this interview process would come with a survival-type goodie bag—one filled with a compass, map, two-way radio, and plenty of snacks in case of an accidental all-nighter in a dimly lit corridor.

"This place is massive—I think I'd have to hire a guide to find my way around," I marveled as he pushed open the large mahogany door to his office. "I'm guessing it was built sometime around the end of the nineteenth century?"

"Your guess is correct," he remarked, allowing me to take the lead—at least for the moment. Silas didn't seem the type to give up control often. Or easily. "The main house was originally built in 1897, but it has undergone several renovations."

"And the cottages?" I hadn't seen them from the parking lot or even from where I'd been standing in the courtyard, but the two modest cottage-style homes could be seen from the hall windows on the second floor. "Were those added to the property recently?"

"They were built five years ago when we acquired the house. They're the sleeping quarters for our residents."

I wanted to ask more about them. In truth, I could have asked a billion more questions about the house and all its rooms and passageways. I grew up reading Mimi's hand-me-down historical romance novels in settings much like this—just one of our many bonds outside of our shared love for all things fashion. But it was becoming increasingly clear that Silas wasn't interested in small talk. The atmosphere between us had cooled since his retrieval of me from the lobby, and though I hadn't a clue as to why, I wasn't about to sit down with him until I figured out the right angle to play.

I strayed from the desk, where a single manila folder waited, and pointed to the opulent bookshelves at the back of the pristine office. "May I?"

After a brief hesitation, he nodded. I brushed my fingertips along the tiny details engraved in the woodwork. Unlike the shelves in the lobby downstairs, these were filled to capacity. I studied his impeccable organization system, wondering at his chosen method of arrangement. There wasn't a single book stacked haphazardly or laid on top of another. Each book had its own perfectly allotted space. Though I'd often prided myself on being an organizational freak . . . this was next level. I scanned the names of each author— not alphabetical and not grouped by genre, either. His diverse collection included biographies of world-famous leaders, books on teaching trades and social justice, and the random how-to guide. Unwilling to give up my quest, I took a step back and examined the whole picture again.

And then the answer was clear: The man had ordered his library by height and thickness of the spine. Interesting.

"You have quite the personal library," I said, twisting around to reveal my sweetest of smiles, as if that action alone might thaw the iceberg that had encased Silas sometime between the courtyard and his study. The charming Zorro who'd used his body to shield me from my unintended assassination and plucked a bullet from my hair was long gone. This man, who assessed me like a knockoff handbag, was one-hundred-percent business.

Good thing I knew a thing or twelve about charming the hard to thaw.

"I spent many summers as a kid just twenty minutes or so from here at my grandmother's house, but I never knew this road—or this manor—existed." While there was no encouragement for me to continue, I did anyway. "To be honest, I expected something quite different when I pulled up the address this morning."

"How so?" he asked evenly.

"I suppose I expected something a bit more institution-like. Bars on the windows and high-level security. Although Glo definitely surprised me at the front door with her talking hidden camera."

"The Bridge isn't a prison, Ms. McKenzie. Our goal is not to cage our residents inside, but to equip them as they transition to mature, contributing members of society in the outside world."

Ah . . . so we were going with formality now.

Silas pulled out his desk chair, an obvious nonverbal that he was ready to get started with the interview since it was probably three whole minutes past eleven by now. I moved toward the chair opposite him and settled into the cushioned seat, crossing my legs and folding my hands in my lap. If he chose to be a crab apple, so be it. But little did he know that I'd held my own in many a business meeting run by power-driven men. I wasn't easily intimidated.

"Yes, I understand that's your mission, but the other government-subsidized transitional programs I read about online looked vastly different from this one."

"We don't aim to be like the majority of programs already in existence." He leaned forward in his chair and set a hand on the folder, drawing my attention once again to the thick scar winding up his forearm. "We aim to be a home."

I couldn't help but laugh, which apparently was the wrong reaction by the way he hiked an eyebrow. "I'm sorry, it's just that I don't know many people who grew up in a place the size of this one." Some of the celebrity parties I'd been invited to were held on private islands smaller than this place.

"The home life we hope to exemplify has less to do with the accommodations we provide at Fir Crest Manor and more to do with the faith-centered atmosphere we work to create—connection, care, community, conscientiousness." He slid the folder toward him and opened it. I recognized the contents inside immediately: my fourteen-page application. By the handwritten notes in the margin, this was not his first time seeing it.

"A large part of that atmosphere," he continued, "is dependent on the expertise and professionalism we strive to uphold here as a staff. The Bridge is a state-licensed facility for the sole purpose of referrals, and as such, our board receives a small percentage of federal funding each year. But our establishment is privately owned and operated in all the ways that matter. Our reputation in equipping young adults in critical life skills, interpersonal connection, conflict resolution, and stress management is unparalleled in our community and in much of the country."

"That's impressive. How long have the residents been in?" I immediately regretted the phrasing, realizing I'd once again managed to liken the young adults to prisoners.

"The majority here now have been with us for nearly a year. Our program usually follows the traditional school year from fall to summer, though a few have stayed on for a second year due to their studies, and one young lady has only been with us since last winter." He glanced down at my application. "You seem to have a lot of credentials."

I beamed at his praise. "The only thing I enjoy more than making goals is crushing them."

He blinked and cleared his throat. "Miss McKenzie—"

"Please, call me Molly."

"Molly, there are a few standard questions we like to ask our volunteer candidates in person, but first I'd like to go over a few of your responses—for clarification purposes."

Were there any questions left to ask outside of blood type and the color of my favorite pajamas? "Of course. I'm happy to answer anything."

"On question seven, under 'Please describe your relationship with alcohol', you wrote, quote: 'I enjoy the occasional glass of red wine but refrain from drinking cocktails (with the exception of New Year's Eve).' End quote." He glanced up, his expression unreadable.

"Yes, that's right. I'm a red wine girl. Hard alcohol isn't really for me."

"Unless it's New Year's Eve," he repeated dryly.

I smiled, sensing he was trying to make a joke, though I wasn't quite sure what it was. "I can assure you, I haven't taken a Jell-O shot since college, and I've never danced on tables for money."

"While that *is* reassuring," he cleared his throat again, "our residents sign an alcohol-free statement as part of their contract to live on campus. They agree to ten such guidelines in total, but our policy for alcohol consumption while participating in the program is zero tolerance. The statistics for substance dependence in our residents is higher than most—one out of every two young adults here—so it's important for our staff and volunteers to uphold the same expectations we ask of our residents."

"So," I began, drawing a line through the dots he hadn't explicitly connected. "I would also need to sign an alcohol-free statement? In order to volunteer?" Miles had definitely left that little detail out of our phone conversation last night.

"Would that be an issue for you?"

Was that a trick question? If I answered *yes*, would he automatically put me in the same category as an addict? But then again, if I said *no*, would it really mean zero glasses of wine for an entire summer? I straightened my spine, unwilling to let him in on my mental flailing. "Of course not. It's not like I'm in the habit of drinking a bottle of wine each night before bed."

He stared, unblinking.

"I'm kidding."

"Forgive me if I don't find alcohol abuse a humorous topic."

Was anything a humorous topic for this guy? I was beginning to think I'd completely imagined his infectious smile during the team-building session outside. "Fair enough. Point taken."

He reviewed my application for several more seconds, his finger dragging lower and lower down the page until he flipped it over and scanned the next one. "Ah, yes. I was curious about your check mark on the bilingual box. We represent many cultures and languages here at The Bridge, but you didn't specify which languages you speak."

Had I checked that box? My eyes must have been crossed from all the heavy reading and essay writing. Yet something told me that if I admitted such a mistake now, I'd have no more strikes left with Mr. No Humor. I wracked my brain, searching for any possible half-truth I could offer in reply. Even a crumb. And then I had it.

"Yes, that's right. I'm bilingual." For the number of times I'd been made to listen to my college roommate—a music major with a minor in Italian opera studies—practice *La Bohème* and *Tosca* in our shoebox of a dorm room, I could have been her understudy. "I learned Italian in college."

"Italian?" He looked up from the application, his expression unmasked for the first time. I'd wowed him. *Finally!*

"Yes."

"Well, that is unique. Most volunteers who check the *bilingual* box usually have two or three semesters of Spanish or French under their belt." He did not sound impressed by those volunteers whatsoever. "But Italian is a first for us. Did you spend time in Italy?"

"I haven't yet, no, but it's a dream of mine to go someday." Now, that was the honest truth. "I've always wanted to taste their local wi—" I caught myself before finishing the forbidden word while in his presence—"mozzarella and fresh baked bread. I hear the food is out of this world."

"Traveling abroad takes language study to the next level. Conversing with people in their native tongue is a powerful way to connect. I highly recommend it."

I smiled but kept my mouth shut. The flare of passion in his voice, in his brown-sugar eyes, made me want to know more about his experience in this area. Where had he traveled? What languages did he speak?

He closed the folder and sat back in his chair, his overall demeanor seeming to have warmed by at least half a degree.

"So why do you want to volunteer at The Bridge, Molly?"

For a man who seemed smitten by an application form I was quite certain he'd authored himself, this was about the most anticlimactic ending to an interview I could have imagined, seeing as I'd answered that particular question in written form at least six times in six different ways. I tamped down my internal frustration, remembering that I was a professional, a businesswoman with a goal. "Because I care about my community and the needs of the kids who live in it." There. Simple, sweet, and to the point.

"And what needs do you believe you can help with . . . specifically?"

Specifically? "Well." I smiled. "I think we've already established that when in a pinch, I can easily double as a human target." I chuckled, but he did not. Fine. If he wanted serious, then I'd give him serious. "Mr. Whittaker, I built a self-made business from the ground up—first by researching how to upload tutorials to YouTube while filming some daily makeup, hair, and fashion tips from the kitchen pantry of my first apartment. Nobody knew my name or my face and nobody cared a lick about what I thought I could teach women in the beauty arena. My first few videos were only viewed by my friends and some family members. But little by little, I grew a following who shared those videos and commented with their encouragement for me to continue. My first sponsor—a protein bar catering to women's health—found me ten months and a hundred and fifteen videos in. Their partnership provided me better camera and editing equipment, and about seventy-five percent of my daily sustenance, too. I now have a hundred and twenty-four companies who have partnered with my brand and my vision to bring a new level of honesty to the beauty industry worldwide, and with over half a million followers who engage in my weekly videos and livestreams, that number continues to grow daily, as do the products and retailers I endorse. So . . . what I have to offer your residents is a lesson in grit and determination."

If Mr. Whittaker was impressed by any of that, he certainly did not show it. Instead, he leaned forward in his chair and released an exhale that had me itching to pull out my phone and tap into my Instagram account to prove I hadn't exaggerated a single word of it.

But something told me it wouldn't matter.

"You want to teach . . . *grit?*"

"Well, yes, and—"

He gave the tiniest shake of his head and sighed. "Miss McKenzie—Molly," he corrected. "While I can appreciate your ambition and marketing abilities, I'm afraid that *grit* is not a quality our residents lack. Grit is how most of them survived their childhood. Grit is the common denominator for every child who's ever lived through trauma. It's kept them breathing in times most people would wish themselves dead. And it's also kept many of them from experiencing deep and meaningful relationships, because the same instinct that tells them to push away potential failure and hurt has become the only instinct they know how to trust. The youth in our program don't need more grit. They need more grace—to be seen, heard, known. To be real."

It was suddenly difficult to swallow, much less speak. There was so much to digest in what he'd just said, so much to process and make sense of that—

"I want to thank you for your time, Miss McKenzie. Please give your brother my regards, and if we have a need for your services in the future, I'll have Glo give you a call."

He rolled his chair back and made to stand, but my legs refused to obey the signal my mind transmitted. He'd denied my application? I'd failed the interview process?

"Wait . . . does that mean you're not approving my application? You're rejecting me as a volunteer?" The very idea was ludicrous. Who rejected a volunteer?

"I don't think you're the right fit for our program."

"Not the right fit?" Stunned, I shook my head. "I'm not a shoe, Mr. Whittaker. I'm a human being, one who filled out your entire fourteen-page application and answered every lengthy question to the best of my abilities. I'm willing to forgo paid work hours to volunteer at your establishment every week for an entire summer—*for free*. Am I missing something? Have you already filled the summer mentor slots? Because my brother seemed pretty convinced that you were in need of help."

We were both standing now, nothing but a three-foot-wide desk between our egos. "As I've mentioned previously, we have a standard of professionalism to uphold—"

"Professionalism or perfectionism?" I didn't know exactly where the words had come from, but there they were, like a slap across his face.

He reared back.

"Listen," I continued, "regardless of how you might feel about my use of the term *grit*, I've proven that I know how to think—and thrive—outside the box I grew up in. Isn't that what you want for all the residents in your program?"

"I won't allow our young women to become brainwashed by some social media Cinderella fantasy they can't possibly attain."

"I'm not offering them a fantasy, I'm offering them relatability."

"Relatability?" A huff of a laugh escaped him as he scanned the length of me. "Perhaps in all the confusion today with the Nerf darts, you didn't get the best view of the young women in our program in need of a mentor. None of them own impressive clothing or shoes, and most of the possessions they do own have been passed down, bartered, stolen, or are worth less than the coins in your wallet." He clamped his mouth closed and then restarted. "So, in short, no. I have a hard time believing that any of them will find you or your beauty brand the least bit relatable."

"Every young woman wants to be beautiful. To *feel* beautiful. It's one of our most basic core needs."

He paused, as if unsure how to address such a statement. "Seventy percent and three percent."

"Excuse me?"

"Those are just two statistics out of many that we fight against every day—the first being that seven out of ten aged-out foster girls become pregnant before their twenty-first birthdays, and the second that, despite government funding, only three percent of the twenty-three thousand teens who age out of the system each year will earn a college degree. *Those* are just two of the facts that determine how we focus our efforts within the program." He flicked out the fingers on his right hand one by one. "How to budget, how to prioritize a weekly schedule, how to study for an exam, how to fill out a job application and interview for a position, how to cook a meal with more than three ingredients, how to trust another human being and be trusted in return. That's just a sampling of the critical life skills we teach."

"Being confident in your own skin *is* also a critical life skill," I said passionately, recalling my Mimi's favorite quote and arranging it to fit the context of this heated discussion. "'When a person feels good in their own skin, they're far more likely to want to help someone else feel good in theirs.'"

"I disagree."

"I doubt Wren would disagree," I snapped back.

His sharp eyes locked on mine. "You know nothing of her story."

"You're right, I don't. But I do know what it's like to feel trapped in my own life circumstances. And I certainly know how it feels to be judged for my appearance and not for my worth." I let that last sentence hang a few extra seconds before continuing on. "Wren wants something . . . and she likely doesn't even know how to discover what that *something* is yet. I don't have an MBA, but I do have experience with being an insecure woman who found confidence by making something out of her life despite opposition and disapproval. Both are life skills I've learned the hard way. I hope better for Wren, and for all the kids who live here." I lifted my purse off the floor and pulled the strap over my shoulder. "I'll see myself out."

If only my pride had held in that final statement. Because the truth was, I would be lucky to find my way out of this labyrinth before next Thursday if I went at it alone. But that's exactly what I did as I pushed through Silas's door and into a hallway that looked no different than all the others I'd walked down today.

5

Silas

She turned the wrong way.

Miss McKenzie—*Molly*—should have taken a right, but in her hurried departure, she shot out my office door and swung a left. I didn't stop her.

Eventually, the woman would dead-end at the locked doors of the theater room, having no choice but to turn back and walk past my office in search of the main staircase. For as much as Fir Crest Manor had been a godsend to our organization, there was a garish lack of efficiency to its floor plan.

Even still, I doubted her dramatic exit had accounted for a U-turn.

Listening to the tap of those impractically tall shoes against the parquet floors, I swiped her file off the desk and dropped it into the wastebasket. Though she'd hardly been the first applicant I'd turned away over the last five years, she'd certainly been the most vocal. And quite possibly the most disappointing. I'd trusted Miles's recommendation of her, trusted his judgment as a friend and as a fellow servant to our community. But family ties could blind the best of us, a flaw I knew a thing or two about.

I pressed my palms to the cool glass overlay of my desk, seeing her fake charm of a smile in my mind once again as she shot a live video in the lobby of our private establishment for her own personal gain. And without a second thought. I'd been leery of her self-proclaimed career title as an *Influencer* on her application, and I was even more so now. Nothing real or authentic ever came from the personal kingdoms we built online, especially kingdoms that paid as well as hers appeared to.

If not for my respect for her brother and the ministry partners he'd sent our way over the years, I would have canceled our interview right then and escorted her out of the house.

My vetting system might be rigorous and maybe even extreme at times, but I'd never apologize for protecting my residents or their privacy.

A crescendo of footsteps peppered their way toward my office, and I rounded my desk to prop my hip against the inside of the doorjamb, preparing myself for Molly McKenzie round two. In my experience, when it came to people who enjoyed the sound of their own voice, more time to think often equaled more fuel to speak it. And Miss McKenzie, with all her impressive accolades and shiny accomplishments, was not short on words or on show.

Though I remained obscured from her view, waiting in the shadow of the doorway, her pace slowed considerably as she neared. Perhaps she could sense my presence the same way I could sense hers. A hint of her flowery perfume wafted in my direction, and for the briefest of moments, I fought the urge to take a deeper breath.

What exactly was she waiting for out there?

The instant before I stepped out to give her directions back to the lobby, those heels started up their engines again. But this time as she strutted down the hallway past my door, she balanced her purse on her right shoulder . . . as if . . . as if she were a 1980s rapper sporting a boombox. I barely managed to bite back a laugh, half expecting her to moonwalk her way to the stairs.

As a youth advocate and advisor for the last several years, I'd seen my fair share of dramatic displays, but this stunt rivaled for the most amusing of them all—a grown woman using her duffle-sized handbag like an invisibility cloak.

I stepped out of my concealed spot in the doorway. "I don't advise taking that spiral staircase without full use of your peripheral."

She lowered her purse and seemed to take an extra beat to fill her lungs with whatever dragon fire was about to be spewed in my direction. Yet the instant she faced me, something in my chest opened and cracked. Stripped of her superficial charm and practiced pretense, she was absolutely . . . stunning.

"I was wrong," she said, jabbing a sparkly pink-tipped finger in my direction. "I *do* know what Wren needs."

"I highly doubt that." There were few things I tolerated less than a stranger telling me what I didn't know about the kids I'd served for years. Especially someone more in touch with the two-dimensional world of social media fans than the connected world I'd worked so hard to create at The Bridge.

"She's sharp—at least, she's a lot sharper than her insecurity lets on. She told me she wants to learn how to talk to people." She shook her head. "I didn't get that at first, thinking it was a comment about words or vocabulary. But I actually think it has very little to do with that and everything to do with having the courage to speak up for herself. To speak her mind when she feels belittled and overshadowed." She paused, her eyes turning more intense. "And don't even think about telling me that's not a critical life skill. Because that might just be the most critical life skill she could possess as a female living in our world today."

Heat flared in my gut. Who did this woman think she was, telling me about Wren's *true needs*? I'd been the one to refer her to The Bridge after she'd aged out last winter. I'd been the one to ensure her younger sibling remained in-state with a foster family I'd personally referred. And I'd been the one to arrange transport for her weekly grief counsel after school. "And who do you suppose is belittling her? Because if you're going to start throwing around accusations based off the assumptions you made from a four-minute conversation with her, I hope you have evidence to back them up."

Her laugh was an enraged cackle. "Assumptions? You're one to talk about assumptions. Though your website certainly makes a huge deal about your program being a"—she framed her fingers around her face with air quotes as she spoke—"'judgment-free zone,' you've done nothing but judge me from the moment I told you my name. I'd be willing to bet you made your mind up about me before I stepped on campus. And still, for some insane reason, you decided to waste both of our time by continuing with an interview I never had a chance of passing no matter what my answers were." She held her arms out, her purse swinging back and forth. "So why don't you tell me the real reason, Silas? And don't bother holding back, because there's honestly nothing you can say that could be worse than what my online trolls post on the daily. So what is it . . . am I too blond? Too mouthy? Too strong-willed for a female?"

"Don't insult me," I gritted out.

"Then don't insult *me* by saying I'm not the right fit to work with your young women and then offer me zero reason to back it up."

"I don't trust you."

Her lips parted in an inaudible gasp, and I felt an odd sensation, like knuckles digging into my ribcage, as I glimpsed beyond her carefully constructed facade.

I took one step closer to her, only one, and yet it felt too close. "I have little respect for social media or for those who make a profit from its false realities. But I would have been willing to overlook that for the sake of my residents if I hadn't caught you breaking our privacy policy in your first ten minutes inside our lobby without a second thought."

"I . . . *what?*" All the tightness in her face relaxed as my words hit their intended mark. "But that was just an Instagram story, not even eight seconds long. And it was mostly just of my face."

"You were videoing inside a private residence where many of our young adults have chosen to reside because it's the only place they can find solace from their dysfunctional family ties. The Bridge is a safe harbor, one that provides security and confidentiality for those who wish their location to remain anonymous during their time here."

Her gaze drifted to the floor, and I wondered if she was calculating her next comeback or her next dramatic exit. But after a full ten seconds of silence, she simply reached into her bag, took out her phone, and swiped and tapped several times on the screen. "Okay, it's gone."

"What is?"

"The video. I deleted it." She pulled on an expression yet to be determined—perhaps the kind of face that could cry on camera without ever losing composure? I wasn't sure, yet it was impossible to look away from her nonetheless. "I wasn't aware of your privacy policy or your rules regarding social media, but I apologize if my actions put the house or any of its residents at risk. That certainly wasn't my intention. I'm sorry." For the briefest of moments, her voice strained with a sincerity I would have doubted her capable of during our interview.

She swallowed, recovered, and then retreated a full step back, gripping the wooden handle of her purse with both hands. "I appreciate you telling it to me straight, though. I value learning from my mistakes." She stopped suddenly and studied the intersection at the end of the hallway. "I'd also value you telling me how I might find my way out of this maze before my brother reports me as a missing person."

"Two lefts and a right. The staircase will take you to the lobby. Glo can let you out, or . . . I actually have a minute now. I can walk you out." I started toward her when she shook her head and waved me back.

"That's okay. I got it." Her smile left no doubt in my mind of how she'd attracted over half a million followers. It was worth that much, maybe more. "I'll make sure to tell Miles you said hello."

"Thanks," I said, unsure of what else to say but positive I should be saying more than a monosyllabic word. Yet I couldn't seem to wrap my mind around what had just happened. I'd prepared for a defensive outburst, a vent of frustration at the very least. But not an apology. Not remorse.

A familiar tug of intuition surfaced as she walked away, one that had no right to be there. Not when I'd already crossed her name off as a mentor candidate.

Yet my disquiet persisted.

There was nothing inherently dangerous about the woman, unless one could count the level of distraction she would cause for the hormone-crazed males living on our premises. But even still, my decision to dismiss her was valid.

The instant I was back in my office, I opened my laptop and scanned my waiting emails without actually reading a word. Then I picked up the phone on my desk and punched in Glo's extension. I would ask her to pull up the other background-checked women we had on file and schedule interviews for early next week, seeing as our summer program was officially as short on instructors as it was on time.

Glo answered without so much as a hello. "Ms. McKenzie just left."

"Yes, I'm aware."

"And . . . ?"

I clenched my jaw, released, and clenched again. "She's not right for us."

"Huh. That's too bad. I liked her."

"Liking her is not the issue. A lot of people like her." Over half a million, in fact.

"Shall I add a new requirement to our application forms, then? 'Must be unlikable.'"

"Glo." I rubbed my left temple. "She'd be a constant migraine to manage."

"Then don't manage her. I will."

A humorous remark, considering Glo's responsibilities were

already at maximum capacity, like the majority of our staff. "I'd rather focus on who we have on file already. Let's make some follow-up calls, okay?"

"Alrighty."

I set the receiver back in its cradle and closed my laptop with a heavy sigh. Rolling back in my chair, the toe of my shoe bumped the wastebasket housing Molly's folder. And then, before I could stop myself, I reached down and lifted it out of the trash and placed it in the bottom drawer of my file cabinet.

6

Molly

A cascade of silky fabric shimmered over my hips as my hands reached for the sash at my natural waist. My fingers stilled on the knot as my mind added yet another class idea to a syllabus I'd never be allowed to write, much less teach from: *Multifunctional Fashion—How to Get the Most Bang for Your Buck When Purchasing an Outfit.* Most people struggled with how to take a simple article of clothing and either pair it down for a casual ensemble or, on the flip side, add a few meaningful accessories to dress it up a notch or two. One piece could easily serve multiple purposes. Surely not even Silas would criticize such a budget-friendly notion. Clothing one's body could easily be categorized as both a critical need *and* a life skill, depending on the occasion.

"Molly? You there? Can you still hear me? Did we lose audio again?"

I fumbled to locate my phone, hidden under the last outfit I'd tried on in the tiny dressing room I currently found myself in. When I unearthed it, my assistant's smiling face stared back at me. This was our standard practice, Val waking up early to hop on a video call with me while I tried on clothing options in a space suited for Polly Pocket.

"Sorry, yeah. I'm still here." At least, physically I was. Mentally I was back in that too-giant manor again wishing I could tell myself not to start a livestream from the lobby. I raised my phone to the mirror to show Val the second jumpsuit from today's shoot collection. "What do you think about this one?"

"Hmm." She tilted her head to the side and leaned close to her laptop screen. "It's beautiful and unique, but I still prefer the pale pink over that chartreuse. I think it's better for your complexion overall."

One of the biggest myths in the beauty industry was that photo shoots were the mountaintop of a career in fashion. Lies. Don't get me wrong—I was grateful for any and all opportunities to further the reach of my brand, but the constant pinching, tweaking, waxing, plucking, and comments to "suck in" while trying to hold an unnatural pose and not look constipated while doing it . . . well, it was all less than glamorous. As was the 4:00 a.m. wake-up call to catch my flight to Seattle, especially after I'd been awake most of the night rehashing a certain conversation with a certain highbrow director.

"Great. Decision made. I'll wear the pink." Awkwardly, I pinched the phone under my chin and worked the zipper down the side of my jumpsuit, slipping it off easily.

"Decision made? Really?" She laughed. "I think that might be the quickest you've ever decided on an outfit in your life. Much less while at a shoot. You still have a pile of options there from the stylist. Are you sure you don't want to try on a few others just to make sure?"

"I'm sure. I trust you." The instant those three little words came out of my mouth I was transported back to that hallway outside Silas's office, back to when he looked me dead in the eyes and said, *I don't trust you.*

It had been those words that had kept me awake, those words that had rattled inside my brain since the moment I drove away from Fir Crest Manor. *How could he not trust me?* Hadn't I made a living earning the trust of strangers worldwide? Hadn't I become an expert in the art of connecting with people? My word alone had become a profitable stamp of credibility in my industry, and yet astoundingly, someone who had sat with me in person while I shared an honest piece of myself had deemed me untrustworthy due to an eight-second mistake.

His swift and candid assessment of me had stung far worse than the vilest of comments left by an online troll.

But try as I might, I still hadn't found a delete option for real-life rejection. And I'd been searching for one for twenty-seven years.

"Okay, Molly, what is going on with you today? Wait, before you answer that, you might want to flip the camera the other direction, unless you feel like answering a nine-year-old's questions regarding female anatomy. Tucker will be waking up any minute now."

I quickly flipped the camera so it was no longer pointing at my silicone pasties. "Good call."

"So? What is it? You seem . . . I don't know, unusually distracted this morning."

"I'm just tired." I hadn't told Val what had happened at The Bridge. I hadn't even told Miles yet. How could I, when I was still so confused by it all myself? Molly McKenzie didn't fail interviews; she didn't fail at anything. "Nothing some caffeine won't fix as soon as I'm done here." I smiled bigger, hoping the internal shadow lurking within wasn't as obvious to an onlooker. While my makeup artist had been fantastic, masking the dark moons under my eyes and giving me just the right amount of color to lift my cheekbones, she wasn't a magician.

"I'm sorry the delivery service got your order wrong this morning. I even double-checked it all before I submitted the address. I'm still not sure how a triple shot unsweetened coconut milk latte with one pump vanilla translated to an extra hot Americano. If I could deliver the right drink to you myself, I would."

"It wasn't your fault. Besides, technically, according to the anti-inflammatory cleanse I'm on, I'm not supposed to have anything but hot water or green tea until after the shoot. But if you ever decide to personally deliver me a drink, I'd drink whatever you bring me. Promise." She laughed at this, though she had to know I meant it by now. I'd been hinting around for a reason for Val to visit the lower forty-eight—as she called it—since she became my assistant full-time nearly three years ago. But apparently when you're four generations deep in Skagway, Alaska, a single parent to the only grandchild her parents have, and have a crippling fear of flying, there isn't a lot of motivation to leave home. Which is exactly why I'd been promising her I'd take a trip there to Alaska for . . . well, awhile now. I really needed to get that on my calendar. Again.

Thankfully, though, Val was as savvy with technology as she was with current fashion trends, and we rarely went a day without speaking, much less video chatting. Bottom line: I never wanted to do Makeup Matters without her by my side.

"You know what I was thinking about yesterday?" she asked. "That first tinted lip balm company that reached out to us. Remember? We were absolutely giddy at the thought of your lips being on a sponsored campaign ad."

I laughed, and the action seemed to loosen some of the tightness in my chest. That call felt like ages ago. A different lifetime, really, back when I was paying Val an hourly wage I could barely afford. "I never knew how badly lips could hurt from practicing a pout hold for days on end. But at least I didn't have to do a cleanse." My stomach grumbled at the thought of the burrito Ethan was picking up for me later.

"True, but look where you are now. The Fashion Emporium." Val said it with the awe and wonder of a tour guide showing the Grand Canyon to people who'd just regained their sight. "The opportunities you've had this last year since signing on with the Cobalt Group have been nothing short of incredible. And I couldn't be more excited about what's to come."

"The opportunities *we've* had, you mean." One of my stipulations for signing with Ethan was making sure Val was taken care of—and she had been. She was still my assistant, but she was on Cobalt's payroll, since they were able to offer her the benefit package she needed as a single mom. It had been a perfect union in every way.

"Right," she said. "Yes." Her voice wavered, though—enough to make my eyes flick back to her face.

"What?" I asked, scrutinizing her uneasy expression in my phone. "What's that look for?"

By the sound of her sigh, I knew whatever it was, it wasn't something flippant. Val didn't have time to worry about frivolous things. Nor was she prone to creating drama. Quite the opposite, actually.

"I've been debating mentioning something to you all morning, but I certainly didn't want to bring it up before your shoot. It can wait."

"Which means you absolutely should mention it and that it can't wait. Now is as good a time as any. What's up?" I bent down to buckle the ankle strap of my heels, then began collecting the empty hangers.

"I saw something I don't think I was supposed to see . . . an email thread between Ethan and his assistant and a few other staff members at Cobalt. I'm fairly certain I was copied by mistake."

I stopped with the hangers. "What kind of emails?"

"They mostly pertained to building up your brand, networking with bigger-name celebrities, and the possibility of hiring a ghost poster for your account."

"No way. I don't need a ghost poster." It was a subject Ethan and I had hashed out multiple times before. Though I could see the time-saving benefit of someone else posting still shots for me on sponsored products or informal fashion polls, I didn't need someone else pretending to be me when I was more than capable of meeting the responsibilities of my brand head on.

There was only one Molly needed for Makeup Matters with Molly. And that was me.

"I know how you feel about ghost posting, but that wasn't all. Ethan also mentioned he was considering re-staffing your marketing team with more widely known professionals in the industry. He said he thinks your current team is holding you back."

"What? No way. That's insane. I'd never agree to that. Ethan knows how important you are to me. I'm sure that can't be what he meant."

"It's just," she went on, clearly not assured at all, "this job has meant the world for me and Tucker. To lose it would be—"

"Val, listen. *Please.* Whatever you read, whatever unfortunate brainstorming was discussed on that email thread, you being replaced is not ever going to happen. Ethan is just hyped-up right now because of this next big opportunity with the makeover show. He has a lot on the line—"

"But so do you, Molly." She studied me through the phone screen, the same way she'd done for the past three years. "I realize your career has grown beyond what we ever hoped it would, and I want to be realistic about that. I want *you* to be realistic about that, too. I'm not ever going to be a big name in this industry. I'm a single mom who still lives in the same house she grew up in with her parents, in a town of less than fifteen hundred people. I love to research and edit and strategize, and I love working with you, but if you ever start to feel that I'm holding you back in any way, then—"

I jerked the phone to eye level and used the voice my Mimi would use whenever I doubted something true about myself. "That is trash talk. Complete trash. You've never held me back—not for a single minute. But if I keep talking to you like this, then I will for sure crease my foundation with frown lines that will need to be touched up in makeup, which will then delay the shoot time, so . . ." I did a super close-up of my quirked eyebrow, and Val's laughter made my heart ease a bit.

"So by all means please stop making that face," she said, sounding a lot more Val-like now.

"Fine. But this conversation is dead and buried. Nothing more to discuss on this topic. Got it?"

She gave a nod, then twirled her finger in front of the camera. "Now let me see the whole ensemble. With the shoes, too."

I stretched the phone out as far as I could to show her the outfit she'd helped to select from head to toe. I twisted in the mirror, taking in the exquisite drape of fabric that came to a V at the center of my back and the way it hugged the curves of my hips and backside without a single pucker.

"It's perfect. The Fashion Emporium will adore you."

A double knock on the dressing room's door was followed by an announcement that the photographer was ready and waiting for me in the studio.

"Thank you," I answered back in my perkiest non-caffeinated voice. "I'll be right out."

And then to Val I whispered, "Wish me luck."

She laughed. "You're Molly McKenzie. You've never needed luck a day in your life."

I blew her a kiss and ended the call.

◇◇◇

"I trust the shoot went well?" Ethan asked, taking my hand to help me get situated beside him in the limo. Turned out he was flying to New York around the same time I would be flying back home from Seattle today. So, in our customary style, we decided to have a "travel date"—which was an exotic-sounding term for riding in a car to the airport together before going our separate ways. Sometimes I envied the relationship norms of typical couples. Then again, the very reasons we'd found each other were because we were anything but typical.

"It did," I said, buckling my seatbelt and searching for the Mexican takeout I was beyond desperate to devour. The forty-eight-hour anti-inflammation fast was the absolute worst part of these big endorsement shoots. "Although the studio was absolutely freezing, and I had to use a beach towel I found in a prop closet like some kind of shawl from biblical times, so that was kind of funny. . . ."

Ethan was already back to typing on his phone. "Well, you'll be happy to know I'm closing in on a new celebrity collaboration for you. Made some great headway this week on the goals we discussed."

"Great. But um, hey . . . is my burrito in here somewhere? I'm starving." I hoped my nose had suddenly lost the ability to smell melted cheese and green sauce smothered over a hand-tossed tortilla, because maybe that would explain why I couldn't see a to-go box anywhere in this barren rented limo.

"Oh, yes. Sorry, babe," Ethan quipped, opening the fridge next to him and taking out a clear container with three street tacos in it. No melted cheese. No green sauce. Just blackened chicken with pico de gallo, wrapped in disappointment.

He set the container on my lap, and I breathed out slowly. "Did you see my text when you told me you were picking up lunch?"

"What? Yeah, of course I did. Three street tacos. No sour cream. Your usual, right?"

Not even close to my usual. "I'm fairly certain men have died for lesser sins than offering a hangry lady the wrong lunch order when her heart was firmly set on a smothered burrito from Mucho Harvey's."

"You didn't ask for a smothered burrito, babe. You asked for . . ." He exited the screen he'd been on and scrolled back to our text thread as if to prove me wrong, only he couldn't. "Oh. I must have misread it. Sorry." Or he hadn't read it at all because he was likely too busy multitasking seventeen things when it came time to place my order. "I have, however, been working on something that just might steer you away from plotting my demise."

I opened the container of soggy sadness and limp cilantro. "That's doubtful."

"I just got off the phone with one of the producers from the show. I think I got you an early audition."

I paused my first bite. "How early?"

"Late July. But they asked for a compilation of your highest-viewed videos that showcase your talent. Something we can turn into the producers ASAP." He tapped his cheek with a finger. "Pretty sure that deserves a kiss."

He wasn't totally forgiven yet, but I complied with his request, kissing his cheek, as he hated lipstick on his mouth.

Never one to let an opportunity go, I capitalized on the moment. "You know who's excellent at making compilation videos, seeing as she's worked on every video post I've ever done? Val. She'd be perfect for this."

He tapped into his inbox again. "Hmm."

"Yeah, I can't tell you how many times she's taken my raw cut ramblings and made them into something marketable and professional—"

"You don't have *raw cut ramblings*," he chided. "You have first takes. Hear the difference? Success is a mindset, Molly. How you frame your words is often more important than the words themselves."

"Fine, then. Val takes my *first takes* and works magic on them. And we're fortunate to have her level of talent at Cobalt. I'd never want to work with anyone else." There. How was that for framing my words? Pretty clear, I'd think.

He looked up from his phone and studied me. "I've never doubted her talent. But I figured you'd want her to edit all the footage you'll be giving her on that teen halfway house. Was I wrong?"

So . . . I hadn't told Ethan about the failed interview with Silas, either. And I certainly wasn't going to try now. I didn't have the first clue how to reframe that kind of rejection into a "success mindset." Silas hadn't only dismissed my application that day, he'd dismissed me—before I'd even had a chance to brainstorm a list of possible life skills classes I was certain he would approve, if only I were given a second chance. Maybe that was the key. . . .

"Molly?" Ethan's face cocked to the side, his quizzical gaze on me. "Is there a problem?"

"No, no. It's just The Bridge isn't a halfway house. It's more of a home for older teens who simply need a hand up to take their next step in life."

"That's a perfect sound bite. Use it," Ethan said approvingly. "When's your first post scheduled?"

"I'm, um . . . I'm actually still working out some of the logistics." As in hoping I could persuade Silas away from Team Anybody Else to Team Molly. "But yes, I'd want Val working with me on this project."

Just as soon as I could get Silas Whittaker to agree to a second meeting with me, which I would. Now *that* sounded like a success mindset.

I whipped out my phone and started typing up a syllabus in my digital notepad.

7

Silas

Whoever said guys were messier than girls hadn't spent much time poking around the dark side of a female-dominated restroom. Though the personal accommodations at Lavender Cottage seemed more than sufficient, given there were three full bathrooms in a house of twelve women, somehow their facilities were in constant disrepair. Predominantly the issues had to do with drains. Leaky. Clogged. Backed up. All of the above.

On my knees, and eye level with the problematic pipe, I clawed my way through a wall of feminine product boxes under the sink. With a careful sweep of my arm, I pushed the boxes to the back corner, only to uncover an apocalyptic supply of lotions and fruity shower gels.

While there was so much I couldn't control inside this messy and complicated world of teens in transition, I could wrap a leaky pipe with plumber's tape. If only every issue we faced could be resolved so quickly.

"Ya know, the next time I start to doubt if I'm doing enough for the greater good, I'm gonna remember this moment: my big brother swimming in a sea of tampons."

I jerked back and bashed my head on the underside of the sink basin. "*Ouch*. Jake?"

I emerged from the cave of estrogen and rubbed at the sore spot on the back of my skull. He laughed. There were people who winced at the sight of others in pain. Those people were not Jake.

He lifted a clear bag of wrapped sub sandwiches. "I bought us lunch."

I sat back on my haunches, eyeing him warily. "Why? I thought you were still framing that fourplex up north."

"Permits got delayed." He shrugged. "Such is life as a crew lead." Jake reached his giant hand into the bag and grabbed one of the sandwiches.

"Don't even think about opening those up in here." The very thought made my skin crawl. I stood to wash my hands and pumped an abundance of soap into my palm. But in typical Jake style, he did not heed my warning. It was a wonder that I managed to supervise twenty-four human beings for a living when I couldn't control one Jake Whittaker if it killed me. "You are truly disturbed."

He laughed. "If you think this is bad, you should see how my crew eats on the jobsite." He lowered his voice conspiratorially. "Most of them don't even wash their hands first, Silas."

I stretched my neck from side to side and reached for the pink hand towel hanging on the rack before thinking better of it. I'd seen the way these girls cleaned a bathroom. Another point to the gender cleanliness myth. I shook my hands over the sink, working to keep the droplets of water in the basin.

Jake pulled out a napkin stamped with a red logo. "Here, use this. I swear I didn't blow my nose on it first."

I peered at the twenty-four-year-old man in front of me, who still often acted as if he were fourteen. "Who raised you?"

Jake beamed. "The same people who were crazy enough to raise you, brother."

I waved him out of the bathroom. "Go on, we'll head outside."

I trailed his six-foot-six frame down a hallway clearly not meant for people of his stature. When Jake shot up those last six inches during puberty, passing me and everybody else in our seven-member family, I warned him about the dangers of being conspicuous. He would no longer be able to hide in a crowd. He'd be visible everywhere he went, and with that increased visibility would come bigger expectations and greater responsibilities to uphold. Because at some point in his life, his height and presence could easily make him a target if he wasn't mindful of his actions and the company he chose to keep.

As a Hispanic man who moved with his all-white adoptive family to northeast Washington during my teen years, I knew a little something about being different. I was the only non-white face in our high school for nearly two years, until the administration began an international exchange program. Now, of course, things had become much more diverse in our region, but even so, it still wasn't uncommon for me to be the only minority in a room.

As the long dorm-style hallway widened into the open-concept floor plan, I had to give the young ladies credit. They were far less rough on their furniture than our guys, though the food stains were about equal between them both.

Although we encouraged a no-eating-in-the-living-room policy, there were some things at The Bridge I chose to turn a blind eye to. For my sake as well as theirs. In the nine years I'd worked with kids who'd come from hard places, I'd learned a few things about grace—and it was a lot easier to hand out when I didn't hold it with a clenched fist.

As we made our way to the picnic shelter in the common area outside, Jake sat on top of one of the wooden tables and planted his NBA-size feet on the bench while I sat at the next table over, watching as he took a crocodile-worthy bite of his Italian sub. Jake had once been a nationally recognized swimmer with a wingspan and an appetite that could rival Michael Phelps. Six years later, not much had changed, other than his now having a stable job as a framer and a fiancée I thought the world of—Clara was a saint.

My stomach growled the instant I unwrapped my sandwich. I hadn't eaten since after my morning run. "Thanks for bringing this."

I didn't miss the way he eyed me. "So what's up? What's got you so stressed today—I mean, more than usual."

"Who says I'm stressed?"

"Oh, I don't know, maybe the handyman badge you try to wear when you either *A*, hear bad news, or *B*, want to control something that can't be controlled, or *C*, both. So, which is it?"

Definitely C. I finished chewing and set the remains of my sandwich aside. "I heard from Sharon at the county this morning."

"Yeah? And?"

"Two boys on our waitlist died in a drug house last night. Overdose."

I didn't need to spell it all out for him. He'd been around this world long enough to know what that meant. Not only had our system failed them, but so had we. So had I.

I didn't know their faces or the details of their stories, but I knew enough. I knew all about teen boys who'd been turned over to the state with nothing but a pocketful of false hope and empty platitudes.

"That's tough, bro."

I nodded and stared out at the hills just beyond the guys' cottage. "I can't keep turning kids away."

"You're not the one turning them away."

"I may as well be."

He laughed without humor. "You can't only focus on the list of kids you can't help. What about the twenty-four who are here now? Look what you're doing for them. Not to mention the ones who've already successfully transitioned on from here. Don't forget about them."

I huffed a short sigh. It didn't feel like enough. It never did. It probably never would. Not when there were hundreds of kids who aged out in our state each year with nowhere to go and no one to call. "I'm thinking of presenting the expansion proposal at the board meeting next week. It's time. We have this huge house to offer—and yet our hands are tied due to lack of funding."

"You know I'm in. I've already drawn up the plans. As soon as the trustees give you a green light, I'll build whatever you need."

"I know you will. Thanks." If only the board shared Jake's enthusiasm for such a project. But I knew what we were up against. Though the board was made up of five respectable leaders in our community, they were realists. I could relate. Still, no matter how many statistics I quoted or how many personal testimonies I shared with them, it would always come down to affordability and sustainability. Taking in more referrals meant more staffing needs, more bedrooms, more supplies, more of everything we couldn't provide without more funding.

Fir Crest Manor was a dream location without a dream budget. While the main house was used for classes and communal living, it wasn't used for sleeping quarters, not when our program was co-ed. It was hard enough to enforce the hands-free rule, which was one rule we didn't leave open for interpretation. I knew what happened when pink and blue were given too much free time together, and we didn't need any little purples naming Fir Crest Manor on their birth certificates. Thankfully, Glo and Jerry managed the Lavender Cottage and the Bunkhouse well, and what they didn't catch, our security cameras did. We all slept more soundly knowing that extra layer of overnight accountability was recording.

"You know what would help you? A Black Widow type," Jake spat out, as if we shared some kind of common Marvel language.

"Excuse me?"

"It might be time to bring on some kind of fundraising powerhouse. Someone who isn't afraid to kick butt and take names. They can put on one of those fancy shindigs that rich people live for—cash will be flowing faster than Glo can keep the punch bowl filled." He shrugged. "That's my vote."

An immediate image surfaced in my mind. Only it wasn't of Scarlett Johansson wearing black leather but rather of a woman with billowy blond hair wearing heels that could double as a weapon.

"I don't believe in fundraising gimmicks. God will provide the way He always has—in His own timing."

"You also don't believe in using a kitchen sponge. Doesn't mean they aren't necessary at times."

"A sponge is nothing more than a breeding ground for bacteria. It only serves to circ—"

"*Circulate germs.* Save it for your residents, Silas. I've heard it more times than Aunt Barb's coin drops in the swear jar at Mom and Dad's. And that's saying something."

At that, I laughed, and Jake did, too. But when we settled, it was clear by the way his knee continued to bounce that Black Widows and swear jars weren't the only things on his mind.

"Your tell is easy, Jake."

He glanced at his knee and tried to laugh it off, only we both knew there was something he wanted to ask. The same something he'd avoided asking the last three times we were together. "It's just, I've been keeping track. I know Carlos was released on parole a few weeks ago."

"You're right, he was," I said. "Nearly a month ago now."

Jake looked at me, all humor stripped from his gaze. "Has he contacted you?"

"No." Yet I knew he would find a way. Carlos always found me when he wanted something.

Jake leaned in closer, elbows to knees, his gaze focused on the scar on my right forearm as if he were remembering all the gory details I'd done everything in my power to forget. "But you'll tell me if he does?"

The charge in the air thickened immediately. Though Jake was six years my junior, there was nothing young about the fight for justice that ran thick in his blood. He was all jokes until somebody messed with the people he cared about. A dangerous combination, and one I'd never allow him to act upon on my behalf.

As much as Jake wanted a fight, there was more at stake than righting a past that couldn't be righted. It wasn't Jake's job to protect me. It was my job to protect him, as well as everybody else in my life who could be tainted by an addict's lies. "He's been locked away for three years—that's the longest term he's served. There's a possibility Carlos won't want to jeopardize his freedom again." A possibility that seemed slim considering the number of times he'd claimed to be clean. And I'd likely never really know for sure, considering I'd cut off all communication with him after his sentencing.

"I don't give a rip about his freedom or about the lessons he may or may not have learned in prison. He doesn't deserve to call you his brother."

And yet I wondered how many times a day Carlos must have thought the same about me.

· 8 ·

Molly

I figured Glo would be surprised to see me back at The Bridge unannounced. I also figured she would be under strict orders to keep me off the premises, removing me by armed guards with Nerf blasters if need be. But neither of those assumptions appeared to be true.

"Hello again, Glo. I brought you something," I said as she met me in the lobby, wearing an all-black outfit with slip-on Birkenstocks. This time the two straps across her feet were tan colored. Perhaps she considered this her "pop" of color. In all honesty, I hated that made-up fashion term. A person did not need one pop of color to complete an ensemble. They needed synergy.

I turned up my smile several notches, letting go of my internal argument for now, and handed her the shoe box. "So, I obviously didn't know your exact shoe size, but I guessed you to be about an eight. Just to be safe, though, I also bought a pair of sevens and nines. They're out in my car."

Now Glo did look shocked.

"You bought me a pair of shoes?"

Technically, I'd bought three pairs. "I was in Seattle yesterday, and there was this great pre-summer sidewalk sale going on and I couldn't resist—"

"How much do I owe you for these?"

"Oh, nothing." I gave a quick shake of my head. "Absolutely nothing at all. They're a gift." I waved her on, encouraging her to open the box.

It wasn't until she looked at me with such a dazed expression that I realized how foreign this gesture might be in Glo's world. But in mine, the reality of gift packages showing up from companies and small businesses hoping to be mentioned on my pages had become as commonplace as receiving a mortgage statement each month. Whether they be for product placement purposes or for review, there was hardly a day I didn't have a package or two waiting for me to open.

I didn't know Glo well enough to gauge all the things going on in her head, but once she peeked under the lid, she simply stared at the shoes as if they might disappear if she blinked too quickly. I wasn't exactly sure which way to take that.

"It's totally okay if you don't care for them," I hedged. "You are under no obligation to wear them, or even to like them—"

She shook her head slowly, but no verbal response followed. Instead, she went over to the worn couch in the massive lobby and sat, setting the box beside her with a reverence that made the back of my throat tingle.

As she slipped off her worn sandals and lifted the shoes out of the box, I held my breath. I hadn't anticipated the moment to feel like this . . . but then again, I hadn't expected Glo to look as if I'd given her an all-expenses-paid island vacation, either.

She slipped one foot inside the matte-black kitten heel and then did the same with the other one. Standing up, she took a wobbly step forward, righting herself quickly before strutting her way across the lobby. And then back again.

She spun on one heel. "You weren't lying. These really *are* comfortable."

I clasped my hands and held them tightly to my chest. "So you like them?"

"I *love* them." Again, she met my eyes with a wonder that caused something to bump and burst inside my chest. "And they're quite possibly the best bribe I've ever received . . . and that's saying something."

I flashed her a guilty grin. "To be fair, I would have bought them for you anyway, on principle. Because I believe every woman should own a pair of go-to heels to spice up an outfit if she wants them. But yes, I am hoping you might help me with something."

She laughed and tilted her head to the side. "Have you come back for a redo?"

"A . . . *redo?*"

"That's our lingo around the house for a second go. Another chance. A do-over."

I nodded. "Then, yes. I'm here for a redo. I have—" I reached inside my satchel and pulled out a rose gold portfolio folder that contained the syllabus I'd worked on until 2:00 a.m. One I hoped Silas couldn't refuse.

"Ah, good for you, Molly. Silas can be . . ." Glo pursed her lips and dropped her gaze to her tapping foot. "Hmm . . . I could get used to this sound."

I laughed.

"He can be a bit rigid at times."

I bit the insides of my cheeks to keep from saying one of the fifteen hundred comebacks currently scrolling through my mind.

"But," she continued, "he has integrity. More than anybody you'll meet this side of heaven." She paused and looked at me straight on. "We're lucky to have him—not only for all he does at The Bridge, but for the way he believes our world can be." She shook her head, sadness creeping onto her face. "It's a special person who can see all he's seen and experience all he's experienced and still have faith for better days ahead."

Her praise of Silas pinged against a tender place in my subconscious, one I hadn't visited or explored in a very long while. I shook my head, brushing away the lingering impressions of a young girl who so badly wanted to believe that she, too, could be worthy of the praise her family members so often received for their good works and selfless callings.

"Do you think I might be able to meet with him for a few minutes? I have something I'd like to hand him in person, if possible."

Glo smiled. "You're in luck. Our residents are all away at school or work at this time of day, so Silas is actually out on the grounds tending to a few things."

"Oh . . ." I turned uncertainly, attempting to catch a glimpse of him through the windows.

"I'm happy to point you in the right direction. Last I checked, he was doing some repair work in the girls' cottage. I can find out for sure, though."

She lifted her phone, and I held out my hand to stop her. "Actually, if you don't mind, I'd like to just pop in on him for a minute. I won't take up too much of his time. Promise." Also, I was ninety-nine percent sure that if she called to alert him of my presence, Silas would have zero qualms about sending me packing.

Glo hesitated, then seemed to make peace with something in her mind. "How about I walk you to the path that leads to the cottage. Jake, his younger brother, is with him today." The woman's mouth quirked a bit as she opened the front door and gestured for me to follow. "You'll like Jake. Everybody does."

Glo gestured to the path leading to a frothy white and lilac cottage, set off from a gazebo and a common area with a picnic shelter. "Let me know if you need anything more, Kitten Heels. Good luck. And this time, don't take no for an answer." She gave me a wink.

Regulating my breathing to one of high-level confidence, I rehearsed the pitch I'd come up with the night before. He'd be crazy not to say yes to me this time, right? He couldn't keep turning away free help, and if he didn't get another mentor soon, his summer life skills program wouldn't get off the ground.

Lavender Cottage—as the pretty sign read—wasn't large by any stretch of the imagination, but the outside looked charming enough. Did all the girls share this one house? If so, I wondered where Wren's room might be.

I knocked on the door. Waited. No response.

"Hello?" I called out, but again, no one answered.

On my third knock, I twisted the handle. It was unlocked. Using the tip of my pointer finger, I tapped the door just enough for it to groan open. Immediately, the scent of imitation vanilla and drugstore hairspray confirmed I was in the right place.

"Mr. Whittaker—Silas?" I wasn't sure which name he'd respond to best today. Perhaps neither, since I was the one calling out for him. "It's Molly McKenzie. Are you in here? I was hoping we could talk. I don't need more than five minutes." Ten, tops.

I crept through the silent, super-sparse living area, noting the lack of art on the off-white walls. It wasn't that no one had tried to decorate this space—just nobody with an eye for interior design.

I rotated until I spotted a gas fireplace surrounded by river rock in the corner. Okay, so the room wasn't a total loss. This, at least, looked classy and sophisticated. It should be the focal point of this entire space, yet on top of the mantel was a single red candle flecked with gold glitter. I desperately hoped it hadn't been left up since Christmas.

My feet shuffled across the open space, and then I saw . . . *Oh, Great Aunt Wanda.* What had happened to that fridge? The stainless-steel door appeared to double as a weekly menu, chore list, *and* message board for missing items. Strangely, there wasn't a found list.

Missing:
Red flats, size 7—Jasmine
Necklace with gold heart pendant—Wren
Bluetooth earbuds—Amy
iPad for school!!!—Felicia

Black marker was literally all over the refrigerator. I smudged the edge of one of Felicia's corkscrew letters with the tip of my finger and sighed audibly. At least it wasn't permanent. *But come on, ladies. You have enough wall space to set up a theater screen.* Why not get a cute menu board and a chore chart display and add to the charm of this darling space? I made a note to look up some options when I got back home.

Much like the first time I'd visited The Bridge, something outside caught my eye as I looked through the sliding glass door near the kitchen. A man. No, two men. Throwing something at each other.

I moved closer, my lips parting at the sight of Silas pitching pinecone after pinecone at a man who looked close to seven feet tall. Was that the Jake Glo had spoken of? He gripped a rake and looked to be encouraging the onslaught, egging Silas on and smashing four out of the five pinecones in quick succession. These two were brothers? Did Glo mean they were *like* brothers, as in the spiritual sense? Or perhaps they only shared one parent between the two of them? Because, unlike Silas's tawny skin and dark hair, the other guy looked like he could be a Viking.

As noiselessly as possible, I slid the glass door open and stepped onto the back porch, watching in earnest as Silas picked up another round of pinecones to pitch.

"Don't wimp out on me now, old man," Jake heckled. "Let's do five more. Consider this your workout for the day."

"I finished my six-mile run before your alarm went off for work."

"Fine. Then consider this your stress therapy. I'm a lot cheaper than a shrink."

"And you would know that how, exactly?" Silas asked. "You skipped the one session I set up for you with our house therapist, Denise."

"True. But what do I need a shrink for when I have you for free?" The Viking laughed with a levity that caused me to smile as Silas pitched the next few. "Okay, focus. If I miss this last one, then I'll take the garbage disposal job in the main house."

"Deal." Silas warmed up his shoulders and prepared to throw

his final pinecone from his makeshift pitcher's mound. Obviously, Silas had played baseball at some point in his life. And it was then that I had the strangest epiphany: Silas had been a child at one point. And not only a child, but also an adolescent, one who likely stressed about girls and acne and embarrassing pre-puberty voice cracks. What an impossible revelation to have, considering he was quite possibly the adultiest adult I'd ever met.

He pitched the last pinecone, and a smile brightened his entire face as the Viking swung . . . and missed.

"Enjoy cleaning out that disposal, hot shot." Silas clapped the dust off his hands while wearing what any female on earth would describe as a sexy smirk. "I'll meet you at the boys' cottage after you finish raking up the pine—"

But his words died off as he turned to find me standing ten yards away like some deranged stalker in a maxi dress.

He blinked at least three times in a row before his mouth moved. "Molly?"

Whatever I'd rehearsed in my house sometime after the clock struck midnight now felt as tangible as the vapor of perfume I'd spritzed on after my shower.

"Hi," I said first to Silas, and then to the man who may or may not be his brother. "I didn't make an appointment." Not my smoothest opening line ever.

"It would appear not."

"But I wasn't sure you would agree to see me again if I called first."

"So, naturally, you decided to come in person." His even tone gave me absolutely nothing to work with.

I took in a deep breath, squared my shoulders, and glided toward him with ninety percent more confidence than I felt. Why did this guy rattle me so much? I'd pitched dozens of ideas to the agency, held meetings with executives about influencing their products, and even given an acceptance speech once for Cobalt Group's 500,000 Subscribers Club Award last fall. But this guy made me feel like I was trapped inside a living game of Tetris, only I never knew which way I needed to slide or move or flip to make a play.

"I'm sorry to interrupt your day like this." Although pinecone baseball hardly seemed like the most productive use of time for someone who walked around wearing an invisible Badge of Efficiency wherever he went. "But I'm hoping for just five minutes of your time to tell you that I thought about what you said—about the grit—and while I'm still pro grit, I do realize that there are likely more practical, more current needs to be addressed with your residents, and especially your young ladies at present. I typed up a syllabus for the life skills classes I could teach on Tuesday nights and even an outline for possible conversation topics I could help facilitate during the mentor connection time on Friday afternoons." I slipped the portfolio out of my satchel and handed it to him. "I've also reviewed your privacy policies, and I'm happy to sign whatever contractual agreement you might need from me regarding house rules and the like."

From my peripheral, I watched the man who'd just been wielding the rake like a baseball bat begin walking toward us, but I couldn't shift my attention away from Silas now and lose momentum. Not when I was fully aware that any second he might cut in and smash any hope I had of gaining the mentor experience I needed before my audition. "I know you're short on female volunteers, and I also know that the start date for your summer program is next week. Your residents deserve a solid program, and I'm asking you to let me be a part of it. I'm asking you for a redo." I paused for only a blink, hoping the use of this specific vernacular might unlock the deadbolts bearing my name.

There was the slightest movement in his right cheek. The beginnings of a smile, maybe? Or perhaps a tic warning me to take my pretty portfolio off his property before he called the authorities on me for trespassing. I couldn't be sure. "If you give me a chance to be on your team, I promise to run harder and faster than any volunteer you've ever brought on. I will make these young women my top priority."

Silas stared without saying a word for nearly five seconds before he opened my portfolio and studied the typed syllabus as if I'd handed him blueprints for a jewelry heist in Vegas.

"You put all this together in two days?"

"Technically, in an evening—I was traveling for most of the day yesterday, so I just took notes on my phone that I transcribed last night, but yes." I'd edited each page three times before I'd finally printed them out. I hoped he hadn't spotted a typo.

He nodded again, his expression giving zero clues as to what he was thinking.

"'Week One—Dress for Success: How to purchase a professional wardrobe on a budget.'" Silas lifted his eyes to me again, as if waiting for me to expound.

"I know where every sale rack and consignment store is located within a fifty-mile radius. My idea is to teach the residents about appropriate work attire in the first Tuesday session and to match apparel options with job descriptions. Then maybe I can bring a variety of clothing options for the practical steps of choosing outfits on a budget while also demonstrating how nearly every ensemble can be multifunctional with a little tweaking and attention to detail. This idea can be as flexible as you need it to be for the program."

The Viking propped his arm on Silas's shoulder, making him appear much shorter than the five or six inches he had on me. "Wow, that sounds like a winning idea to me. I'm Jake Whittaker. Molly, was it?" Jake held out his mitt of a hand, and I shook it, acknowledging that, yes, he had my name correct.

Jake studied the syllabus in Silas's hands. "I like this one here, too." He pointed at the paper. "'Talk Like a Pro: How to trade the *ums* and *uhs* for confident speech.'" Jake peered down at me again. "These are all super creative. Usually the Tuesday night classes are titled things like 'Baking with Gene.'"

Jake laughed; Silas did not.

Jake read on despite his brother's lack of shared amusement. "'Food Flair: How to assemble a meal for one, two, or a dozen or more.'" Jake smiled and asked, "Are you a chef?"

I shook my head, aware that Silas was tuned in to us, though his eyes still scanned the pages I'd given him. "I do really like to cook, but I actually enjoy assembling food even more. It's a lost art, really—how to arrange food to be an experience and not just a five-minute shovel and go."

"Shovel and go?" Jake chuckled again. "That's probably how my fiancée would categorize my eating style. Maybe I need to take your class—I'm sure Clara would appreciate it."

I was grateful for his interest and flattery, but the growing sink-hole between Silas and me seemed to be expanding.

"There's also 'Decor 101,'" I said, jumping aboard the moving train Jake was conducting. "Which is less about decorating and more about how to orient a space to make it homey, which I define as both functional and aesthetically pleasing." I glanced back at the girls' cottage. "I noticed a few minor changes that could be made to the cottage that could be a hands-on application component to this class."

Jake looked down at Silas and then back at me. "Honestly, that sounds right up Silas's alley. He's an organizational freak of nature, and—"

Silas shot him a narrowed side-eye glance that quickly shut him up.

"What does this asterisk mean at the bottom of the syllabus?" Silas asked.

"Well, I wasn't sure what the financial or physical needs are at The Bridge, but I'm guessing since you mostly rely on donations and sponsors, all of these classes could culminate with a fund-raising event I'd be happy to host at the end of the summer. I've fundraised for many of my brother's mission trips—for him and the teams he travels with—and I grew up in a home where fund-raising was a necessary evil to put food on the table." I stopped there, unwilling to unpack any more personal details regarding my parents or childhood. "I could do the same thing here. For The Bridge. And the residents could all participate by managing specific jobs for the event."

Jake's eyes grew rounder and rounder as I spoke, and even Silas's silence seemed to shift into something of a more stunned nature.

And then out of Jake's mouth came a whispered phrase I had zero reference for: "Um, Silas, does this mean I'm prophetic?"

9

Silas

Molly had returned to Fir Crest Manor with a typed syllabus.
A part of me was still trying to wrap my brain around that fact
alone. The effort she'd put into the formatting, font, and bulleted
list following each bolded class title proved it hadn't been thrown
together. It had clearly taken her hours to analyze the feedback I'd
given her in order to create five specific classes that fit five specific
skills she possessed.

It was impressive to say the least.

Which, of course, I hadn't been able to say, since Jake had filled
every breath break with small talk.

"I'm not sure what Silas has told you about the other volunteers
here," Jake began on yet another change of subject. "But they're
all great. I met my fiancée during a Tuesday night class a few
years back, actually. I was here tearing out a wall in the fireside
room, and Clara was here to teach a class on how to open a bank
account. She's a manager at a credit union downtown and a total
math wizard." He looked at Molly appraisingly. "What do you
do for work?"

Molly glanced my way, as if waiting for me to butt in with my two
cents. But I wouldn't. "I'm an online fashion and beauty influencer."

"Wow, like on YouTube? I don't think I've ever met someone who's made a career that way—although I'm guessing there must be a lot of you since so many people subscribe to social media channels."

Molly remained quiet for a beat, and I discerned from her reticent expression that it wasn't the first time a comment like this had been made regarding her chosen profession. Far from it, I gathered. But just as I was about to remind Jake of his awaiting garbage disposal duties, she answered him. "While I can't speak for every vlogger personality on the internet, I can say that often the people who start uploading videos because they think they can turn a quick buck without a strategic marketing plan are almost never the same people who stick it out for the long haul. As my manager says, 'If your numbers aren't growing, somebody else's are.'"

"You have a manager, too? Is that a requirement?"

"No, it's not. Finding quality representation can be difficult in my industry, but a good agency partnership allows their talent to focus on what they do best. It's been a positive experience for me overall," she explained. "Unlike your fiancée, knowing the numbers behind how everything works isn't my favorite part of being an influencer, but it is a necessary part. I'm glad I don't have to figure out the math anymore." Despite Jake's overstep, the smile Molly offered my brother looked genuine.

"I bet she'd love to meet you—Clara, I mean. She's always watching videos on how to tie a scarf or how to dress for certain events or . . . oh, what do you call that thing with the . . ." Jake's voice trailed off as he mimicked a spastic brush stroke at his cheek, which had my eyes rounding. "It's something to do with dark and light coming together."

"Contouring," Molly interjected with a light laugh.

Jake snapped his fingers. "Yes, that's it. Contouring. Can't tell you how many different tutorials I've watched since we set a date. Anyway," he chuckled and shook his head, "she'll be here Tuesday. I hope you get a chance to meet her."

Molly crinkled her brow slightly, and once again her glance flitted to mine before returning to Jake. "Oh? So is she teaching for the summer classes?"

"She'll be doing some mentoring and teaching. She was originally planning to take most of the summer off, with our wedding in September and all, but Clara didn't want to leave Silas stranded. She's a big supporter of what they do around here, and she loves the residents."

"Sure, right," Molly said slowly, as if breaking down her assumptions into bite-size pieces. "That's great."

I gave Jake a hard pat on the back, a reminder that he had elsewhere to be. "The kids will be showing up soon, and Glo will be wanting access to that kitchen for dinner."

"Which means she'll be wanting a functioning garbage disposal." Jake sighed. "See what kind of grunt work I get stuck with when I show up out of the goodness of my heart to help my big brother for an afternoon?"

"Nice try. You lost a bet," I reminded him. "One you set the stakes for, too. Maybe you'll think twice about challenging me next time."

"It was good to meet you, Molly. I'll tell Clara to keep an eye out for you," Jake said as he retreated several yard-stick-sized steps backward. "And don't worry too much about that one." He pointed at me. "He's all bark. Well, mostly anyway."

"Thanks for the advice." Molly looked straight at me while Jake took advantage of the moment and pointed at her back with the kind of zeal no self-respecting man should possess, mouthing the words *Black Widow* more times than I cared to count.

"So," Molly said, eyeing her portfolio in my hand. "It sounds like you may have already filled your summer mentor opening with your brother's fiancée?"

If there was a hint at nepotism in her query, I wouldn't back down from it. "With Clara's long history at The Bridge and her expertise in financials, she's become an asset around here."

"Sounds like it." Molly's chin remained squared, never dipping an inch, as if nothing I could say would challenge the new shade of resolve she wore. Not even a dismissal.

I respected that more than she knew.

"Our intent was always to have someone train as a mentor under Clara for however long she'd be willing to do that, given her need for flexibility this summer," I said. "But until today I wasn't sure we'd have a candidate I could recommend to her."

I didn't hate being the reason something sparked to life in her eyes.

"Meaning?"

"Meaning that if you're interested in apprenticing as a mentor for our summer program, then I'd be open to discussing the terms with you—"

"Really?" She pressed her hands together as if in prayer and brought the tips of her pointer fingers to her shimmery mouth.

I redirected my attention.

"I like the majority of your class ideas. Like Jake said, they're original and creative, and still relevant to our program. Our continuing residents will appreciate the new subjects. And if you're open to broadening your audience, I'm certain a few of our male residents will find some of these topics appealing, too."

"Of course. I like men. I mean . . ." She shook her head. "Male people are fine with me."

"*Male people*? Will that term be included in your 'Talk Like a Pro' class?"

She peered at me as if trying to read something on my face. "Is that a joke?"

Working to mask the twitch in my left cheek, I moved on and tapped at the second class from the top, the one she and Jake hadn't yet mentioned on this ten-week syllabus she'd handed me. "I'm also interested to hear more about this class here."

She read it out loud. "'How to Master an Interview: Five Simple Steps to Landing the Position You Want.'" She looked up at me again, her cheeks brightening. "To be fair, my interview with you that day was an anomaly and—"

"I'm teasing you."

She stopped abruptly. "You are?"

"I'm impressed by your work here. It's good." I held up her portfolio, and something inside me softened at the way she exhaled. "But I think before you officially sign up for the summer, we should use Tuesday's class as a trial. Make sure it's a match—on both sides. If our residents respond well to you, then we'll go ahead with all the necessary documentation in my office. And then on Friday afternoon, you and Clara can tag team a small group of six young ladies. That will give you some extra experience and Clara some flexibility to attend to other priorities."

"I think that's fair. Thank you." Molly nodded and stuck out her hand, the gesture so unexpected that the grin I'd been fighting since she'd shown up looking like she was ready to take on the Oval Office couldn't be stopped.

"Silas?" Glo called from the path to the Lavender Cottage. "Cecilia from the board called, wanting to confirm a few things on the meeting agenda. I sent her to your voicemail."

Both Molly and I turned to address her at the same time—Molly giving her an excited wave and a thumbs-up while I . . . *What are those shoes doing on Glo's feet?* No matter how I tried to tear my eyes away from them, I couldn't stop staring. In nearly seven years of working with Glo in some capacity or another, I'd never seen her in anything but Birkenstocks or snow boots.

I blinked. "Uh . . . thank you. I'll call her back in a few minutes." I definitely had some agenda changes I needed to discuss for the upcoming board meeting.

"Oh, and Jake's got Alex and Diego in the kitchen using power tools, FYI. They both arrived home from training early. It's quite the comedy show in there. See you soon I hope, Molly," Glo said as she turned and clacked away in a pair of black miniature heels.

"I'm sure it is," I replied absently, still unable to understand what my eyes were seeing.

But then it all made sense. Slowly, I pivoted toward the woman who'd been on the premises for less than three total hours and yet had already managed to hack the closet of my most dedicated staff member. "Those ridiculous shoes are your doing, aren't they?"

With a full-steam-ahead smile, Molly said, "You'll have to be more specific. I can honestly say I've seen zero pairs of ridiculous shoes today."

I sighed and ran a hand over my hair. "Never mind. I'll see you Tuesday evening at five."

"I'll be there."

· 10 ·

Molly

The instant I sent my latest video off to Val to edit—a compare/contrast of the five most popular, budget-friendly denim brands on the market today—Ethan called me. I quickly saved the file, took a swig of my sparkling water, and answered.

"Molly? You there, babe?"

"Yes, sorry, I was taking a drink. Been a long day."

"Oh, yeah? Finally working on those posts for The Path?"

I chuckled, ignoring his slight at the word *finally*. I'd been up since dawn trying to get everything in for my day job so that I could manage my new unpaid job located at Fir Crest Manor. "You mean The Bridge?"

"Oh, right. The Bridge."

"Not quite yet, no. I'm still working on gathering what I need from them." Like signed social media releases and permissions from a certain director. "Actually, I really can't chat long right now." I glanced at the time on my laptop and made a break for my bedroom down the hallway. I had less than fifty minutes to build the most teacher-worthy outfit I could for my big debut. "I have class tonight."

"Well, this news will make your charity work feel a whole lot sweeter, because I just secured a killer new campaign for you. And if all goes according to plan, not only will it be the biggest check Makeup Matters with Molly has ever received, but it will also broaden your reach and visibility by a landslide."

"Oh?" I flung open the door to my walk-in closet and flipped on the light. A rush of endorphins warmed my cheeks as I surveyed the options before me. "Who's it with?"

"The Fit Glam Kit."

I paused my perusal of appropriate blouses. "As in the monthly subscription box with the famous personal trainer who does random workouts in cities across the U.S. in random locations like parking lots and bridges and beaches and parks?"

"Yes, Sophia Richards. She has an incredible branding team."

"Well, that's, wow. That's . . . surprising." Especially considering I was not a personal trainer, nor was I interested in working out till I vomited up a lung. "And her company is wanting me to do what for them, exactly?"

His laugh was light, as if I'd just asked the most obvious question in the world. And perhaps I had, but he also knew how I felt about modeling workout gear, so I sincerely hoped his answer wouldn't be—

"To model some of their summer workout gear. They're looking for a fresh new face with a loyal yet trendy audience. I'm still working it all out with their marketing team, but basically, they'll send me a list of things they want you to promote—specific poses with some of their gear and whatnot. They're set to offer your viewers the biggest collaboration discount yet for this special box subscription. But they want you to be natural, of course. They know your face and personality are what sells the products."

I sat back and stretched my neck side to side, wondering what he might be leaving out. He only talked a thousand miles an hour like this when there was something unpleasant he was withholding. I'd overheard several one-sided conversations with his clients while riding shotgun next to him to recognize what this hyperspeed meant.

Before I could ask him the specifics, he hit me with, "Molly, are you hearing me, babe? This deal could be huge. Bigger than huge. As in buy-your-parents-a-houseboat-for-their-retirement kind of huge. Imagine it with me: your face on a box, your quote on a water bottle, your body on a step-by-step guide on how to stay trim and cool in the hot summer sun. This could be a permanent collaboration if we play our cards right. I just sent back their initial offer, and I have high hopes they'll take my renegotiated price."

Before I could laugh at the idea of my parents retiring from full-time ministry to live on a fancy houseboat, my attention snagged on his last sentence. "You already renegotiated? But I hardly know anything about this yet."

"What do you mean? I just told you about it."

"No, like, I want to know what they expect me to do, what they want me to wear." Because he knew just how much I loathed active photo shoots that involved jogging in place while wearing stretch pants and a sports bra. It just wasn't me. And my viewers knew it. I was their go-to girl for makeup trends and fashion alerts and how-to guides. And while I was all about supporting a healthy body image for young, impressionable girls, I was just as passionate about staying true to my brand. And to my own body comfort level. "I find nothing natural about me sweating on camera and talking about how comfortable workout wear is while I huff and puff and jiggle in places I don't want jiggling in front of the whole wide world. I'm just not the type of gal to promote workout wear, Ethan." I reached for a black pair of straight-leg dress pants and a gauzy cream tunic blouse with a tie at the natural waist. I held the blouse up to the mirror, then tossed it on my bed in search of the right shoes.

"You don't need to worry about any of that. I know what your preferences are. You can trust me. I haven't led you astray yet, right?"

True. "Send me what you have, and I'll try to look it all over tonight when I get back."

"Or I can just take care of it for you since you're busy with the charity stuff. You are good with a pool, though, right?"

"Wait—a pool?" My mind raced ahead to a punchline I hadn't seen coming until now. The subscription box was for early summer usage. That meant towels, sandals, sunglasses, sunblock. "Ethan, is this *summer workout wear* you mentioned actually . . . swimwear?"

"I don't believe they specified that term."

"But they specified a pool? Unless they're asking me to try on a wet suit, my guess is they'll expect me to be in swimwear, and you know how I feel about that." We'd been over it countless times. "I do not want to model swimwear. Ever."

"Hey, hey, I know that. There's no need to get worked up. I'll take care of everything. Promise."

His reassurance eased the cramp in my stomach, and I exhaled a deep breath. Ethan knew me. And he knew my brand—after all, he'd helped build it to what it was now. He'd never let me down before; I had no reason to believe he would now. "Thank you, I appreciate that."

"You're welcome," he said, sounding less like my manager and more like the boyfriend I so rarely got to see these days.

"Hey . . . will this shoot be in California?"

"Malibu. Why?"

"What if . . ." I sat back on my haunches for a moment, thinking of how I might phrase this, of how I might ask him for more time when he already gave so much energy to my projects and my career and future. But it had been months since we'd spent any kind of significant time together. And even longer since we'd had a conversation about anything other than Makeup Matters or endorsement deals or metadata. "What if we did something together after the shoot?"

"What did you have in mind?"

I sighed dreamily and closed my eyes. "What if we went to the beach for a date? Wouldn't it be wonderful to walk on the sand together and eat ice cream from one of those cute little pedal trucks? It would just be so nice to . . . to have a day out of the office together. Like our entire purpose could just be to enjoy each other's company."

At his lack of response, my stomach clenched in a whole new way. "But it's okay if you can't. I know you're super busy and that you don't really enjoy ice cream all that much—"

"I think it's a nice idea."

"You do?" I hated the girlish swell in my voice.

"Let me see what I can work out, okay?"

"Sure, great."

A door opened in the background, and I overheard someone speaking to him. "I need to go, babe. But we'll talk more about this later. Keep next weekend open for travel dates."

"I will. Bye."

With a smile I hadn't worn in quite some time, I rummaged deeper into my shoe shelves, looking for an appropriate pair. Strappy? Tall? Peep-toe? No. No. No.

And then I saw them: my favorite leopard print wedge heels.

I would be teacherly, yes. But I would definitely still be me.

◇◇◇

From the moment I exited my car, my nerves began acting as if tonight wasn't just my first time teaching at The Bridge but quite possibly my first time interacting with humankind. Neither my persuasive speeches nor my late-night syllabus writing could guarantee me a victory tonight. Because tonight was live. As in me, standing in front of an audience, speaking to a group of actual people with real faces and names that didn't start with an @ sign.

"You doing okay back there, Kitten Heels?" Glo asked, leading me down a long hallway upstairs with renovated classrooms on either side.

"Yes," I said, trying to work the moisture back into my mouth while rehearsing the notes I'd talked through on my drive over.

My mind slipped and stumbled in reverse, falling back more than a decade, to that first day of my senior year in high school when I'd questioned my ability to blend with such a new environment. To be accepted. Liked. Approved. And just like then, as the classrooms on the left came into view, I fought the urge to fidget with my blouse, my hair, my earrings.

Only I wasn't a seventeen-year-old girl going to an actual school building for the first time in her life. I wasn't wearing borrowed clothing, makeup, or confidence. I didn't need to remember the cool-kid phrases I'd practiced from watching the CW's *The Vampire Diaries* at Mimi's house.

I was twenty-seven years old. And I knew how to be liked.

That was just so much easier to accomplish from behind a screen.

I concentrated on my steps, how the arch of my foot flexed with each strike of my heel, how my toes compressed with the exchanges of weight. How my ankle steadied itself over and over again. It was a dumb distraction trick I'd created years ago, a coping mechanism birthed on platforms in front of dozens of congregations while my parents dedicated their latest church-planting effort to God.

As I turned my attention to the classroom door Glo was pointing at, a man charged out of the room directly to my left, knocking me halfway to the ground. But instead of feeling carpet fibers smash into my cheek, I felt hands lock on either side of my arms as he used centrifugal force to spin me in a circle rather than fling me to the floor.

"Molly—" Silas blurted, dropping his hands to his sides the instant he steadied me back on my feet. "I didn't see you out here. I'm sorry."

"Don't be," I said a bit breathlessly. "Who knew a surprise waltz would be the perfect remedy for—" The words had tumbled out before I realized what I was saying, or to whom I was speaking. Silas couldn't know I was nervous. I was on trial. Tonight was about proving I fit in, proving I could fit *here*.

"A remedy for?"

Stress. Panic. Anxiety. All of the above. "Nothing. Never mind."

Silas looked from me to Glo, as if she might provide him a reason for my tight-lipped response. Instead, she patted my shoulder and said, "You're gonna do great, kiddo," then excused herself.

Wait—did Glo sound nervous for me? I followed her with my eyes, hoping she might turn around and give me a reassuring thumbs-up. Or even an okay sign would do. But no, nothing more.

"You all right, Molly?"

I bobbed my head unnaturally, willing myself to pull it together. "Yep, great. I'm just curious where you were running off to so quickly."

"Just to the next room over to get your handouts off the printer."

The emergency had been over my handouts? He must have interpreted the question from the crinkle in my brow. "I didn't want you to have to start without them."

"Thanks, I appreciate that."

"Of course. Though I'm sure you'd have no problem winging it without notes."

I wouldn't bet on that, Silas. At this point I'll be happy if I remember not to lock my knees when they start to shake. Passing out on my first night would likely be frowned upon.

I only smiled up at him in reply.

He gestured behind me to the room he'd just exited. "Clara is setting up in there now. She's been looking forward to meeting you."

As he took a step in the opposite direction, I blurted, "I'll come with you." Because at this point, I wasn't ready to step into any classroom without him. Funny how a mere situational change could cause your adversary to become your safety net.

Silas turned back and glanced over my head. "There's really no need. I'll just be a moment. Clara can help you with whatever you need for class."

I exhaled a deep breath but made no attempt to move toward the classroom.

"Molly," he said with a dip of his chin.

"It's just, I think it might be best if—"

Once again he pointed to the open door behind me, to where a short-statured young woman smiled and waved.

"Meet Clara," Silas said. "My future sister-in-law and our math genius extraordinaire. Clara, meet our guest speaker for the night, Molly McKenzie."

As it turned out, Clara was not the embodiment of a member of Mean Girls circa 2004. She was, in fact, a petite midtwenties Asian woman with a cute A-line haircut and an adorable pair of black-and-white polka-dotted glasses.

"Hi, Molly." She offered her hand along with a bright smile. "Your glasses are super cute."

"Really?" She touched the bridge of her nose and slid them upward a half inch. "I just got them. They're actually way out of my comfort zone, but . . ." She snapped her mouth shut and then seemed to think twice.

"But what?"

She leaned in closer and lowered her voice. "I watched your video on how to find trendy frames that fit your face. I followed your tips."

I couldn't have been more surprised than if she'd told me she'd stolen the glasses off some unsuspecting person at a bus stop.

"You watched my . . ." I shook my head. "But how did you even know where to find—"

"Jake." She beamed. "He told me your name, and it didn't take long to find you online. We ended up watching one after another, straight through dinner." Again, she pursed her lips. "I was super nervous about tonight. I've never met a famous person before."

"Oh gosh, I'm *not* famous." I laughed, grateful the classroom was empty minus Clara.

"Maybe not by your standards, but I don't know anybody in real life who has six hundred ninety-four thousand subscribers on YouTube alone. That's definitely celebrity status in my opinion."

Again, I had to laugh. "You really do love numbers."

She shrugged. "I have a weird knack for remembering whatever number I see. Even if it was years ago. They just stick in my head."

I turned back toward the door, hearing groups of footsteps coming down the hall.

"That will be a few of the guys on the set-up crew. They'll arrange the tables and chairs. We still have about twenty minutes before we start, though. So whatever I can help you with, just let me know. Need an HDMI cord for your laptop?"

I nodded, too afraid my racing heart might actually shoot right out of my throat if I opened my mouth. *What is wrong with me?*

"Sure thing. I have one right here." Clara reached into a cabinet nearby and handed me the cord. "I'll erase all this, too, so you can have access to the entire whiteboard if you need it." She began erasing a dozen or more equations—numbers and letters mixed into a queasy blend of math I had zero reference for. "I get here a bit early on Tuesdays to tutor before mandatory starts."

"Mandatory?"

"That's what the kids call Tuesday night classes."

"Wait, like, they're forced to be here?"

Again, she hiked up her glasses and smiled. "They're not led here in chains or anything, but yeah, they have to come. It's a part of the commitment they sign to live at The Bridge."

Great, so not only would tonight's *trial* class not be an elective class they chose to participate in, but these kids were actually required to attend my class to keep a roof over their heads. No pressure.

As if Clara could sense my brain overheating, she said, "They'll love you, though. I know it."

"I'm not too sure about that at the moment," I said with more honesty than I usually allowed myself on a first meeting, but it was too hard to filter my words when I could barely take in a full breath.

"Well, I am. Because you're funny, and these kids haven't had enough funny in their lives . . . humor is one of the best ways to get through to them. Just pretend you're giving one of your fun tutorials, only instead of talking to a camera lens, you'll be looking at a bunch of eighteen-to-twenty-one-year-olds."

Just pretend you're giving one of your fun tutorials.

Somehow, it was that sentence that calmed my breathing, steadied my brainwaves, and reminded me what I did best: improvise.

◆ 11 ◆

Molly

In less than two minutes of sitting on the sidelines of the class-room, I realized just how underpaid our teachers really are in America. Why anyone would subject themselves to standing in front of a room full of students, who looked as if they'd be more interested in picking up lawn clippings than participating in any-thing educational, was beyond me.

Wren had given me a tiny wave and smile combo as she'd come in the classroom, but she'd quickly diverted to a seat at the back of the room, alone, while a group of four talkative girls took the front. They immediately invited two of the guys to sit at their table. Their seating selection didn't feel like an I-don't-want-to-miss-a-thing kind of effort. Rather, they had more of a first-responder-to-drama vibe about them. I could sniff that breed of cattiness anywhere.

"Evening, friends. Good to see you all could make it," Silas said, addressing the class from the front of the room. "First mat-ter of business: I wanted to give a public shout-out to the two of you who stepped up to lead kitchen crew last night so Glo could leave early."

Until that moment, I had no idea Silas had the phrase *shout-out* in his vocabulary, much less that he knew how to use it in a sentence. In all the conversations we'd shared to date, he'd spoken the tidiest form of English of any person I knew.

He pointed to two girls huddled together on the right side of the classroom. "Monica and Sasha. Thank you both for serving. That's the kind of initiative we like to reward around here—which means you can both help yourselves to a free treat from the snack closet after we're done here tonight."

A guy sitting in the front left corner, who was obviously the comedian of the bunch with his backward hat and *Haters Gonna Hate* T-shirt, twisted fully in his seat to address the girls. "Keep in mind, ladies, that my birthday's coming up. For the record, I like sour gummy bears."

"Or perhaps, Devon, you could collect your own reward by showing some of the same initiative. There's ample opportunity in a house this size."

"Keep believing in miracles, Mr. Whittaker."

That got a laugh, even from Silas.

He seemed more relaxed in this environment, and yet, more energetic, too. An unusual mix I hadn't quite figured out, but I was fascinated by the change just the same.

"As you may have noticed, we have a special guest tonight." Silas gestured in my direction, and I waved to the students. "This is Ms. Molly McKenzie. She works in direct sales and marketing, and has spent the last several years as an online influencer within the fashion and beauty industry." He glanced at me, and I couldn't help but wonder if he'd had to practice saying that last part without gritting his teeth. It was obvious he was unimpressed with my work, but like most people, he likely didn't understand what I actually did. There were often more myths associated with my profession than truth. And, unfortunately, some people weren't as interested in the facts. Those weren't nearly as flashy.

"She's taken the time to put together a class on budget-friendly work attire, and I expect you'll show her the same courtesy and respect you've shown to Ms. Clara and our past speakers. With that, let's welcome Ms. McKenzie."

The class clapped, and the girls in the front perked up a bit, whispering among themselves, one of them taking out her phone and using it under the table. I doubted that was allowed, but I was only a guest teacher on trial, not an authority figure. So little Miss Google would get a pass tonight.

"Good evening," I said, situating myself at the front of the class, aware of two dozen pairs of unblinking eyes, Clara's supportive presence, and one lone nod from Silas at the back of the room that I interpreted to mean *There will be no more redos if you screw this one up, Molly.*

I cut my thoughts away from him and made the decision to pretend he didn't exist for the next sixty minutes. He was nothing more than a broody shadow in my peripheral.

I turned my charisma up to the highest degree and spoke in my clearest on-camera voice. "Who can tell me why what we wear matters? And no, this is not a trick question."

A few chuckles and then a hand shot up. Naturally, it was the loud-mouth dude in the front. Before I pointed to him, I addressed the class. "If you raise your hand to answer a question, would you mind telling me your name so I don't have to refer to you as *Backward Hat Guy* in my head?"

The class laughed, and Devon, Backward Hat Guy, took a mock bow before he replied, "We wear clothes so we're not all out there strutting our birthday suits at once—although nothing wrong with having a birthday."

"Stop bringing up your birthday every five minutes, Devon. We get it already," said one of the catty girls from the front. Her frizzy bleached hair looked like it had been dyed far too many times. She could really use a deep-conditioning treatment.

"And what's your name?" I asked her.

"Jasmine."

"And what do you think? Why does what you wear matter?"

She thought for a second. "Self-expression, I guess."

"Absolutely. And our self-expression matters because . . . ?" I paused, then made eye contact with Wren. "What do you think, Wren?"

Several girls in the class turned to look at her, and I could almost feel the way she shrank into herself. If the girl would have had a shell to hide inside, this would have been her cue.

"Maybe because it's how we make a first impression?" she answered quietly.

"Yes, exactly." I wanted to take the spotlight off her as quickly as I could. "Now, I'm going to need two willing participants for this next part." I pointed to Devon, knowing he was the type who enjoyed attention. "How about you, Devon, and . . ." I was about to pick Clara for my female representative when one of the residents Silas had rewarded earlier stood up from her seat at the table.

"I'll do it."

I smiled. "Awesome. And you're . . . Monica, right?"

"Yes." The curvy girl with the thick headband holding back a cascade of gorgeous dark braids and wearing dark jeans and a jewel-tone scoop-neck blouse moved toward the front. She definitely had a sense of style.

"Great. Now, do either of you mind if I take your picture? It'll only be used right here in this room, for the purpose of this exercise only." I made sure to qualify that for Silas's sake. Thankfully, a quick glance his direction confirmed he'd taken note of my disclaimer and didn't appear to be bothered by it. He actually looked . . . intrigued?

Good. Now back to ignoring him.

I reached in my bag and took out my iPhone.

"If you can each strike a pose with your arms down at your sides and your hips squared . . . yes. Just like that."

A catcall came from somewhere behind me and the room erupted again.

I snapped a picture of each of them, getting their approval before I plugged my phone in to my laptop and projected their images on the screen pulled over the whiteboard.

"Okay, everybody, say hi to Monica and Devon as we know them now," I instructed.

They obeyed, the class participating in earnest, invested in the process while still unsure about what was coming up next.

I bent over my keyboard and tapped a few keys on a fashion editing app I had received a few months back in exchange for a positive review. After making a few minor adjustments to the angles and colors, I tapped the *share* icon.

The class *gasped*, and I couldn't help but release a little cheer. Monica was now wearing a crimson power pantsuit, while Devon wore a dry-fit polo and straight leg denim jeans with canvas boat shoes.

"I've gotta send this picture to my mama!" Devon shouted out. "She won't believe it's really me!"

More laughter. Even one unfamiliar laugh coming from the back.

"Now." I held up my hand to hush them like a true professional. "One rule is that we are *not* here to dis anyone's current style of fashion, and we won't be discussing body types or specific features at all, understood?" They nodded. "Good. Our two friends here, Monica and Devon, are simply a social experiment for us to work with. Keeping that in mind, tell me what assumptions you make when you look at this picture of Devon in his new clothes."

No one said a thing.

"Come on, don't be shy," I coaxed.

"Spoiled."

The front row chuckled.

"Okay, and?"

"Like he takes care of himself."

"Great," I encouraged. "What else?"

"He probably has a good job."

"Responsible," said one of the other guys. "A college graduate."

Devon did another one of his seated mock bows. "Thank you, thank you."

I pointed to Monica. "And what about Miss Monica here."

"Rich!" Devon shouted out.

The class laughed.

"Fascinating," I added. "What else?"

"Powerful."

"Focused on her career."

"She looks like a boss!"

"A leader," said a sweet, shy voice toward the back.

Ah. I glanced up at Wren's participation and smiled at her. "Isn't that interesting? All those positive thoughts came from a simple outfit change on two people you already knew. It tells me that clothing, though such a simple thing to change, can create one of the most powerful judgments about us. What we wear speaks for us, whether we want it to or not. It tells a story about who we are and where we want to go. When we project an image to the world—not only to the strangers we encounter, but to our teachers, our co-workers, and even to our future employers—that image fills in the gaps of what is known and unknown, whether we want it to or not. Now," I said, pivoting on my heel, "do you think Devon and Monica would be received well if they showed up at a real estate firm to interview for a paid internship looking like this?"

"As long as their brains can back it up," said Sasha, Monica's seat neighbor, with a sassy bite.

The class murmured in agreement.

"Very true. And from what I understand, it sounds like all of you have made the investment in that area. So while you're taking big steps forward in finishing up school or achieving trade certificates and job experience," I said, "it's also important to keep the big picture in mind as you work to achieve the goals for the next steps in your independence. How you present yourself to the world matters. If you want to be taken seriously, then putting an extra ten minutes of thought into what you should put on your body before you sit down at an interview may have the potential to change the narrative in yourself . . . and the narrative in others, as well."

A girl from the front, one who'd been quiet yet attentive, slipped up her hand. "Do you have more examples? Like, can we all have a turn with that app thing you used on them? Also, Silas mentioned budget tips. Do you have any tips on how and where we can shop on a limited budget and still look this good?"

I could feel the smile welling up inside me. If there was ever a question etched in the sky with my name on it, this was it. And I'd spend the rest of my classroom time giving them every tip and trick I knew. Right after I took each of their pictures and let them play with my Try It On fashion app.

I'd definitely be leaving a glowing review for the creators of Try It On after this evening. Because if the approval I saw on Silas's face was any indication, I'd say it just landed me a summer position at The Bridge. And quite possibly a giant step up in my audition résumé.

12

Silas

We'd had all types of individuals teach life skills classes at The Bridge over the last few years—mechanics teaching car basics, mothers demonstrating easy meal prep, financial advisors showing budget management. And many topical classes on conflict resolution, maintaining safe boundaries, and the pressure of dealing with negative influences. Never had I seen the level of engagement Molly had coaxed from a room of co-ed young adults.

She was magnetic.

Within thirty seconds of beginning, she'd captured the attention of everyone in the room, especially the male students in our program. And it was clear it wasn't just her laptop presentation they were interested in. Unfortunately, a several-year age gap didn't mean much when it came to an attractive member of the opposite sex. And whether I wanted to admit it or not, Molly's physical appearance was anything but unappealing. She was, in fact, as exquisite as her thick golden hair that swung to the center of her back.

As the students high-fived Molly on their way out and asked when she would be back and what she would be teaching next, I watched Wren inch her way toward the front of the room. Likely waiting until the others had exited.

I worried about that girl. Even more than I worried over the majority. Molly hadn't been wrong about her during the interview. Wren was intelligent, bright in a way that surpassed many of her peers, but she was also a loner. And while I believed there were natural introverts who refueled independently, I also believed Wren's tendency to stick to herself was less about personality and more about an isolated grief she didn't know how to share.

In many ways, I understood that. Which was, perhaps, why I'd accepted her mid-program instead of adding her to the wait list for the coming fall. There hadn't been a vacancy when the social worker called last December. But when I hung up the phone that evening, I knew I would pay out of my own pocket to bring her to Fir Crest Manor if I had to. Wren's backstory wasn't the most dramatic account I'd heard in my line of work—no reports of criminal activity, physical abuse, or illegal substances. But there certainly had been trauma, nonetheless. Losing a parent was traumatic no matter what the circumstance or age of the child. But something about a grieving nineteen-year-old being separated from her much younger, adoptable brother was too much for me to walk away from.

I'd been there once, too. Not as the grieving teenager, desperate to keep his family together by any means necessary, but as the adoptable younger sibling who had wanted nothing more than to stay with the only living family member he had left. A hope never to be realized.

The minute Molly finished passing out her *Five Tips to Selecting a Winning Outfit* handouts, Wren approached.

"Hey, girl," Molly practically sang. "Thanks for your participation tonight. I appreciated your answers."

Wren's entire countenance changed. A noticeable difference. Even from where I stood near the back of the room. "I liked your class."

"And I liked that you came. Even though I know you kinda

had to," Molly said in a conspiratorial way that caused Wren's mouth to curve into a half grin. It was the best attempt at a smile I'd seen from her in . . . well, since the last time she had a visit with her brother.

It was obvious why Molly might appeal to Wren; Molly was the type of person people wanted on their team. The kind of advocate a young, impressionable girl would give anything to have believe in her. The two of them were an ironic blend of opposites, to be sure. Where Wren was timid and owned little of earthly value, Molly was enthusiastic, and based on her personal belongings, lacked for nothing. Even still, the common ground between them was notable, as was the absence of Wren's usual monosyllabic responses in conversation.

"Will you be back next Tuesday?" Wren asked, to which Molly's eyes flickered to mine before she simply said, "I sure hope so."

Last week I'd doubted Molly had even the smallest potential at relatability. I'd suspected our young ladies would feel too threatened by her high-dollar lifestyle and stylish clothing to engage deeper with her. I'd even questioned if *Molly* would be able to engage with them. But in the same way I'd chosen to believe my residents were more than the scars they wore from their pasts, I was also starting to believe that Molly was more than the flashy fairy tale she presented to the world. It was a revelation at odds with a sense of caution I still couldn't shake.

As Wren said good-bye and ducked out the door to the hallway, Molly glided over to her laptop and began fiddling with cords as if she'd forgotten all about my presence in the room.

"I'm curious," I said, unwilling to play her game, "how often do you use that digital dressing room?"

Molly made one of those humming sounds in her throat as if my interruption had pulled her out of a deeply meditative state. Hardly. "That was the first."

"As in, you'd never used it before tonight?"

A slight know-it-all smile emerged on her mouth. And I had just started to like her, too. "Nope. It was something I was sent a few months back but didn't think I'd have much use for. But I think it worked out well for tonight's class. They seemed to have fun with it."

Though *fun* wasn't the main objective for our life skills classes, it was certainly a plus. I sat at the edge of one of the long tables across from her. "It certainly made for an engaging visual." As had she.

She glanced up, a glint of humor in her eyes. "Does that mean I'm off probation?"

"I don't believe *probation* was the word I used."

She laughed. "No, you probably used a much longer, much more sophisticated word suited only for the intellectually inclined."

I narrowed my eyes. "I'm not sure what you're referring to."

"Come on, you know what I'm talking about."

I had no clue.

"Silas, you speak like you're . . . I don't know, like you're some kind of dignified aristocrat from the 1800s. Like a duke. You speak like a duke."

"And have you heard many a duke speak?"

She raised her chin. "No, but I have read many a duke's dialogue. Which is basically the same thing."

This woman is . . . I shook my head. I didn't even know how to continue such a nonsensical conversation. It was ridiculous. I took a mental return back to the grounds I knew better how to navigate. "No."

"No?" She put her hands on her hips. "No what? Are you actually going to challenge my prolific reading of historical fiction as a teenager? Because books were pretty much my entire social network from the age of thirteen to—"

"No, you're not on probation, and yes, if you'd like to join our team and work alongside Clara and the rest of our staff this summer, we'd . . . we'd welcome your help."

Her smile grew. "I don't think anybody has ever *welcomed my help* before."

"Is that a yes?"

"Affirmative," she said with a stiff dip of her chin. "I enjoyed them—the residents. They're surprisingly . . ." She paused, seeming to consider her words, which I was now quite interested in hearing. "Well-adjusted. I mean, considering their pasts."

"What had you expected?"

"Um . . ."

"An unruly gang of profane, irreverent vandals?"

"I wouldn't go that far."

"Unfortunately, that's often the assumption. And to be fair, there are plenty of group homes and transitional institutions full of kids whose past traumas have manifested in unregulated behaviors."

"Unregulated behaviors like . . ."

"Rage, outbursts, violence, vandalism, aggression, theft, open defiance—the list goes on."

Molly nodded slowly. "So none of that happens here at The Bridge?"

"Oh, it happens. Just usually not in the same way. We rarely see outward displays of unregulated behavior here, given the steep requirements our residents are asked to uphold to stay in the program and live on campus. But there are still a myriad of unseen behaviors that can be just as dangerous and as damaging. Trauma can't be erased from our histories, but it can be managed through specific techniques taught by trained professionals and counselors."

I took in her stunned expression and felt a pang of envy at her innocence to this part of our broken world. "These residents may not know the correct way to set a dinner table or dress for a job interview, but I guarantee every one of them could find their way out of a burning house while blindfolded. These young adults are expert survivalists. And even after months and months of living here at The Bridge, sitting in mentorship meetings, attending weekly counseling sessions, and being offered support and community on a daily basis, many of them are still just surviving—saying and doing whatever we ask so they can take another step forward."

"But how do you fix that? How do you change such an ingrained mentality? That seems . . . impossible. And I rarely use that word."

I smiled at her astuteness. "You're right. It absolutely does seem impossible. And yet, I've witnessed the transformation dozens of times. Our objective is not to change their instincts but to embrace them. To meet their need to feel safe and provided for head on with every lesson and conversation and experience we offer them. But ultimately, the choice to embrace us, and our program, is their own."

Molly said nothing for several seconds, though I had little doubt of a lively narrative taking place inside her head. "I can't imagine how it must feel to do all that you do here and still watch some of them choose to walk away unchanged."

Devastating was too shallow a descriptor for that level of pain, though that was hardly the most professional response to her question. "Part of our process as a staff is to be prepared both mentally and emotionally for those types of . . . difficult setbacks."

She studied me. "In other words, it's brutal."

"Yes. But I can assure you that as painful as it is to watch some leave unchanged, it pales in comparison to the pain they've yet to let go of." After a moment, I cleared my throat and reached for the folder I'd placed on the shelf at the start of class. "If it works with your schedule tonight, I'd be happy to give you a brief tour of the house while the residents are at D&D—dessert and discussion hour. Unless you'd rather have Glo or Clara show you around next time you're here."

"No, no. I'd be happy to take a tour of the house tonight. I'd like to get a better feel of everything that goes on here and where everything is located," she said as she eyed the folder I'd set on the table in front of her. "Is that the volunteer paperwork I need to sign?"

"Feel free to read everything over at home. You're welcome to bring it back with you Friday."

"Thanks, but I'm fine to sign it now."

And that was exactly what she did. For the next several minutes,

Molly sat at the table and combed through each document, signing and dating them all like someone well versed in contracts. But as she reached the final page, her hand paused on the signature line of the confidentiality agreement.

"Is there a problem?"

"No," she said, but I waited for a follow-up response, because her face indicated her answer was only a precursor to many more words to come. Three taps of her pen later, my intuition proved correct.

"I can understand the reasons you don't want social media used on the premises," she said, "especially for the privacy protection issues you've mentioned before. And I can also respect that you don't want The Bridge's location tagged or mapped." She paused, and I braced for impact. "But it's not all bad—social media, I mean. I actually think it could do a world of good for a place like this, if used responsibly, of course. There are people searching for a humanitarian cause just like this one to partner with." She pulled in her bottom lip, and I redirected my gaze to the blank signature line once more. To my surprise, she signed her name, swooping the arches on each *M* even more dramatically than on the earlier pages. "I'll abide by these rules, Silas, but I'd also like to show you some of the positive aspects that having a social media presence can offer."

"You do realize you haven't even had your first mentor meeting yet?"

"Yes."

"And that you're suggesting I change a rule I've never once compromised on for any of the residents who have come begging me to reconsider it for one reason or another."

"Again, yes. But I'm not asking for the policy to be changed entirely, just adapted a wee bit."

I doubted Molly's idea of a *wee bit* was anything close to mine. I sighed through my nose and rubbed at my temples. The ink had barely finished drying, and I was already feeling a stress headache coming on.

"I won't change my mind on this policy."

"Okay," she said. But once again, I could tell that particular *okay* was only the start of something, not the ending of it. I was just beginning to learn the tiny nuances and fluctuations in her tone. Much of what Molly said or did seemed to hold a broader meaning.

She slid the documents toward me and stood, planting her cheetah heels deep into the carpet fibers. "So what are you taking me to see first? I've been dying to have a look around this place."

I was absolutely certain that was true. Molly seemed the type of person who would open every private drawer and cabinet in a guest bathroom and then inform the host of an expiring prescription. She was anything but subtle.

"First I'd like to drop this signed paperwork off in my office."

"Perfect." She hesitated in the open doorway, then looked both ways as if the hallway were a busy interstate.

"Take a left," I instructed.

She laughed. And something about the lightness of it caused me to do the same.

· 13 ·

Molly

I was on such a high when I left The Bridge that instead of heading home, I drove to the only other place I possessed a key to: my brother's house. Miles lived in a could-be-quite-charming-if-he-tried ranch home nestled on the Idaho side of the Washington State border. As a unique bonus, the house had an attached-yet-separate upstairs apartment he used like an investment property to support his multiple trips abroad. After all, paying off seminary and a mortgage while living on a pastor's salary hadn't left a ton of wiggle room in his budget. His current upstairs renter was a college student who had asked to stay through the summer to be closer to his girlfriend—a concept that was completely lost on my brother, seeing as he hadn't had a date in, well . . . I couldn't even remember how long.

But I rarely complained about his stark lack of decor or how a fresh coat of paint—or five—would make a huge difference to the entire mood of his diamond-in-the-rough home, because the only thing that really mattered to me about his house was where it was located. He might love to travel the world and be a superhero a few months out of the year, but Miles always came back. His home was here, near mine. Which was the exact reason I had declined Ethan's many invitations to move to Seattle near him. I just couldn't.

No matter how frustrating my differences with Miles were at times, I knew I couldn't ever leave him . . . the same way Miles knew he couldn't ever leave me. He was my twin, but in many ways, he was the only family I really had.

I banged on his door, giving him the option to invite me inside before I reminded him of the key I refused to return. As soon as he twisted the deadbolt, a rush of anticipation had me lifting the grocery bag in the air with a smile.

"Hi, I brought snacks!" Likely Miles's favorite phrase ever spoken.

He gestured to the phone pressed to his ear and waved me inside. I gave him a thumbs-up and headed to his sparse, but mostly clean, kitchen. I'd learned over the years that if I planned to make a meal at Miles's house, I needed to provide more than just the basic ingredients for the recipe itself—which meant all necessary spices, sauces, and cooking utensils. Reason enough to eat at my place.

I set out the Raisinets. Whose favorite junk food included raisins? My brother's, naturally. Then I carefully opened a bag of his coveted Flamin' Hot Crunchy Cheetos while listening for any clue to whom he might be talking to in such hushed tones. Hopefully *not* our parents. It was no secret they called him five times more often than they called me; then again, they did have five times more in common with him.

". . . yes, okay. Sure, I'll be there. You too. Thanks, Tom."

Ah, so not Mom and Dad, then. I was fairly certain Tom was one of the guys who worked at the church with him. Or maybe I was thinking of Jim? Or Bob? Whatever the case, there seemed to be a lot of men with three-letter names on staff at Salt and Light Community Church.

"Hey, so what's all this about? You celebrating something?" He reached for the chocolate-covered raisins, tore the end of the box like a savage, and then seemed to reconsider his guess. "Wait. This isn't one of your weird TV show premiere nights, is it? I'm not really in the mood to watch some self-proclaimed organizer guru tell a bunch of hoarders to find joy in their sock drawers tonight, Molly," Miles said in an Eeyore tone.

"First of all, that's not even close to what she says, but no. That's not why I came over." I chose the high road instead of chastising him for attacking one of my favorite guilty pleasures. "Second, why are you in such a bad mood? What was that phone call all about?"

"I'm not. And nothing."

"Um, you are. And it was obviously something." I swiped the box of candy from his grasp. "You don't get to eat my snacks until you tell me."

He gave me an are-you-kidding-me-right-now glare, but Miles couldn't stay angry for longer than about six seconds. A tried-and-true fact I'd proven over and over again.

He shook his head, sighed. "It will all be fine. There's just some turnover happening at work."

"Turnover? How so?" Several alarm bells rang in my head at once. Turnover in a place of ministry was rarely positive. "Will it affect you? Your job?"

"Not at this point." He shook his head and snatched the box right back out of my hand. "But it doesn't help anything to borrow worry even if it does."

"Don't borrow worry." A phrase our parents often said regarding, well, pretty much everything in life.

Miles swiped the Cheetos off the counter before slumping his lanky frame onto the sofa. He twisted to look at me in the kitchen. One of those long, assessing, brotherly looks. "You're happy."

I nearly burst at his astute pronouncement. "I am."

His keen gaze continued to take my measure. "Did you hit a million followers on your Instagram?"

"Since last week? No, Miles." I rolled my eyes, reaching into the grocery bag for my sugary treasure.

"Secure a cover shoot for Vogue?"

I laughed. "Try again."

"Get an audition for a TV show?"

A guilt-ridden jolt zapped at my conscience. I still hadn't told him about the opportunity Ethan had offered me with the Netflix executives, but I would in time. Just not yet. Once things were a bit more secure and I had all the experience the producers needed from me, *then* I would tell him.

"I'm still holding out hope for that one." I riffled through his utensil drawer until I found a spoon.

"Then what? What's the reason for all this?"

I weaved my way from the kitchen to his living room and plopped down on the ugliest chair in the universe to indulge in my treat of choice—a pint of chunky butter pecan ice cream. "I taught a class tonight. And it felt good." I dug into the pint, fighting my way through the boring vanilla parts to the rich caramelly tunnels.

He looked utterly confused. "What class? You mean, online?"

"No, Miles. At *The Bridge*. Keep up."

"How exactly am I supposed to keep up when you haven't mentioned a thing about that place since you went in for your interview?"

I shrugged, unwilling to tell him the back-and-forth drama of it all. "It took a while for everything to be official—you know how it is, with background checks and such. Anyway," I said, pausing to consume an unladylike bite, "I start Friday as a mentor. I'll have six girls in my group during their summer program."

"Wow, really? Good for you, Molls."

Not gonna lie, it had been a long time since Miles had said something like that to me with such sincerity. "Thanks. I'm starting to see why you do this for a living."

"Do what?"

"Look for people to help. It has an addicting quality to it."

He eyed me as I kicked off my leopard heels and brought my knees up. I had a sudden urge to dish out all the rest—walk Miles through everything I knew about the residents, the program, Glo, and the director, who had to be one of the most difficult people to read on the planet. Maybe Silas Whittaker wasn't actually a director for a transitional youth home at all. Maybe he was CIA or FBI or some other acronym that came with masking your emotions and talking like a nineteenth-century duke.

I backed out of that dead-end tunnel and instead steered my mind to something—or someone—a bit easier to figure out. "So there's this girl who lives there—Wren. She's super shy and quiet and doesn't smile very often. But she's also really sweet. I just wish I could scoop her up in my pocket and take her home with me. I'd do a room makeover for her in my house and give her unrestricted access to my closet and my pantry and my best bath bombs."

I could almost imagine it—the delight all those gifts would bring to someone who'd had so little good given to them in life. And to be the one to give it to her! That feeling would be nothing short of elation. Is that how Silas felt every time he approved a new resident's application into the program, too?

Miles stopped popping chocolate-covered raisins into his mouth and stared at me. "You do realize that kidnapping the residents isn't a standard mentoring practice."

I met his gaze. "I'm not actually being serious, Miles." Though, technically, it wouldn't be a proper kidnapping seeing as Wren was a legal adult. But that wasn't the point. "Haven't you ever had that feeling when you first meet someone and everything just clicks? It's almost like you were *supposed* to know them. Like knowing them is part of some bigger, more purposeful plan? Well, that's how I feel about Wren."

"I do know that feeling."

My eyes met his, and I knew his next words even before he spoke them.

"And it's usually an indication that God has something to do with it."

"That's one possibility, sure." But I didn't like pinning things on God that I wasn't completely certain about. And truth be told, I wasn't certain about a lot. Not the way Miles was, anyway. And certainly not the way our parents had always been. I believed in God, and I believed in the stories I'd grown up reading and hearing about from the Bible. But my belief in God hadn't been the issue.

It was the other way around. "I'm just happy our paths crossed the way they did."

"I wouldn't be surprised if she felt the same, but it can be tricky," he said slowly, as if sorting through a bucket of approved statements in search of the right one. "To find the right balance."

"What balance?" I dug into the ice cream carton for another bite.

"Of helping without overstepping. It's difficult to see real needs and not want to rush the process to appease our own desire for restoration."

"Miles, come on. I already said I was joking about stealing her away. I'm not trying to rush any kind of process."

He shrugged and reached into the chip bag for another handful. "I'm just saying, in my experience, there's always a bigger picture to take in than what you can see at first glance."

"Well, while that may be true, I will say that Fir Crest Manor has more security cameras and checkpoints than the airport, so I can assure you there won't be much missed by any of the staff." Hmm . . . I wondered if my new mentor position would classify as staff.

I swung my legs over the side of the hideous chair Miles refused to replace. It was corduroy. Bark-brown corduroy, to be exact. But I'd given up on Miles caring a lick about his poor taste in home decor. I'd once offered to fund a furniture renovation for him myself, but he simply told me to redirect the budget to something that mattered more than where he ate takeout. Unless it cost less than ten dollars or could be consumed in a single sitting, Miles wasn't the best at receiving gifts. "Have you ever seen it? Fir Crest Manor? Silas gave me a full tour tonight."

"No, we've only met at restaurants."

Absently, I wondered what kind of food Silas might enjoy. Perhaps something sophisticated that required three different types of forks? "It's incredible, the house. It reminds me of the mansions I used to tour with Mimi when I was a teen. It's over twelve thousand square feet and has nine rooms, which they've mostly converted into classrooms and community areas, and then of course it has large open spaces, too. Oh, and it even has a theater room with all the wiring installed . . . just no screens or seats yet."

"They have a no-screen theater room?"

I laughed. "Yeah. Actually, some of the rooms are still in the *visionary* stage. There's not a lot of furniture to speak of, either. But the residents don't sleep in the main house. They actually have separate units for the guys and girls on either side of the manor. I think that's where the bulk of their cash went after they purchased the property."

"They didn't purchase it. It was awarded to them—to Silas's organization, actually."

I sat up straighter, eager to hear more of whatever intel my brother knew. How was it I was with Silas all evening and that never came up? "What do you mean by awarded?"

"I'm not sure of all the details. I just know that five or six years ago, while Silas was working with a group home in Spokane, an incredibly wealthy man passed away and left that whole estate to a trustee board. They interviewed hundreds of people from all over the country, because there were some pretty specific instructions on what the house could or could not be used for, and Silas was ready. He'd already been working on his nonprofit plan for The Bridge for years, and, well . . ." Miles shrugged. "From what I can recall, his proposal was approved unanimously. I met him shortly after that during a community function."

"Wow, that's incredible."

Miles chuckled. "I'm sure I made it sound much simpler than it actually was. I do know it took him a while to get all the proper licensing and through all the red tape."

I leaned back in my chair, wishing I could hear the story from Silas's mouth and subsequently wondering how he'd tell it. Somehow, I couldn't imagine him bragging on his achievements.

"I'm glad you decided to volunteer out there this summer, Molly," he said. "I don't think I've seen you this happy since you reached one hundred thousand followers."

I crinkled my nose. "That was years ago."

"Just an observation."

"For the record, I'm happy often. I love my life."

He simply nodded, doing his whole quiet reflective thing that drove me bonkers. "And Ethan's good with you spending so much time away from your duties?"

"My *duties*, as you call them, are managed on a scheduled timeline. Val keeps me organized and on track."

Miles chuckled. "Ah yes, good ol' Video Val."

"Stop calling her that. She's a real person."

"How would you know? You've never seen her in real life. She could be a really expensive hologram, or part of an AI militia. I just watched a docuseries on that."

"You and your docuseries." I rolled my eyes. "She's not a hologram or any kind of artificial intelligence. She's a single mom and a brilliant editor and a great friend. See? She's three in one. Like the trinity of virtual assistants."

"Your jokes prove you've been out of touch with humanity for too long."

"*Anyway*," I said, dragging the word out, "to answer your question, Ethan is thrilled I'm volunteering."

Miles did nothing to mask his disbelief. "What's in it for him?"

"A happier girlfriend, obviously." I flashed a smile at him, and Miles shook his head once but said nothing more on the subject. And neither did I.

We sat with our own munching sounds for the next few minutes until Miles finally picked up the remote and tossed it at me. "Fine, we can watch your organizer lady if you really want to."

"Ha! I *knew* you secretly liked that show."

"Nope. But anything's better than hearing you scrape the bottom of that ice cream carton."

I threw my wet spoon at his chest.

Molly

Ethan

> Good news. The paperwork for The Fit Glam Kit is set for you to sign.

Molly

> Did you figure out what they want me to do at the shoot? To wear?

Ethan

> Yes, they sent me the fine print details of everything that's in the box. It's their five-year anniversary box—all specialty summer must-haves. Perfect for you. Oh, and a bonus creation from Sophia Richards herself. She's excited for you to reveal it.

Molly

> Bonus creation?

Ethan

> She's a big fan of your work. Did you see she shared your post about date night looks? You're up at least 5K followers.

Molly

> Wow. That's super nice of her!

Ethan

I only find you the best.

Molly

😊 Just send all those details to Val, okay? I'll look them over tonight.

Oh, did you look at your schedule for that weekend?

Ethan

?

Molly

👫 🕯 🍧 🍦 😊 👫

Ethan

Is this a game? I give up.

Molly

😵 Our walk on the beach while eating ice cream and kissing on our sunset date!

Ethan

Sorry, babe. I couldn't make it work this time.

Molly

. . .

Ethan

Mr. Greggorio needs me back in New York the next day. I'll need to fly out after the shoot.

Molly

. . .

Okay.

FaceTime call.
Canceled FaceTime call.

Ethan

Why aren't you answering?

Molly

I just arrived at mentor group.

Ethan

Didn't you just do that? How many hours a week do they have you there?

I hope you're not letting anybody guilt you into doing more than you have to.

Molly

I'm fine. Need to go.

Ethan

Call me later.

◇◇◇

"Hi, Molly!" Clara waved me over to the group waiting under the pavilion outside. Though it was still a bit chilly to sit in the shade, there was something refreshing about being outdoors with the promise of summer in the air.

I heaved my giant beach bag over my shoulder and trotted across the grass. I hadn't seen Glo or Silas today, but I'd briefly met Jerry, the house manager for the guys' Bunkhouse. Turned out he was the Santa look-alike I'd seen on the brochure in the lobby and online.

"Hey, ladies," I said, joining the group of women and smiling directly at Wren, who sat at the end of the bench seat. "How was everybody's day?" I plopped my bag down on top of the table and noticed a not-so-subtle eye shift as I reached inside for one of the six goodie bags I'd assembled for each of the girls. I hadn't embossed them yet, but I figured that could be a great project for later. Perhaps a fun team-building activity? "I have a little happy-start-of-summer gift for you all."

Just as I'd hoped, the girls perked up. I recognized three of them immediately—the Front Row Populars from my class the other night. Their name tags read Felicia, Amy, and Jasmine. And the other two were the Snack Pantry Reward BFFs: Sasha and Monica.

"Oh, uh, Molly . . . before you hand those out, can we chat for just a minute?" Clara asked.

"Sure," I said, before addressing the girls. "I'll be right back. You'll love the lip glosses in these bags—it's my top pick for the summer, actually. Has an all-natural SPF with a hint of iridescent shimmer."

A couple of them giggled while Wren's expression matched the puzzled worry on Clara's. Had I done something wrong? How was that even possible when I'd only been on campus for all of twenty seconds?

I rounded the picnic table and followed Clara to one of the large pine trees next to the pavilion shelter.

"Sorry, Molly. I hate to have to be the one to tell you this, really, but there's a fairly strict policy about not giving the residents any material gifts. Silas usually has the volunteers sign something about it . . . but it's understandable that you could have missed it tucked in with all the other paperwork." Her face was so hopeful it was almost comical.

I thought back to the paperwork I signed several nights ago, briefly recalling an agreement regarding money and possessions. "Oh, right. I figured that was only about money or expensive items like jewelry or electronics," I said. "I wouldn't think it would apply to cute summertime gift bags?"

Clara couldn't have looked more uncomfortable than if she'd told me a thorn was lodged in her big toe. "Well, yes, you're right about that. We definitely can't give money or jewelry, but we're not supposed to give any kind of material items that can't be shared with everyone. It can create tension and jealousy among the girls."

"Jealousy?" The idea of a group of young adults being catty over tinted moisturizer felt more than a bit odd to me. "But they're all over eighteen."

"True, but age is often relative when it comes to kids who've grown up in trauma. Everything is filtered through a lens of *fairness*. It can seem like favoritism if only half the girls in the house receive a special gift. I'm sorry, I know your heart is totally in the right place with these bags, but I think it's best we don't hand them out today."

This new realization left me dumbfounded. "So no gifts . . . unless I can provide them for all the girls who live on campus?"

"Unfortunately, yes. I'm guessing you don't happen to have twelve goody bags with you?" Again, her optimism was endearing.

"Unfortunately, no." I'd handpicked every last summery product I had from sponsors present and past to make these gift bags. "But I'll be sure to bring another set next week. For Hannah's group." I glanced to the other girls' group sitting inside the gazebo, eyeing Hannah's third trimester belly and wondering if she was even going to make it to the end of August.

"I'm really sorry. It was super thoughtful of you."

I touched her upper arm. "It's totally fine. I just didn't know before and now I do. It's all good." And if it wasn't, I'd take it up with Silas.

"Thanks for being so understanding." She nodded once and then glanced at our girls, eyeing my beach bag with anticipation. "I was thinking earlier that since this is your first mentor meeting, I could lead things off to show you the structure we try to follow. But you'd be welcome to jump in whenever you'd like. Oh, maybe you'd want to lead prayer time today? It's the last thing we do as a group before the girls are dismissed for reflection time to journal."

Three words pecked against my skull. *Lead. Prayer. Time.* "You know, I think it would be best, for continuity sake, if you went ahead and closed us out in prayer this time. I'm happy to follow your example."

"Okay, sure, that works."

As we met up with the girls again, Clara's steps were much peppier than my own as I wondered just how to un-gift the presents I'd brought. Luckily, Clara took over that part, as well. She simply made it out to be a math blunder that would all be sorted out by the next meeting. And it would. I'd make sure to come back with twelve.

Clara was good people.

She opened our time asking a series of questions about everyone's day, to which the residents seemed to know the routine well.

Each of the girls took a couple minutes to give an update, bringing up issues like co-worker disputes, classmate problems, homework deadlines. Wren passed on it all.

I wondered how often Wren skipped these personal questions. Whatever the answer, Clara didn't seem bothered by her lack of response whatsoever.

"Great. Well, once again, I know we're all so happy to have Molly joining us this summer. She and I will be co-leading, so I wanted to invite you all to get to know her a bit better. If you have any specific questions for her before we move on to reflection time, please feel free to ask."

Five hands went up at once—all except for Wren's. She simply studied me from the end of the picnic bench without a word.

From Monica: "How many total followers do you have on your social media pages—like combined? Is it over two million?"

From Felicia: "Do you think you could give us all makeovers sometime?"

From Jasmine: "Yeah! And could we see a picture of your closet? You must have so many nice clothes. Is it true that you get sent free stuff from all kinds of companies?"

From Amy: "We looked you up on Tuesday night and saw that Selena Gomez follows you! Have you met her in real life? Do you get invited to celebrity parties? Have you ever dated anybody famous?"

From Sasha: "Is this really all you do for money? Make videos of yourself and talk about makeup?"

Ouch. Okay, so Sasha wasn't exactly the warmest of young women.

"Oh, well, wow. That's a whole lot of questions." I glanced at Clara, hoping for a rescue plan. Somehow, I doubted Silas would approve of Makeup Matters taking over the small group study handbook we were supposed to be following. But Clara was no help; she looked as curious as they did.

And then I had an idea.

"What if . . . what if we had a slumber party here at some point?

Like a whole evening dedicated to makeovers and hairstyles, and I could bring some yummy snacks and we could watch some cute romantic comedies or something? That might be a better time to get into the details of all your questions."

Hoping I hadn't broken some kind of protocol by making the suggestion, I glanced at Clara. But she was already bobbing her head in agreement. "We actually try to plan a dedicated girls' night each month—but I don't think we have a plan for later in the summer yet. Let me see here." She opened a spiral-bound planner on the table and flipped through weeks and months, her finger roaming past each date box overflowing with blue and black ink. Apparently, somebody needed to get this girl a second calendar. Finally, her finger stopped and she tapped an open weekend in July while offering me a hope-filled smile. "Any chance this date could work for you? I'd still need to run this all past Silas, but I can't imagine he'd have an issue with it."

She couldn't? Really? Obviously Clara and I knew two very different sides of Silas Whittaker. And for whatever reason, I seemed to evoke his irritated side far more often than any other person I'd encountered here. But perhaps things would go smoother overall if Clara was the one to ask the Duke of Fir Crest Manor for a makeover night and not me.

I picked up my phone, seeing notifications of four hundred forty-six comments on the photo I'd posted to my Instagram before I left the house. It featured a cream clutch handbag with gold hardware, a linen bullet-point journal, and a pale pink coffee mug boasting the hashtag #MakeupMatters propped beside a blush throw blanket. All items were twenty percent off today if they used the promotional link in my bio. Apparently, my followers had wildly approved.

The muscle memory in my trigger finger narrowly escaped clicking into my favorite social media outlet, but instead, I swiped into my calendar and double tapped the date she'd asked about.

Outside of some loose work notes specific to video themes and shoots, my days were wide open. I had exactly zero social engagements scheduled on any given date in July. Just like the majority of my evenings and weekends for much of the summer . . . and beyond.

In general, if Ethan wasn't flying in from Seattle for a spontaneous date night or flying me to some VIP conference or fashion shoot, I had little else going on outside of working at my home studio: taking pictures of new product lines, making and arranging food I'd eventually drop off to Miles, replying to hundreds of online friends, and video chatting with Val while I tried out the latest hair mask recommendation.

I swallowed, squinting at the blank calendar box on my phone before glancing up to the girls again. "Hmm, I think I can make something work for that weekend. I may have to juggle a few things, but it shouldn't be too much of an issue. That's the glory of owning your own business, I suppose." My laugh fell short as I realized the audience sitting in front of me. *Stupid, Molly.* The majority of these girls didn't even know what it was like to have a paying job, much less owning a successful company.

"Great!" Clara said. "Then I'll work on setting something up with Silas and Glo."

The squeals from five of the six girls were electrifying as talks of what kind of makeup they wanted to try first ensued. I happily obliged in this conversation, offering brands and insights and eventually pulling out my phone to show them a folder of products I had on hand at home. More giddy squeals as they passed my phone around.

"What about you, Wren? Is there anything specific you'd like us to plan for our girl's night?"

"I don't think so. I'll probably just watch," she said quietly.

"No way. I have a very strict policy of my own. If one girl goes glam, then we all go glam," I said as if I hadn't just made up the rule on the spot.

Her lips twitched. "You're going to do glam makeovers on twelve girls in a single night?"

Hmm. She had a point. That *was* a lot of makeovers to do all on my own. "Nope, I'll need an assistant. And I volunteer you as tribute."

"Now, that's a perfect job for you, Wren. This girl has skills when it comes to hair," Clara piped in.

"I know, I've seen some of her intricate braid work." Much like the one she wore now that looked like a rose in full bloom.

Clara stood up from the table and waved to Hannah and her girls from across the field. They were on the move, spiral-bound journals in hand. Obviously, our group was late on dismissing the girls for reflection time. Which meant I'd likely bulldozed right over Clara's allotted prayer time with talk of going full glam. *Way to be spiritual, Mentor Molly.*

As Clara asked for prayer requests, I whispered across the table at Wren. "What do you say? Will you be my assistant?"

Wren shifted her eyes to the girls at the opposite side of the picnic table who were staring at us both—Sasha and Monica. But then, shockingly, she gave me a nod. I spent the next several minutes of Clara's prayer closing my eyes while fighting off an all-teeth grin.

I might have lost out on a romantic beach date with my workaholic boyfriend, but somehow Wren's little head nod had just more than made up for it.

· 15 ·

Molly

I flopped back on the sofa and crossed my slippered feet at the ankles. My black charcoal beauty mask was already starting to feel like shrink-wrap on my skin. I faked a yawn to test the crusty layer forming over my cheeks. It didn't budge. What was this stuff made of? Rubber cement? I picked up the tube to examine the ingredients list, but who was I kidding? No human with average eyesight could read the minuscule print on the back.

I grabbed my phone to take another scroll through all my feeds, noting the stats of my latest post and stopping to *heart* each comment—or in some cases leave a response—when I noted the top right corner of my opened app. My direct message inbox showed over a hundred waiting messages.

I went in prepared, knowing that half the senders would be trolls—some telling me I was fat, ugly, a poser, or a horrible human being for profiting from the products I promoted, while still others would be asking for a variety of inappropriate pictures. Sometimes I'd even receive a marriage proposal or two. The only response I'd give to any of those was an automatic *block*. One of the first rules I'd learned in this business: Never engage with the crazies.

But a single message near the top caused my delete-happy finger to pause: Felicity Fashion Fix.

Well, this was curious. Felicity hadn't said a single word to me since the debacle that involved both our legal teams having to intervene on account of her stealing my series idea and using it for her sponsor's products. Unfortunately, her crime against me had fallen under the legal header of "intellectual property," and not much could be done.

Her message simply read: *Way to hit seven hundred thousand. What's it like dating an agent who controls all your content for his own gain? Oh, wait, I already know. Word of free advice: Hold on to your soul before he finds a way to sell that, too.*

I stared at her words, my breathing growing shallower by the second as I took in her backhanded compliment and her clickbait lies. She'd never dated Ethan—I'd asked him point-blank before I said yes to going out with him the first time. I hadn't wanted to be one in a long line of clients-turned-girlfriends. But not only had she *not* been his girlfriend, she'd only been his client long enough for Ethan to gauge what an absolute train wreck she was to work with. From the stories he'd told me early on, Felicity was a demanding witch of a woman who threw diva tantrums often and schemed her way to the top. I witnessed this firsthand when she stole from me by hacking into Cobalt's active marketing campaigns—a violation that was rectified with tighter internal security and a termination of her contract. Shortly after the breach, Ethan decided he would only take on one beauty influencer in his agency at a time.

For a moment, I debated responding to her, debated starting a thread with all the reasons I believed she was a fake and why I'd never in a billion years take life advice from a manipulative cheat like her. . . . But instead, I breathed in through my nose and out through my mouth.

And then I deleted her poison.

The instant her message was cleared from view, a local number I didn't recognize lit up my screen. I swiped left and sent it to my voicemail. Not thirty seconds later, my phone vibrated with a waiting audio message.

I clicked to listen to the recording. Within the first syllable, I knew exactly who it was, and I smiled when his dignified and professional voice came through my phone speaker. I immediately saved his contact information as *The Duke of Fir Crest Manor*.

"Hello, Molly, this is Silas Whittaker. I'd like to follow up with you when you have a few minutes, regarding today's mentor meeting with the young ladies. I apologize that I wasn't on campus this afternoon to ask you in person. Please give me a call at your earliest convenience. Thank you."

I couldn't help the laughter that bubbled up inside me. Why Silas had felt the need to tell me his last name, I'd never know. There was only one Silas in my world who spoke like a nobleman, and he was it.

I called him back.

He answered on the first ring. "Hello, this is Silas."

"Hello, Silas, this is Molly McKenzie." I fought the laugh behind my voice. "How are you?"

"I'm well, and yourself?"

I smiled at the properness of it all and then immediately regretted the action. My face suddenly felt like it was being sucked through a vacuum hose. "Ouch." The mask tightened around my mouth, nose, chin, and eyes. What kind of torture device was this?

"Are you okay?"

"Yes, sorry. I just have—*ouch*—something stuck to my face."

I could almost imagine the crinkle forming in the middle of his forehead as he worked to interpret what I was saying, because I'd suddenly become the Tin Man from *The Wizard of Oz* in desperate need of his oil can.

"As in . . . what exactly?" he asked.

"A mask." I scraped and tugged at the dried peel under my chin. It didn't budge. Obviously, this mask had been mismarked, seeing as this was the opposite of a self-care routine. It was more like a bad prank.

"Isn't it a little early for that?"

"Huh?" I squeezed my watering eyes closed.

"Halloween. It's only June."

At this, I stopped all futile attempts at peeling back a mask that refused to be peeled so I could fully register his words. And once I did, I lost it—completely undone by the thought of Silas envisioning me lying on my sofa on a random Friday night in June with a Halloween mask stuck to my face. "No, no. Not . . ." I couldn't catch my breath. ". . . a . . . costume. . . ."

"What? Molly, I can't understand you."

"A beauty mask," I said through a wheeze. The tightness in my face cracked at the untamed laughter, releasing approximately ten percent of its death grip on my skin. "It's black like tar and made from a dead sea urchin that lives in some special sea."

"In some special sea? Sounds complex. Although I'm still unsure why you'd choose to apply it in the first place. Isn't your face a critical part of your . . . of whatever it is you do online?"

I couldn't stop. Tears poured from my eyes for a whole new reason now. Picturing Silas's expression, a look of shocked horror at the words I'd just spoken out loud, had to be the funniest thing happening on the planet today.

"If you don't stop wheezing," he said, "I'll be forced to contact the authorities."

"I can't even handle this conversation right now." Tears dripped from the corners of my eyes.

"That makes two of us."

Incredibly, Silas did not hang up. And even more incredibly, I had the distinct impression that he might actually be enjoying himself. Maybe even as much as I was.

"How exactly does one go about taking something like that off?" he asked.

"It was supposed to peel off with ease," I said, recalling the words on the package. "But I can assure you, there is no ease happening here."

"Perhaps you need to apply the Band-Aid strategy to this predicament? Take a deep breath and tear it off."

He obviously did not understand the severity at hand. "I can tell you with some level of certainly that if I applied that strategy to this, I would lose my nose."

"So what's your plan B?"

"Hope it disintegrates by morning?"

Silas laughed, and I laughed with him. And even with a black sea urchin suctioned to my face, I couldn't remember the last time I'd laughed like this. Weeks? Months?

I sighed. "I'm gonna try a warm washcloth, though I'm fairly sure it's gone straight through my pores and into my bone structure at this point."

"A case for job hazard insurance if ever there was one."

"You could have been a lawyer."

"I almost was."

I placed my slippered feet to the floor, shocked by this admission. Not because I couldn't imagine Silas in a courtroom wearing a pressed three-piece suit and carrying a briefcase. That was pretty much the way I saw him even when he was wearing a T-shirt and jeans. But the fact that he would admit something about himself so openly to me was . . . surprisingly nice.

"Really? Why weren't you?"

"I realized I could do more for these kids by doing the kind of work I'm doing now. Although, I did pass my bar exam."

"You passed the bar exam but didn't practice law?"

"That's correct. But I have been able to use my understanding of certain policies and practices to help the community I serve."

Quietly, I padded my way into the bathroom and reached for a fresh washcloth before running it under warm tap water. I hoped the sound wouldn't interrupt his line of thought, because I wanted to hear whatever Silas was willing to share about his life. It'd been a long time since I had a phone conversation with someone other than Miles or Val. Ethan and I primarily communicated through text.

When Silas didn't volunteer anything else, I prompted him. "Miles told me you were the one behind The Bridge receiving Fir Crest Manor after it went to the estate board."

"There was a team of us involved. It certainly was not a solo effort."

And yet, even from that one sentence, I knew Silas had more to do with the acquisition of that giant house for his program than anyone else. That was the kind of guy he was. No one who met Silas in person would ever think of him as someone who'd be okay with doing anything halfway. Silas was the kind of person you wanted to be next to when the world turned upside down. Because while chaos ensued, he would be the guy with the clear head and the strong voice, the one mapping out the next right steps for us all.

"Well, I'm glad it was awarded to The Bridge. I can't imagine that gorgeous manor being used for anything else." I pressed the damp cloth to my face, feeling instant relief as the warmth soaked into my dehydrated skin.

"We've come a long way, but we still have a long way to go."

His words prompted a familiar question. "What's your off-the-page goal for the program, Silas?"

"My . . . off-the-page goal?"

"Yes, sorry," I said, realizing how normal that question was to me but how weird it likely sounded to the outside person. "It's a phrase Miles and I made up years ago when we started goal setting every January. Although that makes him sound like a willing participant, and he's not. He complains about coming over for days beforehand every year, and then only agrees because he can never say no to my white chicken chili. But we coined that phrase for the goals that are too big for just one page. I'm curious: What would it be for The Bridge?"

The hard sigh that followed made something in my chest constrict as I made my way to the sofa once more, wiping my under-eye area gently, then folding the warm rag in half to do the same on the other side of my face. Silas was under no obligation to answer this dig-deep question of mine. We weren't friends. We weren't really even colleagues. We were just . . . two people who existed in the same time and space on Tuesday and Friday.

"Interesting timing," he all but murmured. "I'm actually just arriving home from a trustee meeting where I was asked a variety of questions about the future of our program. I can say with some level of confidence that your approach is far more appealing than theirs."

The idea of a trustee board peppering Silas with questions did not sit well with me. It was difficult to imagine anybody challenging his authority in an area he had proven himself an expert in. "Is everything okay?" I tucked my feet beneath me before reaching for my mug of now-cool ginger tea, my stomach suddenly unsettled. "I mean, I'm sure you're not at liberty to discuss details, but is the program okay? The kids?"

"Yes." Only it wasn't the kind of *yes* wrapped in a sigh of relief. It was the kind of yes that seemed contingent on a list of other *yeses*. I knew that version of the word quite well, seeing as it was most often used during my meetings with the Cobalt Group while Ethan was wearing his manager hat and not his boyfriend hat. Those hats were starting to look more and more the same these days.

"Well, good. Because I've got a drawer full of pointy hair accessories that could easily double as weapons if I needed to give some old dudes the what for."

"There are several women on the board, as well."

"My accessories drawer is equal opportunity."

He chuckled as I heard the jangle of keys, a door opening and closing, and footsteps walking on some kind of hard surface floor—definitely not carpet. Wood? Tile? What would the personal residence of one Silas Whittaker look like? Did he organize his spice cabinet and food pantry like he did his office bookshelf? "I'll keep the offer in mind. Thank you."

"You're welcome."

Tap water turned on in the background, hitting a sink basin before filling something. A glass? A container?

"What are you making right now?"

A pause. "Tea."

"You're a tea drinker? So am I! What kind do you like?"

"Chamomile."

"Huh."

"I suppose you have an opinion about this?"

"Not exactly. Though it is curious why you would choose such a flavorless option as your tea of choice," I said.

A quiet chuckle, and then, to my utter shock, Silas switched gears entirely. "I'd like to see every name that represents a teen in transition not only have a bed but a home, people to rally behind them and believe they can be more than the cards they've been dealt. I'd like to see every room at Fir Crest Manor used to its fullest potential—even our barren lobby. I'd like to triple our staff, providing jobs to weary case workers who need respite yet still want to be part of the solution to improve the system. We'll need several more cottages built for sleeping quarters, and someday, I'd like to provide an option to extend our program into independent apartments for those older than twenty-one but who still need some guidance and a safe place to land. On that note, I'd like to have a dedicated closet of supplies for graduates who are ready to move on. I want them to leave with more than the worn-out luggage they came to us with." The high-pitched whistle of a kettle sounded in the background, and I pressed the phone closer to my ear to hear Silas's voice. "Ultimately, I want Fir Crest to feel like a home, especially to the residents who've never had one." He paused a beat. "Does that qualify for your off-the-page goals?"

"Yes," I whispered, though I could hardly exhale, my mind already whirring away with ideas—the first being to submit a formal request to Mr. Greggorio at The Cobalt Group. I'd heard stories of large donations being awarded to special organizations connected to his clientele. In my opinion, The Bridge had to be one of the most honorable nonprofits in the nation.

And then a new thought struck me: *What would it be like to help somebody else reach their off-the-page goals?*

"Good." He cleared his throat. "Because I actually did have an agenda for this phone call when I made it originally, and it wasn't to discuss sea urchin masks, bar exams, or my boring choice of tea."

I set the cold washrag down on my coffee table. "To be fair, you were the one who said *boring*."

"I spoke to Clara, and I wanted to check in with you on how your first mentor group went."

"It went great!" I said, a little too excitedly, hoping she'd left out a certain summertime goodie bag debacle. "I mean, the girls seemed comfortable with me being there, and they answered all Clara's questions—well, except for Wren. She was pretty quiet, but we made a plan to—" I squeezed my eyes shut, remembering at the last possible second that I wasn't going to be the initiator on said plan. Clara, the person Silas actually trusted, was in charge of that.

"Is this plan related to a makeover and movie night at Lavender Cottage?"

I mouthed the words *Thank you, Clara!* to my empty living room. "That would be the one, yes. Would that be something—" I hesitated, searching for the right angle, though the words pained me to ask—"we'd need your stamp of approval on?"

"It would be, yes."

I took a deep breath, prepared for a fight that might cause me to retrieve my hair chopsticks from the drawer, when Silas said, "But I've already given it. It's already on the calendar."

I may have squealed a tiny bit. "It'll be great, Silas. The girls were so excited about the idea, and you won't have to worry about anything. I'll take care of all the planning. I've already pinned the snack tray I'll be bringing to my Party Foods Pinterest board so there won't be any need for food preparation at the cottage itself. I can bring it all with me."

"You can submit receipts for whatever food items you purchase."

"Oh, well, thank you." Though I'd never in a million years ask a not-for-profit to buy food for a makeover snack tray. "I'm just thrilled you approved it!"

"You're welcome."

I took a breath as a mix of unexpected gratitude and vulnerability rose inside me, compelling me to speak. "Silas?"

"Yes?"

"I realize you took a chance on me—saying yes after you'd already said no . . . but I want you to know that I'm really looking forward to spending the summer with these girls." A truth that was becoming more and more apparent. I loved having a set time and place to be each week, with actual people who expected me to simply show up. To sit. To listen. To share. To be nothing more or less than Molly McKenzie. It was such a different reality than the one I lived in most of the week. And there was something surprisingly refreshing about that. Something right. Something I hadn't even known I'd been missing.

"Many of our young ladies have said the same thing about you. We're glad to have you with us, Molly." He went quiet for a few beats. "And I'm glad you didn't take my first no as a final answer."

The validation I heard in his voice caused my throat to swell and my eyes to sting. I worked to push the unexpected emotion away and simply said, "Have a good night, Silas. Thank you for calling."

"Good night."

"Bye."

I stared at my darkened phone screen for the longest time, replaying his words and blinking back unshed tears. It was easy to dismiss the compliments I received from my followers online—always begging for more videos, more entertaining reviews, more affordable bargain wear and comparisons. Because those kinds of compliments were consumer based, a satiation that lasted only until my next post. My next campaign. My next VIP deal link.

But this kind of affirmation felt different. Personal. Honest. Real.

And something inside me yearned for more of it.

◇◇◇

Silas

I stared at my phone screen for the longest time. Replaying Molly's words back to me. Hearing her voice inside my head as she said good-bye. Wondering if I'd misinterpreted the tears I swore I'd heard in her voice before she ended our call.

I rubbed at the stress headache presenting at the front of my skull, pressing my thumb into my right temple. As usual, I'd steeped the tea bag for double the recommended time. The first sip was always the worst. The flavor was as bland as Molly had said, but I didn't drink it for the taste. I drank it for the anti-inflammatory qualities I'd researched for reducing tension head-aches. It was worth a shot. So far I hadn't noticed much change, and after tonight's meeting with the board, I doubted an eight-ounce cup of hot water would bring much relief.

But what plagued me wasn't just the fact that the trustee board had turned down my proposal for taking out a loan against the equity of Fir Crest Manor for the sake of an expansion that could save hundreds of lives—it was the number they'd attached to the project. A number so beyond radical it felt as fictitious as if we'd been asked to slay a dragon or chase after a legendary ring.

We needed to raise a million dollars before we could break ground on new sleeping quarters or hire new staff or save teen-agers who believed their only chance of survival was prostitution and pushing drugs. I dismissed the scarred face that materialized in my mind with a single shake of my head. I hadn't been able to save my brother from a life of ruin, and as much as I'd fought to make a difference in the lives of other kids like him . . . a million dollars may as well be a hundred million to a nonprofit that barely managed to scrape by as it was.

Steaming mug in hand, I swiped my phone off the counter once again and tapped on an app I rarely used unless I needed to launch a private investigation on one of our residents or one of their associates. Social media wasn't entirely useless. While I'd likely never understand the people who felt compelled to air their dirty laundry so freely to a world of perpetual strangers, they were also the easiest types to get a read on.

But this time, I typed *Molly McKenzie* into the search bar.

Several options came up at once—including one with a blue check mark, indicating the official page of Molly McKenzie of Makeup Matters with Molly.

My finger hovered over her picture, as if debating the real reason behind this unwarranted perusal. Because this had nothing to do with personal safety. Nor was it about scoping out a potential threat.

This was one-hundred-percent about satisfying my own curiosity.

I clicked on the first video that came up—Molly, looking into the camera with her cascade of golden hair and sea glass eyes, talking away about some magical towel that offered a remedy for frizz while drying shower-wet hair in record time. Her animated expressions were as inviting as they were intoxicating. At one point, she tossed the towel and did a slow-mo of shaking her damp hair while she lip-synced to the chorus of "Natural Woman."

I laughed out loud and clicked on another one titled *Yoga Pants or Dress Pants—You Be the Judge!*

Again, Molly hammed it up on-screen, strutting down a hotel hallway and interviewing the innocent bystanders about her pants. Were they better suited for the gym or for the office? Or were they interchangeable? Naturally, there was one pair that could work for either, and there happened to be a special deal on them for only the next twelve hours if her viewer clicked on the link below. Not shockingly, there was a comment with more than three hundred sad face emojis stating that the pants had sold out.

I leaned back against the edge of the countertop, navigating my way through post after post—some were replays of past livestreams, some were reviews of products she tested out right then for the first time, opening packages and reading instructions as if they were the next great American novel. Others were time-lapse videos following a sequence of events. But the common denominator was the same—Molly. In her element. Funny, bright, opinionated, classy, smart, and always, *always* stunning.

I viewed her poll requests, asking her fans to vote on specific products or event outfits. And vote they had. Thousands and thousands of times. She honored the popular vote with a picture every time, these posts securing far more attention than the majority.

I scrolled through her replies. Not surprisingly, Molly was nothing but perfectly polite in all her responses. No matter what the commenter posted, she never failed to thank them for their feedback. Negative or positive.

I didn't know how long I studied her page, but by the time I switched to the other profile platform she mentioned during her videos, my tea was cold and my lower back had begun to complain.

My finger halted almost immediately as a grid of small squares loaded on my screen. Though almost every picture of her could have stopped traffic, there was one that caught my eye more than the rest. The one with a man sleeping on a sofa behind her sad-face selfie, captioned *Jet lag is the thief of romance.*

Heat flared in my gut.

I didn't need to click on the image or read any of the comments to know the answer I'd find waiting there, yet I did anyway. And the revelation put a sharp end to whatever warped reality I'd allowed myself to briefly entertain.

Molly McKenzie had a boyfriend.

· 16 ·

Molly

Because our flight times hadn't lined up, Ethan the Boyfriend had promised to meet me at the shoot location in Malibu, while Ethan the Manager had promised he'd taken care of all the details of my contract. My electronic signature had barely spit out a confirmation receipt to my inbox before I was sent a first-class ticket to LAX from The Fit Glam Kit. A rare but welcome perk!

With the poolside photo shoot looming, I'd raced home after finishing up my second official mentor group at The Bridge—which had gone swimmingly after handing out all twelve goodie bags to each girl at the house—and started the detailed process of applying my favorite tan-in-a-can secret potion to my ghostly white self. After living in a winter tundra for five to six months out of any given year, this girl needed some big-time help in the self-tanning department. Thanks to my tried-and-true method, it was a simple fix. I'd even documented my entire tanning process once—showing specific techniques for known problem areas around fingers, heels, knees, and that problematic elbow skin region. *The Ten Commandments of Fake Tanning by Makeup Matters* was one of my first breakout videos. Something like a hundred thousand views within the first forty-eight hours.

But really, "Thou Shalt Not Apply Tanner Without Proper Exfoliation" is a rule that should never be violated, lest you find yourself looking like you were caught in a rusty rainstorm. There were few things as unattractive as a bad self-tan.

Outside the tinted window of the black Escalade I'd been riding in since the airport, palm trees, rocky cliffs, and glimpses of the Pacific Ocean blurred together. I rolled down my window just a tad, breathing in the salty air and wishing once again for someone I could enjoy the moment with. At least Ethan was on his way soon.

I'd been to California for work-related reasons many times over the past couple years, but never for an on-location photo shoot at a celebrity's poolside patio simply because *there was no better place to shoot.* Ethan had made sure to copy and paste that sentence from The Fit Glam Kit's marketing team.

As the Escalade pulled up to an automatic gate leading to Sophia Richards's Malibu estate, my jaw unhinged. The mansions in Malibu were next level. This kind of wealth and glamour never failed to boggle my mind.

A text chimed from inside my purse. It was from Val.

Val

> You there? How is it? Is Ethan there with you?
> Why do I feel like a nervous mother?

I smiled.

Molly

> I'm fine, Mom. 😊 I just arrived! Estate is crazzzzzy. He's not here yet but should be soon.

Val

> Rooting for you! Have fun! Text me later!

Molly

> <3

I started to slip my phone back into the pocket of my purse when it chimed against my palm.

The Duke of Fir Crest Manor

Any idea why this was delivered at Fir Crest today? There's no name or information attached to it. Just instructions to put it in the lobby and have a happy day.

I smiled as a picture of an oversized black leather sectional and chair set appeared in the new text thread, and then shoved my phone back inside my handbag. I may not be able to fund an apartment complex on Fir Crest Manor's campus, but I could surely furnish the lobby. And as of yesterday morning, I'd received Mr. Greggorio's stamp of approval on my request for a donation from Cobalt. His written response had been far, far beyond my wildest hopes! Not only was he willing to donate to the growth of The Bridge's program, he'd actually gone one step further and offered his annual Dream Big Scholarship! As soon as he veri-fied all the facts and presented the nomination to his board, the check would be signed and sent. I bit my lip, imagining the mo-ment I could announce to Silas that he would soon be handed a one-hundred-thousand-dollar check to use as seed money for his off-the-page goals.

"Molly!" A stunning, bronze-skinned woman with a satin floral wrap dress descended a sweeping staircase attached to the open-air second floor of the mansion. "You are even more gorgeous in person." She greeted me with a kiss on each of my cheeks. "I'm Truella Agate. Let me be the first to welcome you to Sophia's Malibu estate. Unfortunately, she's currently at her NYC residence this week for a project, but rest assured, our team is ecstatic to work with you. Sophia's been a fan of yours since that dollar store cosmetic makeover you did last year." The high notes of her forced laugh were an assault to my ears, but amazingly, I with-held a grimace. "Now that was some funny stuff. When she sent it around to her staff, we were howling. We must have replayed the part where you tried to smoke out that hideous eyeshadow for an 'evening look' like a hundred times. Your content is always so clever!"

"Oh, wow. Thank you. That was a fun series to shoot," I said, still a bit shell-shocked that someone like Sophia Richards would even know my name, let alone the work I'd done. "It's lovely to be here."

"We're just thrilled your manager could make the timing work so quickly—when Victoria dropped out it left us in quite a bind. Legal can sometimes hold these things up for weeks, months even. It's fabulous when all the stars align."

As I followed her up white marble steps and onto a balcony boasting billowy sheer curtains and white linen patio furniture, I let her words soak in. Had I known I was a fill-in? Had Ethan mentioned that I'd been a Plan B for this collaboration and it somehow slipped my mind? I could almost hear the reply he'd give if I could ask him now: *When you position yourself for opportunity, opportunity will position you for greatness.*

Two enormous sliding glass doors were the only dividers between the poolside area and the house, and from what I could see, the inside was just as elaborate as the outside. Palm trees shaded the stamped concrete, where at least two dozen patio loungers bordered an infinity pool. The extensive bar in the corner, with tastefully lacquered wood that reflected the pool water, had shelves stocked full of more liquor than I'd seen in three of my local restaurants combined. It was certainly not a Silas-approved outdoor living space, that was for sure.

As I turned my eyes back to Truella—was that really her name?—a strange and overwhelming sense of I-don't-belong-here washed over me. An odd sensation, since I'd been in homes of grandeur and opulence before, but this was something else completely. I couldn't shake it. Not when Truella pointed out the snack table with every kind of fresh fruit and chopped veggie known to mankind, or even when she introduced me to the artists in the makeup tent who offered me bottomless flutes of champagne I declined.

Suddenly I wished I were somewhere else entirely. In a different large-scale home without any of this glitz or glamour. And with people who were far more down to earth. People who could probably build twenty Fir Crest Manors for teens in need of a home off the sale of just one of these Malibu mansions.

"So what did you think of the Tubee? Ingenious, right? I think it's gonna be one of our most popular items this summer. Sophia designed it herself. She figured you'd have the most fun with it, given your peppy personality."

I scanned my memory for what she might be referring to, but I came up empty. *Tubee?* No idea. "Oh, yes. Totally ingenious for sure."

She twisted back, smiled, and left me to get glammed up by Danny in the makeup tent. Sometime during the bronzer-and-highlighting stage, I texted Ethan.

Molly
You get lost?

Ethan
In limo now. Everything good so far?

I snapped a side profile picture of Danny adding another few swipes of bronzer to my jawbone, then sent it to Ethan.

Ethan
Perfection.

After fiddling with my favorite photo filter for indoor lighting, I asked Danny if he minded me posting some pics to my Instagram story as long as I tagged him. He laughed me off, adding that I was "too cute for even asking" and "of course not." I captioned the story *Surprise Summer Shoot . . . TBA!* Within minutes, my notifications blew up and the heaviness pressing down on my shoulders began to melt.

See? I told the unsettled feeling inside me. *This is fine. Everything is just fine.*

Turned out, going *full glam* in Malibu was an intense process. I was quite certain I'd have to scrape this foundation off later with a spatula. But I'd definitely have to circle back to the highlighter stick Danny used on my cheekbones. I wanted to buy a few for the upcoming sleepover in Lavender Cottage.

Just as I was putting my phone away after getting dressed in the one-piece swimsuit and sarong ensemble that had been waiting for me in my dressing room—*thank you for that, Ethan!*—my text chirped another time.

Clara

> Hi, Molly! We prayed for your big shoot today during our Saturday morning pancake feed (Jake never wants to miss Glo's pancakes). The girls just watched your IG story, and they're currently texting all their friends to like your pages and to watch for your updates. You have quite the fan club here now. Pretty sure you'll win the popular vote for Mentor of the Year! Haha. 😊 Good luck today! P.S. You look radiant!

For some odd reason, the kindness of Clara's text message—a woman who had known me for no more than two weeks—caused the tip of my nose to tingle. The Bridge girls had seen me just now? They'd shared me with their friends? Somehow the idea was as flattering as it was terrifying.

"Molly?" Truella called out. "We're getting everything set up at the pool for you. Our producers thought it might be fun to do the whole kit reveal on camera—though I know you already saw the items. Just do your best to act surprised at everything." She laughed at herself.

"Of course." I stuck the phone in my purse and followed after her again, tightening the sarong knot at my hip. The fabric was itchy, woven with metallic ribbon that scratched my skin, but hey, I was grateful for the coverage.

The crew positioned me directly behind a table, commenting several times on my Malibu Barbie hair. With the pool water shimmering behind me and my sarong blowing in the warm breeze, I couldn't help but contrast this tropical reality with the one from yesterday: sitting at a picnic table with all six of my mentor girls as we zipped up our sweatshirts in the cool shade up north. I touched the pink-and-white box in the middle of the tabletop surface, thinking about how much they'd love one of these summer kits and how none of the sparkly items inside would be something their limited budgets could afford. Maybe I could ask for twelve boxes to be shipped to The Bridge for the girls after we were through here today.

"We're just about ready here, Molly," Truella purred. "Just making final adjustments to the lighting."

I glanced at the cheat sheet she'd taped between me and the box, just in case I needed more than what I could ad-lib on my own. It was a nice but likely unnecessary gesture. From the email exchange I'd read on the plane between Ethan and the marketing director, I'd learned more about their Anniversary Campaign. It was an honor they'd asked me to influence their products and company, even if I was on their B list.

Truella primped my hair and tucked the tail of my sarong behind me. "We're gonna try to do this video in two takes so we can get the most authentic reactions from you when you open the collection for the first time. Since you're used to doing lives, I'm figuring that won't be an issue. The first one will be an intro where you'll make sure to mention your love for Sophia and her company, as well as to remind viewers about the twenty-dollar discount code when they request their first subscription month."

"Sounds good." Though wasn't it strange for me to talk up a woman I'd never interacted with before? Although, I supposed many of my followers did the same thing with me every day. How many of them did I know in real life? How many had I spoken to or shared time with? I didn't need to be a math whiz like Clara to know the number was far closer to zero than I cared to admit.

As the cameraman made some last-minute adjustments, I posed with my most practiced of smiles, the one I used on all my video openers. The one that wouldn't create a weird still frame once the segment became a minimized icon on someone's phone screen. This post, however, would be a sponsored promotional ad that would run on all major social media platforms, be emailed directly to customer leads, and be played throughout binge-worthy TV shows that matched the keyword algorithms of the viewers who watched. Viewers like the girls I mentored at The Bridge.

Truella pulled my tousled hair forward to cascade over my shoulders and down my chest. The producer signaled, and Truella gave me a we're-ready-when-you-are nod and finger point.

"Hello, everyone! I'm Molly McKenzie with Makeup Matters with Molly. And I'm absolutely delighted to be at Sophia Richards's gorgeous Malibu home to celebrate with her and the entire Fit Glam squad on their five-year anniversary! So many of you have enjoyed this incredible box subscription over the years, and I'm telling you right now, they have saved the best of the best for this summer's glamorous collection!" I leaned forward to pretend whisper to the camera. "And a little birdie told me this July box holds over two hundred dollars *more* in value than usual."

Truella gave me a thumbs-up followed by a wrap-up sign, which was my cue to drop in the promo code commercial.

"And cut. Wow!" Truella exchanged impressed glances with her camera crew. "I think that might be our best first take ever. You're such a natural at this, girl!"

"Thanks." I did a quick scan of the outdoor area, wondering once again where Ethan was.

"This next run will be easy. Just you opening the box and giving a few seconds to each item. We'll do a few shots later with you using a few of the featured items we mentioned in the email, and then we'll splice them all together for the promo. Sound good?"

I nodded, and she pointed at me to begin. My finger was already hooked under the lid of the box, where a dozen individually wrapped items in pink-and-white polka-dotted pieces of tissue paper waited. I unwrapped them all, *oohing* and *aahing* over the summery nail polishes, sheer lip glosses, cooling after-sun gel, a hibiscus body spray, soothing eye cream, and the travel toiletry bags. And then in the back, along the flat edge of the cardboard treasure chest, lay a narrow piece of tissue. Smiling, I unrolled it, wondering what the slender piece of fabric could be used for.

I did a quick glance at the cheat sheet and tried to recover without having to stop rolling. "And this specialty item is the Tubee: a no-show tan line alternative created by Sophia Richards herself."

The elastic-like stretch of it confirmed my first suspicions as truth. It was most definitely a headband, perfect for holding your hair off your face so no flyaways could block your face from the sun. I began to put it on, talking up its comfort and styleability, while inventing unique terminology to compliment a piece of fabric that somehow retailed for $49.99—given the notes attached to the table in front of me.

But when I glanced up at Truella, her shoulders were shaking while laugh tears coated her cheeks. She was trying to mouth something to me, but it wasn't her words so much as her chest-pointing gestures that finally clued me in.

This was not a headband, but a . . . breast band?

I pulled it from the confines of my wild mane with a just-joking kind of laugh as the sensation of molten lava filled my belly. "Oh, I just love these multi-use products, don't you? But of course the Tubee's main objective is to be a"—I read the words straight from the laminated description sheet on the table—"'perfectly sheer barrier to tanning a lady's most delicate feminine parts this summer.'"

A barrier I hoped with every inch of my fake-tanned body I wouldn't be expected to model for the promotional video montage Truella had mentioned only a few moments ago. But not even my most optimistic self could be fooled into thinking that Ethan had somehow protected me from such a fate. Not when this celebrity partnership represented an *opportunity for greatness*.

And it was right then, with the Tubee dangling from my fingertips like it carried a transmittable disease within its single sheer layer, that my boyfriend strolled up to the scene looking as if all was right in Malibu.

"Cut. Let's take ten," Truella called, wiping the smeared makeup under her eyes. "That was pure brilliance, Molly. Leave it to you to give the Tubee such a fun personality! That was the best laugh I've had in months."

Only I wasn't laughing. Not even close to laughing. Because this was exactly what I'd been afraid of. This was exactly what I'd asked my manager-boyfriend to shield me from. And from the expression on Ethan's face, none of this was a surprise to him.

Truella continued on, unaware of the fire blazing from my retinas. "Go ahead and get changed in the dressing room, and Danny will touch up your makeup. We'll regroup by the lawn chairs near the bar, where Travis is getting everything set up for your still shots now."

While Truella and the camera crew talked strategy for the next sequence of shots, I excused myself and grabbed the sleeve of Ethan's crisp linen shirt. Without a word, I hauled him to the closest closed-door location I could find to ensure privacy: the hut-like sauna near the bar. The instant I closed the door behind us, I recognized this was a mistake of epic proportions, as the tiny room had to be over a hundred degrees. But we were committed now; there was no going back.

"Molly, come on." Ethan pulled away and brushed off his shirt. "What's the issue?"

I anchored my hands on my hips as sweat prickled my chest and shoulders. "Please tell me you didn't know about the Tubee? Tell me you didn't alter the product email they copied me on so that I wouldn't see it included in the lineup."

"Molly, babe, just calm down a minute—"

But I was already shaking my head. "I'm not putting that thing on." I couldn't even imagine putting it on. How was I supposed to show my face at The Bridge ever again? To my girls, who already spent far too much time fantasizing about my on-camera life? This was not the influence I'd hoped to have on them: me, posing for as-close-to-topless-looking photos as could be allowed by the flaggers on every social platform.

"They only need a few shots of you in it. I made sure of that."

"You . . . you made sure of that? Ethan, did you even see it?

Maybe you missed it because it's practically see-through. Not to mention, it has zero support for my . . ." I glanced down at my ample chest. "A flimsy piece of nylon will be *way* too exposing."

"Babe, stop." He set his hand on my bare shoulder. "Listen to yourself for a minute. Whatever this fear—about, I don't know, about being seen as immodest or something equally as irrational— it's ridiculous. You're not some prudish virgin with a religious platform. You're a gorgeous woman with a popular fashion platform who has a killer body and a paycheck to match. There's a level of compromise in every deal we make. And this is the compromise for a six-figure check." He wiped at his forehead. "Now, let's get out of this hot box. You're gonna ruin your makeup, and I'm gonna ruin this Italian shirt." He slipped a finger under the wooden door latch, but I gripped his arm, pulling him back as my nails dug in a bit deeper than necessary. He couldn't actually be serious right now.

"Do not open that door. You got me into this, Ethan. And now you need to get me out of it. I won't put that on. I can't."

He turned, this time looking far more irritated than he did when I'd first hauled him in here.

"*You will do it*. You already signed the contract." His eyes flicked south to my chest before he lowered his voice and touched his fingers under my chin. "Your body is nothing to be ashamed of, but if it's a little lift you want, I'm sure their editors will take care of it for you. It's standard practice now for swimwear shoots everywhere."

I wanted to scream, yell, push him into the eco-friendly coals sweltering behind us both. "Swimwear is not in my brand. I told you that from the very beginning. And even if it was, that *thing* isn't even swimwear! It's more like something from the *Emperor's New Clothes*—invisible wear."

I braced for the pushback that was coming, because Ethan's hardening, reddening face told me I'd just crossed an uncrossable line. I'd seen this expression before while he vented about former clients, but it had never been directed at me. "*Your brand* is whatever product pays out the most. Do you remember the Molly who filmed her videos in a snack pantry?" His voice held an edge I'd only heard him use on his *problematic clients* . . . not the favored ones. "Because I do. When I signed that girl, she was grateful for every fifty-dollar check that cleared her account."

"Yes, I do remember, but that girl only made videos of the products she believed in—sponsored or not. I have the followers I have because I've worked hard to earn their trust."

He stepped close, his voice so quiet, so chilled I could barely hear it over the roaring heater. "You have the followers you have because I've bent over backward making deals and partnerships for you while you kept your pretty face on camera. Cobalt made your brand what it is today, not you." Though he'd never said it quite like that before, I realized with sudden clarity that the assumption had been there for quite some time, hanging over my head whenever I felt the least bit antsy or uncomfortable representing something that didn't feel fully me. I wasn't free to be Molly McKenzie. I had to be Makeup Matters with Molly . . . which, I was finding out, was not always the same woman.

Hand on the door, he twisted around, sweat beading off his scalp and running down the sides of his face. "Do you even know the real reason we're here today? Why of all celebrities I partnered you with *the* Sophia Richards? Because she just happens to be married to the man overseeing the auditions for *Project New You*—Al Richards. I wanted to surprise you, but this diva tantrum has been the real surprise today." Disdain fueled his gaze. "Pull yourself together, Molly, and act like an adult. I'll see you outside at the pool."

A whoosh of cool air found me as he pushed out the door, and I could hear him making up an excuse as to what we were doing in there together. The feeling I'd had before, the one that knotted my insides and warned me of something I didn't quite understand until this moment, wrapped around me now like a suffocating blanket.

I hit the wall timer on the sauna coals, turning them off, and wished I could think *and* breathe fresh air at the same time. Because I wasn't ready to go out there yet. I wasn't ready to face that dreaded article of clothing that held my future between its sheer fabric.

I pressed my palm to the wall and focused on breathing, on talking myself down, or was it talking myself up? Was he right? Was I the one making too big a deal of all this? I was twenty-seven years old. And I certainly wasn't a virgin anymore. But did that mean I should willingly expose my body to the world? Without considering my own personal values? My own personal . . . convictions. I realized my life hadn't always stuck to the straight and narrow path, but that didn't mean I was willing to jump onto a superhighway traveling in the opposite direction.

The faces of six impressionable young women surfaced again in my mind. Six young women who needed strong female guidance in their lives. Six young women Silas had worked tirelessly to steer away from the jaws of all things fake and toward something real. Something honorable and life-giving. Something true and purposeful.

This shoot was not that.

I'd made a lot of compromises to get to this point in my career . . . but this wouldn't be one of them, not when I'd sat with, talked with, even prayed with several of my recent followers in the flesh. Not when they looked up to me as if I was someone who could help them. Someone who could maybe even . . . lead them one day.

It was one thing to sell myself out, but not for the price it might cost these girls. I wouldn't hurt The Bridge. Not even if it meant losing a large paycheck and a potential Hollywood connection. Or a boyfriend who'd just treated me like an ex-client.

I exited the sauna and shook my head in disgust as a single phrase assaulted me like the crisp air against my sweat-slicked skin: *diva tantrum.*

Truella gasped. "Molly . . . what . . . ?"

Aghast, she took in my sweaty face, neck, arms, and then finally my legs. "What happened to you?"

Without needing to see my reflection in a mirror, I knew her horrified expression couldn't only be due to my overheated body. No, what she and the crew and even Ethan were all staring at were the tiny pinpricks of speckled brownish orange oozing from my every pore. Because like some kind of self-tanner novice, I'd just violated my fourth commandment: "Thou Shalt Not Use a Sauna for the First 48 Hours After Application."

Only this perfectly timed violation had just given me what I needed most: a way out.

I locked gazes with Truella. "I'm so, so sorry to do this, but I'm not going to be able to finish the shoot today. There's been a big misunderstanding that I'll leave my agent to explain. But please give my sincerest apologies to Sophia."

Without stopping to look back, I snatched up my purse, flung it over my shoulder, and fled the pool area. With shaky hands I fumbled in the depths of my handbag, searching for my phone. The instant I found it, I scrolled to the only app I knew that could send a getaway car in a matter of minutes. I typed in the airport as my desired destination, and the app quickly provided my rescue—a Maria in a tan four-door sedan, who was only six minutes away.

It would likely be the longest six minutes of my life.

"What do you think you're doing?" It was a hiss more than a question, but I refused to face Ethan. I refused to look into his lying eyes.

"Leaving," I said with a calm I did not feel.

His hand gripped my bicep and spun my flip-flop feet on the slick concrete to face him. "Don't be ridiculous, Molly. You aren't leaving. Your tan can be fixed—"

"My tan? I don't care about my tan! I care about my reputation, my value as a woman, and as a—"

He laughed as if I'd gone completely bonkers. "Your value as a woman? Are you hearing yourself right now? Molly, you promote beauty products. Nobody is asking you to dance on a pole or become a lady of the night."

"Let go of me," I said, raising my volume higher.

He didn't let go. "You are embarrassing yourself—and me."

"Oh?" Fury shot from my glare. "Is my *diva tantrum* too much for you, Ethan?"

For a minute, he had the audacity to look confused, as if he'd completely forgotten the dozens of times he'd spoken that phrase to me in regards to his problematic ex-client. Or perhaps, I realized with shame-induced clarity, his problematic ex-girlfriend. "You dated her, didn't you? You dated Felicity Fashion Fix, and then you cut her as a client when I came along."

"Are you serious right now?" He fisted his hair and lowered his voice even more. "You're about to walk out on a six-figure paycheck because of a past girlfriend who doesn't even matter? Who *never* mattered?"

The confirmation made me want to retch. How many other lies had he told me this year? How many other compromises had he made on my behalf? How many other times had I been an oblivious accomplice to . . . *no.*

"Did you . . ." But the words logjammed in my throat. "Did you steal Felicity's vlog series idea and then pass it along to me after I signed with you?" Worse, had I participated in a witch hunt based on a false accusation?

"Those products were sponsored by a company I found for her—a company she lost when I signed you. She had no right to post that vlog series."

I closed my eyes, dizzy from the mountain of deception I'd just been pushed from.

"She was the one in the wrong, Molly," he continued, stepping closer to me, his breath hot on my cheek. "I gave her a more than fair Plan B option, and she refused it. But you're too smart to follow in her footsteps. You and I—we're the same, baby. The reason we work so well together is because we know how to put all the other stuff aside and focus on what needs to be done in the moment. And right now, what needs to be done is for you to go back inside Sophia's mansion, put on that million-dollar smile of yours, and finish up this shoot. I'll smooth it all over and then we can go somewhere private and—"

Maria pulled up at the gate, waving at me from inside a beige sedan I could have purchased ten times over with the paycheck I was about to give up.

I broke Ethan's hold on my arm as tears tiptoed up my throat. "You're wrong. We're not the same." Not anymore.

"Molly." The warning in his voice was clear. "If you step foot off this property, Sophia Richards will sue you for breach of contract, and given the assets inside her home, you will stand to lose every cent you've ever made."

And yet, as I looked into the back seat of Maria's car, and as I slipped my shaking fingers under the door handle, I knew which option I'd advise my girls at The Bridge to take given the same compromising scenario.

"Then it's a good thing I'm signed to an agency that shares my paychecks and my liability."

17

Molly

I hadn't spoken to Ethan in nearly thirty-two hours.

I hadn't returned his calls, his texts, his emails, or posted a single picture of the giant bouquet of orchids he'd sent to my house this morning. Because not even a three-hundred-dollar flower arrangement was enough for me to contact him.

This wasn't fixable. Not our personal relationship, and likely not our professional one, either, though that would be harder to terminate, seeing as I was still bound to him by a contract. Or at least Makeup Matters with Molly was.

Whatever issues Truella or her boss had with me departing from the set so quickly after my self-tanning blunder and escape, she and her team could take those issues up with Cobalt Group. Or, more specifically, with Ethan. After all, he'd been the one to misrepresent his fancy new sponsor *and* his client whose net worth was far too great for him to cut. Hence the apology flowers and phone calls.

I dropped my head into my hands. My eyes were glazed over after trying to review two legal contracts that may as well have been written in hieroglyphics: my contract with The Fit Glam Kit and my agency contract with Cobalt Group. If I did find a way out of this mess, what would that even mean for me? And . . . oh gosh. What would it mean for Mr. Greggorio's Dream Big Scholarship offer? My gut twisted to the point I could be sick. I was currently living out the plot of a bad TV drama titled *Why You Never Date Your Talent Manager.*

Only a lawyer could understand the vocabulary in either of these contracts.

I threw myself back against my desk chair and rolled to the far side of the empty studio space, careful not to bump the expensive camera set up behind me. And then I had what could be my worst idea ever. I breathed out a shaky breath and scrolled through my contacts to find The Duke of Fir Crest Manor.

> Molly
>
> Does passing the bar exam mean you might be able to offer me some legal advice?

I sent it off, then immediately regretted it. What was I doing? I couldn't involve Silas. First of all, he had enough responsibilities to attend to for The Bridge. Second of all, it's not like I could ever tell him about the whole Girls Gone Tubee incident at Sophia Richards's house. And third of all, he was Silas. *S-i-l-a-s!*

Just as I contemplated sending him a *just kidding* with a laughing face emoji, he responded.

> The Duke of Fir Crest Manor
>
> You need help?

Why did his response make my throat burn? I hadn't even told him the issue yet, and his first thought was to ask if I needed help? It was difficult not to do a mental compare and contrast of Ethan and Silas. I wouldn't even need to create a social media poll for that one. The answer to *Who's the better man?* was shockingly clear.

> Molly
>
> What if I told you I'd just robbed a supermarket?

> The Duke of Fir Crest Manor
>
> I'd ask if you used your hair accessories as weapons.

I pressed my lips into a flat smile, returning to my laptop again and sobering quickly at the reality staring me in the face.

> Molly
>
> I'm concerned I might be in breach of contract, and I'm not sure what all that entails. I know you're busy, so there's no obligation to help me. But if you had a minute, I would gladly pay you for your time.

This time his answer came slower.

> The Duke of Fir Crest Manor
>
> Can I call you in ten minutes? Do you have the contract with you?

> Molly
>
> Yes and yes.

> The Duke of Fir Crest Manor
>
> Do you feel comfortable sending it to me?

Heat flushed my cheeks. The real answer? No. I wasn't comfortable sending anything I didn't understand. Especially when it involved my brand and my body.

> The Duke of Fir Crest Manor
>
> Would you rather meet in person?

Oh gosh. I stood up, paced several steps away from my desk, and then sat back down. Why did an in-person meeting with Silas seem a lot more serious? *Because this is serious. Potentially, this could be very, very serious.* Truth was, I didn't know how much trouble I was in or how much liability I could pin on Ethan and Cobalt. My final words to him had been spoken out of sheer desperation and a teensy bit of hope.

> Molly
>
> I could meet you, but I don't live close to Fir Crest.

> The Duke of Fir Crest Manor
>
> I'm just leaving my parents' house, actually. I'm in Harper.

Harper was only ten minutes from my house.

> **Molly**
>
> Do you know the old Western Burger House on 7th and Applewood? I could meet you there in fifteen minutes?

> **The Duke of Fir Crest Manor**
>
> I'll be there.

> **Molly**
>
> Thank you.

◇◇◇

His back was to me as he walked through the old ranch style restaurant, but even if it wasn't, I could have pointed Silas out of a crowd anywhere and anytime. And that had little to do with the striking shade of his skin or his midnight-black hair.

Though he was dressed in the most casual outfit I'd seen him in yet—army green cargo shorts and a black cotton tee—he could just as easily have been wearing an Armani suit. Silas carried himself the way royalty did: with a posture of unmistakable authority and confidence.

I gave a small wave as he turned toward the back of the dining area, and something flipped in my abdomen the instant he registered me. Self-consciousness heated my body from the inside out. Though I'd zipped up my navy Adidas jogging jacket to my chin and tugged the sleeves down to cover my entire speckled hand, I was under no false illusions about my hideous appearance.

I looked like I had a bad case of freckled jaundice.

The two swipes of mascara I'd added to my top lashes, along with a squeeze of lip gloss on my lips, weren't nearly enough to distract from my radioactive glow. But when faced with a time frame of only a few minutes to get legal advice for a possible breach of contract or apply a full face of makeup . . . my contour compact did not have a chance at winning. Well, maybe a small chance. But still. This meeting took priority.

Silas pulled out his wooden chair, sat, and looked me over. I prepared for his first words to be one of the following: *Did you contract a tropical skin disease since last we spoke?* Or *If you create videos about makeup, then why aren't you wearing any?*

I didn't expect his quiet yet contemplative, "Are you okay?"

Again, something in my stomach flipped. This time, for a very different reason.

"I had a self-tanning faux pas."

He said nothing as he kept his questioning gaze steady on mine.

"It's why my skin looks like this," I continued nervously. "You see, the solution reacts to intense heat and sweating, and I did both within the first twenty-four hours. The heat and the sweating part, I mean. At the same time. It was a rookie mistake. Anyway, that's why I'm orange in case you're wondering."

The slowest of nods, followed by, "And is that what you need legal advice for? Your . . . skin color?"

I chuckled nervously. "No, no, I was just trying to clear the air. Make it all a bit less awkward."

"And do you feel less awkward now?"

Not even slightly. "Yes."

He closed his eyes briefly, his lips curving. "Good, well I'm glad we settled that."

"So . . ." I began, grappling for something I could create a natural conversational transition with. "You just came from your parents' house? Do you go there often? Were Jake and Clara there, too? I'm sure there is a lot of wedding talk to discuss, seeing as—"

"Molly, what can I help you with?"

I clamped my lips closed as sweat dampened my palms. This was a mistake. I hardly even knew Silas. One long phone call didn't suddenly make him my life coach. He probably thought I was some kind of mentally unstable hot mess of a woman. And at the moment, I couldn't exactly blame him for that assumption. All of this was wrong. What if I'd just committed career suicide? Worse, what if I was about to get sued by Sophia Richards? I had a comfortable savings account and several investments in my name, yes, but my 401K plan was pennies on the dollar to what Sophia Richards and her husband brought in. I only needed to look as far as the inside of her bathroom cabinets to figure that out.

"This is probably a huge waste of your time. I'm sorry, I don't know what I was thinking to ask you to come here and get involved in this." I squeezed my eyes closed in renewed humiliation; then I felt his hand touch mine.

I opened my eyes and stared down at it, taking in the long corded scar curling up his right forearm.

"I'd like to help you, if I can. Do you mind if I view the digital contract from your phone? Or do you have it printed out?"

I eyed him cautiously. "You're sure?"

"I never extend offers I don't intend to follow through on."

My throat tightened. "Thank you. I'll pay you for your time, Silas."

"Let's worry about that later, shall we?"

I slipped the paperwork I'd printed off at home from the inside pocket of my purse and slid it across the table to him. "I suppose you'll need to know what I could be in breach of, right?"

"That would be helpful, yes," he said with a comforting smile. And I couldn't help but wonder if this was the same expression he wore when he first sat across from his new house residents at The Bridge. If these were the same kind eyes they saw when Silas told them they were safe, provided for, and welcomed into a home they could call their own for however long they needed.

Unlike what I'd planned to do when I arrived—skip all the self-incriminating details regarding my foolishness and use only vague terms when it came to certain unmentionable tanning wear—in actuality, I laid it all out for him. The whole ugly saga. With one minor exception: I didn't tell him about *Project New You*. Or about Sophia's connection to a producer. There simply wasn't a good way to share that part without Silas figuring out why I'd volunteered at The Bridge in the first place, and I couldn't lose whatever ground I'd finally gained with him in these last few weeks.

"So this Tubee top . . ." Silas seemed at a loss for words after that. Like he'd attempted to start a sentence and then quickly realized he had no direction to go with it. Understandable. Expecting him to wrap his mind around a grown woman fleeing a photo shoot in a beach sarong, dripping orange sweat while fighting with her manager in the driveway of a Malibu mansion was certainly not the easiest of stories to process.

"You're concerned about the repercussions of refusing to wear the tanning garment they provided and then fleeing the shoot before it was finished."

"My ex said I'd be sued for breach of contract if I left the way I did," I said, trying out Ethan's new title for the first time.

A brief yet quizzical look crossed his features. "I thought you said your manager told you that?"

So I supposed I'd left that little detail out, too, then. "They're actually two in one."

"Who is?"

"My manager is my boyfriend. Well, now he's my ex-boyfriend."

Silas said nothing, but I *didn't* miss the slight hitch in his eyebrows as he read through the first two pages of legal jargon.

"And yes, I do realize how that sounds," I said.

"How what sounds?"

"How dating my talent manager must sound."

"I'm not asking you to defend anything to me."

Yet I wanted to do just that. I wanted to explain that while Ethan had called me his girlfriend for several months, these last several hours of being single had brought more clarity than I'd had in the entire time we were a couple. Because that was the thing—we hadn't ever really been a couple, at least, not in the ways that mattered most. There was always something more pressing, more urgent, more engaging to tend to than the health or growth of our relationship. And I had told myself to be okay with that. To be okay with playing the arm-candy role at every social event. To be okay with engaging in the shallowest of small talk with colleagues and sponsors who spoke to me like my brain was filled with helium. To be okay with being labeled a *progressive power couple* who didn't need romantic expectations or emotional connection to fulfill them.

But as it turned out, I wasn't nearly as *progressive* as I thought I was.

I reached for the salt and pepper shakers on the table and spun them around each other like dance partners, dipping one and then dipping the other. It was a game I used to play with Miles as we waited for our food to arrive after enduring never-ending church meetings as kids. Whoever invented the most creative dance routine for the bride and groom without spilling a single speck onto the table would get to—

"Are you hungry?" Silas asked, plucking me out of my childish memories.

"No." I stopped the imaginary bridal dance. "Oh gosh, are you? Sorry, I asked the waiter to come back once you arrived since I wasn't sure what you might want, but I guess he forgot. I can go and find him if you—"

"I'm fine." Silas's mouth stretched into a sly grin. "I was just concerned that your salt and pepper dancers were going to get rowdy if they didn't find a hot plate to season soon."

I smiled back at him. "You know, you can actually be funny sometimes, Silas."

"Don't tell anyone." He moved to the third page of The Fit Glam Kit contract, sliding his finger down. And then he stopped. "Ah, here we go. 'The Brand Ambassador retains the right to refuse to create content that may injure, tarnish, damage, or otherwise negatively affect the reputation and goodwill associated with Makeup Matters with Molly or that of the Brand Ambassador's existing sponsors.'" He looked up at me again. "There's your out."

"That's it?" I looked down at the document.

"That's it. According to the Brand Ambassador's protection clause of this contract, you have the legal right to refuse to create any content you feel will damage your reputation. There's no breach of contract."

Relief rushed over me. "Thank you, Silas. Thank you."

He gave a nod. "You're welcome. I can write up an official statement if you'd like me to. To send to your . . . manager, or to the sponsor herself. I'm not a practicing lawyer, of course, but I can make it sound pretty convincing if you need me to."

"You'd do that for me?"

"It's the right thing to do after such an unfortunate occurrence."

I released a self-deprecating sigh. "I should have read it all over first."

"No, your boyfriend never should have put you in such a compromising position. I'm sorry that happened to you."

As my eyes met his, I felt it anew. The drastic divide between the man across the table and the man I'd shared far too much of myself with over the last year.

"You're right," I said with adamant resolve. "He shouldn't have. And he won't have the chance to again." A statement I'd said aloud for the first time yet knew it wouldn't be the last. "Would you mind taking a look at one more legal document for me? I think I understand this one a bit better, since I had a lawyer present when I signed it, but I'd like to be sure."

"Of course."

I slid the rest of the Cobalt Group contract on the table, asking him the specifics of the consequences of an early-exit strategy. But unlike the first contract, Silas's finger never stopped trailing the clauses. He didn't get that *aha* look on his face as if he'd just reeled in a marlin when he'd been expecting a catfish. Instead, he confirmed what I already knew: My contract with Cobalt was ironclad until it renewed at the end of this calendar year. If I broke it, if I exited early, I'd not only forfeit any profit brought in by the sponsors, endorsement deals, and campaign promotions that they'd secured for me during our business partnership, but I'd also lose the $100,000 Dream Big Scholarship I'd secured for The Bridge.

No matter how much I was beginning to despise him, I could tolerate Ethan as a manager for six more months. I'd have to.

"I'm sorry," he said. "I wish it was better news for you."

I shook my head, sighed. "It's okay." I'd make it be okay.

I reached for my phone to pay him through Venmo. "How much do I owe you for your time tonight?"

"That's not necessary."

"Yes, it really is, because if I end up needing something more—like a written statement, I want to be able to ask you without feeling like I'm taking advantage of your generosity."

"I can respect that," he said, eyeing me cautiously. "But I don't want your money."

Something grabbed in the pit of my stomach at the change in his tone.

"But I could use your help," he continued. "If you're willing."

"Of course, with what?" I set my phone down, giving him my undivided attention. Silas wasn't the kind of man who asked for favors. Whatever this was, it certainly wasn't an easy or casual ask for him.

"That fundraiser idea you mentioned in your syllabus. Is that something you might be willing to take on? I know it will require more volunteer hours and more time away from your work responsibilities, but the head of the trustee board called me this afternoon. It's why I was out at my folks' house this evening. I was consulting with my father."

"What did he say—the head of the trustee board?"

Silas smiled. "She's a woman, actually, Mrs. Cecilia Harleson. She told me about a fundraising option called the Murphey Grant. Essentially, it's a dollar-for-dollar matching grant for nonprofit organizations like ours looking to expand. There's a lot of red tape to the application process, a lot of documentation needed to prove our program meets their requirements, plus an approved building plan by our trustee board."

"How much will the Murphey Grant match up to?"

"Five hundred thousand." He put out his hand like a stop sign before I could let my excitement explode across my face. "But the catch is that we can only apply for this particular grant once every five years."

I crinkled my brow, thinking through the implications of his statement. "Meaning that if they approve your application but you don't quite reach the financial goal you need, you can't re-apply next year."

"Correct." But something like doubt remained cemented on his features.

"So, what's the issue? If the grant is willing to match whatever you can fundraise, it seems like a no-lose situation."

"The issue is that the trustee board at Fir Crest Manor will only approve my proposed expansion plan on the condition that we secure the entire sum of money needed to complete the project before we break ground."

"Ah, so the Murphey Grant won't approve the release of their matching funds to The Bridge without an approved building plan, and the trustee board won't approve the building plan without securing the total funds." I sat up straighter, my focus becoming more and more clear. "So what do we need to raise? What's the total sum?"

"A million dollars," he said, as if the impossibility of that num-ber was greater than the possibility of it. And I didn't believe that for a second.

"Silas," I said, no longer able to contain my enthusiasm, "that's amazing! You only need to fundraise four hundred thousand dol-lars for a project that's worth one million! Why aren't you more excited about this?"

"Because we'd have to secure it all before September first. The funds actually have to be in and accounted for by the morning of August thirty-first—that's the cutoff date for the Murphey Grant. Less than three months from now. And the total we have to bring in is five hundred thousand, not four."

"Nope, numbers may not be a strength of mine, but I promise I'm not wrong on this math story problem. We only need to fund-raise four hundred thousand out of the five hundred thousand we need matched, because . . ." I beamed, nearly coming out of my skin. "Because I recently secured a one-hundred-grand scholarship for The Bridge through my agency. It's a pay-it-forward perk that Mr. Greggorio runs every year with nominations from his clients. He already chose mine and approved it. I don't have the check in hand yet, but it's solid. And don't worry, the scholarship has nothing to do with Ethan."

"Molly, I . . ." I'd never seen Silas speechless before, and I had to admit, it was kind of nice. "I'm not even sure what to say, other than . . . thank you."

Outwardly, I waved off the compliment, but inwardly I was melty and warm. "We have several weeks to raise four hundred grand. Totally doable."

This time when he shook his head and laughed, I laughed with him, lowering my chin to catch his eye. "No more debating or consulting necessary. Apply for that Murphey Grant, Silas. We've totally got this."

Because whatever part I could play in making Silas's off-the-page goals come true . . . I would do it. And for once in my life, I wouldn't do it for my own personal gain. I would do it for Silas. And Glo. And Clara. And for all the kids who'd spent way too many years of their life struggling to get ahead of their circumstances.

◇◇◇

To: Ethan@cobaltgroup.com
From: Molly@makeupmatterswithmolly.com

Ethan,

Despite the unfortunate events occurring last Saturday at Sophia Richards's private residence in Malibu, I am prepared to honor my contractual agreement with Cobalt Group until the time of its expiration at the end of the calendar year, unless there is just cause for early termination—see clause 5.6 located on page 4 of our agency contract.

In the meantime, please respect my personal and professional boundaries regarding all further communication. My business hours will be 9 a.m.-4 p.m., M-F, via my assistant, Val. Also, for your consideration, I've sought legal counsel regarding any and all circulating rumors regarding a breach of contract due to the incomplete The Fit Glam Kit photo shoot. Clause 3.2 of The Fit Glam Kit contract states that I have the right to reject any content that could damage my brand's reputation. It also states that all damages and/or fines will be directed to my sponsor and talent agency.

Sincerely,
Molly McKenzie

◇◇◇

To: Sophia@srenterprises.com
From: Molly@makeupmatterswithmolly.com

Dear Sophia,

First off, please allow me to say thank you for your kindness in sharing my videos on your fan pages, and for the invitation to your beautiful Malibu home. I'm sure, at this point, you've heard from your staff and my agency about the failed photo shoot last Saturday. And while I know this personal contact from me likely goes against wise counsel, I hoped I might appeal to you—woman to woman.

You see, I love all things glittery and pink and summery and fanciful. Almost all the items you included in your campaign box are things I'd happily promote without reservation. That being said, the Tubee is not a product I feel comfortable modeling or endorsing to my audience.

My goal with this email is not to offend you any further than I'm sure I already have, but I'd love the chance to explain my decision to leave the shoot unfinished. I've recently started mentoring a group of young women at a transitional home for youth who've aged out of the foster care system. They've never had much in the way of support or guidance, and to say they're impressionable would be putting it mildly at best. Though the goal of the program is to equip the residents with life skills and confidence to thrive in the real world, their role models have often been 2-D filtered photos of celebrities and social media influencers who've made a living doing much of the same publicity work I have done over the last few years. And while I'm grateful for the platform and reach I have, I'm becoming increasingly aware of the audience my influence impacts.

I have no doubt the Tubee will bring in many sales for The Fit Glam Kit, but I can't, in good conscience, attach my name to anything I wouldn't recommend to these six young women I'm now responsible to mentor. Please know I'm deeply sorry for the time, money, and energy your company has lost due to my decision to leave. I wish you and your company the very best.

Thank you for understanding,
Molly McKenzie

18

Molly

Despite the new boundaries I'd placed on Ethan, I'd been anticipating his phone call. Or, at the very least, a string of text messages. But there had been nothing from him at all since my email, and it was almost noon on Monday. Had he read it? Had he been angry? Indifferent? These mentally draining questions were likely why email wasn't advised as a communication strategy between exes.

I clicked out of my email inbox for the twentieth time since I'd woken up and tightened my high ponytail, letting the ends of my hair hang over my right shoulder. No matter what kind of emotional tug-of-war I was in, today was a work day.

Val had slated the Fresh Summer Faces tutorial to go live later this week, which meant I needed to do my part and actually film the compare/contrast of this year's trending tinted moisturizers and top blemish balms—BB creams—and get it uploaded to her by the end of the day. Tomorrow would need to be reserved for selecting a dozen or so professional outfit options for another session of "Dress for Success" at The Bridge . . . as well as a brainstorming session with Silas on the upcoming fundraiser. Pulling together such an important event by the end of August and working a full-time job would be tight. Then again, I didn't have to do any of it alone. There were twenty-four able-bodied residents I could recruit for help, plus my secret weapon—Val, the most resourceful woman I knew when it came to finding deals and generating fresh ideas on a budget.

I switched the camera remote to record, thankful the special exfoliant I'd concocted had removed every last trace of my self-tanner, and lifted the first foundation toward the red blinking light. While my mouth chatted away about the pros and cons of each product, my mind continually drifted to questions not even my subconscious wanted to face: *What kind of woman dated a guy for nearly a year and didn't feel much of anything when it was over?* I definitely *would not* be googling such a question. The last thing I needed was for my social feeds to be consumed by sympathy offerings for a broken heart. Or worse, the unwanted encouragement to engage in risky behaviors. Like bang cutting. When would the world learn that hasty haircuts never solved anything?

After a solid first take, I squared my chin and smiled before signing off with a promise to be back soon with more from Makeup Matters with Molly. And I would be back. Because I didn't need a manager like Ethan to be successful. And I certainly didn't need a boyfriend like him to be happy. I'd learned how to make a living— meager as it was—before he'd ever come along on his flashy corporate horse and swept me into a world of wealthy campaigns and celebrity connections.

All I needed to do now was play my cards right where he was concerned. I'd push through these contracted months ahead the same way I pushed through every challenging hurdle in my life: by powering through and working hard.

Ethan might own a piece of my brand, but he didn't own my face or my personality. He didn't own me.

As soon as I plugged the camera in to my laptop to start the upload of the raw footage to Val, I saw a notification on my phone. *New email from Ethan Carrington @ the Cobalt Group.*

My stomach twisted at the thought of reading his reply. Only the email wasn't addressed to me at all. It wasn't a personal reply, but a group message. An interoffice memo.

Immediately the blood in my hands, arms, and torso cooled to a temperature that should be impossible midsummer. I zoomed in on the message, as if the words would make better sense if only they could be viewed in a larger font.

I was wrong.

Subject: Announcement: New assistant and editorial manager for Makeup Matters with Molly!

Let's all congratulate Rosalyn Bronswick and her team members on this well-deserved promotion. Rosalyn comes with years of experience and glowing referrals from her past clientele. As you all know, Cobalt strives to acquire only the best and most reputable staff today's marketing industry has to offer. Please accept our warmest Cobalt welcome to you, Rosalyn!

-Ethan

My hands shook as I fumbled to click out of the email screen and into my contacts. How dare he do this to me—*to Val!* I slid my finger down to Ethan's name, making a mental note to change his contact name to something far more sinister once I had a moment to think.

After only half a ring, his voicemail cut in. "You have reached the voicemail of Ethan Carrington, vice president of the Cobalt Group. Please leave a message, and I'll return your call as soon as I can. Ciao."

"Ethan, what exactly do you think you're . . ." I clamped my teeth together until my jaw throbbed, realizing I was breaking the first rule of the new boundaries I'd set for our new business-partners-only status. Despite his juvenile behavior, *I* was a professional. And I had to act like it. For Val's sake. As well as my own.

I couldn't afford to lose at whatever game he was playing with my career.

I released a static-filled breath and cleared my throat. "Hello, this is Molly McKenzie. I just received notice of a staff change that pertains to my editorial team. As I've expressed before, I am not in need of a new personal assistant, as Val has both impeccable work ethic and creative ability. So if you'd kindly redirect your hiring of Ms. Bronswick to another influencer seeking her qualifications within Cobalt, I'd greatly appreciate it. Thank you."

I hung up the phone, wanting nothing more than to smash something breakable into a thousand pieces, because I knew, *I knew*, there wouldn't be any sort of contractual discrepancy that could clear this matter up. No, this could only be cleared up by a change of heart. And seeing as I was starting to think Ethan was void of that particular vital organ, that outcome seemed less than feasible at the moment.

On a long exhale, I held my eyes closed, remembering how I'd pushed Cobalt into hiring Val as a *Cobalt employee* as part of my initial representation negotiations with them. At the time, the idea had made the most sense. They had the big bucks after all, and I'd wanted Val's salary to reflect both the growth of my channels *and* of the competitive industry as a whole. Upon signing, Val received full employee benefits—medical and retirement, and an annual performance bonus. It had been the perfect scenario: Val worked exclusively for me and my brand, while her monthly paychecks came directly from Cobalt.

What could I even say to her? Being let go was her worst fear, and I'd . . . I'd allowed it to happen. *Urgh!* What kind of heartless jerk fired a responsible single mother out of retribution?

If I couldn't smash something, I needed to move. To walk. To think outside this room furnished with camera and lighting equipment appraised at twice the value of my car.

Forgetting the makeup tutorial waiting for me in my studio, I shoved my phone into the back pocket of my jeans, ripped open the front door, and shot down my porch steps to the sidewalk. I marched at a pace that should have been a sprint if not for my wedged sandals. I needed a solution I could offer Val before I called her. Something positive and concrete. Something that would make this all seem—

The buzzing in my pocket cut my thinking session short.

Val.

Her name sent a hot jolt through my chest. *Help me, help her, God.* A prayer so immediate and desperate it shocked me.

I answered mid exhale and threw myself into problem-solving mode. "Val? Okay, listen. I just read the email. It's horrible, yes, but we can figure all this out together. There's absolutely no reason to panic. I've already thought of a few options, we just need to process them out loud."

But apart from a sniffle, the other end of the line was quiet.

"Val?"

"He already gave me two options."

"Who?"

"Ethan."

He'd given her two options? When? "What are they?"

"To take two months' severance pay and leave the company . . . or take a promotion with twenty percent higher pay with full benefits and monthly bonuses."

"Wait, I'm sorry." I stopped walking. "He said he'd give you better pay if you do what exactly?"

"If I transfer away from your brand," she finished.

For the better part of five seconds, I stood frozen in place in the middle of the sidewalk as my neighbor's cotton ball of a dog panted at me from the other side of their picket fence, his face as confused and expectant as my own felt.

"Well that's not happening," I finally said through a bubble of hysteria. "That's just . . . that's absolutely ridiculous. He can't possibly think you'd take that. We're a team. There's no Makeup Matters brand without you."

Again, Val was so quiet I pulled the phone from my ear to check the connection.

"I took it. I took his offer."

Though my ears heard the words, my mind refused to process their meaning, as if an *Out of Order* sign had just been stapled to my forehead. A guttural decompression of escaped air was my only response.

"I have a son, Molly. I have to think of him. The tourist industry is in bad shape here, and I can't rely on my parents' business to help us when they can barely pay their store rent and—"

"You . . . you . . . took his offer?" The words stumbled from my mouth like a drunk spotting sunlight for the first time in days. "Without talking to me first?"

"Actually," she said with an assertiveness I'd never heard from her, "I took his offer after you failed to talk to me."

"What? No. That's not true. I told you the photo shoot hadn't gone as planned and that we'd had an argument—"

"You and Ethan had more than an argument. You had a breakup, Molly. A breakup that put both our careers in jeopardy, and you didn't bother to tell me."

"No, I was planning to tell you that we broke up—"

"When? Before I read the email about my replacement, or after?"

"That's not fair. I had to meet with my . . . ." What was Silas to me exactly? "With my legal representation first, because I was afraid I was going to be sued for breach of contract, and then I needed to communicate my new professional boundaries to Ethan. I didn't want to worry you over nothing if he responded . . . rationally." The word soured on my tongue.

Ethan wasn't rational with the people who had wronged him. He was ruthless. I only had to think back to Felicity Fashion Fix for proof of that.

"You didn't listen to me." Her soft voice pulled me down a new path.

"What? When?"

"I told you what he was planning. I told you that he wanted a new team for your brand, and you didn't listen to me. You said it would never happen, that you'd never let it happen."

I spun around and stomped my foot, sending the dog on the other side of my neighbor's fence scurrying away. "And I won't let it happen now. He can't do this—you're *my* assistant, Val, not Ethan's."

The silence between us was different this time, charged with an invisible energy that pulsed through my phone and wrung my insides out like a damp towel.

"I'm your . . . *assistant?*" Tears slicked her question as panic wove through my ribs.

"My assistant *and* my friend. You know what I mean." She had to. "We're partners—me and you—and as long as I have a channel, you'll have a job with me. I'll hire you as an employee again, pay your salary. And your benefits, too. Whatever you need, just say it and I'll make it happen." For however long I could, even if it meant taking out a loan.

"Partners don't hide critical information from each other."

"I was only trying to protect you."

"I didn't need you to protect me. I needed . . ." Val's sigh was synonymous with many I'd heard before. Not a sigh of reconciliation but of rebuff. "I needed you to be honest with me. That's what *friends* do; they tell each other the truth no matter what it might cost them to tell it." She paused. "I have to think about what's best for me and Tucker."

"And you think that's taking a job with Ethan? He's manipulating you, Val. The only reason he's even offering you this is to get back at me. He wants to hurt me, and if you say yes to him, he'll end up hurting you, too."

"I'm not stupid," she said in a voice so quiet and chilled I strained to hear her over the gang of adolescent skateboarders who crossed the street. "I understand the risk I'm taking."

I gripped the fence at my back and swallowed against the unfamiliar lump in my throat, against the pain of the accusation she'd just unleashed: that I was the bigger risk. "Please . . . we can figure this out. Please don't do this." *Please don't choose him over me.* But even as I thought it, I knew I couldn't compete with him. No matter what I offered, Ethan would always have something better and shinier to flaunt. Larger financial reserves, bigger career opportunities, far more stability for a single mom raising a child.

A muffled sob sounded on the other end of the phone, and my hope climbed. Maybe our friendship was worth more than all those things, more than the money or the job security or the—

"I want to thank you, Molly, for these last three years," she said.

"You took a chance on me when Tuck and I needed it most, and I . . . I won't ever forget that. I'll always be grateful for the time I spent working with you."

The past tense of that sentence was too much. I moved to the edge of the sidewalk, my knees collapsing under me as my heart galloped a thousand miles in my chest. *No! Stop! Don't do this!* were the only phrases cycling through my brain.

"Also," she said, then cleared her throat, and I could almost imagine her slipping her glasses off and wiping under her eyes with whatever zip-up hoodie sleeve she was wearing today. "I'll do everything I can to make the transition smooth. I can finish up editing those last videos you're sending, and I'll . . . I'll update Rosalyn on your summer post schedule so you can stay on track after I'm gone."

After I'm gone.

This time, I was the one without words. I didn't care about a smooth transition. Or about Rosalyn being updated on my summer post schedule. I didn't want her calling me or messaging me or pretending to know anything about me.

I wanted Val.

I tied off the hurt in my heart the way I'd done after my parents had left the States and after my Mimi had died and after Miles had devoted his life to a ministry that held little space for a sister who talked about fashion and makeup and social media campaigns, then simply said, "Fine. That all sounds fine. Thank you."

And while I hadn't been able to squeeze out a single tear for the loss of a man who hadn't actually loved me, the pain of losing a friend I'd never even seen in person was truly incomprehensible. I'd hired an assistant three years ago when keeping up with the demand of my pages had become unmanageable on my own. But what I'd gained was the best friend I'd ever had.

In many ways, Val was my only friend.

And I'd just lost her to my ex-boyfriend.

19

Molly

If I'd worried about how I looked when I met Silas at the diner with my uneven tan hidden under a track suit, tonight was a new kind of low. After a wholly unsatisfying resolve to the Fresh Summer Faces tutorial I'd been working on prior to Val's call, and a few mindless surf sessions on social media for anything that might pull me out of this funk, I simply got into my car and drove. And somehow, I'd ended up here. In the driveway of The Bridge, eating a supremely large sleeve of hot, greasy French fries I couldn't even recall ordering. Yet the evidence was in my hand, a glaring reminder that while I'd agreed to shun wine for the duration of the summer, I certainly hadn't agreed to turn my back on deep-fried potatoes covered in salt.

As the sun descended behind the old estate, the manor basking in shades of brilliant marmalade and sherbet, I counted the silhouettes that passed by the windows I could see from my parking spot. There were a total of eleven cars sharing the lot with me tonight—many of them older, unattractive vehicles, most of which likely belonged to the residents. Glo said several used public transportation to get around, but a few of them shared vehicles, carpooling to school, work, internships, and the like. Why hadn't

I noticed before tonight how much my car stood out in this lot? My new red Tesla Model X, with the wing doors that opened like a spaceship, was about as commonplace as a glittering pot of gold sitting in the middle of a junkyard.

I shoved another few fries into my mouth, remembering the cashier's check I'd signed over to the dealer for the total purchase price of the car. The salesman had tried not to react when Ethan told him I wouldn't be needing finance options. A top-of-the-mountain triumph had rushed through me. *This is what success feels like*, I'd thought. Because I, Molly McKenzie, the girl who'd worn secondhand clothes for as long as she could remember, whose parents always owned vehicles at least ten years old, had finally arrived. After navigating her way through a world so strikingly unfamiliar to the one she'd been raised in, she was now the proud owner of one of the most enviable cars on the market today.

Or so Ethan had told me.

The car-purchase date had been a celebration, a just-rolled-over-the-five-hundred-thousand-follower mark with another eight high-paying sponsors who simply couldn't get enough of my influencer magic.

And yet here I was tonight: that same successful woman, sitting in her flashy, depreciating-by-the-minute car, with more than seven hundred fifty thousand subscribers to her Instagram, and nowhere in the world to be. Not one person in the world to call.

As Val's face surfaced in my mind, I reached for my depressed drink of choice—a giant Diet Dr. Pepper, light ice—and drank until the carbonation outburned the tears in my throat. Because I couldn't—*wouldn't*—cry about what Ethan had taken from me. Nor would I dwell on the fact that his only reply to my voicemail was an email reply that read:

Ms. McKenzie,

As per your contract, third page, paragraph five, all Cobalt employees who manage Makeup Matters are subject to our discretion for hiring, promoting, and dismissing. We hope you find Rosalyn Bronswick an exceptional replacement, and we look forward to the work she will produce with you.

Ethan Carrington

I gave the parking lot another once-over—in case I'd somehow missed Silas's black sedan the first several times I'd searched for it. But his car hadn't appeared. And perhaps that was the disappointment that had done me in. Because if I hadn't fully realized it when I'd first parked out here, I could no longer pretend I didn't know it now: I'd driven here for Silas. I needed a slice of his natural calm, his exceptional self-control, and whatever else he possessed that made circumstances seem more bearable whenever I was around him.

I wondered where he was tonight. His parents' house again? A work commitment? A date?

That last thought came with a needle prick of envy. Could Silas be out on a date right now? I huffed and tossed the carton of fries to the passenger seat beside me. Scrunching up my nose, I imagined the sort of woman Silas might take out to dinner on a random Monday night. Because naturally, he would go out on a Monday night. It was the most practical of date days after all—no crowds to fight, weekly specials on dinner menus, and no pressure to stay out late due to an early Tuesday morning work schedule.

As for the woman, well, she'd be poised for sure. Elegant, yet principled, with some sort of social justice–oriented career just like Silas. Maybe she was a social worker, a human rights advocate, or something equally important having to do with writing policies for changed legislation. And her name would be something sophisticated like Catherine or Caroline or Camille. And certainly, she would be the epitome of emotional stability.

Definitely not the kind of gal who'd sit in a darkened parking lot eating the very food featured on a this-is-what's-wrong-with-America docuseries.

I shifted in my seat and swiped an abandoned fry off my knee to the floor mat.

I supposed a woman like Catherine would find Silas attractive, seeing as she'd probably be into know-it-all attitudes and likely enjoy a calculated approach to pretty much everything in life. But I'd never been into those honest-to-a-fault types. No, I'd been into the type of man who would swindle his girlfriend's work assistant with a job offer she couldn't refuse.

A text came through the console of my Tesla's touchscreen.

The Duke of Fir Crest Manor

> Technically, sitting in a parked car for 34 minutes on private property is loitering. A code orange security breach.

I looked around again. *What . . . how does he know I'm here? Where is he?*

The Duke of Fir Crest Manor

> But also, technically, you're the most popular event that's happened on our security screens in months. Glo is about to make popcorn.

A fluttering sensation filled my entire being. But where was Silas—inside the house?

The Duke of Fir Crest Manor

> Your growing audience is eagerly awaiting a wave.

And because I'd built a life on pleasing an audience I couldn't see, I did exactly that. I waved. And then I tapped my console screen and flashed my headlights, too.

The Duke of Fir Crest Manor

> You coming inside?

Molly

> . . .

I started at least five texts in response, erasing them all as I fumbled for a suitable reason for why I'd been sitting in my car for thirty-four minutes and counting. Something that wouldn't make me sound entirely lame and pathetic. But not even my most creative excuses seemed good enough. Because no matter how I tried to spin it or pretty it up, the truth was getting more and more difficult to disguise: Though I was one of the most liked personas on the internet, I was likely one of the most lonely, too.

For the second time that day, tears blurred my vision. I started the "most efficient engine" on the planet. I reversed out of my parking spot, tires crunching over gravel, when I heard a voice shouting after me.

"Molly! *Wait!*"

I craned my neck to see Silas jogging down the cobblestone path.

I stopped my car and fought the urge to shrink to the floorboard. But it was too late to disappear now. And there wasn't a handbag large enough in all the world to block him from view this time. He was headed straight for me.

He knocked on my window, and I reluctantly pressed the button to lower it.

"Where are you going?"

It was perhaps the most profound of all questions he could ask me at the moment—to which my answer would be the same in every area of my life. "I have no idea."

Though I focused on the steering wheel, the intense way he studied my profile stripped the pretense from every cell of my body.

"I figured you were waiting to come inside until you . . ." He tilted his head to glance at the spot beside me—at the supersized cold fries scattered across my seat like a game of 52-card pickup. "Finished your dinner."

"No," I said, hoping the tear balancing on the rim of my bottom eyelashes wasn't as obvious as it felt. "I just . . ." *Had no plans at all and didn't want to be alone tonight.* "I didn't think you were here."

"You came because you didn't think I was here?" Confusion laced his voice.

"No, that's not what I—never mind." I shook my head and swiped the stupid tear from my eyelash. "Do you think we can just

. . . can we pretend you didn't see me on those security cameras? I think that would be best for everyone."

"Unfortunately, pretending has never been a strength of mine," Silas said, lowering himself further and resting an elbow on my open windowsill. "But I do have an alternative option for you."

My eyes flittered to his for all of one second, followed by an electric current that shocked my nervous system.

"You could come inside and join us for D&D—dessert and discussion hour. Diego baked oatmeal cookies." Silas seemed to consider something more. "Wren's inside, too, and I'm sure she'd enjoy seeing you tonight. She's had a hard day."

My full attention snapped to his face. "Why, what happened to her?"

"I'd rather Wren talk to you about it herself, in her own words. That is, if you're willing to stay awhile longer."

I knew exactly what he was doing. Wren was quite possibly the only hook he had to lure me into the house at this point, knowing my lonely fry binge had just been viewed by Lord only knew how many people. Yet I couldn't say no. If something was wrong with Wren, then I wanted to know about it.

"Don't think I don't know what you're doing." He shrugged, and I sighed. "Fine, I'll go park."

Silas reached a few more inches into my car, set his hand on my shoulder and gave it a squeeze. "Great. Thank you."

We didn't talk as Silas escorted me from the parking lot to the fireside room at the end of the east corridor. My silence was a conscious decision on my part, as there were too many jumbled thoughts rolling around my head to filter them into words. Yet I was fully aware that Silas was drawing his own unvoiced conclusions about my reserved mood by the way he eyed me at every turn.

A few paces out from the room, Silas touched my arm. "One word of advice—coffee helps the cookies go down easier."

"Diego's cookies?"

"Yes. Let's just say he's not our most skilled baker in residence.

But it was his turn on rotation, and Glo never misses an opportunity to instruct one-on-one in the kitchen when she can. D&D is her baby."

"Is it also mandatory—for the residents?"

"No." He smiled. "Technically, only Tuesday night classes are mandatory, though mentor time on Fridays is highly encouraged. We find that most of our young adults work to arrange their schedules to be here each D&D. It's often the highlight of their weeknights."

I nodded, though I wasn't entirely sure what he meant. "Okay."

"Molly," he said, with a brief touch to my back as we entered the room together, "I'm glad you're here for this tonight."

Thankfully, Glo was waiting on the other side of the open door, pulling me straight into an unexpected embrace that allowed me to hide the rush of emotion Silas's gentle words had provoked.

Glo rubbed my back and spoke directly into my ear. "I was sure hoping you'd decide to come inside, Kitten Heels. These are always good nights to stop in for a visit. We'll be starting things up in just a few. Oh, and sit wherever you want. We're casual around here."

"Thanks," I said, turning to the room as a wave of insecurity washed over me at the sight of happy faces gathered together in clusters of four or five.

Though Silas had pointed this room out to me during the official tour, I hadn't stepped inside it until now. And without a doubt, it was my new favorite space at Fir Crest Manor.

The room was oriented around a tiny platform next to a retired corner bar, where several residents swiveled on stools, sharing a laugh as they mixed hot chocolate packets into actual mugs, not disposable foam cups. A nice touch, presumably by Glo.

I scanned the unlit fireplace hearth, where to the left several girls from my mentor group sat on pillows, chatting near the built-in cabinetry stocked with board games and puzzles. A few waved at me and smiled, and I returned the gesture, although one of them gave me a look that couldn't be classified as anything but dismissive. Sasha, the tall, too-thin girl with wispy, faded pink hair who wore eyeliner as thick as a black Sharpie, had an obvious dislike for me. It seemed whatever I had to offer her peers in the program held little to no interest where she was concerned. I needed to ask Clara what was up with her. I never saw Sasha speak to anybody but Monica. Those two always seemed connected at the hip.

The random pockets of seating around the room mimicked a downtown coffee shop. Cozy chairs, sofas, love seats, and tables of all sizes filled the space. Two mismatched round tables near the center of the room had been pushed together for a game of Yahtzee, where Devon kept score on the back of a paper plate. Silas had just pulled up a chair to join them, catching my eye and tipping his head toward the back corner of the room.

It took me all of two seconds to understand why. Wren's unmistakable Celtic hair, plaited in a double Dutch braid, spilled behind the wingback chair she sat in. She sat alone, focused on a picture on a phone screen.

Armed with no plan and no real experience in the area of comforting another human being, I made my way toward her. As quietly as I could, I sat beside her on the edge of the sofa and glanced at the image she'd been staring at for quite some time.

"Hey, Wren. How are you?"

Startled, she dropped the phone to her lap. A fairly obvious indication that I'd already failed the empathy test straight out of the gate.

"Hey . . . I didn't know you'd be here tonight."

That made two of us. "Yeah, it was kind of a last-minute thing."

She nodded. "Oh, sure."

I tapped my thigh as if I were typing an SOS message for immediate rescue. "Did you go to school today?"

I'd learned from Clara that Wren had just been accepted into a two-year program to become a physician's assistant after she finished her associate degree.

"Yes."

"And it was . . . a good school day?" I asked, hopeful she'd give me a clue.

"It was fine."

And now I understood why my parents used to despise the word *fine* whenever Miles and I would use it in response to their daily check-in questions. It was a dead end. No conversational trail to follow.

I'd have to make my own trail, then. "Who was that picture of? The one you were looking at on your phone?" I smiled. "I'm pretty sure I saw a hint of hair color like yours."

Behind those crystal blue eyes was a debate I knew all too well: to trust or not to trust. "My brother. He's ten." Slowly, she turned the phone back over and handed it to me as if offering me the most precious gift.

"Okay, um, so he's stinkin' adorable." I stared at the face of a ginger-haired boy with a splattering of freckles and a grin that tugged at my chest. "I've never seen a set of dimples so pronounced. What's his name?"

"Nathaniel—Nate," she clarified. "He's cute, but he can be crazy, too."

"I hear ya. I have one of those myself—a crazy brother, I mean."

She gave me one of those half smiles as several questions popped into my head at once regarding this sweet child. I suddenly wished I could redo my quiet parking lot walk with Silas and prod a bit deeper on the subject matter of Wren. A little heads-up to a younger brother would have been nice.

"Do you get to see him much?"

"Twice a month for our hour visitation. But I'm allowed to see him more than that as long as I can get to the bus stop on time from my last class." She looked back at the picture. "I'm used to seeing him at least once a week, but now that won't be possible."

"Why not?" I asked, glancing from his picture to Wren again.

"Nate's foster family is moving to a farm outside of town. There's no bus route I can take out there."

Nate's foster family. Those three words punched me the hardest. Wren's younger brother had a foster family, while Wren was here, only a year into adulthood, living at The Bridge with twenty-three other young adults. My heart ached for her.

A shrill female voice called "Yahtzee!" from somewhere in the room, but my gaze held to Wren's. "How long has he been with them?"

The muscles in her neck tensed as she swallowed. "Since our mom died last year."

"Oh, Wren . . . I'm so sorry to hear that."

She sniffled, but no tears came. "They're a nice family—the Coles. They have three sons."

"Good," I said, absently. "That's good."

"He's excited because they're getting baby goats, and they told him he can name one."

"Well, sure, who wouldn't be excited about that?" I teased. "I might need to become friends with the Coles so I can visit your brother's goat."

She laughed a little before turning her face away on a sigh. "It's just . . . I wanted to take care of him myself. I promised my mom I would never let anything or anyone separate us, and I tried to keep it, I did, but . . ."

But she was barely nineteen years old with no means to support herself, much less a dependent. "I'm sure he knows how much you love him." Though I meant the statement to be comforting and supportive, it felt weak. Feeble in the light of such a difficult circumstance, one I only knew a tiny part of.

She wiped her nose on her sleeve. "I just really miss him."

"Can the Coles take Nate to see you more often?"

She shook her head. "They said they'll do their best to figure something out since I don't have a car, but they both work full-time and have their other boys to take care of, too."

At this she swiped at her face, smearing her light layer of mascara onto her cheek.

"Then I'll take you," I said.

She blinked up at me, her eyes narrowed and questioning.

"I can take you out there once a week. I'll pick you up from school and take you to the farm. Just send me a screenshot of your schedule, and we'll figure out the best day and time, okay?"

Her glossy eyes rimmed with doubt. "Mentors don't usually do that kind of stuff."

"This one does," I said with such confidence I'd be willing to go to the mat with Silas over it. But as my eyes met his from across the room, I knew a throwdown wouldn't be necessary, at least not over this.

"Really? You're serious?" The hoarseness in her throat caused my own to ache.

I touched her knee, smiled. "I absolutely am. I don't know what I'd do without my brother."

"Thank you," Wren said, still staring at me as if I might take back my offer at any moment. But I wouldn't.

"Fresh baked cookies!" Glo announced to the room, carrying a tray as Diego trailed behind her. "Who's going to be first?"

"First? What does she mean?" I asked Wren as she wiped a finger under her eyes and chuckled at my confusion.

"For sharing the high points and low points of their day. The warmest, freshest cookies go to the people who volunteer first."

Just as I was going to ask her more on the subject, Devon and Monica raised their hands and made their way up to the platform.

· 20 ·

Silas

I couldn't make out the exact words shared between Molly and Wren, but body language often spoke the loudest. Whatever exchange had taken place just now had been a positive one. Quite the gamble on my part, given Molly's parking lot mood not even fifteen minutes ago. Yet I knew from experience that serving others was a sure-fire way to shift an off-kilter focus to a new perspective.

By the look on Molly's face, she was likely experiencing such a shift.

It was the same look I saw reflected in her eyes last night at the restaurant when she agreed to help raise funds for the Murphey Grant. And like then, I wondered what such a sacrifice might cost her. How it might change and challenge her. How it might unsteady her beliefs, or uproot whatever current torment she was working so hard to hide even now.

Her gaze tracked Devon and Monica as they trailed through the room and stepped up on the platform, and I forced my own to do the same.

As Devon reached the step first, I raised an eyebrow and nodded in the direction of the young lady behind him. A silent yet pointed reminder that he would be a gentleman and allow Monica to go first. After a short bob of his head, Devon took a step back and gestured for her to go ahead of him. Smart guy.

Though I didn't usually address the entire group on these evenings, as our routine was often as casual as it was fluid, for the sake of our newest volunteer and mentor, I decided a heads-up would be beneficial. From the floor below the platform, I smiled at the young adults I'd spent the better part of a year serving, counseling, coaching, and hanging with. "Evening, ladies and gentlemen. As all of you know, tonight is about answering one of three chosen questions, depending on what's happened in your day or week." I looked to the group sitting near the fireplace. "Amy, would you mind reading those questions out loud for us tonight?"

"Sure." Amy stood and pointed to the questions printed inside the frame Glo had placed on the mantel two years ago when she'd envisioned D&D: "Question one: What was the high point of the day or week, a moment when you felt closest to God and to the truest version of yourself? Two: What was your low point today, a time when you felt tension or regret or most unlike your truest self? Three: What were you most grateful for today?"

"Sasha," I directed. "Would you be so kind as to remind us of the three sharing guidelines?"

Sasha, who quickly veiled her frustration with the shield she so often wore in the form of indifference, stood and ticked off her fingers one by one. I hadn't failed to notice the way she'd rolled her eyes as Monica made her way up. Though the two were usually inseparable, Glo had reported a dispute between them that had yet to be resolved. "Don't interrupt others while they're sharing. Keep your sharing time focused on *I statements* only. And encourage others by modeling good listening behavior when it's their turn to share."

"Thank you, Sasha." I made sure to wait until she acknowledged me with a nod before moving on. "As usual, the goal of these evenings is to grow in authenticity and in vulnerability. When we're willing to risk being real with others . . ." I stopped the sentence there, prompting the room to finish.

"We teach others how to be real with us," they said in unison.

I stepped aside for Monica to share, noting Molly's attentive posture. How foreign would this exercise be from her daily routine? I'd become increasingly aware that perhaps it wasn't only our residents who needed Molly, but Molly who needed them.

"I'd like to answer question one tonight—my high point." Monica swayed side to side as she spoke. "This morning I was able to buy a muffin for one of my classmates. She'd got to the front of the line and realized she'd forgotten her wallet in her car. She was freaking out a bit, throwing out all her books to search for loose change in her backpack. I only had a ten-dollar bill on me, but I felt like I could help her. So, I stepped up and gave the cashier my ten. Just like that." She looked around the room. "It reminded me of all the times someone stepped up for me, and also of the times when nobody stepped up, and I felt my only option was to steal what I needed." She shrugged as if that wasn't one of the most profound statements she'd ever made. "But I think God was proud of me today. It's like what Glo's always saying about how it's better to give and all that—well, it was. Even though I was short on cash for myself, paying for Becca was even better than my double white mocha and slice of banana bread." Monica smiled at Glo, and Glo blew her a kiss. "That's all. Thanks."

God wasn't the only one proud of her. Monica was big on personality and on influence. A natural-born leader. And yet it had only been recently that I'd seen her use that powerful combination for people other than herself or Sasha. I smiled up at her, like the delighted father she'd never had, yet deserved nonetheless. "Proud of you, Monica. Good job."

Glo met her offstage, wrapped her in a quick hug, then offered her a warm cookie as the room whooped and clapped for her. Devon then took center stage, which was likely his favorite spot to be in.

My brief glance at Molly proved she was up for another one. *Good.*

I braced for Devon's speech to come, hoping he'd stay on track or at least on a single topic. The kid reminded me so much of Jake when he was nineteen. "I'll take question *numero tres*." The room laughed, and I quirked an eyebrow at him. Though we had some native Spanish speakers in this room, Devon was not among them. He gave me his signature apologetic grin and addressed the group once more. "Today I'm most grateful for this." He reached in his pocket and took out a new iPhone, held it up.

"Devon," I cautioned in a volume only he could hear.

"No, no really. Hear me out. This isn't just for laughs. For a long time I could only afford the pay-as-you-go service plan, but the data was so expensive and my minutes would always run out before the end of the month. But today I got my first-ever service plan. Because I actually have some credit now—the good kind, even." The class laughed, and he did, too. "But I got to talk to my old foster dad this afternoon, and I gave him my number. And . . ." Devon paused, swallowed. "He told me he was proud of me. And that he'd been praying I'd check in with him and let him know how I'd been doing. So yeah, today I'm grateful to have a phone, but even more grateful that I have someone to call on it."

I stood and clapped Devon on the back, pulling him in to a quick hug as the room erupted once again. That kid had come so far since his first few weeks here. There was a time I hadn't been sure if Devon would ever let go of the facade he wore long enough to let us in. But once again, God continued to prove His timing was right on schedule. Even when that schedule wasn't made by me.

I cut another glance at Molly; this time her expressive eyes were on me, only I couldn't interpret the thoughts behind them before she shifted her gaze to the other side of the room.

Amy and Alex and Jasmine all stepped up after Devon, each sharing a high or low, and reminding me for the thousandth time why it was worth it. The sacrifice, the long hours, the trustee meetings, the minimal pay, and the pending approval on a matching grant that would require everything we had to give and more.

And still, I'd do it all over again.

As the line dwindled, I moved to wrap up the evening before we prayed out and dismissed for the night, when I saw a flash of copper. There were few things in life that left me dumbstruck, but watching Wren make her way to the platform counted as one. She'd never participated in this portion of our community activities. But here she was, coming to take the stage, her hands trembling as she addressed her peers.

"Um . . ." Her lips quivered, and I prepared for her to bolt under the pressure. But Glo set her cookie tray down and went to stand beside her. We had a house rule about not rescuing one another from moments of vulnerability, but one way we encouraged support was simply to stand or sit beside the sharer.

I'd never been prouder of my staff.

I looked to Wren, willing her to open her mouth, to engage with her housemates and connect with the community God had given her.

"I'd like to answer number two and number three." She took a shuddering breath, and I was sure more people than not were holding theirs in anticipation of Wren's next words. I was one of them. "I spent most of today pretty upset about a change in routine I had no control over. For a while, it was looking like my weekly visitations to see my brother would be cut back to twice a month due to transportation issues. I couldn't imagine seeing him less. He's the . . . he's the . . ." She closed her mouth, knotted her fingers. "He's the only reason I've kept going when I haven't wanted to. That was my low point." Her eyes cut from me to Molly, and Wren's chin started to quiver once again. "But tonight I'm grateful for my mentor, Molly. She's offered to take me to see Nate each week." She choked on a sob and placed her hand to her mouth. "I'm not sure if I can say what feeling close to God feels like exactly, but I imagine it feels a lot like this."

As Wren stepped off the stage, her fellow housemates stood and cheered, not only for Wren, but also for Molly, whose own tears were now a steady stream down her cheeks.

With a single glance in Glo's direction, I communicated my

next move, and without a moment's hesitation she understood and took the stage to close out the evening in my place. Because in roughly ten seconds, I would be needed elsewhere. If there was one thing I'd learned to recognize after years of working in social services, it was a flight risk.

And Molly was about to make a run for it.

◇◇◇

Molly

Despite the weight pressing against my ribcage, I'd summoned a feeble smile when Wren had come back to her seat and thanked me once again for my offer. It was then she'd hugged me. An actual hug that had likely cost her far more than it had me, and yet, something about it had forced all the air from my lungs.

The instant Monica approached to encourage Wren, I excused myself and bolted for the exit at the back of the room. For once in my life, I prayed the attention would not be on me—the crying mentor who hadn't a clue what her life was even about anymore.

I was halfway across the dusky lot when Silas called my name from somewhere behind me. For the briefest of moments, I considered the odds of outrunning him. If I could sprint to my car and engage the zero-to-sixty-in-two-point-six-seconds perk that Tesla fans raved about before Silas could catch up to me. But then what?

Where would I even go? Instagram didn't have a destination I could drive to.

"Molly," he said again, his voice closer, calmer than the first time. As if he couldn't sense the panic invading my every labored breath. "You don't have to leave."

His words were so unexpected that I actually stopped, right there in the middle of the gravel driveway, and spun to face him. "But I should leave. And you should want me to."

Not a flinch to his face. "Why?"

Because I can't breathe here. "Because you were right. I'm not a good fit for your program. I'm . . . I'm not the kind of person you want as a mentor."

He narrowed those deep dark eyes of his. "And what kind of person is that?"

I shivered, though I wasn't cold. "Someone who's selfless and caring and isn't constantly looking out for her own personal gain wherever she goes. Someone like you and Glo and Clara." And even Miles. Tears gathered in my eyes again, spilling over my cheeks once more.

Another step closer. Another too-calm question. "So if you're so sure you don't belong here, then why did you come tonight?"

"Because I didn't know where else to go." I shifted my focus to the forest of trees, wishing I could hide among them. "And yes, I realize how absolutely pathetic that sounds. But it's true."

"Then it's not pathetic, it's real."

"*Real*," I repeated with a self-deprecating laugh. "You know, people talk about how important *reality* is, how the world would be better if we could just *be real* with each other. But nobody really wants that, Silas. Not really. If they did, there wouldn't be multibillion-dollar companies built on bettering ourselves in every possible way—physically, mentally, emotionally, even spiritually. It's why I have a job."

I pointed to the red Tesla behind me. "It's why I have that car and this purse and these shoes." I rotated my ankle to show off my newest Coach slip-ons. "Nobody wants to see images of empty ice cream cartons and piles of dirty laundry. They want pictures of pristine living rooms with fluffy throw pillows and white shiplap walls and huge vases of fresh wildflowers. They want contouring compacts that promise a face like a Kardashian. They want chins without blemishes and clothing without the stains of last night's chili cheese dog. Because that's where hope actually lives—in the hustle. And if they can just hustle a little harder, a little longer, a little faster . . . then maybe all those pretty things can be theirs. Maybe life will finally make sense. Maybe something they do will actually matter." I swiped at the tear trailing my jaw. "Reality isn't enough. It's never been enough."

In the made-for-TV version of this conversation, the camera would zoom in on Silas's face, panning away to a commercial break only after his broodiest of micro-expressions had declared me wrong.

But naturally, Silas never played to my expectations.

"You're right. Our present reality isn't enough; it was never meant to be. The danger, as far as I see it, is not in promoting the stuff you enjoy, it's in believing that something so temporary can bring you actual joy. Peace. Acceptance. Fulfillment. Because if that were actually true, you wouldn't be here tonight. You wouldn't have parked in front of this building looking for something you can't buy or sell." He stepped closer. "And you wouldn't have offered to drive a nineteen-year-old orphan across town once a week for any other reason than to bring *her* joy."

I closed my eyes, my chin quivering in a way I hadn't felt since I was a young girl. But Silas deserved better than my half-truths, better than my stories and my spins. He deserved better than anything I could offer him. And though I knew he'd cut me from the program the minute I confessed, I would keep my end of the deals I'd made. I'd get all the donations he needed for the house, and I'd even hire a driver to take Wren to her brother's farm once a week. But I couldn't hold back the truth of who I was for one more second.

Because confessing had to be better than the guilt pumping through my veins right now and poisoning my heart.

"I have an answer to question two," I said. "The one about tension and regret and about not being the truest version of yourself."

Silas said nothing in response; he just waited.

"Before this moment, I believed my low point was losing my virtual assistant today. I felt sorry for myself, for the fact that my best friend—my only real friend for these last three years as Molly McKenzie of Makeup Matters with Molly—was just bought off by my ex-boyfriend."

"I'm sorry to hear that."

"And see? That's exactly how I want you to feel—sorry for me,"

I said, tears swimming in my eyes. "Because maybe then I can be a Catherine type—the kind of woman who wins your respect by rising above her own sufferings and lends a hand to those in need of justice and support. . . ." I shook my head. "Only that's not who I am. And no matter how desperately I want to be more than just a pretty face with an addictive personality . . . the truth is, the only person I wanted to help when I first came here was me and me alone."

The confusion clouding his face crippled something inside my chest. Whatever trust I'd managed to swindle from Silas was about to die a hard, quick death. "Care to expound on that?"

"I didn't sign up to be a mentor because of some undying passion for my community or its underprivileged youth. I came for . . ." My stomach roiled, and for a moment I thought I'd actually be sick. Right there, in the parking lot with Silas. I forced the words out. "I filled out the volunteer application because I was being considered for a network show that dealt with disadvantaged teens and young adults. And I was told to—" No, I wouldn't blame Ethan for this. I was an adult woman who needed to be held responsible for her own life choices. Her own deception in this plan. "I got your contact information from my brother under false pretenses. And then I sought you out and applied for the summer mentor position with the sole purpose of gaining experience with these residents so that I could use the experience to further my own career." Again, nausea churned as the last of the truth sputtered out. "And to grow my following."

"How?" he asked, his tone low and flat.

"By linking my brand to a human-interest cause. To your program here."

"And have you?"

"No." I shook my head adamantly. "I swear to you, I haven't, Silas. I haven't posted a single thing. I've only filed some notes away on my computer. Some future ideas and a few pictures I was planning to get your permission to post once you . . ."

"Once I what?"

This exhale hurt. "Trusted me."

The silence that followed was excruciating. But I wouldn't escape it. I deserved this front row seat to the disappointment I'd caused. After all, I'd conned one of the most respectable men I'd ever known for my own personal gain.

"I'm sorry, Silas. I'm so terribly sorry. I know nothing I can say will change what I've done, but if you'll allow me to keep my commitment to Wren, then I'll hire a driver to take her out to see Nate weekly—a background-checked driver, of course. And I can send you and Clara all the information I've collected so far on the fundraiser—that is, if you'll accept my help from afar. But I understand if you won't."

Another several beats of silence until he finally opened his mouth. "Is that all?"

I glanced around the parking lot. Was that his way of telling me he was done with this conversation? With having to stare at my pitiful face? Was this the beginning of his dismissal, where he'd hammer me in place, one coffin nail at a time?

"Was that all of them? The lies," he said in a detached voice.

"Yes," I whispered. "Wait—no it's not. There's something else."

He arched both eyebrows, inclined his head.

"I don't . . ." I bit down on the insides of my cheeks. "I don't actually speak Italian. Not conversationally. Unless that conversation happens to be in opera form."

I thought I imagined the twitch in his lips, because it disappeared faster than I could blink.

"I figured as much."

"You . . . did?"

"Yes, just like I figured there was something you were hiding when you sat in my office for that first interview. Several somethings, as it turned out."

It was my turn to be confused. "Wait, you knew I was hiding something and still said yes to me being a mentor? *Why?*"

"Because I believed you needed this house and these residents even more than they needed you. What we did tonight in the fireside room—the high and low points of their day—it's only a small peek into the collective challenges these kids have faced in their young lives." He glanced up at the sky. "When I first started in this line of work, helping these youth navigate a life path they hadn't been prepared for, I didn't want to praise every baby step forward. I wanted to see them run through the finish line. I knew how far they had to go, and the progress I could see in the moment didn't feel worth the time. I wanted to rescue them—to pay their way, to cosign their debts, to remove the hardships they faced on a day-to-day basis. I wanted to be the faithful authority figure they never had." He looked at me. "But more often than not, the best rescue plan we can offer someone we care about is our support for each step they take forward."

His words cracked something open inside my chest, something I'd worked to dam up a long time ago.

"Are you saying you might . . ." I rubbed my lips together, too afraid to even suggest the idea of yet another second chance with Silas. "You might allow me to stay with the program?"

"I'm not making this decision based on where you were when you started, but where you are now. No more lies, Molly. No more half-truths. No more trying to custom-make the rules. If there's a question, you ask first, act second. It's the only way I can assure the safety of our residents and our staff, including you."

Stunned by a pardon I never in a billion years believed I'd be granted, another chin-quivering episode took over my face. "I promise. I don't ever want to hurt anyone here."

He studied my face. "I believe you."

And then, before I had time to react to the one statement I'd longed to hear since our first meeting, Silas crossed the divide between director and volunteer and folded me into the kind of hug that could make even the loneliest of hearts feel reconnected again. And as I laid my head against his chest, listening to the strong beat of his heart, I realized I didn't want to be a Catherine type after all. Because as much as I craved his respect and approval . . . those weren't the only things I desired from a man like Silas.

A man I could so easily care for, and yet could never deserve.

Silas

Glo set her Diet RC Cola on the coffee table and sank lower into the couch cushion, laying her head back against the high leather back and exhaling deeply. A clear indication she was in no rush to wrap up our Tuesday lunch-hour meeting. Strangely enough, I wasn't, either. While I'd come to enjoy this new meeting location, one she and the residents had deemed the "lobby living room," my mind still had at least seven tabs open. Six of which had to do with the woman I held responsible for outfitting this new homey meeting space.

The same woman I'd held against my chest approximately three hundred feet from where I sat now.

I rubbed my hand down the length of the sofa arm, thinking back to the delivery of such a generous yet anonymous gift. The residents were correct. This was the most comfortable piece of furniture inside Fir Crest Manor to date. But the donations hadn't stopped there. This once bleak room now included a swanky rug, a dark-stained coffee table, a couple matching side tables, and four lounger chairs. And two shelves' worth of books. The note on that box had simply read *No historical manor is complete without a good mystery or romance novel.*

How is she today? I'd asked myself this question more than a dozen times as I replayed Molly's teary confession, hearing her bold words again and again, remembering the way her hair had brushed my chin as I'd pulled her to me.

"I've been sensing a weird vibe. In the cottage," Glo said ominously, pulling me back to the present. She opened her eyes, lifted her head. I'd known Glo for a long time. She'd lost a husband, a son, and about a decade to the bottom of a whiskey bottle, and yet somehow this house was where she wanted to be most. With these residents. Doing this work. Living out the hope she wished she'd found while navigating her darkest days. So while *vibe* wasn't an active part of my own vocabulary, I would never discount the word when she used it. Glo's sensitivity meter was set to a higher level than my own could ever be.

"What kind of vibe?"

As she leaned forward and settled her elbows on her knees, her long gray braid swung over one shoulder. "Something isn't right with Sasha." She sighed. "I can't quite put my finger on it, but there's something going on with her."

"Have things escalated with Monica?"

"No. They aren't even speaking to each other now. At least, not when Wren's in the picture."

"Jealousy, then."

Glo nodded. "I've pulled her aside a few times to try and walk her through her feelings to get a better grasp of what might really be going on, but . . ."

"She's a fortress." Though I'd had deep concerns over Wren's isolated existence when she first moved into the house, Sasha's version of social withdrawal was altogether different. The kind of hiding done in plain sight. Every one of her moves was calculated, a survival technique that did little to heal the festering wound she'd strived to avoid at all costs. Life had taught her how to play the game of getting what she needed without actually having to engage herself in the process. Though we'd seen the warning signs during her initial interview, we'd hoped and prayed her walls would crumble over time as she learned to trust her leaders and housemates. Instead, Sasha had continued to give lip service to all the right answers with no real growth to show for it.

"And nobody here seems to have the key. She's even shut Clara out now."

"Have you searched her room?"

"It's clean. I went through everything a few days ago when she was working at the coffee shop. No signs of drugs or alcohol. No proof of anything out of the ordinary, but . . ."

"What?"

"I have a feeling she might be involved with a boy. Someone here."

Exactly what I'd been dreading. Life on a co-ed campus was never boring. "I've had no camera alerts of late-night activity, so if something is happening, it's not happening on campus. Who do you suspect?"

Glo shrugged. "Hard to say. Possibly Jessie. Possibly Alex."

"Alex wouldn't be that stupid. He has too much on the line to risk getting kicked out."

Glo chuckled. "Wouldn't be the first time the allure of an attractive woman turned the head of a goal-oriented man."

I kept my expression neutral. Her slight eyebrow hitch hinted at a suggestion I wasn't ready to discuss. Not even with a woman who was second only to my mother.

"I'll do some digging around, too. In the meantime, I'll get her in to see our therapist again this week and see if Hannah might meet with her a few times in between if she's shut Clara out." I slid my phone out to schedule a reminder to do just that.

"Hannah's pregnant and needs to be resting right now, not trying to crack the code on a vault." Glo pursed her lips and then lifted her drink from the table. "I wonder . . . I wonder if Molly might be able to crack her."

"No." I shook my head. Molly was too fresh and too unversed in the ways of trauma.

"Why not? She's sharp, confident, classy, and she has her own unique way of—"

"I'm aware of who Molly is, but Sasha needs a professional."

"She's had professionals, Silas. Lots of them. Maybe she needs someone different to talk to, someone with a bit of spunk and style to mix it up."

I could feel the beginnings of a headache coming on. "Sasha will eat Molly alive."

"Maybe. Maybe not." Glo took a long pull of her soda. "But why not let her try? Sasha's already in her small group, and Clara and I can help coach her, too. Look at the progress she's made with Wren."

True. But Wren was a different situation altogether. Her heart was hurt, but open. Sasha was walled and defensive, a striker when agitated, not someone who shrank back when she felt threatened.

"Just think about it. Molly's a . . ."

I met Glo's eyes, curious to hear how she'd choose to conclude her sentence.

"She's a soft center," she finished.

As I thought back to Molly's confession last night, to the truth she'd chosen to reveal, knowing the outcome could mean dismissal from the program . . . I had to agree with Glo's assessment. Strong, yet also soft.

The overhead *ding* of the lobby door being opened by someone with the correct access code cut our conversation short as our attention zeroed in on the very woman we'd just been discussing. A woman who wasn't due here for another five hours. Only this Molly wasn't draped in any of the extra flourishes I'd come to expect—no vibrant colors, patterns, or prints. No outlandish shoes set on stilts or slices of cork.

And something about this subdued version of her made my gut twist in revolt.

I stood as she approached us in her muted pastel T-shirt and light denim jeans. It was as if she believed that by dialing down her fashion selections she could turn off the very thing that made her so unique, so Molly.

"Sorry," she said. "I didn't mean to interrupt; I was just hoping

I could take some measurements of the east lawn. For the fundraising event. Thought I should ask permission before walking out there." She pressed a pink notebook flat against her abdomen like a protective shield.

Glo pushed up off the couch and headed straight for her. "No apologizes necessary. Silas and I were just finishing up here."

We weren't, of course, but I appreciated Glo's on-the-nose perception like usual. "Yes, thank you, Glo. I'll be sure to follow up on everything we discussed," I replied, though my eyes never left the woman in front of me.

I observed the way Glo pulled Molly into a hug and then pushed her back to assess her feet with suspicion. "I thought you said you didn't wear flats. Those sneakers look pretty flat to me, Kitten Heels. Next thing I know, you'll be asking to borrow my Birkenstocks."

Molly's laugh was thin. "Maybe so."

Glo squeezed her shoulder and quirked a telling eyebrow at me as if to say *Fix this, Silas* before she clacked away in the shoes she hadn't taken off since Molly first gave them to her.

"How are—"

"Is everything—"

I gestured for Molly to go first.

She studied the floor. "Your meeting wasn't really over, was it?"

"It was over enough."

She glanced up. "Is everything okay—I mean, it seemed serious when I walked in."

If only to put her mind at ease that the subject matter Glo and I had been discussing had nothing to do with her, I pulled back the proverbial curtain. "We have some concerns about Sasha."

"About what?"

"Several things, but currently, we're concerned about the possibility of an inappropriate relationship. Between Sasha and one of the male residents."

"Who?" she asked.

"Not sure yet. We don't have actual evidence to go on right now, just a suspicion."

Molly nodded. "And if you find evidence, what happens then? Do you call the two of them in for a meeting and ask them both outright?"

The optimism in her response caused me to smile. "Have you ever cornered a toddler who had melted chocolate on their fingers and asked if they knew anything about a missing cookie?"

"You don't think they'd confess?"

"No one ever has before." I paused a beat, weighing my words. "Given their age and freedoms, it's impossible to account for every moment of a resident's day, but we do try to make it as difficult as possible for our residents to break the rules on campus. And due to our long waitlist, they know how serious we are when it comes to the consequences."

Her eyes rounded slightly. "Getting caught means they'd have to leave?"

"It depends on the circumstances, but if there's evidence that things have . . . evolved to a certain extent, then we have no choice but to ask them to go. Everyone here has signed a commitment statement. They are well versed in the expectations."

"Is there anything I can do to help?"

Glo's words boomeranged in my head. *Why not let her try?* "As you've likely noticed, Sasha can be . . . challenging. But her past has been marked by tragedy and rejection. She was born in Ukraine and adopted as a young girl by an American couple from Oregon, but that adoption dissolved two years post placement due to certain behavioral issues the family felt underprepared to deal with long-term." I cleared my throat, unwilling to debate the morality of such a life-altering decision, even inside my own mind. A disruption like that was damaging for everyone involved, but it was nothing short of devastating for the displaced child. In this case, Sasha. "She was never adopted again and instead was raised in and out of several foster homes up and down the West Coast. The manifestations of the kind of trauma she's faced in her young life are more evident than in some of our other residents, but even still, we've tried our best to connect with her, to help her understand the value of real, trust-based relationships."

"That's so sad." Molly's face contorted with compassion. "I never would have guessed that about her."

"Like many kids raised in traumatic situations, she's become an expert at concealing her pain." I hesitated. "Maybe, if you see an opportunity, you could try to talk with her, too."

"Of course. I'll do my best."

And I knew she would. "Thank you."

She nodded, then slowly glanced away, the sparkle in her eyes dimming to match the rest of her uncharacteristically sheepish body language today.

"Molly," I hedged, unsure of how to start such a conversation. "You and I—we're good. There's no need for you to tiptoe around here as if last night was—"

"I feel like such a fool, Silas." When her eyes met mine, it took every shred of willpower I possessed not to reach out for her. "I have no clue how I should be now after . . . after everything I said to you last night. I don't know how to act around you or what I should say or when I should—"

I worked to douse the flame of heat her words ignited. "I don't want or expect you to be anything other than who you are."

"But do you really even know who that is? Because I'm not even sure I know. What if I'm just a fraud through and through and the hope of me actually being able to offer something of value to one of the residents here is nothing more than a really bad joke?"

I studied her, working to unscramble her fears one by one, sorting the obvious lies from the truth I'd come to believe about her in such a short period of time. While I was in no way blinded to her faults or flaws, the number of positive adjectives I'd use to describe Molly McKenzie had only multiplied each time I was near her.

"You are confident and eager, witty and inviting. Empathetic and invested when engaging with our young ladies, and you've shown generosity in providing for needs spoken and unspoken alike." I let my gaze linger on the sectional sofa beside us. "All of those are valuable qualities to offer a hurting world." I waited until her searching eyes met mine again, and when they did, I spoke the rest, unfiltered and unrestrained. "You are everything you were last night before we talked, minus the burden you were carrying. So if anything can be called fraudulent here, it's the timidity you came in wearing like a cloak."

After a silent moment, her lips quirked. "Only a duke would use the word *cloak*."

"Doesn't make it any less true."

She released a heavy exhale, and as she did, the notebook she held slacked away from her chest just enough for me to make out the corner of a glittered word. I reached for it, prying it away from her hands to read the shimmery pink phrase in its entirety: *Sparkling Is My Favorite Sport.*

A laugh erupted from my throat. If ever there was a life motto to describe someone by, this was hers. Molly sparkled wherever she went, even now, when she was trying her best to conceal it from the world.

She tried to pluck the notebook back from me, but I shook my head. The last place it belonged was pressed against a T-shirt that couldn't decide whether it was peach or tan. "What exactly were your plans for such a notebook today?"

"Like I said earlier," she said with about twenty-five percent more spice than before, "I was hoping to take some measurements of the lawn and garden area. I was also hoping I might find a corner where I could work in the house and sketch out some plans. It's easier for me to visualize it all if I'm here." Absently she touched the side of her head where she'd pinned her golden mane into a style I'd seen her create in one of her hair tutorials. A weaving together of loose curls that somehow required more hardware than my kitchen cabinets.

"Seeing as this house is twelve thousand square feet, I think we can do better than offer you a corner to work from." Though there were a dozen possibilities, only one registered as the suggestion I'd offer. "There's an empty room directly across the hall from mine. It's yours for however long you need it."

"Thank you," she said with a smile much closer to her natural brightness. "I might need to ask your opinion on a few details later—in regards to the dinner. I had some thoughts about the decor and agenda for the evening."

"That's fine. But, Molly, you should know that our budget will be limited as to what we can afford to host here on the grounds." The subject made the headache I'd managed to suppress throb yet again.

She shook her head. "And you should know that it's my goal for The Bridge not to have to pay a cent for hosting it at all. I just need to think through some of the bigger details a bit more first, but between my sponsors and my platforms, I'm fairly certain I can build a strategy that can pay for it all without dipping into your accounts." Her smile grew, and once again, I was taken aback not only by her beauty but also by her resilience.

"Okay," I found myself saying. "Just let me know what I can do to help."

"I will."

◇◇◇

While Molly walked the grounds, sketching in her notebook and taking notes, I carried some temporary office furniture from downstairs into the room across the hall for her to use once she came back inside. As I pushed the table to the window, I saw her. She wasn't alone. Both Monica and Wren had joined her—all taking giant yard-stick size steps and falling into fits of laughter I could hear, even from two floors up. As I continued to watch, something undeniable tugged inside my chest at the sight of her here. Something I wasn't yet willing to admit, even to myself.

Perhaps Glo had been right. Maybe Molly's soft center was exactly what someone like Sasha needed. Maybe it was what we all needed.

The harsh shrill of my phone shoved the tranquil moment aside and yanked my thoughts away from the woman twirling in circles outside my window and to the unknown number on my phone screen.

"Hello, this is Silas."

"Silas, *mi hermano*."

A familiar cold crept over my skin at a voice I'd know anywhere. "Carlos."

"You sound good, brother. You're healthy?"

I turned my back to the window and lowered my voice, working to recall the many hours of therapeutic roleplay I'd endured after the incident. "I've asked you not to call me." Though boundaries likely didn't mean much to a convict.

"The judge released me two months early—for good behavior. I wrote to tell you, but I wasn't sure if you—"

"Is there something you need from me, Carlos?"

The pause on the other end of the phone caused me to prepare for whatever manipulation web was waiting to be spun. My brother's lies were often as subtle as his breath.

"I'm not your enemy, brother."

"The scar on my arm would disagree."

"That was a mistake. I'm not that man anymore. I'm clean— I've *been* clean. For over two years now. Everything is different, I've explained it all in my—"

"A mistake implies a moment of misjudgment, not a lifetime of bad decisions." My words lacked warmth but not sincerity. Though I had prayed my brother would change, that he would find a true and lasting faith in God, I no longer believed I would be the one to lead him there. Not after he'd left me for dead at the bottom of a cement staircase in the pursuit of another hit.

"I called to ask if you would meet me—you can pick the place. Any day or time. If you need me to bring Peter, I will. He's the pastor I've told you about—the one who visited me in prison every week. He's my sponsor, too. He gave me a Bible and a job stocking food at a warehouse in Bellingham. That's where I'm living now. He said I could take a day off to meet you."

Though I worked to guard myself against his every word, the cramp in my chest expanded. If the man could watch his own brother be beaten and thrown down a staircase, he certainly wouldn't think twice about using the Bible for ulterior motives. "A meeting won't be possible."

"I'm telling you the truth, brother. Call my sponsor, *please*. His name is Peter Rosario. He works at Applegate Community Church in Bellingham, and he'll vouch for me. For everything I've said. I'm not asking for anything more than your time. For just an hour or so to talk. To start to catch up on what we've missed. Nothing more."

Nothing more? Surely he didn't actually think we could catch up on all we'd missed in an hour or so. We'd missed a lifetime. And not by my doing. By his.

I worked to keep myself in check, to stay in control of the guilt card Carlos loved to play. My temples began to pound, blurring my vision enough for me to reach out for the office chair I'd carried in for Molly earlier. I kneaded my right temple with my knuckle.

"I won't be calling him." It was hard enough to pray for Carlos most days, much less track down all the trails his lies would lead me to. I'd taken that dead-end path before and lost.

"Silas, brother, I'm not the same addict you remember. Things are different now. *I'm different*." The catch in his throat ratcheted the throbbing in my head to a new level. "You're the only family I have."

That sentence never failed to hit me in the gut, no matter how many times I'd spoken it aloud or written it down or tried any of the tactics my therapist had insisted would release the stress my body refused to let go of—long after my concussion and broken bones had healed.

I slammed my eyes closed, seeing and hearing it all again. The lure of lies he'd used to draw me in for the last time, to a drug house full of addicts, money, and nauseating sin.

I'd been arrogant enough to believe I could save him. To think I could rescue him from the same clutches he'd willingly run to once again. The D. A. had said I should count myself lucky. That often altercations involving an enraged addict ended in a fatality. Much less six enraged addicts. And even though my brother wasn't the one to throw the first punch or steal my wallet or shove me down a flight of cement stairs and leave me for dead, he also hadn't been the one to stop them.

He'd been too high to do anything but watch, much like the way he looked at his sentencing trial, where the paranoia behind his erratic, shifty eyes matched the panic that spewed from his mouth—accusations and explanations too disgraceful to repeat as the judge demanded his silence.

I'd changed my entire career and future for this brother. But not even The Bridge could fill what he'd stolen from us both that night.

"We aren't family anymore, Carlos. Please don't call me again."

I dropped the phone to my lap, cutting off his voice with a single tap of my screen, knowing without a doubt it wouldn't be the last I heard it. Because even if Carlos honored my wishes, his voice was forever locked in my memories.

With elbows pressed to the desk in Molly's office, I dug my knuckles deeper into my temples, exhaling hard—

"Silas?"

I started at the sound of Molly's voice in the doorway and tried to stand, but I immediately collapsed back into the chair as the mixture of light, sound, and movement crashed over me at once.

"Oh my goodness, Silas." She rushed toward me. "Are you okay?" I felt her hand on my back. "It's a migraine, isn't it? Ocular?"

How she knew that, I'd—

"My Mimi used to get them. Do you have a prescription somewhere?"

"Top drawer of my desk. Right-hand side. It's locked." Gingerly, I reached into my pocket and handed her the key ring. "The small silver one."

"Okay. Be right back."

I could hear her feet patter across the hallway to my office, and then she was back just as quickly, with the pills and a bottle of water I'd left on my desk earlier.

"Here, take this." She placed a single pill in my hand and unscrewed the water, bringing it to my mouth for me to take.

"Thank you," I said after I swallowed it down.

I heard her rummaging somewhere behind me—in a bag? Her purse maybe? A moment later she was beside me again.

"Okay, so this might sound weird, but since I don't have a rice compress to warm for you, I swear this is the next best thing. All you have to do is inhale."

"Inhale?"

"Trust me. I lived with my Mimi during my senior year of high school and this was the remedy that helped her most. Take three deep, slow breaths in."

The powerful fragrance of lavender filled my nostrils as I did what she asked.

"The other thing that helped her was . . ." But her words faded out before she finished the sentence.

I hated that it hurt too badly to open my eyes, but I was next to blind until the pressure passed. The impairment to my vision didn't usually last longer than thirty minutes, but I felt every sightless second with Molly more acutely than I thought possible. Interpreting her facial expressions had become a critical factor to the way I communicated with her.

"What?" I probed. "What else helped her?"

"It's just, I'd have to touch you. On the back of your neck, I mean. Is that okay?"

A prickle of heat climbed my spine in anticipation. "Yes, that's fine."

Tentatively at first, she pressed her fingers into the back of my neck, trailing a path into my scalp. Her touch alleviated the pressure inside my skull almost immediately.

"Do you see dark spots when it comes on? Or does everything just blur together?"

"Both."

She braced each side of my head, her fingers gripping the space under my ears as she pushed her thumbs into my tensed muscles, ushering instantaneous relief.

"Who is Carlos?" But before I even had a chance to answer, she rushed on. "You don't have to tell me, it's just that I couldn't help but overhear the tail end of your conversation when I came in to find you."

At the sound of his name, the tension in my neck returned. I willed the words to come out clear, strong. Detached. "My older brother. My only blood relative." Though we'd shared the same mother, there'd been little else we'd shared in common after the day protective services had separated us.

A soft intake of air. "Oh."

"He was just released from prison. For the second time."

"Oh, Silas, I'm sorry. I didn't know."

"It's fine." I swallowed as she tilted my head to the left, rubbing her thumb along the tendons below my ear. "As you probably heard, we aren't close."

"Still, I'm sure that's hard. It might even make it harder," she said. "I don't have much of a relationship with my parents anymore. I know it's not even close to what you must be going through with your brother, but sometimes I think the strained way things are between us now makes me think of them more, not less. They're always hovering close. In my thoughts. My memories."

It was the first time she'd mentioned her family—outside of Miles or her grandmother. And even though I couldn't see her face or the way her eyes likely shifted to the floor, the significance of such an admission was unmistakable.

"Where do your parents live?"

"Where haven't they lived?" Her exhale came out as a tired laugh. "They work for a ministry organization that takes them all over the U.S. and sometimes abroad. They're church planters. To impoverished communities. These days, they rarely stay anywhere for longer than a year or so."

Interesting. "Was it that way growing up, too? You and your brother traveling with them from church plant to church plant?"

"Yes, though it was a slower process back then. We lived in six states in ten years, from ages seven to seventeen. But we always spent a few weeks here every summer."

"With your grandmother. Mimi, you called her?"

"Yes. Miles and I moved in with Mimi for our last year of high school. Our parents went to the Philippines that year, and I begged to stay back. Miles didn't want to leave me, so he stayed back, too." Her sigh was filled with an angst I could feel through her touch. "It's strange, though. When I think back on it, on being homeschooled by our mom and traveling in the back seat with my brother in our little compact car, my memories of that time, of that part of my childhood, are mostly positive." Another weak chuckle. "Ten-year-old Molly would never have imagined she'd become an adult who didn't have the support of her parents."

"Why don't your parents support you?" Though I'd heard hundreds of abandonment stories in my line of work, the idea of Molly's parents willingly walking away from her as an adult seemed unthinkable.

"It's hard to support someone when you don't take the time to understand them. And my parents haven't tried to understand me for a very long time." A simple explanation that was likely tied to a much deeper root. "Sometimes I wish I could pinpoint the exact moment the distance between us began. Like if I could look back and recall one of those big holiday meal blow-ups where everybody hollers their opinions at one another over a tray of sweet potato soufflé . . . but that's not what happened with us at all. It was more like a slow erosion of indifference over time. The more I pursued interests and hobbies outside of what they knew, the further the distance. Miles is about the only thing we have in common now, and even that feels strained."

"Because Miles is a pastor?"

"Exactly." The finality with which she spoke the word was sobering. "The truth is, I don't know how to fit in their world, and they don't know how to fit in mine. That's one of the reasons I loved living with my Mimi. She was precious to me." Molly's voice took on an ethereal quality. "She always smelled like lavender and honey and was as assertive as she was graceful. She used to say, *'God has uniquely shaped gifts for every one of His uniquely shaped people.'* She'd tell me it was okay that my gifts didn't fit inside the same box as my family's gifts did. But as a kid, that was pretty hard for me to understand. It still is sometimes." She was quiet for a few seconds before adding, "I suppose that's something we all want in life, no matter how old we get: to find that special place where we fit."

"I suppose you're right."

Her fingers paused for a beat. "Were you adopted by the Whittaker family, Silas?"

"Yes. Just after my tenth birthday."

"And did you feel like you fit with them immediately?"

"No, but at the time I hadn't wanted to fit anywhere." Especially not with a family who didn't look or speak like me. And who hadn't known my mother or my big brother. "But I was a boy with a lot of confusion and anger to work through after my mom died of an overdose. I was the Whittakers' first emergency placement, and I was anything but easy on them. Eventually, though, they became everything to me, and I'm grateful to be their son. Their brother."

"And Carlos . . . was he ever adopted?"

"No," I said, unable to hide my grief or my guilt. "But I imagine so many things would have turned out differently for him if he'd been given that chance." Or even a place to feel safe during his transition from teenage boy to adult man.

As her fingers slowed and eventually stilled on the nape of my neck, Molly asked, "How is your pain now? Better?"

Remarkably so. "Yes, thank you."

"Good. I'm glad I could help." I felt her distance as soon as she stepped away from me.

"Molly." Slowly, gingerly, I opened my eyes and reached out for her wrist, feeling her delicate pulse thrum against my fingers as I stared up at her. "You fit here. At The Bridge. I hope you see that as clearly as I do now."

She pressed her lips together, swallowed, nodded. "Thank you, Silas."

· 22 ·

Molly

If there was a prize awarded for the least interaction one could have with their new personal assistant, I would win first place. If I hadn't seen Rosalyn with my own human eyes, I could be convinced she was actually connected to the artificial intelligence conspiracy Miles loved to prattle on about. The woman had the personality of copier paper. And not the high-gloss variety, either—the one-ply, standard stock.

Over the past two and a half weeks, she'd emailed me twice a day. First to let me know the titles and times of the scheduled posts Val had edited for me weeks ago—as if I couldn't see them waiting in the queue myself—and second to let me know how each of those posts performed in their first twenty-four hours. Again, as if I didn't have the log-in information to my own social media platforms. But those were far from her most annoying transgressions, as Rosalyn's favorite form of communication seemed to be the automated group text message she sent out every morning at exactly 7:00 a.m. A motivational quote. But not one for each day of the week—nope, the same one. Every. Single. Morning. And the more I read it, the more unmotivated I became:

"Working hard is not the same as hard work."
—Rosalyn Brunswick

What kind of person sent out a daily *anti-motivational* quote that they wrote themselves via group text message? Not Val. That's who.

I sat at my computer, wishing I could copy/paste my latest Rosalyn encounter—an unnecessary reminder to *please respond to your viewers within an hour of your most recent postings for best visibility and reach*—to Val, since she was the only person in my life who could truly understand what I was working with here. But every time I scrolled down to Val's name, I'd get that same awful prickly feeling in the pit of my stomach. Because I'd be forced to see the last of our text messages to each other. Those brutally polite exchanges recounting her final days and hours as my assistant. Simple logistics absent of personality or emojis.

Who was I to Val now? A former boss? A former friend? Both?

I wasn't sure of the new rules. What were the boundaries for such a strange arrangement? I didn't know. Just like I didn't know how to push the constant swell of grief and regret away whenever I thought of her. Why hadn't I visited Val in Alaska when I'd had the chance? I knew all about her fears of flying, her obligations to Tucker and her parents, and yet I never actually booked a flight. I should have surprised her, shown up with balloons and a cake for her birthday one year. I should have planned a girls weekend at a spa retreat on a snowy mountaintop as a thank-you for her countless overtime hours and loyal dedication to building my brand. I should have put one of my many work trips aside to do something that actually mattered for *someone* who actually mattered.

And yet, I'd done none of that.

I forked another bite of chilled wedding cake samples. Perhaps one of the only things I did know how to answer was the call to eat my feelings, and thanks to Clara's generous donation to the Late Night Emotional Eating Fund for Molly McKenzie, I'd be on a sugar high for at least another hour. Possibly two.

When Clara had asked if I wanted to go with her to Bake Me A Cake two days ago to pick up the samples, I'd figured she just needed a ride since Jake was at a job site across town, but as it turned out, we ended up spending the entire day together. After the tasting, she'd asked my opinion on a going-home outfit to wear after the reception, which had led to several more store visits and then to the purchase of iced coffees and a long stroll around the Riverwalk. It had been an unexpectedly fun day, yet like so often over these last few weeks, I couldn't help but think of Val. I'd reached for my phone countless times to snap a picture of something I knew she'd find amusing or cute or post-worthy for an upcoming feature. But then I'd remember how things were between us now, and that terrible gut clench would return.

I stuffed the last piece of orangesicle-and-limeade cake into my mouth and swiped to the home screen on my phone. It wasn't the first time I wanted to start a music playlist entitled *Friendship Breakups are the Worst*.

An email notification appeared at the top of my device, and I prayed it wasn't from Rosalyn. I couldn't be held responsible for a professional reply after 11:00 p.m.

But it wasn't from my new assistant. It was from Sophia Richards.

I fought to swallow the too-big piece of cake and sat up as if Sophia herself were walking into my living room and not confined to my inbox. I clicked into the body of the message.

Dear Molly,

I apologize that it's taken a couple weeks for me to respond to your email. We've been in Barbados, celebrating the launch of a new product line before my husband gets back to the Hollywood grind.

To address the outcome of the photo shoot, yes, I was disappointed by your decision to leave. However, we all have times when our personal convictions override obligations. In this case, I applaud you for sticking to your convictions and considering how the choices you make on your platform might affect the impressionable following you've grown. As a former foster child myself, I'd be interested in hearing more about the organization you mentor through. I was adopted prior to my twelfth birthday, but not without much struggle and hardship.

Due to some recent feedback within the industry, we will be implementing an alternate pattern to the traditional Tubee: a halter tank which will cover more chest and midriff with a less translucent fabric. I'd be honored if you'd consider it for future endorsement.

Stay in touch,
Sophia Richards

I read the email over three times in a row, my eyes growing wider and wider with each pass. And then I stood up and paced my living room. Sophia Richards applauded me? She applauded me for leaving her photo shoot early?

I glanced back at the clock. Ten after eleven.

Miles would for sure be asleep. Plus, I would have to spend thirty minutes filling him in on everything that had happened that day at Sophia Richards's house, and by the time I got to the punch line, all the happy endorphins I felt right now would be dead. At least, that's what I told myself as I picked up my phone and fired off a text.

> **Molly**
>
> If you're sleeping, then I sincerely hope your phone is set to DND and that you wake up rested. In that case: Good morning, Silas! But in the case that you might have your phone set to emergency alerts only and you happen to see my text, then know this is not one. An emergency, I mean. Unless you happen to count a certain celebrity emailing with some very interesting information as an emergency? Then yes, it is one.

The Duke of Fir Crest Manor

> No. Yes. No.

I rolled my eyes, laughed.

My phone rang an instant later.

"Hey," I said. "You really weren't sleeping?"

"No," he said, with an amused voice. "Reading."

Silas would never be accused of wasting words.

"Okay . . . well, I just got a pretty insane email."

"I gathered that."

"From Sophia Richards. You know, the Tubee lady."

"Is that actually her title of choice? I'd think a woman of her means would have a more creative marketing team."

"Silas. Sophia said, and I quote . . ." I pulled up the email to read directly from her message. "'I applaud you for sticking to your convictions and considering how the choices you make on your platform might affect the impressionable following you've grown.'"

"How did she know your reasons for not wearing it?"

I scrunched up my nose, knowing without a doubt that any person with half a business brain would have advised me *not* to email her after such a professional disaster, and yet . . . "I emailed her."

"You emailed her." For some reason he sounded slightly less shocked than I'd anticipated. "And I suppose Cobalt Group doesn't know you did this?"

"If you're asking if I was granted some sort of permission before I emailed her, no. But I did make it clear that I was reaching out to her just as Molly, not as Makeup Matters with Molly. There's a difference."

He groaned, and I heard the unmistakable sound of a book closing and a mattress shifting under his weight. "I'm not sure a legal team would see it the same way."

"Good thing I only care about what *my* legal team—Silas Whittaker Minus Associates—thinks, then."

He chuckled at that, the way I hoped he might. "I'm sure her high-powered entourage of lawyers might know a little more than a guy who passed his bar exam five years ago and then never practiced law."

"Yeah, but I doubt any of those hotshot lawyers are as trustworthy as you." The compliment slipped easily from my mouth.

"I appreciate that," he said.

"Good, because I mean it."

The natural pause indicated that this brief but informative exchange of ours was winding down. As it should, seeing as it was nearing midnight, especially when I knew Silas ran several miles at the break of dawn. It wouldn't be kind to keep him on the phone any longer.

"Well," I began, "thanks for letting me interrupt your reading time to—"

"Glo said you asked her to go on a shopping trip this weekend," Silas said, steering the conversation in an entirely new direction. "Something about rental furniture for The Event?"

I smiled at his terminology. No longer was it called the fundraising dinner, but The Event. Silas had come a long way from the early vision I'd cast, but we still had much to sort out. I hadn't intentionally withheld information from him, but Silas wasn't the type who would willingly stand under a waterfall of details, either. Not unless he could check each one of them out from every angle. That's the stage I was at with him now, the *let's look at one piece of party preparation at a time*, because everything at once was way too overwhelming for a man who asked if a simple taco bar could replace the multi-course menu I'd carefully selected. To which I had politely and emphatically told him, *"Not a chance, pal."* Four hundred thousand dollars wouldn't come out of a mass taco feed, no matter how fabulous the guacamole tasted.

"Yeah, I was just hoping to get a second opinion on a few things, and it sounds like Clara and Jake already have plans this weekend. Don't get me wrong, I'm glad Glo is taking time off to spend with her niece and nephew. She deserves a break."

"I'll go with you."

For half a second, I thought I'd understood him wrong. "You'll go with me . . . to the rental place?"

"Unless you'd rather go with someone else."

Though I couldn't imagine Silas wanting to spend an entire day selecting table settings and figuring out which of the three themes I would choose for The Event, I suddenly couldn't imagine going without him, either. "If an entire day of party supply shopping doesn't scare you off, then I'd be happy to have the company."

"I grew up with three older sisters, Molly. I've done many a long shopping excursion in my life."

"Okay, then, it's a date." As the word escaped my mouth my eyes widened, ready to reel it back in, or at the very least, soften the blow by furthering the statement. But Silas didn't seem bothered by it in the slightest.

"I can drive if it makes sense for us to ride together?"

"Sure, that works," I said. "One of the stores is out in my neck of the woods. How about if you drive us around town for the day, then I'll buy you dinner for your impeccable patience."

He made a *hmm* sound as if he were considering my proposal carefully.

"What?" I asked with a laugh. "Believe me, you will need a reward by the time the day is over."

"Mind if I trade in my meal ticket for a different reward, then?" A most un-Silas-like request, but an intriguing one for sure.

"What did you have in mind?"

"Driving a Tesla Model X."

I laughed as I stood up from the sofa, reaching to switch off the lights in my house one by one, starting at the studio and working my way through the kitchen and down the hallway. "I should have known. No man can resist her allure."

"I will pretend not to be offended by that comment if it means I get to drive a Tesla for a day."

"Deal. She's all yours on Saturday."

"Then feel free to add a few more stores and errands to your list."

I imagined the curve of his mouth and the way his eyes crinkled at the corners. It was a look I'd seen him wear far more often in these last few weeks than in the early interactions we'd shared. Or perhaps I'd just noticed it more often because I had a clearer vantage point of his office across the hall from mine at Fir Crest Manor. In either case, his relaxed demeanor with the residents had caught my attention more than once—especially his merciful and tolerant responses to their obvious shortcomings. Even when he'd had to address bigger issues with higher-level consequences, Silas's reprimands were a blend of authority and grace. Never shame. Never anger.

"Do you have to wake up early for your run in the morning?" I asked, turning on the tap water and rinsing my electric toothbrush before loading it up with toothpaste.

"It might need to be an evening run at this point."

"Sorry," I said, talking around my toothbrush head. "But hey, a change in routine can be good, right? Muscle memory and all that?"

"Are you brushing your teeth right now?" he asked, as if it was the wildest concept in all the world.

"Yeah? Don't you brush your teeth before you go to bed?"

"Of course, I just never considered it a social activity I'd include on a phone call."

"You should really reconsider. It saves time."

"In the same way your half twist bun saves time?"

I nearly choked on a minty gasp. I quickly rinsed out my mouth, tapped my toothbrush on the side of the sink, and patted my lips dry on a towel. "Silas Whittaker. How do you know about my half twist bun trick? And don't even try to say one of my mentees told you."

I waited for him to break his sudden muteness and speak the words into a complete sentence, because as far as I was concerned, Silas was not capable of telling a lie. "I watched your video on timesaver beauty hacks."

My mouth smacked open in triumph at the thought of Silas engaging in a social media video for entertainment purposes. And then another thought hit me. That video had been smack-dab in the middle of a three-part series. "Wait . . . how many?"

"Excuse me?"

"How many videos have you viewed, Silas?"

"I don't see why that's a relevant question."

I laughed. "You *so* should have been a lawyer."

At his own chuckle, I laughed even harder. "More than five?"

"I'm not doing this."

"Ten?"

"Molly."

The rising heat creeping up my neck reached my cheeks. Had Silas social media stalked me? I simply could not envision it. He had been so adamant, so against it all—the posting, the promoting, the product endorsements for personal gain. Yet again, Silas hadn't been nearly as uncompromising as he'd been when we'd first met. He'd actually agreed to my idea of doing a livestream for donations during The Event as long as it met his security criteria for the house and residents.

"Silas Whittaker . . . have you seen *all* of them?" A whispered accusation.

"I wouldn't say *all*, no." He cleared his throat. "But quite a few."

I tried to purse my lips together, tried to keep the sound in, but it wouldn't—couldn't—be stopped. "I don't even know what to say."

"Are you . . . upset?"

"Upset?" Was he serious? A laugh burst from my throat. "Of course not. Those videos are my job. My literal, actual job. It's what I do. Why would I be upset that you watched them? If anything, I'm shocked that you'd stoop so low as to break your personal convictions on my disgraceful career path."

"I've never said your career is disgraceful. In fact, I think you're quite entertaining at what you do. I'd planned on watching one video, and the next thing I knew I ended up down a rabbit hole of *Molly's Fashion Do's and Don'ts*."

I lifted the covers off my bed and slipped between the cool sheets, a bit light-headed over the idea that Silas had watched not only my bobby pin techniques but so much more. "I'm sure it was all pertinent information to your life, too."

"You're gifted," he said. "It's easy to understand what your Mimi saw in you all those years ago. What she said about God having uniquely shaped gifts for each one of His uniquely shaped people. She was right about you."

His recall of what I'd told him weeks ago sent a tingle skipping down my spine. "That means a lot, thank you."

"You're welcome."

I heard him stifle a yawn.

"Okay, it's time. I've kept you up way too late. You might not even have energy for an evening run tomorrow at this point."

"I will. I'll just have to work a bit harder for it. But hard work never killed anybody."

I groaned. "But bad motivational quotes about hard work do, I can assure you of that."

"What?"

I laughed, pulling my face away from the phone and calculating the few hours between now and when Rosalyn would be texting out her quote. "Believe me, you don't want to know. Sleep well, Silas."

"You too. Good night."

As I plugged my phone in on my nightstand, my mouth curved into a grin I couldn't wipe away. Because somehow I'd managed to make Silas a cyber stalker. What had the world come to?

· **23** ·

Molly

> Do you think we could make a stop on the way to the Coles' house after mentor group today? I need to pick up a birthday gift for Nate. Oh, and Silas said yes about the Star Wars sleepover tonight. Thank you! 😀

Molly

> Oh that's wonderful! 😄😄😄 And yes, of course! I never need an excuse to shop.

Wren

> Thanks! :)

Despite my momentary frustration over Rosalyn's unwanted input—via Ethan, I was sure—on my latest post upload schedule, stating that I "didn't have enough content to satisfy my contractual agreements with specific sponsors," I smiled down at Wren's text.

I pushed away from my desk in my makeshift office at Fir Crest Manor and peered across the hall into the open door of a certain program director. The Coles had invited Wren to stay the night after her brother's big Star Wars bash, and I'd gone to bat for

237

her, pleading with Silas to allow her to stay, assuring him that I'd arrange transport there and back. He'd voiced reservations, concerned that bending the rules would seem like preferential treatment and be cause for animosity among the girls. But I disagreed. Ever since Wren's moment of vulnerability in the fireside room that night at D&D, I'd seen the start of a transformation in her. A budding friendship between her and Monica, participation in extra activities around the house, and particularly her sharing during mentor group time.

Both Silas and I had met the Coles, and we trusted they were a safe family with a safe home life. Plus, it would do Wren's heart good to have some real connection time with her brother, a fact Silas couldn't deny. She had a phone to contact us if she needed to, which I would gladly be on call for. Ultimately, the final decision was Silas's to make. I was thrilled he'd chosen to give Wren a night away to spend with Nate.

I caught a glimpse of him now as he strolled out of his office with his brother Jake and down the hall beyond my view.

I clicked out of my email screen and into my bulleted task list on my phone for The Event.

"I hear you're making dreams come true around this place with your magic fundraising wand." Jake's voice nearly startled the phone from my hands.

He smiled good-naturedly and sauntered inside my office. My eyes flicked over his shoulder, wondering if Silas had made a quick U-turn as well and followed his brother. A niggle of disappointment settled in my gut when he didn't appear.

"Hey, Jake. How are you?" I rose to give him a quick hug. He and Clara always seemed to be at the manor doing something or another. Sometimes I wondered how they managed it all—their jobs, their relationship, their constant service to the needs of these residents and this house. Then again, my own work-life balance had changed quite dramatically since I'd taken on planning The Event. I'd written somewhere in the ballpark of fifty donation emails to my current sponsors, informing them of the black-tie, invitation-only affair that would benefit a worthy cause and offer them a tax break.

So far, with the Dream Big money I'd been promised from Mr. Greggorio, and all the other sponsors who'd pledged, we were in for just over two hundred and eighty grand—a fun little secret I couldn't wait to tell Silas on our date tomorrow. Or, rather, our shopping trip and dinner outing.

Jake looked around my cozy office space and reached his hand out to the wall. "What are these things?" He touched one of the giant summery flower decals I'd added this week to brighten up the room. "Stickers? Are they permanent?"

Men. "They're decals. And as I've already assured Silas, they are temporary. They'll peel right off if I ever get fired as a volunteer."

"Fired?" He chuckled. "Yeah, that's not gonna happen."

"I don't know, I'm pretty sure Silas put a big check mark by my name after the edible glitter fiasco in the kitchen last week. We're all gonna need a bit more practice on our dessert platter arrangements before The Event."

Again, he laughed. "Nah, you're good, really. I haven't seen Silas smile this much in . . . well, years."

Warmth flared in my chest. I didn't want to assume that statement was directly related to when I'd joined the ranks, but—

"And yes, in case I wasn't clear enough, it's you. You're the reason. Clara and I are certain of it."

The compliment thrummed though me. I so badly wanted his words to be true.

"Oh, that's right," Jake said, cutting through my happy haze with a snap of his fingers, "Clara wanted me to tell you she's under the pavilion. She's hoping you might have a free minute to chat about event numbers before mentor group."

"I'll make time, thanks." I closed my laptop and slipped my phone into my pocket. "I'd be lost without her budgeting brain."

"I'd just be lost without her, period." The smitten, sincere way he said it caused my heart to swoon. They were young, yes, but they were also deeply in love with each other. What must that be like?

As I took the stairs that led outside to the pavilion, I wondered if I would ever truly be capable of sharing that kind of connection with another human being.

I hoped so.

◇◇◇

Clara crossed the pavilion and gave me a hug as soon as I stepped off the grass into the shaded area. "I told Jake only to bother you if you didn't look too busy. I know you're trying to juggle two big jobs right now."

There'd been less juggling and more ball dropping happening as of late, but The Event was more pressing than my socials. Dialing back on my posts wasn't the end of the world, no matter what Rosalyn—or Ethan—believed. "It's fine. Chatting with you was actually in my task journal today. I think it's good for us to stay connected; then there's less chance of me straying too far off track with the budget."

Clara had been crunching all the fundraiser numbers for me from the beginning. And there'd been a lot of numbers to crunch. "Right, I agree. It's best to stay on track." Though her words were informational, I couldn't help but hear an undercurrent of unease.

"Did you print out the latest report?" I sat my satchel on the picnic table and smiled down at her. "I always have an easier time with numbers when they're not on a screen."

"Yes, I did." Again, with the obvious hesitation. "I have the numbers right here . . . including the updated ticket price." She handed me a color-coded budget spreadsheet without looking at it.

"What? Is it more than we talked about?"

"Considerably more." She wrung her hands in front of her petite frame.

"Hey, let's not borrow worry. Whatever it is, we'll work it out." That was one of my dad and brother's favorite phrases, and it brought a wave of pleasure to use it, knowing they would be pleased to hear me say it. Maybe . . . maybe they'd even come to this event if I invited them? After all, it was for the benefit of those in need.

I tried to focus on the numbers blurring in front of my eyes and not on my growing freebie invite list. "Okay, what am I looking at here? What's the bottom line?"

Clara looked ill. "To raise what you want to raise *and* cover all the overhead plus entertainment fees . . ."

"Clara, it's really okay. Just say it."

She tapped the sum at the bottom of the page. "We'll need to charge two thousand dollars a ticket."

"Oh." I gripped my chest, huffing out a laugh of relief. "Gosh, for a minute, I thought you were going to say a number close to triple that. But that's totally doable."

Clara didn't blink. "Molly, two grand a ticket is . . ." She shook her head. "It's not something people around here can afford. Our monthly supporters are small church congregations and faith-based bookstores and family-owned restaurants."

"Exactly. Which is why I haven't limited our invitations to local businesses and their patrons." I bit my lip, debating with myself. "Can you keep a secret?"

She nodded, albeit hesitantly at first.

"I've secured commitments from twenty of my sponsors already. With those donations and the scholarship from my agency, we have nearly three hundred thousand already in the bank. The livestream auction from my platforms will make up the deficit, no problem. So those ticket prices, they won't even be relevant in the end. Most of the sponsors who pay won't actually RSVP to the event anyway."

Clara's mouth gaped open like a fish needing to be thrown back in the lake. "Molly . . . really?"

I nodded excitedly. "Yes! Really! I wanted to wait until we set up the account link and had the transfer confirmations, but yes. Everything is going perfectly on schedule."

"I just . . ." Clara shook her head, amazed. "I'm speechless. That's *so much* money. I can't believe you've managed to raise all that in such a short amount of time—and basically all on your own, too. Silas is going to be thrilled, shocked." She pinched her lips together, her eyes teary and soft. "It's been his dream to be able to do more for the community, for the kids on the waitlist."

For possibly the first time since I'd created a beauty brand from the meager beginnings of my social media platforms, I saw a bigger picture. A more purposeful connection to it all. The followers. The sponsors. The shares and views and comments and link clicks. What if everything I'd built had been for this? For this moment right here? To use my years of networking and beauty product testing to help a group of people in need.

The hope set a fire deep in my chest.

"So you really don't think most of your sponsors will actually attend?"

Her question pulled me out of my introspection. "They're all welcome to, but it's easier for most people in their positions to just write a check." The flippancy of such a statement stung as I recalled all the moments I'd done exactly that. How Miles would mention a need within his church or abroad, and I'd simply send him money without a second thought of how else I might be of help. Of service.

"I guess that makes sense," she said, in a way that told me it didn't actually make sense to her at all. Because Clara couldn't imagine herself being anywhere but *here*, no matter what else was going on in her world. She found the time. No, she *made* the time. For these young adults. "At least it will free up more spots for some of our locals who otherwise couldn't afford the price of admission."

I cleared my throat. "Exactly. I have a list of names going for complimentary tickets if there's anybody you'd like to add to it."

Unexpectedly, Val's face surfaced in my mind. She would have loved working on an event like this—organizing the schedule and doing the website and all the social media prep work. Val shined when it came to roles like this, and yet . . . and yet I had no right to ask her to help me, not after all that had transpired. I was realizing more and more the many ways our relationship had been built on my needs and on my timeline. Maybe things between us would heal if I gave her space to tend to her own—and to Tucker's.

Clara's watch beeped a calendar alert for the start of group, and we both looked across the lawn to the open door of the girls' cottage, where our six mentees trailed into the sun with their journals in hand. "Here they come."

Though this was only our fifth Friday mentor session of the summer, my connection with the girls had grown in a way I hadn't anticipated. At first they'd been fascinated by my following and the famous people I'd met. And sure, they enjoyed talking beauty and fashion trends with me. But our last couple mandatories and mentor meetings had had nothing to do with my social media persona at all. Last Tuesday night, as we'd sprinkled cookie dough with the edible glitter Silas despised, we'd talked about all the happenings in the house—who hated what chores, which girls had known each other prior to The Bridge, and what they hoped for after they moved out. All normal life stuff.

I'd loved every single second of it. And based on how long they'd stayed in the kitchen with me after mandatory hour was finished, they'd loved it, too.

Monica's gregarious giggle sailed over the grass as she shoulder-bumped Wren in response to whatever she'd just said. The sight of them together made my heart yearn for a friendship like that. One friendship in particular. Interestingly enough, that was the exact topic we were discussing in group this afternoon.

The girls took their seats at the picnic table, the day a perfect blend of heat, sunshine, and a light breeze that trailed under the shelter. Throughout the weeks we'd been meeting, Clara had gradually off-loaded more and more of the meeting responsibilities to me, though I'd yet to say the closing prayer. On the agenda we followed each week, the words *lead group prayer* taunted me like a playground bully. I'd prayed out loud before—of course I had—hundreds of times while growing up. And dozens of times since, mostly before an opportunity to expand my business. Although, I couldn't recall the last time I'd done even that.

"Afternoon, ladies," Clara said. "I have a special announcement I've been waiting to make all week: You've all been approved to attend my wedding in September."

Amy and Monica let out a squeal, and the other girls reacted in their own more reserved ways. Everybody but Sasha, that is, who hadn't stopped eyeing Wren since she sat down. I didn't know what that was all about, but if wedding talk didn't distract her, I didn't know what would.

"And you can thank Molly for that," Clara continued. "She's arranged for special permission and transportation."

Yet one more conversation I'd had with Silas recently.

"Aww, really?" Monica asked. "Thanks, Molly. Will you help us figure out what to wear?"

"Absolutely. I'll start collecting some outfits now so that everybody has something special to wear on the big day. Maybe we can plan to figure out hairstyles when we do our big glam makeovers at the sleepover, too." I glanced over at Clara. "It's not every day the best mentor on the planet gets married."

She tilted her head so that her dark, chin-length hair swished over her cheek and mouthed *thank you*. I knew it would mean a lot to her to have the girls there. Some of them had been with her for a couple of years.

She gave me a small nod to get started with group, and I clasped my hands and inhaled deeply. I opened our time with the icebreaker question from our handbook that had been swirling in my head for days: "What qualities do you look for in a good friend?"

As I asked it, I wondered if Sasha's mood might soften with a little extra warm-up time. But based on the pointed glare she made no effort to conceal, my optimism died a quick death. What was up with her today?

The answers to the icebreaker question were kindness, compassion, authenticity, trust, and honesty. As the natural conversational lull occurred, indicating it was time to move on to the next question, Sasha piped up as she shifted her glare from Wren to Monica. "I'd like to say loyalty, but that seems to be a hard one for some people."

Monica rolled her eyes, and for a moment, I wondered how far this tiff between them would go. Thankfully, in typical Clara style, she'd already slipped out of her seat to sit next to Sasha. She whispered something in her ear, and a second later, the two of them were walking away from the table to have a private conversation. Probably for the best. I'd witnessed a few of Clara's talks. She had a gift for drama reduction.

"How about an example of a time when a friend helped or comforted you?" The questioned lingered for a few moments before Amy raised her hand. She was a practical girl with clear skin, no makeup, and an affinity for western wear, never seen without at least one pattern of plaid on her person and her trusty cowboy boots on her feet. "I broke my leg when I was in eighth grade. There was this girl at school who didn't have many friends, but she was always kind. The whole time I was on crutches she carried my books to class, and then we ended up eating lunch together almost every day for the rest of the year."

"That's a great example, Amy. Thanks for sharing. Anybody else? Maybe something from the past like what Amy shared, or it can be something more recent, too."

Wren glanced at Monica before addressing me. "Last week I had a friend volunteer to do my chores for me so I could get extra phone time talking to Nate. He was missing our mom and needed to talk to me."

"Aww, that's super sweet. A great example." I gave Monica an approving wink, and she smiled in response and added her own story.

"Well, *I* have a friend"—she nudged Wren—"who helped me with a huge English assignment on a book I so did not understand at all. She stayed up late with me and walked me through all the symbolism my brain was refusing to get. But I aced it. And because of that, I passed the class. Thank God for that, too. No more English for me ever again!"

Jasmine and Wren laughed as Monica danced in her seat.

Gratitude rippled through my heart as a pang of another kind pinched my next intake of breath. I'd had that kind of friendship once, too, with Val. Sure, I hadn't ever been with her in person. But it was real—our friendship. At least, on my side it had been. Had it been on hers, too? Surely her job as my assistant hadn't been the only reason she'd answered my calls. Or why she'd checked up on me when I traveled alone to a campaign shoot. Or why she'd spent hours researching fresh ideas for my next series shoot even when there were plenty of average ideas that could work. She'd gone the extra mile for me time and time again, and what had I done for her in return?

"So . . . do you have a Scripture for us this week?"

"What?" I blinked at Jasmine's expectant face as the image of Val's faded once again. "Oh yes. Of course. There's actually two."

Just as I picked up the leader's guide and focused on the meditation Scripture for the week, Clara escorted Sasha back to the table, taking a seat next to her on the bench.

"'A friend loves at all times.' Proverbs 17:17," I said.

"Glo loves that verse," Wren said. "She even bought a picture with that and put it in the front room of the cottage."

My chest tingled at the thought of this very Glo-like thing to do.

"The second Scripture is found in John 15:12–13. Can you read that one for us, Sasha?" I took a chance in asking her, as her non-verbal language was still all kinds of off, but she opened her book and read the words in red font.

"'My command is this: Love each other as I have loved you. Greater love has no one than this: to lay down one's life for one's friends.'" And though I'd read that verse dozens of times, heard it preached in sermons, and seen it written in calligraphy as an Instagram quote more than once . . . it hit me anew in this moment. The enormity of such a command.

I scanned through the next questions, the ones written for a far holier leader than myself, and then closed the book.

"Do you think that's even possible?" I asked the girls, unscripted. "To love another person in that way?"

Every eye shifted from me to the tabletop.

"I'm not asking because I have the answers. I don't. Not even close. I'm asking because I'm learning this, too. How to be a real friend who puts someone else's needs above my own. Even when it's hard."

Jasmine lifted her gaze. "I don't really understand it, either. The love I've seen hasn't looked anything like that. Not between my parents—when I lived with them, anyway. And not even the love I've had with friends or boyfriends. Usually it ends because somebody is selfish. Or, I guess, both people are selfish."

I nodded. "I've experienced that, too."

"So have I," Amy said.

"Me too," Monica agreed.

"So what do we do about it? How can we be a different kind of friend? One who loves selflessly?"

Once again the question lingered in silence, and this time it was Clara who spoke up. Likely the only one at the table who could speak to it. "I think we first have to understand just how deeply we are already loved that way—by God. Then we can love each other out of the response to His love for us."

A profound truth that left a deposit in my soul.

As we bowed our heads to pray at the end of group time, my voice was weak, yet shockingly, my words were not. I wasn't sure what was happening in my heart, but something most definitely was. And it was something I wanted to embrace for the first time in many, many years.

24

Molly

Parked in Silas's driveway, I raised my sunglasses to the top of my head, pinning back my hair, which I'd chosen to wear down today. My white sailor button crop pants and airy yellow blouse couldn't have matched this summer day any more. The few cottony clouds in the sky only added to the perfection of the sunshine and low-eighties temperature.

Silas's home was a modest rambler, painted a cool gray with crisp white trim, parked on the right curve of a generous cul-de-sac. The shockingly green grass surrounding his house was well maintained and not at all dissimilar from what I'd pictured.

As I climbed his porch steps in my white heeled sandals that ribboned around my ankle in a wispy bow, he opened his front door. My stomach flipped at the sight of his damp hair and the waft of his freshly showered man scent. But perhaps what surprised me most was that he, too, had chosen to wear a yellow shirt today. It was only half as bright as my canary shade, and could possibly even hold a case for beige, but *wowzers*—if a color could be responsible for making a set of biceps sing like his . . . then I could be convinced to call it purple.

"If I'd known you wanted to match, I would have called ahead to discuss our shoe options," I said.

He glanced at my feet and chuckled. "I can assure you I have nothing in my closet with a ribbon."

I smiled but couldn't help a wandering glance toward the private world of Silas Whittaker's home.

"Would you like to come inside?" Silas asked with a trace of amusement.

"Oh no, that's all right."

"Which is Molly code for *yes, but only if I have time to snoop in your cabinets.*"

"First of all"—I laughed, holding out my pointer finger—"you don't know me well enough to speak Molly code fluently yet. And second of all, I was only hoping for a quick glance around. And maybe also to see how you've organized your spices and canned food."

With a sweeping, duke-like gesture, he pulled the door open wide, and I held my breath as I stepped over the threshold and into his home. Had I really just been invited into the home of the same man who'd once rejected my volunteer application at his nonprofit? My life seemed full of irony these days.

I scanned the clean lines of an uncluttered living room, my gaze lingering on the running shoes he'd left next to his front door. I could envision him putting them on at the first wink of the morning sun. Just like I could envision him standing in his kitchen, filling a glass of water at his sink, or making a meal for one after a long day of work.

His watchful gaze tracked me as I moved through his house, but his smile indicated I hadn't yet overstayed my welcome. As I cut through his living room, past his sleek kitchen to poke my head around the corner, I recalled our late-night phone conversations this past week. Now that I had the added visual of his floorplan, I could imagine him moving about his space as we talked together. It was like a movie playing in my mind, one I could rewind and pause now at my leisure.

My attention turned to a lacquered wooden dart board at the end of his hallway. "I don't think I've ever seen a dart board like that."

"It was a gift. From my father. He made it."

"Wow. It's beautiful."

"Yes. It's a hobby we've shared for many years."

"That's really special." Slowly, I turned toward him, realizing just how little I knew about Silas's world. Though he'd told me bits and pieces about his adoption, his siblings and folks, and his altered career path in his midtwenties, there was still so much I'd yet to learn about him. And I wanted to learn it. I wanted to know anything Silas was willing to share with me.

He smiled quizzically, and I broke the spell his dark eyes had cast with a gesture toward his living room. "Well, it's official. You have the nicest bachelor pad I've ever been to." At the gleam of humor in his eyes, I realized how a statement like that might sound. "Not that I've been to a ton of bachelor pads or anything. I haven't. Just a few. One of them being my brother's."

"Molly," he said. "I understood what you meant."

"Right, okay."

"Okay," he said, smiling. "Need to see anything else while we're here?"

"Nope, I'm good now. Wait." I held up a finger. "Inquiring minds still need to know how you arrange your spices."

"Is the answer a prerequisite to driving your car?"

I laughed. "It is now, yes."

"They're alphabetized."

For some unexplainable reason, his answer delighted me.

"You passed. Let's go." I tossed him the keys, and he stared down at his palm as if I'd just given him the deed to a private island. The corner of his mouth ticked into a sly grin.

Silas didn't say much as he opened the driver's door and listened to the voice prompts from the talking computer that was, in fact, my car. He buckled his seatbelt and shot me a glance I couldn't quite decipher as it rattled off current statistics—mileage total, battery charge, road conditions, weather conditions, the current time.

"What?" I asked. "What are you thinking?"

"That I'm about to drive a brand-new Tesla, and Jake's not even here to witness it."

"It's just a car," I offered nonchalantly.

He laughed and pressed a button to adjust the mirrors to his height. "Right, and you're just a woman."

Though I wasn't entirely sure what he meant, if the way he accelerated was any indication, his comment had been anything but negative. Silas wove through his neighborhood, fiddling with every button and testing out the brakes several times.

"Mind if I take a more scenic route through Spokane?"

"Of course not."

Neither of us spoke as we passed fir trees, streetlights, residential neighborhoods, farms, and then eventually the more industrial districts of downtown.

For some unknown reason, it didn't feel odd in the least to hand over the driver's seat to Silas. In fact, it felt just the opposite. Like I could close my eyes and relax my head against the back of the passenger seat as he grinned like a teenage boy who'd been let loose with a brand-new license.

"I can't get over how smooth the acceleration is. It's incredible."

"Yeah," I said a bit dully. "It's great."

"I take it you're not much of a car specs gal?"

I chuckled. "Not at all. The specs weren't why I bought it." A painful admission I rarely shared. I hadn't bought it for the cool tricks or the fuel economy–saving statistics. I bought for status, a shiny symbol of my success. I bought it because Ethan had pointed to an image on a magazine with a quote that read, *"This year's most coveted car for under a hundred grand!"* The memory of it caused shame to swirl in my lower abdomen. What could a program like The Bridge do with money like that? I knew the answer, of course. It's the reason I agreed to work so hard on the fundraiser, so that Silas's vision could be made into a reality. So that more kids like Wren could sleep in a safe home and be given a hope for their future outside the disheartening statistics.

"So why did you buy it?" Silas asked.

The story seemed too unreal to retell, like it was connected to another life outside of mine. And yet, somehow, I often told Silas the things I usually reserved for my brother—and sometimes not even him.

"I'd just hit a big milestone on my platforms. Five hundred thousand followers. I celebrated by buying a new car." *With Ethan* was what I left out. "To be totally honest, I probably spent more time deciding what to wear to the car lot than I did on this purchase." The admission soured in my mouth as I waited for Silas to say something about the wastefulness of it all, of the poor financial decision I'd made when there were thousands of better options for me to invest that money in. And yet his face remained pensive as he drove on without comment.

As we neared the mall, I changed the subject to one we both had stock in. "Have you heard anything from Wren today?"

He glanced at me before looking back at the road. "No, you?"

"Not yet. But I just keep thinking about how happy she was when I dropped her off last night. The Coles seem like a great family."

"They are," Silas said, turning into a parking garage. "I've known them a long time. They attend my parents' church, actually."

"Really?"

He nodded, which I used as the only encouragement I needed to ask something I'd been burning to know since hearing Wren's story. "Why wouldn't they take Wren in, Silas? I know she's nineteen, but she's such a sweet girl, and she adores her brother so much. Why can't she just live with him there? It would make everything so much better for her."

Silas pulled into a spot and parked, and the computer once again told him all the updated statistics. He muted the volume and swiped to the display image of the engine.

"Silas?"

He twisted to focus on me fully, and I could almost see the neurons firing in his brain, pondering my question. "They have three young sons. Taking on an older teen comes with more responsibility and more liability than another boy who stairsteps their biological children."

"But she's not a risk at all. She's wonderful." His answer had done nothing to assuage my heartache. "And she still needs a family, parents who will guide and love her. Nineteen shouldn't even be considered a legal adult in my opinion. I made all kinds of foolish mistakes at her age, and I grew up with both my parents and a brother." I cupped my hands as if holding an invisible flower. "She's like a delicate little daisy, and I just want to protect her."

The smile Silas offered me was of a different breed this time. It wasn't amused or enchanted or driven by the dry wit that often separated our two worlds. It was, in fact, an expression of empathy that seemed to say *I get it. I understand.*

"And that's exactly why The Bridge exists," he remarked softly. "Because age doesn't replace the need for a hand up from someone who cares where you are or where you're going. It's why this expansion project to allow more kids to have a home after they age out of the system should matter more to our community, to our state and nation as a whole. We're failing our youth every time we have to turn them away due to lack of funding."

His words took root inside me, under layers of soil I once believed were too shallow for planting. I was wrong. "I wish I could do more to help."

A twitch in his cheek drew my eyes to his lips. "You're doing more than you realize."

"It doesn't feel like enough."

"It never will."

My eyes flicked to his again. "And what if I can't accept that?"

His grin spread slowly as his gaze roved my face. "Then let's hope The Event and the Murphey Grant will do more than either of us can imagine."

25

Molly

By two in the afternoon, we'd been to three party rental stores.
The first for linens—tablecloths, napkins, and chair coverings. All
easy decisions, given the swatches and available stock they had
for our chosen date at the end of August. Silas had stood beside
me without complaint, patiently nodding as I asked the associate
questions and compared sheens and combinations of fabrics to
my notes and swatches. But the next two stores were not nearly as
successful. Due to the high demand with summer weddings, the
place settings we had to choose from were few and far between.
And none of them matched the vision I'd sketched in my notebook.

Silas had made some phone calls in the parking lot while I'd
begged the manager at Bridal Bliss to rush their backorder supply
of the china I wanted in time for our event. Apparently, short of
an act of God, it could not be done. Not even for *the sake of the
children*. Which was exactly how we'd ended up here: a random
rental store in a deserted strip mall in a town I'd never heard of.

A heavyset midsixties woman in a lavender maxi dress clasped
her hands together at the sight of us walking into her tiny store.
To be fair, Silas hadn't said it was in a prime location, just that
my plates were available for the coveted August twenty-ninth date.

The woman greeted Silas by name, somehow knowing he was the man who'd called in.

"Aww, and you must be the bride-to-be. You're positively glowing. I can always spot a young face in love, and you most certainly have been shot by Cupid's arrow." She laughed and rushed to shake my hand. "I'm Bea, like the bumble and buzzing kind." Her grip nearly knocked me off my feet.

"Nice to meet you. I'm Molly, but we're actually not—"

"Oh, Molly, your fiancé is an absolute sweetheart. Such a chivalrous man to call and check up on the place setting you've been searching for." She grinned up at Silas, showing all her teeth as she did. "It's so rare that I get to speak to anyone but the bride or her bouncer these days." She lowered her voice to a conspiratorial whisper. "That's what I call the coordinators. A bride acting like a bridezilla is mild in comparison to the nicknames I've made up to describe some of the 'wedding planners' I've been subjected to over the years." Bea used air quotes around the words *wedding planners*, and if not for the too-snug store, and Silas at my back, I would have taken a step back. Maybe two.

With one hand planted firmly on my shoulder, Silas reached around me and offered his other hand to Bea. Shockingly, the first words out of his mouth were *not* a correction on the whole fiancé bit. "It's good to meet you in person, Bea. Thanks for putting a hold on those plates for us."

"Wouldn't you know, but I've had two calls for that same place setting since I hung up with you. It's like the whole wedding world's gone mad over blush pinks and rose golds. We're a little shop, but our footprint is growing with each wedding season." Bea had a bit of an infomercial presence about her: the constant tilt of her head as she spoke, the smile that never seemed to dim.

"Well, thank you again," Silas said. "Would you mind if we took a look at them to make sure it's what Molly wants before we sign the rental agreement?"

"Not at all. I went ahead and set it all up for you both to see. It's in the back here, next to a few other choices." Bea bustled to the back of the store, where a few display tables covered by white linens were set up. And there, sitting right on top of the center table, was my vision in physical form. All of it, even down to the stem and flatware.

"It's perfect," I said, fingering the rose gold rim, mesmerized by the glamour of it. "They're even prettier in person."

Bea's voice broke through the spell I was under. "By the expression on your fiancé's face, I'd say he's thinking the same thing about you." Her tinkling laugh vibrated the sparkling wine glass I'd reached to inspect. "Gotta love a man who adores making his woman happy."

I glanced up to find Silas's eyes not on the gorgeous table setting before us, but on me. Once again, I struggled for breath, and for the reality check I so desperately needed. Because this was perhaps the biggest fantasy moment I'd created on record. And I'd once stood beneath a clear umbrella as a thousand cherry blossoms tumbled over me from two stories up—all for the sake of the ideal image.

But this moment at the bridal shop was even less real.

There was no upcoming wedding, no fiancé, no lovestruck man admiring his soon-to-be bride. All of this was the by-product of a marketing guru so practiced at playing pretend that she often missed the cues for reality. I stared down at the pretty porcelain. How many times had I created the perfect image in hopes of procuring a future happiness that never came? Didn't I own a shiny expensive car for that very reason?

Bea gripped Silas's arm and gave it a squeeze. "You two take your time. I'll be at the register with the paperwork when you're ready."

"Thank you," I heard myself say. "We'll be up in just a minute."

I worked to exhale the building static in my chest.

"Is this what you want?" Silas asked the loaded question while I picked up a plate to study the microscopic print on the bottom, as if that had any reflection on the decision at hand. But squinting at the words *hand wash only* was easier than facing the truth pumping through my veins with every squeeze of my heart.

I set the plate down and glanced at the classic settings to the right and left. Both beautiful in their own right. Both sturdy and sophisticated and wholly suitable in every way. And both half the price and a quarter of the demand.

I slipped around the table and picked up the setting to my right—an all-cream number with a single watermarked flourish in the center of the salad dish. A far more practical option with far less pretense. I thought back to the highlighted figure on the budget sheet Clara had shown me. No matter how many sponsors I secured or how much money was pledged, whatever I didn't spend on the showy extras would go straight to the house. To the future residents. To Silas's off-the-page goals that would ultimately be matched one-to-one when we secured the Murphey Grant.

And suddenly, that's what I wanted most.

I smiled up at Silas. "Actually, I'll take these ones."

Silas stared at me, unblinking. "Those ones? Are you sure?"

I nodded, a bit exhilarated at the thought of telling Clara I'd come in under budget for our party rentals. "Yes, I'm sure. I appreciate you calling on these, though, and for taking me out here so I could see them in person. It helped me process through a few things."

By the confused expression Silas wore, I could tell he hadn't a clue what had just happened. Fair enough, since I wasn't totally sure myself.

"Okay," he said with a nod. "I'll go let Bea know."

"Thank you."

As soon as he left for the lobby, I touched the fantasy wedding plates one last time, admiring their beauty and feel, and whispered, "I'll be back for you someday" as I walked out of the room to meet Silas and Bea.

◇◇◇

After the plate decision was made, it was only fair that Silas get to choose the restaurant, a point that I argued for going on five minutes in the parking lot of Bea's Bridal. Finally, he acquiesced and consulted his phone, as neither of us knew the area. When he tried one last time for me to at least give him a food genre, I simply reclined the passenger seat and closed my eyes as the last of the day's sun warmed my face. "You choose, Silas."

And choose he did. The most un-Silas-like place I could have imagined.

"A bar?" I asked as he parked and unlocked our doors.

"And grill. A bar and grill," he repeated, as if that made it any less bar-like.

"You do know what goes on in an establishment like this, right?" I lowered my voice in a mock whisper. "I hear they serve *forbidden beverages* here. Aren't you worried this might break my volunteer contract at The Bridge?"

"Not as long as you promise to refrain from all Jell-O shot table-dancing endeavors," he deadpanned.

I rolled my eyes but couldn't help but smile at his reference to the worst interview in history. "I promise to be on my best behavior."

"Good. Because we're here for a very specific reason."

I looked from him to the entrance of the most stereotypical small-town bar in America. "And what's that? The sticky floors? The anti-nutritional dinner menu?"

"Neither." He pushed out his door and came around the car to open mine. "We're here for the darts."

"Ooh, really?" A thrill of excitement rushed through me. "I approve of this plan one-hundred-percent. I was hoping I'd get to see you play ever since I first laid eyes on that dart board in your house this morning." I tucked my clutch purse under my arm, and Silas lent me his elbow as if it were the most natural gesture in the world for the two of us. "Also, just so you're aware, I'm a secret bar nachos fan. So no judgment when you hear me order extra cheese."

He chuckled. "Noted."

Like every bar scene ever captured on the big screen, this one was no different. Dark, dank, a bit too loud and echoey around the billiards table, and yet somehow it was the most perfect place to be on a Saturday evening with Silas.

◇◇◇

He was on his third iced tea, and I was on my second club soda with a twist of lime. Yet despite my sober mind and good intentions, throwing darts was not nearly as easy as Silas made it look.

"Okay, okay. This is getting ridiculous. What's your trick?" Hands on my hips, I stared him down. "Because unless you cursed my darts ahead of time, I have no clue why mine are bouncing off the board, while every one of yours is sticking in the center of the bull's-eye."

"My trick is twenty years of practice."

I huffed and reached in the front pocket of my purse for a hair tie. Time to get serious. I pulled my mane away from my face and off my neck. "Call me crazy, but that's not exactly helpful advice."

He watched as I wrangled my hair into a messy bun and then plucked his last thrown dart out from the center, ruining our current game, which was pathetic at best. "Would you like me to give you a few pointers?"

"About thirty minutes ago, yes."

Silas laughed, and so did I.

He was different tonight. Less authority figure, more dart-throwing, nacho-cheese eating, everyday man. And I honestly couldn't decide which version I liked more. Although dart-throwing Silas was gaining on the sexier of the two versions.

"What? What's that look for?" Silas asked, studying my face with a bit of a smirk.

I shrugged. "Nothing, I was just thinking." I reached for a dart, but he moved his hand away.

"About?"

"About how I expected we'd spend the whole day talking about the house and the residents and the current drama issues between

Monica and Sasha. Kind of like parents who go out for a night on the town and can't stop talking about their kids even though they promise not to."

An incredulous laugh boomed from his chest. "That's really what you were thinking?"

"Pretty much." I swiped a dart from his hand. "And how I have excellent reflexes."

"A distracting mouth is more like it."

I gaped at him, certain he hadn't meant it the way it sounded, but . . . that half grin of his would disagree.

"First thing," he said, after setting his iced tea back on the table. "Your throw is abysmal."

"What? My throw is *not* abysmal."

"Do you want pointers, or do you want to keep collecting your darts off the floor?"

Touché. I pinched my lips together as he angled my right arm with his hand, slipping the dart between my fingers in a different configuration than my previous *abysmal* grip. "Okay, so this time, when you step forward, make sure your weight is completely on your right foot before you pull your arm back. Keep your wrist level. And don't drop it until after you release. It should feel fluid and balanced. Go ahead. Try."

I nodded, recalling the entire sequence of actions before I let the dart fly.

It stuck in the outer ring.

"Oh my gosh! It stuck! It actually stuck!" Unconcerned by the close proximity of other patrons, I window-washed my arms back and forth and shrugged my shoulders to the beat of whatever top-forties song belted through the bar speakers. With the help of my slick sandal bottoms, I slid into an impromptu moonwalk, all while Silas continued to smile at me in a way that could have convinced me to add a backflip to my routine. And I didn't even know how to do a backflip. "You want to join in, right? A little moonwalk is good for the soul."

"That may be, but I'm actually thinking that if you dance like that after you score a twenty, then I definitely want to see your bull's-eye dance."

"Does that mean my lesson isn't over?"

"Not unless you have somewhere else to be."

I eyed him as I reached for my drink. "You don't think I'd give up before I hit the bull's-eye, do you?"

"You're a lot more like me than I realized."

"Yeah, how's that?" I asked, my cheeks heating at the comparison.

"When I first learned how to play, I was determined to figure out the secret to throwing a perfect game."

"And did you?" I leaned my back against the bar table, taking another long sip of my drink, content to listen to whatever story Silas wanted to share with me.

"Yep. I already told you."

I sighed. "Not the whole twenty years of practice thing again?"

He laughed. "Afraid so."

I groaned, but Silas was undeterred. "You know, all that practice time on the board ended up being the best thing for me. A quick win wouldn't have taught me the lessons I needed to learn most."

I studied him as he sailed another dart straight into the bull's-eye. "What lessons?"

He turned those brilliant brown eyes on me. "Self-control. Patience. Perseverance."

"Sounds like you're halfway to preaching a sermon on the fruits of the Spirit."

Silas chuckled, hiking an eyebrow at me. "I suppose that's exactly what my father was trying to teach me when I first came to live with them. I didn't want his help or his advice; I just wanted the quiet space his tool shop provided—a place away from all the noise inside the house and inside my own head." Silas held the dart in his palm, drawing my eyes to his open hand and then up to the thick, corded scar on his right forearm. "I hated meeting with my social worker and the trauma counselor in those early weeks and months. I was so angry, I'd refuse to say a single word for the duration of the visit. That's when my dad figured out a way to reward me. My cooperation equaled time in his shop, with his dart board. He'd always come with me, of course. But he'd be content to sit in the background, keeping one eye on me and the other on whatever project he had going on his workbench, only speaking to me if I initiated the conversation first."

"So that's why the dart board in your house is such a treasure . . . it's symbolic of the connection between you and your father."

"Yes." Silas continued to stare into his palm. "We still have our most important discussions around a game of darts."

"I love that."

He dipped his chin and looked to me. "Your turn."

My breath hitched as he placed the dart inside my open palm with an intimacy that surpassed both our location and our entertainment of choice. Not trusting myself to speak, I rotated toward the board, rehearsing Silas's instructions in my head several times.

"Don't overthink it, Molly." His breath heated the top of my left ear. "There are plenty of darts, plenty of chances for do-overs."

The now-familiar phrase caused the tension in my chest to relax. Before The Bridge I hadn't really believed in second chances, and I'd certainly never been the recipient of them. I'd been too caught up in my own goals, in my own overachieving perfectionism to ever allow failure to be an option. I was either on or off, hot or cold, running hard or hardly moving at all. The in-between was too uncomfortable, too unsettling with all its unknowns and possible outcomes. And yet here I was, completely out of my element in nearly every regard: volunteering at a youth home, mentoring young women on topics I likely needed to be mentored in myself, and playing a game of darts with a man I admired most for the way he invested in people who could never repay him.

I let the dart fly, and it hit the triple bar on the middle ring. It wasn't the bull's-eye, but it also wasn't the floor. It was progress. For what might be the first time in my life, I was okay with that.

I beamed back at Silas. "Progress."

"Yes," he said, his gaze skimming my face. "Excellent progress. Want to throw another?"

I shook my head. "Actually, I think I'd like to sit for a bit and eat some bad-for-me nachos. You good with that?"

"Sounds like a winning plan to me."

As we reached the table, I squirted my hands with sanitizer and then reached for his palm to give him some too. He rubbed his hands together as he sat down across from me, our knees bumping under the table and sending a quiet tremble through my body. I pushed the platter of nachos in his direction and set one of the small plates in front of him.

"This is my brother's favorite meal. He is a nacho connoisseur. Only, if these were his, he'd have every kind of ridiculously hot pepper sprinkled on top."

"You're close. You and Miles." A statement, not a question.

My immediate response wanted to be *Absolutely, we're the closest. We're twins! That's how it's supposed to be.* But my actual response was much closer to the truth. "We're as close as we choose to be. Or, rather . . ." I contemplated my words. "As close as I let us be."

"How's that?" Silas pulled a cheesy chip off the tower of nachos.

"Hmm. How do I explain it? It's like there's this giant ocean just beyond the safe-for-swimming area where we now tread water, but for so many years he used to beg me to venture farther out, to take a risk with him in the big water so I could learn to love it the way he does. Sometimes I think I've said no to his invitations so many times that he doesn't know how to ask me anymore." I'd never articulated this thought before now and wasn't even sure my metaphor made any sense to someone not in my head. I picked at a piece of chip I'd dropped on my napkin.

"So what's the ocean?"

"Faith. The kind he has, anyway."

He nodded. "And what kind is that?"

I looked up into Silas's eyes, besotted by the earnestness I found there. "The kind that requires me to take off my life jacket, but I'm not sure I'm ready to do that yet." Or if I ever would be.

Silas didn't try and tell me I was. And he didn't try and tell me I wasn't. He simply listened, which, as it turned out, was the exact response I needed from him.

Without an invitation and without permission, I reached across the table and slid my palm up Silas's forearm, running my fingers over the bumpy length of his scar. "Can I ask what this is from?"

"Carlos." There wasn't an ounce of hostility in his voice as he spoke his brother's name. His tone was resignation more than accusation.

"How?"

This answer took a bit longer for him to articulate. "After he was released from prison the first time, my parents offered to take him in, as a favor to me. They had a basement apartment with a separate entrance. The deal was that he had to stay clean and sober, attend meetings, and hold down a job. That only lasted about two weeks. And then one night my mom called to say Carlos hadn't come home after work and that she'd noticed a few things missing from the garage. Within twenty-four hours, his parole officer was asking questions my folks couldn't answer. Nobody could find him for almost three days until I finally tracked him down."

"Where was he?"

"In an old condemned apartment complex downtown, out-of-his-mind high. I hadn't thought much past what I'd do after I found him, and I certainly hadn't anticipated the six men inside, counting cash and prepping bags of substances I could only guess at." He touched his glass, spun it on his napkin. "I was in the wrong place at the wrong time. I didn't have a chance. It was over before it even began."

I was barely breathing as I tried to imagine the scene. "What did they do to you?"

"Charged me, beat me with whatever they had on hand. It's a wonder I wasn't shot at. After a few blows to my head, they threw me down a flight of concrete steps at the back of the complex."

Silas paused, and every cell of my body seemed to pause along with him. "All while Carlos looked on." Silas stared at his arm and flexed his fingers into a fist. "Nobody really knows how long I was out there, unconscious, or how I didn't bleed out. But the police found me the next day after they were tipped off by a jogger. By the time I got to the hospital, the surgeon was concerned I'd lose all function in my right arm. My bone had been shattered in sixteen places. It took four surgeries, but I have just over eighty-five percent functionality back."

"Oh, Silas . . ."

"Turned out, I'd walked straight into a drug ring. Once the DEA found them all, I testified against them, my brother included. Carlos served three years as an accomplice with a prior, getting a break for his testimony against the others involved."

It was so much worse than I believed possible. Horrifying. "Is that when you started getting the migraines?"

"Yes. The doctor believes they're from the concussion I had."

I traced the path of his scar one more time, trying to imagine the surgeries he'd endured. "And he's out on parole again now?"

"He's in Bellingham, or so he says."

The revelation raised the hair on the back of my neck. "Did you stay in contact with him while he was in prison?"

"No. He sent a few letters to my parents' house at first, but I told my mom to toss them. I couldn't . . ." He shook his head. "I just couldn't do it again. I can't keep reopening the same wound, believing things will be different. No matter what he claims now."

"You mean, that day he called you at the manor—while you were in my office. He was asking something of you?"

"He wants me to meet up with him. He claims some pastor he met in prison has been mentoring him and that he's a changed man."

My expression lifted, along with my hope. Miles had done prison ministry in years past. If that pastor was anything like my brother, then—

Silas shook his head, something desperate in his eyes as he spoke to me. "I can't let him into my life again, Molly. I know I lead a ministry to save the kids who can still be saved, but my brother isn't a seventeen-year-old drop-out anymore. He's a thirty-seven-year-old convict who's caused massive destruction at every turn and to every relationship he's ever had."

I had no words to offer him. No condolences that could touch the kind of pain I saw in his eyes. But I got it now. I understood why Silas had given up everything to serve the kids in our community. Because I'd be willing to bet that he saw his brother in the eyes of every single one of them.

He looked down at my hand, smoothed his thumb over my knuckles, and contemplated something I wished I could hear. But even though he didn't speak, he also didn't let go. Not at the table while we stayed and talked for another two hours. Not as we walked through the parking lot to my car. Not even as we drove back to his place so I could drive myself home.

He'd simply held on to my hand, and I held back.

As we parked in his driveway, ready for me to switch from passenger to driver once again and end this perfectly imperfect day, I slipped my hand from his, not wanting to manipulate him in any way. Because if Silas wanted to hold my hand as a friend he'd come to care for, one he'd entrusted an intimate piece of his story to, then I needed to be okay with that.

I would *make* myself okay with that.

But if there was something more, even at the smallest of levels, then my heart needed to know it. I needed to know it.

"Today has been one of the best days I've had in a really long time. Thank you, Silas. For offering to drive around town and for teaching me how to play darts and for telling me about your family and . . . for all your patience with my indecision about the place setting. You've been a perfect gentleman."

He turned to me, his dark eyes steady on mine. "I would have driven you a thousand miles for the right place setting. I'm glad you found one that made you happy."

Heat flamed in my chest at the risky admission that rolled over my tongue. "Turns out, it wasn't the place setting that made me happy today. It was the company I was with. Somehow, every time I'm with him, he helps me see things more clearly."

"Turns out, she helps him see things more clearly, too." My throat constricted as his gaze dipped to my mouth. "This will complicate things, Molly."

"I'm not afraid of complicated."

He smiled and brought his hand to my cheek. "I'm not, either."

And then Silas's lips were on mine and his hand was at the back of my head and all the fantasies I'd ever had about a first kiss were forced to bow to my present reality, because this man kissed the same way he drove. The same way he threw a dart. The same way he passed a bar exam while working full-time with the forgotten youth in his community.

Like a perfectionist with something to prove.

• 26 •

Silas

I arrived at Fir Crest Manor early to run the trailhead only a half mile away from the house. It gave me a chance to clear my head, meditate, pray. To focus not on the things I couldn't control but on the one thing I could: my immediate next step and then the next after that.

My feet pounded the dusty trail as the early morning sun beat against my neck and cut through the dense branches of the fir trees lining either side of me. In only a few more strides, I'd see the roof of the guys' Bunkhouse, and then not long after that I'd see the back of the estate, where Molly had envisioned an entire black-tie affair to take place at the end of the summer.

My cadence picked up at the thought of her—at the way she'd looked at me last night when I told her about Carlos. At the way she'd traced my scar with her delicate fingers. At the way she'd pressed her cheek into my palm and told me I made her happy.

I'd kissed her.

And not a single part of me regretted it. Not even the part that hadn't a clue how we'd coexist in the same work space, under the same roof, separated by a hallway, when all I wanted to be near her. I didn't understand how it had happened, and I certainly hadn't planned for it to happen, but falling for Molly had been as quick as it had been all-consuming.

I'd never experienced anything like it.

As I rounded the wild rose bushes that lined the trail up to the street, I spotted the blue SUV I'd been expecting. My mom had texted early this morning to say she'd be running errands out this way and would stop in. I jogged to where she'd parked, grabbing my towel and water bottle on the way to her car.

She unlocked her door and stepped out of the vehicle in her typical cycling attire—dry-fit tank, workout pants, tennis shoes, and a bright smile. "Hey, sweetheart. Perfect timing."

As I wiped my forehead and face, she reached for me. "I'm pretty sweaty, Mom."

"Do you think a little sweat bothers me after all my years raising kids? Especially after raising Jacob?"

I laughed. "True, he still smells like gym socks and chlorine."

She put her arms around my middle and squeezed. I kissed the top of her head, and when she pulled back, she planted both her hands on my cheeks, her gaze nearly eye level with mine. Jake's height and athleticism had come from our mom's gene pool, not our father's. And while Jake had been their only biological child, the youngest of five, with four adopted children, our father's genes had rubbed off on me the most, despite our lack of shared DNA. Daniel Whittaker was a studious man, never without a book, and serious about his hobbies, darts ranking near the top.

Mom assessed me in the way she had since I was a young boy, with a probing but gentle gaze. "Jake was right. You look good, Silas. Happy." She patted my face, her dark, short curls bouncing as she did.

My mother may be in her early sixties, but age would never be what slowed her down. She cycled with a group of friends in the mornings, and she was as healthy as most of the early twenty-somethings we had in our program. "Did you want to come inside? I'm sure Glo would warm up some breakfast for you while I rinse off. I'll only be a minute."

"No, I wish I could, but I'm babysitting for Emily in less than an hour, so I probably shouldn't."

It wasn't exactly rare that my mom stopped by the house, but it was rare that she'd stop by and decline to come inside to say hello to Glo. The two had been friends for decades. Her eyes drifted from mine, as if to search the parking lot beyond me. "Unless . . . unless there's a chance your adorable new friend might be inside?"

I blinked to clear my focus, certain I'd heard her wrong. "My . . . my what?"

Her laugh was half nervous energy, half meddling mother. "I googled her, Silas. We all did. When you missed family dinner last night, well . . ." She shrugged. "Clara and Jake were just raving about her and all she's doing for the house, and then you know how your sisters are. They asked to see her picture, and one thing led to another, and the next thing we knew, everybody was crowding around Dad's laptop until Emily suggested we just put her channel up on the TV with that special cord your dad has. We ended up skipping a movie to watch Makeup Matters with Molly."

The clock had barely chimed the twelve-hour mark on my relationship status change with Molly, and already my family had stalked her online over dinner? Though I could hardly pass judgment on the addicting quality of Molly's videos, the idea of the entire Whittaker family watching her as entertainment felt all sorts of wrong.

By my lack of response, my mother picked up on this fact quickly. "She's an absolute doll, Silas. We all think so."

"She's more than that." The words shot out before I could filter them. "Molly. She's more than what you can see in those videos."

"Oh yes, of course. I'm sure that's true." She placed a hand on my arm, studied me. "I'm sorry if we overstepped any boundaries by watching them. We were just so caught up by her engaging personality."

"I understand, but Molly's personality is only a small part of what makes her a stunning human being."

At my words, my mother's eyes glistened with tears. "Oh, Silas . . ." She pursed her lips together. "I wondered if Jake had been exaggerating, but it's true. You really do care for her."

"Yes, I do."

She nodded. "Then I absolutely cannot wait to meet her. I've always told your father that the woman who turns your head and gets you to take a second glance when you've been so focused on the goals in front of you . . . well, she'll have to be someone really special."

A statement I wouldn't—couldn't—discount. Molly had turned my head. But it was the turn she'd been making to my heart all summer long that had been far more significant. And yet, I couldn't quite believe my practical mother had driven all the way here on the off chance she'd catch a glimpse of my *adorable new friend*, as she'd called her.

"That can't be the only reason you drove all the way out here—to tell me about the events of family dinner?"

My mother's elation drained in a matter of seconds, leaving behind a tension as unsettling as her answer. "You're right, it's not the only reason I came."

"Then what? Is it Dad? He said his cardiology appointment was routine only."

"It's not about your father, Silas. It's . . . well, it's something I need to show you—to give you—in person."

She reached into her SUV and retrieved a letter, one with handwriting I recognized. She set it in my hands, and immediately my insides were at war.

"What is this?"

"Carlos wrote a letter to your father and me. It arrived three days ago, and we've been praying about what to do with it." She touched my hand reassuringly. "We felt it was time for you to make a decision for yourself. Not just with this one letter, but with all of them."

How was it possible for my mother to shock me twice in the same ten-minute period?

"All of what?"

She turned back to her car once more and took out a shoebox. "This box is full of the letters your brother wrote you while he was in prison. They arrived steadily, at least one a month for the past three years. I know you told me to toss anything that came for you, but . . . I couldn't do that, Silas. We were all so angry at the time he was sentenced, but even still, I couldn't throw them away, not when you'd lost so much history with him already." Her eyes brimmed with tears. "There may be a time you'll need these. I'm not telling you to read them today or even next week. But you'll know when the time is right. And whenever that day comes, I'd simply ask that you start here first." She touched the letter in my hand as my mind became a tangle of bitter memories too painful to revisit.

I studied the box still clutched in her hands. "Have you read them?"

"Not these, no."

I nodded, too stunned to ask any of the multitude of questions that raged inside me.

"I love you, Silas. You've been on a journey only few can understand, and yet you've made me so proud to be your mother. So very, very proud." She placed the box in my arms. "This is just one more step, for someday."

For someday. Two words my mother had used with her kids often. A hope attached to no immediate deadline or pressure. Two words I'd needed often as a boy. And now once again as a grown man.

◇◇◇

Though I stored the shoebox of letters in the locked cabinet in my office, their presence couldn't be concealed so easily. Nearly every hour since I'd come inside, I wondered if and when I would read them. Or if and when I should read them. By noon I left my office, needing a break from the internal monologue inside my head. Molly's absence across the hall this morning had never been more acutely felt. I was certain she had a good reason for coming in later than usual, and yet I hoped she'd be in soon. And with that thought, an entirely new monologue took over. One that started with the kiss we'd shared in my driveway last night.

As if she'd timed her dramatic entrance perfectly, my phone buzzed in my pocket.

Molly McKenzie
Hi 👋

Silas
How are you?

Molly McKenzie
Smiling

Silas
Last I checked, that's a verb.

Molly McKenzie
Maybe I'm a verb type of woman.

Silas
Are you planning to grace us with your presence sometime today?

Molly McKenzie
That depends.

Silas
On?

Molly McKenzie
If you're planning on apologizing for last night.

I read her text three times, trying to translate her meaning.

Silas
Is there something I need to apologize for?

Molly McKenzie
😬 No. Absolutely not.

I smiled.

Silas

Where are you now?

Molly McKenzie

In the parking lot. I just pulled in. I was trying to prepare myself for what might happen today. In case you decided last night was a complete mistake? I would understand, I mean, if you'd changed your mind. I could respect that. I just wanted a heads-up before I saw you in person.

I didn't respond because I was already walking, already heading down the hallway, down the stairs, out the front door of the lobby to the cobblestone path where Molly was staring at her phone, waiting for a reply.

I'd give her one.

Her eyes held a hint of surprise as she watched me stride toward her and then stop roughly three feet from where she stood. Aware of the many eyes that could be viewing us from any number of places around campus, I was mindful of the rules I'd set for appropriate conduct between members of the opposite sex. Though I wished for the sake of this moment that I could make a few exceptions to those rules now.

"Because there seems to be some doubt about where I stand, I'll make it clear. I care about you," I said. "Quite a lot, actually."

She blinked, stared. "Same here. About you."

My fingers twitched at my sides, tempting me to reach out as the breeze blew a long strand of her hair across her pink lips. She slipped it behind her ear, her eyes trained on mine.

"I'm not sorry about last night. Not a single second of it. And if we weren't currently the focal point of three security cameras, I'd show you just how not sorry I am."

"You would?"

I smiled. "I would."

She studied me a few seconds more, then glanced at the house. "So how do we do this, exactly? This whole caring-about-each-other-quite-a-lot thing while working under a roof with a no-kissing-each-other-at-all thing?"

"I've been deliberating that since the moment you drove out of my driveway last night."

She laughed lightly. "I'm guessing there aren't many loopholes to The Bridge's no-touch conduct agreement I signed?"

"Believe me, Molly, if there were, I wouldn't be standing three feet away from you."

Her smiling face rivaled the sunshine. "Good to know."

❖ 27 ❖

Molly

By the following Friday, I felt as if I'd lived a month in the span of a single week. The house had been extra busy, and Clara had been off for the week, working overtime at the bank to ensure she had enough vacation days for her honeymoon in late September. I'd encouraged her to do it, of course, pushing her to believe I was more than capable of taking over the group, closing prayer and all.

I was wrong. She should have been worried.

"That you, Kitten Heels?" Glo called over her shoulder as she filled a giant pot in the undermount sink of Fir Crest's main kitchen. There were several rooms in the manor that registered less than their full potential, but the kitchen was not among them. Bright, open, cheery, and resembling what I pictured as every chef's dream, I understood why Glo spent so much time in here instructing the residents on the basics of cooking and baking. Although today, she'd graciously offered to make me a recipient of her reputable skills.

"You might want to throw the lock on that door so we don't ruin the surprise before it's time, though by the sounds of it, Silas is up to his eyeballs dealing with Devon's run-in with the parking meter."

I cringed as I latched the door behind me. "I know, poor Devon. He seems really upset. I saw him when he first got back from school." And I'd also seen Silas—that look of fatherly compassion in his eyes as he led the shaken young man upstairs to his office. I almost hadn't recognized Devon at first. There had been no trace of his usual humor, which, for a kid who always had a joke to tell, was heartbreaking in and of itself.

"Poor Silas is more like it," Glo chided. "He'll be the one cleaning up the mess with the college, not to mention paying whatever fines are involved in mowing a parking meter over. I hope that boy's thanking Jesus he only dented a metal pole and not a human being with that scooter of his."

I opened my mouth to respond—because how many times had I been guilty of the exact same offense, checking my phone instead of keeping my eyes on the road—but suddenly I was too stunned to speak as I took in all the ingredients strewn along the counter. The supplies we needed for today's special cooking lesson.

"Wow, Glo. I didn't realize just how involved this recipe was. I hope you didn't go to too much trouble."

"Nonsense. There are few people in this world I'd do just about anything for, and Silas is right near the top. He's like a son to me." Her eyes reflected admiration, and yet her statement had to be connected to a deeper grief than I could ever grasp. Silas had mentioned the son she'd lost many years ago, and though I didn't know the details, I did know that Glo's past had been anything but easy. Somehow she'd found a new life for herself here, with people who adored her as much as she adored them. "Besides," she continued, "it's about time I taught someone else how to make Silas's favorite meal. Judy, his mother? Bless her." She shook her head and laughed a little. "There's not a more lovely woman in all the world, but she's no cook. And she'd be the first to tell you that, too. At least *you* already have some skills in the kitchen."

Scanning several unrecognizable ingredients, I questioned her assessment. I enjoyed cooking and experimenting with new flavors and techniques, but I was beginning to think taking on such an authentic meal from scratch might have been above my pay grade. Especially since tonight was technically only our second date.

"Don't fret," Glo assured, as if she could hear my doubts. Maybe she could. Silas seemed to think she had some sort of sixth sense about people. "I'll teach you how to make a mean Mexican tamale dish. I may be Nez Perce by blood, but you'll be hard-pressed to find someone who can make authentic masa as good as mine."

Glo's laugh loosened one of my own, and I quickly washed up, ready for her expert instruction on how to begin making Silas's favorite meal. He told me he hadn't eaten many tamales growing up, but when he traveled with his dad to Mexico the summer after he graduated from high school, they'd quickly become his favorite. His retelling of that trip on one of our recent late-night phone calls had made every one of my senses come alive. I wanted to taste what he'd tasted that first time in Mexico City, drinking Coke from a cold glass bottle. What I wouldn't give to smell the spicy chicken and hand-pressed masa, swaddled in silky corn husks the way he'd described it. That thought had led to a craving, and that craving to an idea. Thankfully, Glo was more than willing to humor me.

Not only did she show me the proper way to prepare and soak the husks, but I also learned the techniques that "made her masa dough second to none," as she put it.

"Don't be afraid of lard. That's the first rule. Young people are too afraid of lard, but there's just no good substitute for it."

"Right. Got it." I listened, mixed, and poured tablespoon after tablespoon of chicken stock into the masa flour mixture as she watched my every movement and instructed. And then came the float test. According to Glo, the masa dough was only ready when it could be balled up, placed into a glass of water, and float to the top. If it sank to the bottom, it would need to be mixed for longer, adding in broth little by little until it was ready for a second try at the float test.

"Good. We're going for a creamy peanut butter texture with the masa. The dough needs to be slightly sticky to spread on the corn husk, but also smooth. You probably have about a minute more, and then we'll start layering the husks with the masa and then the chicken. Good job on the chicken, by the way. I tasted it."

"Thanks. I followed your recipe." I'd slow cooked it overnight in the Crock-Pot and added the green chilies halfway through, then stuck it into the fridge first thing today, but not before I'd tried a piece. Mouthwateringly good.

"And then all we have to do is roll and tie."

I smiled at Glo's youthful energy. This was definitely her element, though she was fantastic with the residents, too. Stern yet always gracious. Which made me wonder about her thoughts on Sasha. Maybe she had some tips on how to get the girl to respond to . . . well, anything for starters. Today's mentor group had been a challenge at best. While I'd seen huge strides in Wren and Monica, Sasha couldn't have been more closed off. And it was becoming more and more difficult to look past her cutting glares and eye rolls.

"You can't make it personal," Clara had told me once after Sasha huffed at one of my blatant attempts to draw her in to conversation. But the thing was, it did feel personal, considering the way she'd crossed her arms and spouted off robotic-like responses whenever I asked one of the questions from the study guide. She seemed to be sending me a message. And it wasn't the thumbs-up kind but rather the kind involving a different finger altogether.

Sasha had a way of telling a person off with her eyes even when her mouth said exactly what you'd hoped to hear.

Glo set her hand on mine, switching the mixer off. "I said creamy peanut butter, not puree."

"Oh, oops." I tapped the mixer on the side of the bowl and reached for the wooden spoon on the counter. "Is it okay?"

"Should be," she said, balling up a handful and testing it out in a glass of water. It floated. "Where'd your head go, Kitten Heels?"

I sighed. "Sorry, I was just thinking about group today. It didn't go so well."

"Don't apologize. What good are two women in the kitchen together if we don't use it to sort our issues out? Or someone else's issues." Glo laid out the soft corn husks, then scooped a tablespoon of masa on one, covered it with plastic wrap, and then pressed the sticky dough over the glossy husk. She gestured for me to do the same. "So? Let's hear it."

I followed her movements, careful to apply the right amount of pressure to each tamale. "It's just that Sasha . . ."

Glo side-eyed me, saying nothing.

"She doesn't seem to like me much." I grimaced at how incredibly middle school I just sounded. *Teacher, teacher, the girl with the winged eyeliner is giving me dirty looks.*

Glo laughed. "Sasha doesn't like most people."

"I'm sure that's probably true, but . . ."

"But you're not usually disliked by anybody."

The heated humiliation that crept up my neck indicated just how right she was.

"That's not a bad thing, Molly. Most girls here have taken to you extremely well in such a short period of time. It's not always like that, you know. Look at Wren. She was completely curled into herself, and somehow you coaxed her out of her shell, something neither Clara or I had managed to do before you came."

Then what am I doing wrong with Sasha? She was a puzzle I couldn't figure out. "So how do you suggest I connect with her— Sasha, I mean?"

Glo set her spoon down and studied me for several long seconds. "By continuing to try. That's all we can do."

For all her wisdom and obvious life experience, I'd been expecting something a bit more profound—a poignant proverb maybe, or at least some kind of recipe parallel. But instead, Glo seemed to operate on the same wavelength as Silas and his twenty years of dart practice. The whole slow-and-steady-wins-the-race mentality. A mentality that certainly didn't come naturally to me. I understood that *trying* had its place, but things had not been progressing for the better with Sasha the way my dart game had. It actually seemed like the more I tried with her, the worse things became.

"You seem disappointed by my answer."

I shook my head, pasting on a cheery expression that had Glo chuckling and bumping my arm.

"You can't fool me with that pretty smile, kiddo. I know it's not the flashiest advice around, and maybe there's some well-educated therapist somewhere who can say it better. But in my experience, showing up after a rough day or a hard meeting is worth more than the fanciest words in the universe to these kids. That said, you can do everything right and still be rejected in the end. We don't get to control how someone else chooses to respond." Her cheeks lifted into a knowing grin. "About the only thing you have control over is your attitude and your heart."

I reached for the shredded chicken, adding a small scoop to the masa layers one at a time while Glo started the rolling and folding process. "Well, then I think I might be failing as a mentor, because today my heart was full of eye rolls when she spouted off the same rote Bible verse for two different questions before anybody else had a chance to answer."

Glo pressed both palms on the counter, bent at the waist, and belted out a laugh I wished I could record as a cure for depression. "Molly, some days my heart is full of eye rolls, too, and I've been working with these types of kids longer than you've been alive. Just keep showing up. That's the only difference between a good and not-so-good mentor. Sasha will either let you in, or she won't. The choice is hers to make."

As she rolled the tamales into a tight funnel-like wrap, showing me how to tuck in the edges and stack them into a pot I'd steam them in at home, I thought about her words, about all the time she had invested here and elsewhere. "Okay." I sighed. "I'll keep showing up." *Eye rolls and all.*

"Good. Because if you think dealing with some teenage angst is bad, then you obviously haven't dealt with a disappointed Silas. And I can tell you with great certainty, your absence here would cause quite a stir."

This time, my neck flushed for a completely different reason.

A reason that had me counting down the minutes until he would arrive at my house in T minus two hours.

◇◇◇

As he texted he was on his way, a part of me expected to see Silas a bit off his game tonight. It had been a long week, and dealing with the consequences of damaged property on a college campus on a Friday afternoon was hardly the best start to a weekend. But when Silas arrived, his disposition looked anything but stressed. He actually looked . . . invigorated.

"For you," he said as he handed me a summer bouquet that could have graced the cover of a *Martha Stewart Living* magazine. "Thanks for inviting me to dinner."

I lowered the billowy bunch of wildflowers and smiled over the top of them. "Thank *you* for being my guest. Come on in. Can I get you something to drink? Ice water? Tea? Sparkling water, soda?"

"I'm good at the moment." Silas strode inside with a confidence I'd come to revere, unapologetic and unhurried. My home wasn't overly spacious or breathtaking the way Fir Crest Manor was, but it also wasn't a minimalist's dream like Silas's one-story rambler. My fully restored 1955 craftsman-style bungalow, nestled in a quiet neighborhood renowned for its large lot sizes and mature fir trees, was somewhere in between. The recent remodel had kept its vintage appeal, displaying splashes of femininity and texture, pillow-soft nooks and well-lit reading corners. Custom, sophisticated artwork hung purposefully throughout.

I loved it.

I'd poured paycheck after paycheck into fixing up each room, paying contractors and designers and even Miles at times—with fresh apple fritters from our favorite bakery, naturally—for every eye-catching improvement. But for as homey as I'd made it look in all the perfectly filtered photos I'd posted, I couldn't manufacture good company to enjoy it with me.

And I certainly couldn't manufacture whatever feeling I was

experiencing now as Silas's gaze shone with the kind of admiration I'd been searching for my whole life long.

"Somehow, your home is even more Molly-like than I realized possible. It's beautiful."

"Would you like a quick tour? We have approximately"—I glanced at the timer for steaming the tamales—"twenty-two minutes before dinner is ready, though I do still need to make the pico and guacamole."

"I'm happy to help with either of those. Whatever you're cooking in there smells delicious."

Good! That meant he still hadn't a clue what Glo and I had been up to in the kitchen this afternoon.

I filled a vase with water and set it on the farmhouse dining table, then added the flowers he'd brought, a centerpiece I'd likely move from room to room to get the most enjoyment from them. With an uncontainable giddiness I hadn't felt since I was an adolescent, I reached out and slipped my hand into Silas's. Quite the novelty, considering we'd stuck to the parameters of the no-touching agreement for the last week. But there was no such agreement here. "Can I tell you something a little bit outrageous?"

"A little bit outrageous," he repeated cheekily. "From you? Always."

"So this one time, I was asked to go on this super strict diet for a skincare campaign. It was only a seven-day plan, but the options of the things I *couldn't* eat outnumbered the things I could eat nearly twenty to one."

"That does sound outrageous."

I shook my head. "No, that's not the outrageous part yet. The thing is, I'd actually been fairly content with the food on my plan until I saw the giant list of the foods I *couldn't* eat printed out in black and white. It about drove me crazy. I started having these forbidden food fantasies over things I'd never once cared for, like dried fruit and Wasa crackers. I mean, really, who has fantasies about Wasa crackers?"

Silas laughed. "I'm not even sure what a Wasa cracker is. Is that the outrageous part?"

I huffed an exasperated sigh as Silas's grin stretched wider. "No, Silas, the outrageous part is still coming. Don't rush it. Anyway, when I could *finally* eat those pre-diet foods again on day eight, it was so disappointing. They tasted nothing like the fantasy in my head." I looked down at our joined hands. "All week long at the manor, whenever I saw you walk by my office or enter a room I was in, all I could think about was how much I wanted to reach out for your hand—and just so you know, I've never wanted to hold a hand more in my entire life than in these last several days. But there was also this tiny part of me that worried it might be like my Wasa cracker and dried fruit experiment. That touching you again wouldn't possibly be able to measure up to the way I'd remembered it." I blinked up at him. "But it's even better. And that, Silas, is the little bit outrageous part."

With a grin brimming with amusement and something I couldn't quite interpret, Silas walked me toward him, tugging at our joined hands until our noses were only inches apart as he tilted his mouth to mine. "It's good to know I'm not the only one who's been count- ing down the hours to tonight." His minty kiss was light against my lips, hinting at promises and secrets yet to discover. I logged the moment away in my memory for safekeeping. Something to hold on to when we weren't allowed to hold on to each other. "We should probably take that tour."

Reluctantly, I nodded, unwilling to unlace our fingers as I guided him out of the dining room on unstable legs. "Right this way, Duke."

Though I hadn't left a single inch of my twenty-six-hundred- square-foot house out of the tour, Silas had been most intrigued by my work studio. He'd walked the length of it, taking in my camera equipment and the built-in shelves heavy with products— both reviewed and those still to be reviewed. I didn't miss the way he noted the neglected table in the corner full of mailer boxes I'd yet to go through this week. Perhaps a little too symbolic of my Makeup Matters with Molly life as of late.

"So this is where the influencing magic happens," Silas mused as sunlight beamed through the large picture windows overlooking my covered front porch. When I was in active filming mode, those windows remained fully draped to block out unwanted shadows, but their current wide-open status was yet another indication of how behind I was on my summer schedule. A fact Rosalyn reminded me of often. *You are currently not meeting the minimum requirements of posting on Makeup Matters with Molly. Mr. Carrington has hired a ghost poster who will be posting as you twice a day. As per your contract, you are expected to have at least one video series each week and two livestreams. If these requirements are not met . . .*

"Yes," I said, cutting off the spiraling thought trail with a slow spin in the middle of the studio. "This is it."

Perhaps Silas detected the disenchantment in my voice, or perhaps he wasn't nearly as interested in the dusty monitor he'd been staring at, but whatever the case, his face had morphed from curious to concerned. "Everything all right?"

"Yes." A lie. There was an imposter posting as me because I was failing at a brand I'd started. A brand that bore my given name. "I just haven't been in here as much as I usually am."

Instead of easing the crinkle in his brow, my response had intensified it. "Molly, if I've overtaxed you with responsibilities at the manor, please know you can pull back at any time—"

"You haven't overtaxed me. I've enjoyed it—being there. With you and the residents and Glo and Clara." *I'd rather be there in all the hustle and bustle and high drama of life than here, in the incessant silence* was what I didn't say out loud but was sure he'd read on my face. That truth seemed to sing from every pore of my body as of late. When I hummed in the shower, when I took spontaneous coffee breaks in the west garden with Glo, when I hung out with the residents in the lobby until their dinner chores began. I arrived home in the evenings tired in a way I hadn't been tired in years. From real-life interactions and not just from the constant eyestrain of being on and off screens for sixteen hours a day. And somehow, while I was at Fir Crest Manor, the absence of Val and the constant conversation thread we once shared was just a little more manageable than when I was sitting alone in my studio. "I just need to find a new groove is all. And I will. This happens from time to time."

Only it had never happened to me. Not since I first started filming in my kitchen pantry. The drive for more followers, more success, more fame and sponsors had always been motivation enough. And it just wasn't now. Not even a little bit.

Silas didn't seem to believe me any more than I believed myself, but thankfully he only recaptured my hand and asked if he could help make the pico de gallo. My career goals might be suffering, but at least tonight my personal goals were soaring, starting with chopping onions next to a sexy, salsa-making Silas and comparing our guacamole techniques. His won by a landslide. The man knew how to twist a lime.

With much argument from Silas, I made him leave the kitchen and go sit at the table while I served the surprise tamales on a platter. My stomach fluttered with nerves and exhilaration as I arranged them. "Ready? Close your eyes."

I could hear him laugh from the dining room as I carried the porcelain platter from the kitchen to where he waited, but he'd obeyed. His eyes were closed. I set the meal down in front of him, Glo's perfectly tied tamales next to my slightly less than perfectly tied ones. But goodness, their aroma was nothing short of delectable.

"Okay, so before you open your eyes, you should know this was a joint effort. So I hope it's right. Okay, you can—no, wait! Hold that thought." I ran back to the fridge and searched for what I was missing on the table.

"You're killing me, Molly."

"Just a sec!" I popped the cap off the glass bottle of Coke and set it next to his plate. "All right, *now*. Now you can open your eyes."

Silas did, and for a moment, I wasn't sure if he was happy or upset. He blinked at the steaming mountain of tamales in front of him. "You made . . . you made me tamales?"

"With Glo's help. She taught me. We holed up in the kitchen while you were dealing with Devon and the parking meter. I just couldn't stop thinking about the story you told me about that little place in Mexico City, the one you visited with your dad. I know I can't possibly replicate what you had there with him, but I wanted to make something special for you anyway."

"You've more than achieved that; I promise." The conviction in his voice caused my breath to hitch and my chest to swell. "Thank you, Molly. This is . . . it's . . ." His gorgeous brown eyes crinkled at the corners. "It's just a little bit outrageous."

Suddenly, there was no better compliment to receive in all the world.

• 28 •

Molly

Somehow nearly three weeks had passed since our dart-throwing date. And I was certain I hadn't ever smiled more in my life than I had when I was with Silas, which was often, considering I'd basically commandeered the once makeshift office across the hall from him into my all-the-time office.

But today wasn't about office work at all—it was about makeovers and pampering and watching movies with my favorite young ladies. Upon delivering a suitcase of full-size hair and makeup products to the girls' cottage, along with a closet's worth of selected outfits for them to try on, I was now on the hunt for some wildflowers in the west garden. In addition to the treat tray I'd arranged on the counter, I wanted to find something fresh and pretty to brighten up the cottage.

But instead, I found something else entirely.

The garden shed door, which was usually latched in the top right corner by a padlock, was ajar.

I looked behind me, in case I'd missed seeing some groundskeeper while I was trying to roll my gigantic suitcase over the grass. But, alas, there were no groundskeepers at present, because there was no budget for them. I knew this well, as I'd had to hire a special crew for The Event.

I approached cautiously.

"Hello?" I had no idea why I said it as I pushed the shed door open. It wasn't like I thought someone was living in there and would invite me inside for tea and a chat.

But as it turned out . . . someone had been living in there. By the looks of it, two somebodies.

I gasped at the pillows and the blankets and then . . . *oh, dear heavens.*

An open box of condoms.

I suddenly felt woozy and sick to my stomach. Not at all like how I'd imagined a detective on *True Crimes* would feel after stumbling upon such a scene. For all my years obsessing over Nancy Drew and wishing my life held the same kind of adventure, I certainly did not feel that way now. If I had the option to unsee this, to go back five minutes and five hundred steps ago to where my biggest concern involved making the cottage's countertop *party pretty* with flowers and decorations, I'd choose it in a heartbeat. Because *whoever* was involved here, they had not only broken their commitment to the house but also endangered their place in the program.

And that was a reality too heavy to carry alone.

I slipped my phone out of my pocket and called Silas. He'd know what to do.

He didn't pick up. Instead, he sent an immediate text.

The Duke of Fir Crest Manor
> Still with Diego and Alex at the mechanic shop. Everything okay?

Oh, that's right. Today was the final exam for their certification program.

I snapped a picture of the love shack and sent it off to him.

Molly
> Discovered this just now. In the garden shed.

Why was it that time never moved slower than when you were waiting on a critical text message to arrive? I turned on my phone flashlight, scanning the darkened interior for more clues. With an ever-sinking heart, I pinched my lips together and searched for something identifiable.

> **The Duke of Fir Crest Manor**
> Okay. I'll deal with it when I get back. There's a protocol we need to follow.

> **Molly**
> Want me to find Glo? I can be discreet.

> **The Duke of Fir Crest Manor**
> No, I'll talk with her when I'm back.

> **Molly**
> So what should I do in the meantime?

Perhaps instead of makeovers, we could sit around in a circle and talk about how secrets and lies hurt people and then maybe one of the girls would start to cry and—

> **The Duke of Fir Crest Manor**
> Nothing.

> **Molly**
> Wait . . . it seems like you just told me to do nothing about this?

> **The Duke of Fir Crest Manor**
> I can't text right now. Diego is up. We'll talk tonight. Just leave it for now.

I reread his response several times over, and though I didn't want them to, his texts bothered me. He and Glo weren't the only ones who cared about the shenanigans that went on around the manor. Or the residents who lived in it for that matter. I'd practically become a part-time resident myself over the last few months. After all, I was here on the grounds constantly, rubbing elbows with everyone in the house multiple times a day. I had finally started to believe I was done having to prove myself to Silas.

I guess not.

The thought stung. It more than stung, actually.

As I turned to exit the shed, my gaze snagged on a lidded container shoved in a shadowed corner. I swallowed down the rising bile in my throat, because surely the answer I dreaded most was inside. I pried off the thick plastic lid and stared at a sea of random electronics: laptops, iPads, cords, earbuds. I reached into the box to shift the contents and then immediately squeezed my eyes closed as realization struck hard. There was nothing random about the findings in this box.

The glint of a necklace with a gold heart pendant was the first item to confirm my suspicion. And then a pair of name brand red flats. And then a pair of stud sapphire earrings that Wren had recently reported missing. On the fridge. In the Lavender Cottage.

Which was where most of these items had been listed.

This container was filled with the spoils of a lost-and-found list I'd read a dozen times over, one I'd begged the girls to copy onto the cute chalkboard I'd hung in the living room a month ago. One I'd even contemplated adding my Gucci sunglasses to several days ago, though I'd convinced myself I'd simply misplaced them in the manor somewhere. But apparently, they'd been misplaced for me, by a housemate—or a pair of housemates, I couldn't be sure.

If I had to guess, this box, with all its stolen contents, was likely to be sold to the highest bidder. A crime not even the most gracious program director in the world would be able to overlook. With shaky fingers, I slid my sunglasses atop my head, sealed the lid closed, and latched the shed door behind me, praying my hunch was wrong about who might be behind such an act of deception.

◇◇◇

As I waited for the girls to file in from the main house with Glo, I kept my hands busy in the cottage—fixing and primping and cleaning and displaying—though my mind was far from the Glam Night I'd promised to deliver tonight. How could it not be, when a new piece of evidence was seared into my memory as if with a branding iron?

Out of the twelve ladies living in the cottage, ten names had been listed on the fridge, each with at least one complaint of a misplaced or missing item jotted in black. And of the two unlisted ladies, one of them was Monica.

The other Sasha.

I'd never been great with math story problems, but in my mind, there was only one of two solutions here. Either Monica was the best actress I'd ever encountered, or Sasha's ever-increasing defiance was directly linked to a stockpile of stolen property and inappropriate relations in the garden shed.

As the girls burst through the front door of the cottage, full of giggly energy and excited chatter, I willed the tumultuous roller-coaster in my gut to halt. I had one chance to check my theory, and if I was correct, then maybe, possibly, it might be enough for Sasha to finally let me in. After all, she'd never needed an ally more than she did tonight.

"Wow! Is this for real?" Jasmine and Amy squealed as they entered the living room, noting the dining room table I'd dragged in there earlier and set up like a makeup counter kiosk.

"You brought all this makeup for us? Oh my gosh! Look at these cute pink washcloths and hair clips! I've never seen so many products in one place."

Immediately, the girls found their sparkly name tags marking their individual stations. Each was equipped with a mirror, skin-care set, and full-size makeup and hair products.

A chorus of *thank-yous* rang out around the room, and I worked to match their enthusiasm.

"I hope you all have so much fun tonight. Feel free to play and experiment as you'd like, and I'll make my rounds to help anyone who may want some extra pointers. I recommend starting with the skincare. Just follow the tips I've printed on the card there."

I'd been looking forward to their reactions for weeks, only now, in light of my recent discovery, my joy felt muted at best. I glanced at Sasha's empty station, and again my stomach roiled. What would be worth giving all this up for? A guy? Surely that couldn't be all of it.

"I'll start taking before and after pics when the rest of the girls get here," Amy said, slipping her phone from her pocket. "I don't have the best camera on here or anything, but they'll be fun to look at later. Jas, maybe we can make a collage for the bulletin board in the fireside room."

"Great idea," I said, moving to the open doorway to scan for Sasha's arrival. But instead of seeing her faded pink hair and sharp features, I saw a giant popcorn machine being shoved down the cobblestone path and into the cottage by a tiny woman I'd come to adore. Clara was on a mission.

"On the count of three," she instructed Monica and Wren from somewhere behind the red and white mass. "One, two, three!"

A collective grunt followed as the popcorn machine was pushed over the threshold and into the kitchen, leaving me no place to go but out the back door, into the grassy common area. Though it was dusk, it took me only a second to register a nearby silhouette. Standing alone, backlit by a moody skyline of swirling grays, blues, and fuchsias, was Sasha.

"Sasha, hey," I said, my pulse galloping as I approached. "I've been looking for you. How's your day been?"

She gave a half twist of her hips at my words, enough to indicate she'd heard me, seen me, and wanted absolutely nothing to do with me.

"Don't make it personal, Molly." Clara's peppy voice circled in my brain, and I continued without missing a beat. "Yeah, I get it. Sometimes it's nice to have a minute of quiet, especially after you've been surrounded by lots of people all day. Sunsets are a great time to do that." Squaring up to her, I almost missed the way her gaze shifted to the corner of her eye. It was a minuscule reaction, but one I'd roll with anyway. "I was actually out on a quiet walk earlier today myself. Didn't go anywhere too far, just kind of stayed around the west garden. Such a pretty area. I especially love those

wild teacup roses. I think that's what they're called; I'm not very good with flower species. Glo's constantly pointing new greenery out to me, and it seems like no matter how many times I walk that path, there's always something new to discover. Some bush or plant or tiny bird's nest that I didn't take note of the time before."

Though her eye roll and sigh were clearly meant for me, I was too far in to back out now. My pulse thudded loudly in my ears, so much so that I wondered if she could hear it, too.

"In fact, just this afternoon I saw something new. Something I would have missed completely if the door to that cute little garden shed hadn't been cracked open." I casually slipped the stolen sunglasses off my head and onto my face, shading the amber glare of the setting sun from my eyes as Sasha's ever-cool façade was replaced by an expression I'd never seen her wear. Her body went rigid beside mine, a visible panic flashing in her eyes.

I remembered then how Silas had responded once when I'd asked him about confessions, as if the very idea of a resident admitting wrongdoing prior to getting caught was ludicrous. And perhaps he was right.

Then again, perhaps he didn't have to be.

"You can't prove anything." Her words were clipped, icy.

"You're right. I can't yet, and to be honest with you, Sasha, I don't want to have to prove anything. Because I'm hoping you'll let me help you."

"I don't want your help."

Which was exactly what I'd figured she'd say. "That's probably true, but I think you need it."

Sasha twisted her body to face me head on. "And so what? If I play nice with you, tell you all my dirty secrets, then you'll keep my sins hidden from your boyfriend?"

I hadn't expected that. Not even a little bit. Glo and Clara knew about Silas and me—we'd told them, of course—but we had been so careful while on campus. We didn't touch, we didn't flirt, and we definitely didn't discuss the status of our personal relationship with the residents.

Her laugh was nothing more than a weakened rush of air. "Secrets don't keep long here. Obviously."

I willed myself to dig deeper. In all my time at the house, this was the most Sasha had ever spoken to me. Times three. "I would imagine that carrying around such a heavy secret would start to weigh on a person. That at some point, even if they wanted to come clean, they might feel like it was already too late. Like there was no hope left for them even if they wanted to change."

This time, she had no response.

I lifted the glasses away from my eyes and folded them into my hand. "But there is hope. We all make mistakes. We all choose the wrong path at times. Nobody has to stay there, though. *You* don't have to stay there, either." I took a breath and silently prayed she would accept my next words. "I can't promise you there won't be consequences, but I *can* promise that if you're willing to come clean and confess, those consequences will be less."

Her jaw ticked back and forth, an inner battle raging behind her veiled expression.

"I bet if I were Wren, all I'd have to do is bat my pretty little eyelashes and all my sins would be forgiven."

Deflection. I recognized the tactic immediately. "We're not talking about Wren. We're talking about you."

"But maybe we *should* be talking about Wren." She glared me down. "It's her fault."

Though I felt an instant defensiveness flare up in my spirit, I worked hard to keep my voice in check. "How so?"

Sasha shook her head, and I knew she was calculating how much she could say. "Forget it. It's not like someone like you could ever understand."

"Someone like me?"

She rolled her eyes. "Yeah. Like you. Pretty. Rich. Gets everything she's ever wanted just by matching her lipstick to her designer handbag. Your life is like a freaking fairy tale, only worse. More pathetic."

It was getting more and more difficult to channel my inner

Clara as I breathed through my nose. "My life hasn't been a fairy tale—"

"Whatever. Just . . . do whatever you need to do. I don't care anymore." She started to turn, and I reached out for her arm, just above her elbow.

"I don't believe that for a minute. I think you do care, Sasha. I think you're angry because of how *much* you care."

She ripped her arm away from me as if I'd burned her. "You don't know anything about me."

"Then tell me." The internal fire stoked in my gut matched her intensity. "Tell me what you think somebody like me can't possibly understand about someone like you."

Fury erupted from her throat. "How 'bout how it feels to lose your only friend? Let's start there!"

Her words knocked the breath from my lungs as the image of Val's face swam just out of reach. Unfortunately, I did understand that. Too well. It took me a minute to recover, to push the sting down the way I always did when the guilt of losing Val over my own stupidity slipped back into my subconscious. "I understand more than you know, actually. It's horrible. A pain I wouldn't wish on anybody. I'm so sorry."

She sniffed and glanced away.

In her silence, I took another stab in the dark. "Am I right to assume you're talking about Monica?"

"She's a traitor."

"What happened between you two?" Because maybe if I could understand what went wrong between them, I might understand how she got to the place she was in now.

"We had a plan. And she ruined it." She sharpened her glare. "Life sucks."

Though her explanation brought more confusion than it did clarity, I could tell she was closing off to me again. Pulling down an iron gate I likely wouldn't be able to get through again, even if it meant her walking to the gallows alone.

Timidly, I touched her shoulder. "Sasha, I want to help you, but I can't keep what I found this afternoon a secret from Silas. I do want to give you an opportunity to tell him yourself, and you wouldn't have to do it alone. I would go with you."

The back door to the cottage opened behind us. "Ah, there you two are. Everything okay out here?"

As I turned to answer Glo, Sasha's unblinking gaze focused on me. Like a dare.

Like a test.

"Yeah, we're okay," I said.

"All right. Well, Silas is waiting for you out front, Molly. Oh, and Clara's made each of you a bowl of popcorn. The girls just started *The Proposal* a few minutes ago. They have their clay masks on. Looks like a Halloween party in there."

"Great. Thanks for the update," I said as casually as possible while a nineteen-year-old stared at me like she could sift through my soul. "We'll be right in."

Glo closed the door once more, and I mentally prepared for the conversation I'd need to have with Silas in a matter of minutes, wondering if his protocol would mean Sasha would be forced to leave tonight or—

"Can you at least wait until tomorrow?" The defensive edge in her voice was as off-putting as her body language, but I didn't immediately dismiss her request.

"Why?"

"Because I know as soon as I tell him, I'm gone. Even if the consequences are less, I'm still gone. I know the rules. We all do. But I want one more night here. Just one. So if I promise to do as you say and confess everything to him in the morning, can you promise not to say anything to him or the others until then?"

It was a hard bargain to make, one I wasn't entirely sure I should agree to. But then again, wasn't Silas always saying that trauma didn't play by the rules? Hadn't Sasha had enough hard breaks in her life? Yes. Undoubtedly so.

"Okay," I said. "We can wait until the morning."

There was no thank-you as she steered her svelte frame back

to the house, just a lonely resolve that caused my heart to ache with such unexpected sadness I suddenly wished she was wrong about the consequences. Because though I could understand the pain of losing a best friend, that was hardly the only pain Sasha carried inside her tonight.

◇◇◇

As I ventured into the dark field to meet Silas, midway between Lavender Cottage and the guys' Bunkhouse, I worked to shake the unsettledness in my gut over the bargain I'd just made. But the moment I saw Silas up close, my promise to Sasha faded into the background. He looked exhausted. No, he looked weary. Even in the darkness, I could see the half-moon indents under his eyes.

"What's wrong?"

"Diego didn't pass his exam."

"Oh no, not again." Sympathy filled me for the young man with such a sensitive nature. This was his second time around at the trade school. "I'm so sorry. So what does that mean for him?" But I already knew what it meant. Silas had told me yesterday that this test was the make-or-break determination of Diego's place at The Bridge. If a resident wasn't actively enrolled in an internship, job, or education program of some kind, then his eligibility to stay in the program and have a place on campus would be over. The waiting list was too long, and the stipend he received from the government had already paid for two rounds of his trade school and exams.

"I'm not sure yet." He scrubbed his hands over his face, a gesture that worried me more than his words. "I've been on the phone since we got back, trying to figure something out for him, but it doesn't look good. And he knows it. Worst case, he'll have two weeks left here. Max."

"Oh, Silas."

"Yeah, he's pretty upset. It didn't help that Alex aced his exam on his first shot."

I sighed. "Not the night you'd planned." At least on that point, we were on the same page.

He blew out a hard breath. "Devon's still pushing for a group poker game, but I'm not sure he's gonna get his wish. It's pretty tense in the house right now. I might just rent a couple movies for us to watch instead. We could all use an evening off. It's been a long, draining day."

"Is there anything I can do? We have lots of mini cupcakes we can share. I ordered way more than we needed."

"Imagine that." He chuckled softly. "Jerry bought a few snacks, but they're almost gone. Some cupcakes might be nice."

"Okay, I'll send a couple of the girls over to deliver a tray."

A beat of silence passed between us, and his hand reached out. Midway to me, he withdrew it and shoved it deep into his pocket instead. Though we were in the middle of a darkened field, there were dozens of illuminated windows all around us. It was why I stood four feet away from him even now, barely able to detect the scent of his aftershave. And even still, there were some residents who'd apparently figured out that we'd become more than friendly colleagues.

"I need to apologize to you, Molly. For earlier," he said. "I was short with you over text. But my responses had nothing to do with you. I was stressed about Diego. I'm sorry I didn't handle that better."

Though I now had context for his curt responses, there was a dull burn in the pit of my stomach that hadn't been fully extinguished by his apology. "I was only trying to help."

"I realize that. But that's a difficult matter to deal with over text."

And he didn't even know half of it yet.

"The good news is," he continued, "nothing more can happen with that tonight. Not with all the extra staff on campus, and not after I had Jerry switch out the padlock after you texted me. Nobody's getting in there tonight. Unfortunately, he confirmed that the security camera aimed at the west garden has been offline for over a month. My guess is that our offenders knew that." He sighed. "It's likely why they left the evidence in there. They figured they were a long way off from getting caught."

Yet the box of condoms wasn't the only piece of evidence I'd found. I opened my mouth to tell him about the deal I'd made, about how I knew one of the offenders involved and that I'd promised her we could talk to him in the morning together, when Jasmine hollered across the field for me. She wanted help with her eye makeup.

I glanced back at him, my hesitation dying in light of his exhaustion. Silas wasn't even going to start the official investigation until tomorrow anyway, which meant I could honor Sasha's request and allow him to get a good night's sleep tonight. Hadn't he earned that much?

"We should both probably get back to our people." I pointed at the cottage behind me and slowly retreated. "I'll see you tomorrow at the pancake breakfast."

"I certainly hope so. Good night, Molly. Sleep well."

"You too, Silas."

As I neared the cottage, I glanced over my shoulder to find his gaze waiting for me there, offering me a quiet strength, despite his own weary state.

I gave a little wave, and he waved back.

It was incredible how such a short interaction with Silas could have such a profound effect on my psyche. In just a few moments, he'd managed to restore the balance I'd lost, that tipsy uncertain feeling all but gone now. At least, until I reached the front door and heard the unmistakable sound of a chair knocking to the ground and an impossibly high curse word screeched over the rom-com movie soundtrack.

I threw open the door and pushed inside, stunned at the sight of Wren braced in what could only be described as a Warrior One yoga pose, her frail body blocking Monica from a seething Sasha. A palette of makeup and a broken mirror lay on the floor between the two ex–best friends.

"You shouldn't have done that," Sasha hissed through her teeth.

Monica tilted her chin higher in the air, clearly unafraid. "Yeah, well, there's a lot of things I shouldn't have done. You should know, you've been involved in most of them."

"Okay, that's enough, girls," said Glo, rounding the giant popcorn machine and heading straight for the trio. "Clean up this mess and meet me on the porch. No need disrupting everybody's evening because you three are struggling to keep your manners intact."

"What's the point?" Sasha snapped back. "It won't matter soon anyway."

Visibly stunned by her outward defiance, Glo's eyes ticked back to her. "The point, Sasha, is that I've given you a direct instruction, so unless you'd like to add another round of chores to your list for disrespect, you'll do what I've asked without further argument. That goes for you two, as well."

But Sasha didn't move. Not even a single bat of her eyelash.

"Sasha," I pressed softly. "Come on, let's just get this cleaned up so we can go outside and talk."

Sasha turned from Monica to me, her voice breaking. "It won't matter. You get that, right? No matter what I say, no matter what story I tell, it will always come down to me against them."

"And who do you think made it that way?" Monica blurted. "*You!* You're the one who doesn't know how to have more than one friend at a time."

Sasha spun and glared at the two girls with such venom I felt the bite from where I stood by the door. "I would rather rot in a halfway house like your mother than be caught dead with a snitch like *her*."

"Stop! No!" Wren screamed as Monica pushed her aside and threw Sasha to the floor, taking another two makeup palettes and a bowl of popcorn down in the process.

As Glo dropped her full weight onto Monica and twisted her arm behind her back like a secret service agent, I blocked Wren from getting sucked into the mosh pit and shouted for Clara, who'd just walked in through the back door. She ran over immediately, assisting Glo in removing a now completely hysterical Monica from an utterly stoic Sasha. Had the girl even blocked her face when Monica swung?

"I'll go get Silas," Clara said, heading for the door.

"*No!* Don't," I called out after her. "We can handle this."

She whipped around. "But Silas is——"

"Dealing with his own crisis at the boys' house tonight. Leave him. We got this."

She studied me, wide-eyed, then looked to Glo as if for confirmation.

"I'll text him in a minute," I assured. "But for now, take Sasha to get ice for her cheek, and I'll help Glo with Monica. We'll separate them all for the night and work through the same conflict protocol Silas would if he were here."

Glo's face was awash with reluctance, but after a minute, she nodded her approval. "Text Silas, Molly. Let him know there's been an altercation but that we have it covered." She pointed at Monica. "Go sit in my room and wait for me there."

"Yes, ma'am." The remorse in her voice tugged at my sympathy.

Wren's made-up face had paled considerably, and everything in me wanted to wrap my arms around her, but since I'd been the one to call the shots, I had to finish them out.

"Jasmine?" I asked. "Would you oversee the clean-up here, please? We should probably call it a night."

"Yes, ma'am," she said, as she stole a glance at Wren.

"I can help, too," Amy offered, followed by Liberty and two other girls.

"Molly. Clara." Glo waved us both into the kitchen. "I agree that we need to separate these two tonight, but our policy is clear when it comes to pairing off. We can't allow a mentor to be one-on-one with a single resident overnight, which means I'll need you both to stay with Monica this evening. I can keep Sasha here at the cottage with me and the others."

"Right, sure," Clara said in confirmation. "We can do that."

I felt much less certain about this plan than Clara appeared to. "Maybe I should be the one to stay back here—"

Glo zeroed her authority on me. "There's a bunk room up at the manor, bottom floor, far right. You'll find bedding in the linen closet next to the theater room. Clara knows where. Would you both agree to stay in there with Monica for the night?"

We both nodded.

"I'll keep Sasha close to me tonight. I'll pull her and Amy into my room with mattresses on the floor. That's all I can do at this late hour."

I nodded again and glanced back at Wren, who swiped at a silent tear. I didn't know how far this feud between them went, but something told me I'd only seen the tip of the iceberg. Whatever secrets had gone on in this house, they clearly didn't begin and end in the garden shed.

Glo must have read my thoughts because she put a hand on my arm and said, "I'll talk to Wren once I get Sasha settled in for the night. You can follow up with her in the morning. For now, I need your help with Monica. Try to get to the bottom of what's really going on."

I nodded again. "I will."

> Molly
>
> More Sasha and Monica drama at the house tonight. Separating the girls after a minor altercation in the living room. Glo has Sasha at the cottage and Clara and I will be in the bunk room with Monica in the main house. We're all good now, everything is handled, and we've followed protocol. No need to worry. Good night.

Morning couldn't come soon enough.

29

Molly

Something shrieked inside my head. No, not shrieked. Wailed. A shrill that dipped and circled and never once stopped to take a breath. It just kept going and going and going and—

"Molly! Molly! Wake up!"

My eyes snapped open in the dark room. Was it morning? Where was the sun? I blinked several times, trying to remember why I was in a cold room on a hard bottom bunk, when Monica's face cleared into focus.

"Hey," I said a bit groggily. "What time is it?"

"Wren's hurt," Monica said, rubbing her arms and shivering so hard her teeth chattered.

Her words sobered my groggy mind. "What? Where?"

And that's when I noticed the tears glistening on Monica's cheeks. "Clara ran out about ten minutes ago, and I followed her. The police are here, and Silas is—"

I didn't wait for the rest. In socked feet, shorts, and a ribbed tank, I barreled out of the unfamiliar room and down the long hallway, slipping and sliding around every corner and curve. The wail of emergency sirens still hadn't halted as I slid over the hardwood into the lobby.

But nothing on earth could have prepared me for what I saw. Wren.

Only not *my* Wren with the auburn braid that fell over her shoulder and the quiet disposition that wouldn't harm a blade of grass. No, this Wren was curled up on a stretcher, grasping her head in both hands and sobbing to the point of dry heaves. Because her hair, her stunning Irish hair that she'd grown long in honor of her mother, had been hacked off above her ears.

And the anguish that twisted her face was far more gruesome than the blood that trailed the cut on her cheek.

"*Wren!*" A cry squeezed from my lungs as I ran toward her. But before I could reach the gurney, arms were around me, encircling my waist and holding me back, pulling me away. I fought against them, desperate to get to her. Desperate to touch her, to know she would be okay.

"No, Molly," a low voice said as I watched Clara go to Wren. "I need you to stay here. Clara will go with her."

"*What?* No." That wasn't right. I should be the one with her. I was her person. Not Clara.

But it was Clara who rubbed Wren's back, Clara who spoke comforting words into her ear, Clara who stroked her butchered hair as the medics covered her bloodied sleep clothes with thin white blankets. All while Wren sobbed herself sick.

What had happened? Who had done this to her?

I fought to break free once again, twisting against Silas and pleading for him to *please just let me go with her*. But his arms were as firm as his voice in my ear. "Molly, listen to me. I know you're upset, but I need you to be calm. I need you to help us understand what happened at the cottage. To give your statement to the police. Glo said she saw you talking with Sasha last night, outside."

"Sasha?" The shutter in my mind's eye shot in reverse. The fight. The bargain. The discovery.

"They've opened an investigation on the house."

My mind couldn't quite make sense of his use of the word *investigation*. But even still, my muscles slacked beneath his hold as the last of my shallow breaths squeezed from my lungs. For the first time my eyes roved the lobby to where two officers stood at attention, reading the room. And at the moment, reading me.

With all the willpower I could muster, I nodded my head and straightened my spine in an attempt to stand on my own.

Slowly, Silas let me go as I tested out the strength of my legs, actively reminding myself to breathe. "You okay?"

Again, I nodded, though my body felt as detached from my brain as the part of my heart being wheeled out of the lobby on a stretcher.

"Are you Molly McKenzie?" the larger of the two officers asked me.

"Yes." Something heavy draped over my shoulders. A gray hoodie. Silas's. Robotically, I slid each of my arms into the sleeves and zipped it to my chin. The thick hem fell to my mid thigh, blanketing my sleep shorts but failing to hide the involuntary shiver that had overtaken my body.

"Will you please come with us? We'd like to ask you a few questions. About last night."

About last night. A phrase at war with another that had finally registered in my brain. *They've opened an investigation on the house.*

On numb legs, I followed the officers down the cold corridor, stopping only once to look back at Silas, searching for any ounce of strength or comfort he might offer me in his steady gaze. But Silas's eyes weren't tracking me this time. Instead, they were tracking the ambulance as it pulled away from the manor, carrying an innocent victim he'd done everything in his power to protect from the viciousness of this world.

A victim whose attacker I'd struck a deal with only hours ago.

◇◇◇

I tossed my keys on the breakfast bar in my kitchen, flinching at the harsh sound of metal on granite.

My house felt quieter than usual. Emptier, too. I'd spent so little time at home over the last month, leaving at the break of dawn and coming home after the sun had set, that I'd nearly forgotten how this place looked in the daylight. Dust particles gathered in clumps on the textured hardwood, scattering with my every step as muscle memory carried me down the hall to the room responsible for helping me pay off my mortgage within three years of Makeup Matters.

The chill in the studio caused goosebumps to rise on my bare legs, the only skin Silas's hoodie wasn't long enough to shield. Pained by the smell of his aftershave near the collar each time I inhaled, I wondered if this piece of clothing would be it—all I'd have left of a man I'd actually started to believe could care for me.

But I couldn't process that yet.

I couldn't process any of it.

Silencing that heartbreak, I reached for my laptop on a desk I hadn't worked from in weeks, then clicked onto the smiling image of a woman who looked so much like me and yet not like me at all anymore. Still, I needed this. I needed this escape into an old familiar routine that would welcome me back without question and ease today's wounds and troubles with mindless quizzes, click-bait articles, and hot new trends. Anything to keep my thoughts off The Bridge.

Unbidden, the image of Wren burned through the barriers of my subconscious. *Butchered. Bleeding. Broken.* That ever-present internal shiver wracked my body once again. The same way it had when I'd given my statement to the police through chattering teeth. Twice.

And still, the facts I had weren't enough.

Sasha had been taken into custody, led out in handcuffs, escorted by the same two officers who'd sat with me for hours in the fireside room. All of it felt so foolish now as I pictured Wren lying bloody on a stretcher. The evidence in the shed, the bargain I'd made with Sasha, the altercation at the cottage, the separation of the girls overnight . . . the hopes that somehow I could be the one to save the lost.

All of it replayed in my mind—in full color and full surround sound, like a bad movie I wished I could turn off. Because I knew how it ended. With Wren's agonizing sobs. Butchered. Bleeding. Broken.

And Silas. That despondent expression on his face as he tracked the ambulance. A look I could have prevented if only I hadn't tried to be the hero.

My notification bubble showed more than seven hundred new interactions since the last time I'd checked in: new followers, new likes, new commenters, new shares. An easy distraction to get lost in for hours. I scrolled through several dozen comments of people asking why I hadn't posted many selfies, when my next livestream would be, and where my latest series was.

I scrolled farther down to where the trolls lived, their word daggers the same as usual: *fat cow*, *not even that pretty*, *just another stupid blonde looking for attention.* My finger hovered over the last one: ". . . only famous because of her fairy-tale hair."

Her fairy-tale hair.

It was a trapdoor comment that led me right back to a memory I was trying to avoid. To Sasha saying, *"Your life is like a freaking fairy tale, only worse. More pathetic."* And maybe she wasn't all that wrong. Maybe she'd seen exactly what I'd wanted her to see. What I'd wanted the entire world to see. The lie.

A lie so masterfully created, so flawlessly engaging, that not even a daily ghost poster could break its momentum.

I squeezed my eyes closed, seeing Wren's trembling hands as they clutched at her shorn head, mourning the loss of something so distinctively her. The sight was a pain I wouldn't wish upon anybody. Not even the girl who'd done it to her.

Had Wren seen it yet? Had she seen her reflection? Bile inched up my throat at the remembered torment on her face, at the shock she'd feel at seeing herself for the first time.

I did that to her. A self-accusation I'd heard approximately five thousand times since leaving the manor. Not only hadn't I protected her, I'd been the one to put her at risk. Each and every time I'd bent the rules on her behalf. Each and every time I'd encouraged her friendship with Monica. Each and every time I wanted to be liked more than I wanted to do the right thing.

I'd been the one to make her a target.

Numbly, I clicked on the opened tab to my email inbox, scanning over the sender names with absolutely no interest in reading a single one. Most of them were daily reminder emails from Rosalyn, but three of them were recent communications from Ethan. All marked urgent with subject lines like *Where are your live videos? Where have you been? MANDATORY video call at 9:00 a.m. Monday.*

With a frustrated groan, I pushed my chair back and slammed my laptop closed. *This is ridiculous!* I didn't care about any of that! I cared about Wren! That's where I wanted to be—at the hospital, with her. Only I couldn't be. Because Wren needed Clara. No, Wren *deserved* Clara. Even-tempered, considerate, thoughtful, empathetic, selfless-to-a-fault Clara.

The antithesis of Molly McKenzie.

I reached for a glass in my kitchen cabinet, flicking on the tap water and filling it to the brim before dumping it all back down the drain.

I left the glass on the counter and forced my feet down the hallway to the bathroom on the right, to the vanity with the special cosmetic lighting for all the live videos I'd recorded right here in this spot.

In the mirror, I stared at a naked face I no longer recognized as my own. I studied the pair of sapphire eyes to which I'd applied countless colors of eyeshadow, dozens of magnetic lashes, and brand after brand of anti-smudge liquid liner. I stared past the dark pupils into an even darker soul, asking the only question I knew how to voice: *Who are you?*

Because I was no longer the practiced smile and perfectly made-up face I was two months ago. Nor was I the selfless leader I'd tried and failed to become. I was a woman lost to the in-between, an identity divided between two versions of herself she could no longer accept. Because neither was complete.

Unlike Wren, my identity hadn't been compromised while I'd

slept unaware. It hadn't been taken from me without consent or cut off my body without my knowledge.

No, I'd given mine away—one click, one like, one sponsored post and livestream at a time. For everything temporary and nothing eternal.

I unzipped Silas's sweatshirt from my body and hung it on the towel rack behind the door. Then I tugged off the elastic tie at the top of my head. My hair tumbled down my neck and around my shoulders, swinging to the center of my back. The same hair that had started it all once upon a time—just a simple updo that had sparked the match that lit a roaring fire.

With measured calm, I slid the second drawer in my bathroom vanity open and reached for my heavy-duty scissors. They weren't the cutting shears I'd left behind at the girls' cottage after layering Amy's bangs last Friday, the same shears Sasha had used on Wren as a weapon last night. No, those were now in the custody of the Washington State Police.

These scissors were the ones I used most often on plastic packaging sent by sponsors around the globe. They were nicked and dulled and completely unworthy for the job at hand. Which made them perfect.

The first cut brought a surge of power, an addicting rush that hummed through my arms to the tips of my fingers. I repositioned my hair for another snip and sliced through the thick lock without resistance, watching it slip to the floor and fall listless at my feet. A death I embraced with each and every cut.

The scissors continued to weave under my jaw and around my neck, until only a small section of beach-waved hair remained, dangling over my right shoulder. The last of the picture-perfect woman I'd spent my lifetime trying to create. For the final time, I raised the scissors and closed the blades.

A new, uncharted freedom coursed through me as the last blond ribbon spiraled to the ground. I may not know who I was . . . but at least I was starting to understand who I wasn't.

· 30 ·

Silas

I didn't know what state I'd find her in when I arrived at her house.

But I did know that for the last seven hours, while I'd been held up in meetings, placed on hold with board members, dealing with Alex's confession to sneaking into the garden shed with Sasha for the past month, and processing the subsequent discharge paperwork, my concern over Molly's distress had increased tenfold. Her pleas to stay with Wren had haunted me, as had the feel of her tensed muscles against my hold as she'd tried to break free from me this morning.

But what concerned me most was her disappearing act sometime after her interview with the police.

Had she really believed she could just slip out of the house without question or care? That her absence would go unnoticed? That if she silenced her phone I'd forget all about her and just move on with my duties at the manor?

Not a chance.

Molly was as much a part of The Bridge as I was now. Her presence was irreplaceable.

I knocked on her door, impatience thrumming in my veins with each passing second. I needed to see her. To touch her. To tell her that despite whatever she might believe, she wasn't at fault.

But when she opened the door, all previous thoughts were over-ridden.

Her damp skin was pink, her hair twisted into a towel atop her head, her body clad in the same gray sweatshirt I'd given her this morning.

A sight that had me actively remembering how to breathe.

Quiet surprise lit her eyes. "Silas."

"You left." The only two words I could drum up, apparently, after a thirty-minute car ride where I'd had nothing but time. To think. To pray. To plan out my next steps.

But I got the feeling that Molly had also been planning out some next steps of her own. Something was different about her. And I couldn't discern exactly what it was yet.

"I thought it would be best," she said. "After everything that happened."

"For whom?"

She swallowed, turned her head, her eyes everywhere but on me.

"For whom?" I repeated, stepping toward her. "Because I've been calling you since I got out of my last meeting. Glo said you didn't say good-bye, didn't tell anyone where you were going. We've all been worried."

She didn't respond, just continued to stare at a spot in the yard beyond me.

"Molly." The fear that had gripped me for most of the day gave way to hurt as I stared at her clean face. "Talk to me."

"Is she all right?" she asked. "Is Wren . . . okay?"

"Yes, she's back home now. She's asked about you."

It was the slight tremble of her bottom lip that undid me. I'd been polite and professional and every kind of patient as the cops searched each nook and cranny of Fir Crest Manor, asking questions I chose not to be insulted by for the sake of our program. But here, now, with Molly . . . I was done with the pretense and the pleasantries. I didn't wait for her invitation to come inside. The sweatshirt she wore was invitation enough.

The heat from her shower-steamed skin warmed my hands as I clutched her face. "It wasn't your fault. What happened to Wren. You understand that, don't you?"

Her eyes were slow to meet mine. "Didn't the police tell you?"

"They told me a lot of things."

"I mean about the deal I made with Sasha." The pain in her eyes shot through my chest. "I thought I could help her, Silas. I thought that if she confessed everything to you this morning that her consequences wouldn't have to be so extreme. That maybe we could find a way for her to stay in the program." She shook her head. "Instead, my neglect made Wren a target."

"Listen to me. Neither you, Glo, or Clara neglected the welfare of any of our residents last night. You all did exactly what I would have done given the same scenario and circumstances. I've said that at least six times today, and I'll keep saying it for as long as I need to. As much as I'd like to hope we can control all the variables, we can't. It's just not possible." I waited until her gaze lifted to mine. "Your job last night was to protect Monica. And you did that."

"At Wren's expense." She closed her eyes, a single tear escaping down her cheek. "I should have told you about the box. I should have told you about the stolen property and the promise I'd made to Sasha."

"Yes, you should have." I'd struggled with that. For longer than I cared to admit. That Molly had kept pertinent information from me regarding the house and the residents was a blow to the gut. But knowing about Sasha's indiscretions or the box of stolen property ten hours sooner wouldn't have changed the outcome, because I never would have sent her away without a formal exit strategy and plan. "But even still, Sasha's choices were her own."

"How long will the house be under investigation?"

"The investigation is a formality more than anything. It sounds scary, but anytime there's an assault or criminal act of any kind, they need to do a walk-through and open a report. In the long run it's what's best for the continued safety of our residents and staff. Based on the confessions and the evidence they found today, my guess is they will close the case fairly quickly."

"And . . . what about Sasha?"

I smoothed my hands down her neck to rest on her shoulders, debating how much I should say now versus later, when Molly was in a less vulnerable state of mind. Then again, after all the interviews and confessions I'd sat through today, I was more inclined than ever to speak the fullest version of the truth whenever possible.

"Silas?"

"The story is much more involved than you or I could have realized. After you left, Monica came forward and gave a statement to the police and to Glo and me as well." I pictured her even now, hands over her eyes, shoulders heaving, inconsolable with guilt—over Wren's assault, and over Sasha's actions. "She admitted that for nearly three months, Sasha and Monica had been stealing. From unlocked cars in unpatrolled parking lots, from their college break room, from the girls' cottage at Fir Crest. Anything they thought they'd be able to sell for a profit, they stole. They had a whole system—one was the lookout while the other was the thief. They'd made a pact to move out together and get a place on their own after they graduated from The Bridge. Apparently, the money was going to be their deposit on an apartment."

Molly's eyes rounded, her mouth opening without sound.

"I know. It was a surprise to all of us. They stored the stuff in Sasha's trunk for a long time, but then Monica started to get more involved with the program and with D&D and small group. When she became close with Wren, Sasha gave her an ultimatum."

Molly closed her eyes. "To choose Wren or choose her?"

"Yes, pretty much. But as Monica felt more and more convicted to come forward with what they'd been hiding, Sasha convinced her that the truth would only get them both evicted from campus."

"But what about the other evidence I found? The condoms?"

"Alex." I shook my head, an equal mix of disappointment and

frustration surfacing over his confession once again. "When Sasha could no longer trust Monica, she moved on to Alex, trading sex for whatever he could add to her stockpile. He admitted to cutting the wire to the security camera that faced the west garden." I took another breath. "Alex will be transferred to an all-male residence called Mercy House for some intensive counseling for the next several weeks, and Monica will stay at The Bridge. She's agreed to some extra accountability steps and to cooperating with the officers working the investigation."

I wiped away a tear from Molly's cheek. "As for Sasha, there's a pair of older sisters in Coeur D'Alene, Idaho, who take in young women with a history like hers as a ministry—actually, I got their contact information from your brother. They attend his church. They returned my call as I was driving here, said they have an opening for Sasha as soon as she's released from custody. Glo's already been in contact with them."

"You called Miles?" she asked.

"I did. I was hoping he might have an idea where you were."

She shook her head. "He's out of town at a conference."

"Well, for what it's worth, he was as worried about you as I was when I told him what had happened."

But instead of showing any sense of relief, the heaviness masking her countenance increased. "But that's the thing, Silas. You shouldn't have to be worried about one of your leaders—not after all that happened today. I've obviously been way more of a distraction than a help to you or the residents these past few months."

The raw edge in her voice stunned me. I'd seen Molly vulnerable before, I'd seen her remorseful and apologetic, but I'd never seen her like this. Willing to lay it all out without any qualifiers mixed in.

"A distraction?" The very idea of her believing such a mistruth made my stomach churn. "Is that really what you think you are to me?" And then a new revelation. "Is that why you left without saying anything?"

Tears pooled in her eyes and then slowly tracked down her

cheeks. "When you kept me away from Wren this morning, it felt like a punishment for all I did wrong last night. I thought you must have figured out that I couldn't handle this part of the job—the hard part that comes with serving others, with loving others. I don't do that well, Silas. I'm not good at loving people. It's what I've known about myself for so long and yet never wanted to accept. I'm not spiritually deep like Miles or my parents. I'm not compassionate like Clara, and as you saw today, I'm not level-headed like Glo. I wanted to believe I had something else to offer the house, the staff, you . . . but I don't think I do. I only made the mess even messier."

"You left because you were afraid I thought you were unfit to comfort a girl who so obviously adores you?"

Her silence thrummed through me.

"I promise you, my decision to have you stay back was based on efficiency and experience, nothing more. Clara has taken trips to the hospital on our behalf several times, so she knows the protocol and formalities involved. She's filled out the insurance forms and filed the necessary reports. She's clear-headed in a crisis, and that's what this morning was. A crisis. You weren't being punished. We needed you at the house. I needed you." My hands slipped farther down her arms and I squeezed them lightly, hoping the gesture would solidify the truth in her mind. "This is one of the complications we'll have to work through, together. I don't always think about the personal or emotional impact of the decisions I make at the house, but that's why I have the staff I have. You're not a distraction, Molly. You're an asset."

Without hesitation, Molly encircled her arms around my waist, pressing her face to my chest as I rested my chin on her turban-style towel. I took a long breath to fill my lungs once again. "Have you eaten today?"

A tiny shake of her head.

"Me either, and I think I'm gonna need some food before I drag you back to the manor with me."

She pulled away, the towel on her head tilting to the side and exposing a crown of familiar blond hair. "I'll make us something, although I'm not sure what all I have on hand. I haven't done much grocery shopping recently."

"We could grab something on the way?"

"No, I'd like to cook."

"Then I'd like to help."

As she turned toward the kitchen, the towel began to slip even more and she stopped it abruptly with her hand, freezing in her tracks. But I saw something, something peeking out from the bottom of her towel. A short tuft of hair I couldn't quite make sense of.

I came up behind her, her hand still supporting the leaning tower of terrycloth as I gingerly touched the isolated lock of blond at the nape of her neck.

"Silas, it's . . . " Her voice wavered.

I slid my hand up the length of her arm and gave a gentle tug at her tight grasp, a curious question more than a demand. For a full five seconds her hold on the towel remained firm, unyielding, as if she, too, were contemplating something she wasn't quite sure of. Finally, she exhaled and loosened her grip enough for me to pull the towel free of her head completely.

And as I did, as I saw what had been hiding underneath, the towel dropped from my hand.

Slowly, she faced me, her eyes wide and braced for rejection. "Say something. *Please.*"

But there was too much emotion lodged in my throat to speak a single word. All her hair, all her gorgeous, creatively styled hair, had been chopped off. Not a few inches, but dozens of inches. To her jawbone.

Just like Wren's.

I raked my hands through her damp, shorn locks, pulling the raw ends through my fingers. Then, with one finger, I tilted her chin to mine and stared into her eyes with a look that left little doubt how I felt about her in this moment. How I felt about her, period. The heated charge in my blood warred with my fight for control, with my convictions, with my need to make her understand.

I crushed my mouth to hers, the cool of her lips melding to the heat of mine and stoking an internal fire with each exploration of our kiss. She gripped the counter behind her back with one hand as I pressed in close, unable to pull away. Unable to stop touching her. As if everything in me needed everything in her to know the whole and unbiased truth.

That I wanted her in a way I wanted nothing else.

After seconds blurred to minutes, Molly placed a gentle hand to my chest, causing me to slow, to still, to be grateful for her sweet breath still fresh on my lips. I reached for another lock of her mostly dried hair and wound it around my finger. "Don't you ever say you're not good at loving people again." I planted one more undoubtedly telling kiss on her inviting lips. "Because I think you're outrageously good at it."

· 31 ·

Molly

Even though it had only been twelve hours since I left The Bridge, a lifetime of events had occurred since then. Not only had something significant taken place with Silas in my kitchen, but something even more significant had been taking place in my heart since the moment I emerged from my shower. Or perhaps, from the moment I snipped off my first lock of hair.

As I followed Silas back to Fir Crest Manor, past fir trees and through neighborhoods and then finally into the darkened parking lot, I spoke to the God I'd believed in as a young girl. Back before my family had gone our separate ways. And back before I'd felt disqualified by my lack of ministry vocation. My words were far from eloquent, and yet an unfamiliar peace seemed to quiet my anxieties as I pulled up to a house that had become a home in more ways than one.

I'd taken only a few minutes to dress before we left my house, adding a couple strokes of mascara to my lashes and slipping into some cropped leggings and flats. I still wore Silas's hooded sweatshirt—which I warned him he was never getting back. The usual pressure to be perfectly presentable and polished . . . that was absent now. And I wasn't sure if it would ever return.

Truthfully, there was still a lot I wasn't sure about.

Silas walked beside me on the cobblestone path to the cottage, so close I had to stop myself from looping an arm around his waist and leaning into his side. But instead, he placed his hand to the small of my back and led me to the familiar door.

"Are you good?" he asked.

I nodded, a nervous flutter alive in the base of my belly. I was good, yes, but I was also aware that Wren was only a few rooms away from where I stood, and that I had no idea where her headspace was at in this moment. What if she was angry with me? What if she blamed me for what happened? What if she asked questions I couldn't answer? What if I couldn't be who she needed as a mentor?

I tugged the hood farther over my head as Silas peered down at me.

"You planning on wearing that over your head all summer?"

"No." I sighed. "I just want to be sensitive to her, and . . . I'm not sure what she needs yet."

"You," he said confidently. "She needs you, Molly. A friend. A confidant. A loyal authority figure who shows up and presses in to the messy and the difficult. That's what you're giving her tonight—your presence and support."

I rubbed my lips together, trying to stop the tingle in the tip of my nose. "Okay."

He offered me that half grin I'd come to love. "It's after hours, so technically that means I shouldn't be around the cottage." Because even though he was the program director of the entire campus, he was abiding by his own rules: no males on the cottage premises after seven. "After I check in on the guys, I'll be in my office. Want to come up when you're finished here?"

"Sure, of course. I'll see you later, then." A bit shakily, I reached to twist the doorknob when he stopped me with a touch to my shoulder.

"Molly. You can do this."

I briefly closed my eyes and exhaled one last time before pushing inside the same cottage that only yesterday had rumbled with laughter as Sandra Bullock and Ryan Reynolds duked it out on screen, the smell of sugary treats and dry shampoo filling the air. But this evening it was quiet. Several girls sat on the L-shaped sofa as I closed the front door behind me, their acknowledgment of me somber yet respectful.

As I started down the hallway toward the second door on the right, Amy cleared her throat behind me and pointed to the door with a shake of her head. "She's not in there."

For a second, panic got the best of me, my mind racing back to that bloody image of Wren being wheeled out of the lobby into an ambulance. I shook my head to stop the spiral. "But Silas said she was here. That he saw her, talked to her—"

"Oh, no, she's here!" Amy backpedaled quickly. "I meant, she's just not in that room anymore." A sheepish smile curved her mouth. "Sorry. They traded beds earlier today. Monica didn't think it was right that Wren would have to go back to the same bed where, you know . . . *it* happened. Glo let us move everything over while Wren was at the hospital."

Relief and something like pride coursed through me. Monica had done that. For Wren. "Thank you for telling me."

Amy nodded and touched my arm before she headed back to the living room. I knocked lightly on the door at the end of the hall—Monica's old room.

"Hello?" I said as gently as I could, bracing for what I might find. Tears? Anger? A full catatonic state of numbness and shock?

But as the door opened fully, the same nineteen-year-old girl who had been curled up on a stretcher this morning was now chuckling softly at something Monica had said. They both looked up at me, Wren's eyes locking with mine.

"Molly?"

And just like that, the sound of her voice made something inside me both collapse and rebuild all at once. Within seconds, I'd wrapped my arms around her in an embrace I'd ached for since this nightmare began. "How are you?"

"So glad you're here," she said.

I pulled her in, cradling the back of her head as my mind struggled to accept the lack of plaited hair against my palm. Seeing Wren without one of her signature braids was going to take some time to get used to. I perched on the edge of her mattress and then reached for Monica's hand, giving her fingers a squeeze. "Thank you for being such a good friend to her, Monica."

Her round cheeks lifted into a grin. "I'm just happy she's okay."

"Me too," I said, turning my focus on Wren once again.

The three-inch gash across her left cheek had been cleaned and sealed by Steri-Strips, forcing my gaze to drift farther up, to the patches of hair sheared off at odd, uneven angles. While the majority had been hacked off at her jawline, there were some shorter pieces, too. I wondered if they could be blended into layers? Or stacked into an A-line at the nape of her neck? I'd never been an expert in short hairstyles, but I supposed I was about to become one really, really soon.

Monica stood and stepped back from the bed.

She hitched a thumb toward the door. "I think I'll grab some dinner with the other girls, if that's okay? Clara went with Jake to get Wren some special takeout from downtown."

"Oh good, yes. Grab yourself some dinner, and would you mind texting Clara to let her know I'm here?" She probably needed to take a breather. At least she was with Jake.

As soon as Monica left the room, I touched Wren's hand. She stared down at the blankets bunched up on her lap.

"Wren, I'm so sorry about—"

She shook her head. "Please, can I go first? I have some things I really need to say to you."

I swallowed. "Of course."

"I knew about it. About Monica and Sasha's secret. About the lying and the stealing."

It took me a minute to sort out what she was referring to. So many conversations had taken place since the argument with Sasha in the living room last night. "Okay, but you realize that doesn't make what happened to you okay, right?"

She nodded. "Yes, I know that. But still . . . I'm not innocent. I should have told you. I should have trusted you with what was really going on here, with how bad it had become between the three of us."

If she only knew just how much I could relate! "I guess we're all afraid to tell the truth at times. Even when it's about what's really going on inside us."

She was quiet for a beat before she said, "Can I tell you something I haven't told anybody yet?"

I braced myself. "Of course."

"My brother's getting adopted. By the Coles. They told me three days ago, and I've been trying to sort through my feelings."

The bittersweet pang in my heart was as much for Wren as it was for little Nate. "Oh, Wren . . . I can only imagine how many feelings you must be wading through."

"Yes, but the Coles have been so kind to me. They even asked for my blessing to adopt Nate, and they want me to be a part of their lives."

I swallowed down the emotion climbing my throat. "And how do you feel about that?"

She took a second to think, and then finally ran a hand through her cropped hair. "It's not what I wanted at first, but I think it's the right thing for Nate. They love him, and he really loves them, too. But it's still hard."

"Of course it is. It's complicated, and you're allowed to process your feelings as you feel them." I squeezed her hand and took an extra second to compose my thoughts. "Now, can I tell you something?"

She nodded.

"I'm sorry. I'm sorry I didn't ask more questions about what was happening here at the house. And I'm sorry I didn't protect you last night like I wish I could have." I reached up and touched a tuft of hair near her earlobe.

"It's not your fault, Molly. My hair will grow back. And the cut on my face will heal." She said this as if regurgitating words she wanted to believe, but couldn't quite bank her life on yet.

Because redefining ourselves wasn't ever simple or easy. Nor was allowing our identity within to take precedence over the identity we saw each day in our reflection.

"You're right. It will. But that doesn't mean you won't struggle with the loss of it. Losing a part of who you've been will take time to work through. And that doesn't make you selfish or shallow or wrong. It makes you human. It makes you real."

Something tugged inside my spirit, beating hard against my ribcage. "I'm working some things out, too."

Curiosity crimped her brow. "You are?"

"Yes, and I think I'll continue working them out for a while. Maybe we can do it together?"

She smiled. "So you're going to stick around for a while?"

"Absolutely I am. I need this place, and I need you and the other girls. I hope you know that. You've all taught me so much over these last couple months." I chuckled softly. "Probably far more than anything I could ever teach you."

Wren blinked up at me. "My mom . . . she wasn't like you. She wasn't strong or brave or confident." Again, she played with the blankets on her lap. "I love her, and I miss her every day, but there were a lot of things she couldn't teach me and my brother because she simply didn't know how. But I want to be stronger. For Nate, but also for me. I know I'm book smart, but what good is that if I never take a risk? If I never speak up about the things that really matter? The way you do all the time."

Oh, how wrong she was. Because I wasn't actually brave or confident at all. And the only risks I'd taken had been calculated endeavors for my gain. I'd lived in a fantasy world of six-to-eight-minute video segments, absent of authenticity and reality even though I'd often claimed those nouns as subtitles to my brand. But Makeup Matters with Molly certainly hadn't trended on the depth of my vulnerability.

"I haven't always taken chances where they mattered, Wren. But I'm ready to change that."

She looked at me funny, as if she'd missed the connection I'd made in my head but hadn't voiced aloud. I slipped the hood still hiding my hair off my head. Wren gasped and covered her mouth, her eyes bright and unblinking. "Molly . . . what . . . did you do?"

"Let's learn how to be brave together, shall we?"

32

Molly

The amber light from Silas's office spilled into the quiet hallway like a beacon showing me the way. His office was a sanctuary for all those seeking answers to unspoken questions. Which fit my needs tonight like a pair of high-quality Italian heels.

Since saying good night to Wren, my head had become a jumble of half-chewed thoughts. And I was desperate to process them in a space that felt even safer than home.

Before I crossed into his open study, I stopped short, pausing in the doorway to observe him without notice. Though I'd seen Silas reading in the corner chair of his office before, I'd never observed him quite like this, with his head bent and resting on his hand, as if the only thing that mattered was the piece of paper he held. My gaze drifted from his hand to the open, overstuffed shoebox beside him. Were those . . . letters?

I debated my next course of action, wondering if I should allow him privacy, but the floorboard creaked beneath the shift in my weight and Silas looked up at me. Though he didn't say a word, his eyes shimmered with a story so heartbreaking I couldn't help but go to him.

"What is it, Silas? What are these?" I lowered myself to the floor, kneeling between him and the table where the stack of letters had been placed.

"They're from my brother." The reading light behind Silas shone through the page in his hand, illuminating the slanted, narrow handwriting as well as the signature on the bottom.

Carlos.

"From when he was in prison?" I asked, wondering if I needed to tiptoe around the subject or if it was better to be direct. I didn't know a ton about Carlos, but what I did know was complicated. Even if Silas had wanted to make it an open-and-shut case, family matters rarely operated that way. No matter how I'd tried to categorize my parents, stuff them into folders with labels of my choosing, they never quite fit. The same way I hadn't quite fit in theirs, either.

"Yes." He rubbed at his head. "There are forty-two in total. My mom kept them all, stored them for me. I wasn't sure if or when I would read them, but . . . here." Gently, he lifted two letters from the front of the box and handed them to me. "Start with the one on top."

"Oh, Silas. Are you sure you want me to—"

"Yes, I'm sure."

I stared down at the letters, the one on top addressed to Daniel and Judy Whittaker. "This is addressed to your parents."

He offered a single nod, as if that was all he could afford by way of explanation. With extra care, I slid the thin piece of paper out of the envelope and read the words Carlos Rodriguez had penned in black ink. Within the first line, his purpose was clear. This was a letter of deep regret, an apology in hopes of making amends.

But it was also much, much more than that. A story of a man, patched together through the insights and context he provided, telling of an older teen boy who'd become addicted to the drug he'd helped his mother and her merry-go-round of boyfriends sell. A testimony of trial and pain. Hardship and bitterness. And in many ways, I supposed this apology was also a confession, because where Silas had been offered a second chance at a happy childhood with a functional family who knew how to love and protect him, Carlos had spent his adolescence trying to find a path of his own. A home of his own.

With shaky fingers, I traded out the first letter for the second, this one causing my eyes to mist and burn the instant I read the first word. *Brother.* It was much shorter than the one he'd written to the Whittakers, only a few lines, yet somehow the words clutched my heart and refused to let go.

Brother,

This is my last letter to you from the inside. Next week I'll be a free man. But I know true freedom isn't the sun on my face or money in my pocket. That only comes from God and His forgiveness of my sins.

I've hurt many people. But I've hurt you most. I've sat with my regrets and bad ~~desisons~~ decisions for three years now. I know there is nothing I can do to ~~desearve~~ deserve your forgiveness. But I hope you will give it anyway.

You have always been the better man and the better brother.

I'm sorry.

Carlos

I finished reading those last few lines while holding my breath. I lowered the letter to my lap and peered into the face of a man I'd grown to care for so deeply. "Wow, Silas. This is . . ." But I couldn't really define what it was, nor was it my place to define it. Carlos was Silas's brother; this was his story to own and to share. "What are you thinking?"

Silas exhaled slowly. "I think it's been a really long day."

"It has indeed."

He stared down at my hand. "Would you mind if we put the no-touching rule on pause for tonight?"

Without a second's hesitation, I answered by reaching for his hand. He slipped his fingers through mine, saying nothing more for several heartbeats.

"Are you going to read them all?"

He nodded. "Yes, and I think I might call the pastor who's been mentoring him, too." He glanced up at me. "What do you think?"

That he would even ask my opinion on such a deeply personal matter made me weepy. "I think that sounds like a great next step."

He rubbed a hand down his face. "I can't always see straight when it comes to Carlos."

"I know," I said, squeezing his hand. "But it sounds like he's processed through a lot and wants lasting change."

Silas planted his elbows on his knees and lowered his head, but he still kept a firm grip on my hand. "How can I direct a ministry based on the notion that with enough guidance and grace the trajectory of any life can change . . . and yet struggle to believe it could be true for my own brother?"

"But you do believe it, Silas." I squeezed his palm. "I know you do, because you believed it was true for me."

"You were different."

"No." I shook my head. "I'm really not. For many years I tried to convince myself that I wasn't lost. That I'd just found my own way to live—a prettier, happier, more sparkly way." I focused on the definition of his jawbone, then sighed. "But really, my sin wasn't any prettier than a junkie looking for his next hit. I only learned how to package it better." I met his eyes. "I was just as lost as your brother, and you didn't turn me away. Just like Carlos, I needed people who were willing to speak truth into my life, willing to show up at my door and drag me back to where I belonged." I stared down at our joined hands, grateful in a way I'd never been. "Before all this, before I came to Fir Crest, I believed my online followers were synonymous with real-life friends. That might sound crazy to you, but it had been so long since . . . " I swallowed and released a deep breath. "It had been so long since I'd let myself truly connect to anybody as just me, Molly. And not as the persona of me."

Silas touched my cheek, sliding his fingers to my jawline and the short hair that still didn't feel like mine. "There is nothing *just* about you."

"Do you think I'm supposed to shut down my channels?"

The sharp change in subject reflected on his expression. "What?"

"Makeup Matters with Molly. I've been thinking about it all day—longer than that, if I'm honest." I chuckled, remembering my revelation in the sauna at Sophia Richards's house. "Since the Tubee incident."

Silas studied me, saying nothing for the longest time. Although he may have found my videos favorable, he'd made his overall feelings about the danger of social media clear from the start. And in many ways, I couldn't blame him. I was becoming less of a fan myself every day.

"Why did you say *supposed to* shut your channels down?" he asked, emphasizing the same words I'd used.

"Because . . ." Though it wasn't one of my usual traits to shrug, I found myself doing it now, shrugging my shoulders like Insecure Teenage Molly. "I feel like today was a redo of sorts. A life redo. I want to be different, Silas. I want to prove that I *can* be different."

"To whom?"

"To . . ." I sighed. I wasn't supposed to be trying to prove myself anymore, right? Was that what he was getting at? That trying to prove myself was the exact mentality that had led me to a self-focused destination I no longer wished to call home: my little island of one. "To God?"

He hiked an eyebrow. "Do you feel like God is asking you to give up your platform? Your influence?"

"I don't know. . . ." My voice trailed off into an uncomfortable silence.

"Because if you gave everything up, He might, what? Love you more? Forgive you more? Accept you more?" I didn't miss the way Silas tried to catch my eye. But I didn't want to be caught. All of that was true. "If that's your goal, you'll never meet it. There's nothing you can sacrifice that's worthy of what God gives us freely."

"Now you sound like *my* brother," I said.

"Then he's even smarter than I thought."

I punched him in the arm. "Seriously, though, wouldn't the bravest thing I could do be to start my life over? With some kind of worthy nonprofit cause? Like . . . " I thought for a second. "Like Bible translation in a tiny village overseas?"

He laughed at that. "Bible translation? Is that a secret passion of yours?"

Twisting my mouth to the side, I shook my head. "No. But it would totally be a Catherine cause." I tipped my head back, staring up at the ceiling fan in his office.

"Who and what is a Catherine cause? Is this the same Catherine reference you brought up in a dark parking lot at the beginning of summer?"

"Yes. Same one." I sighed. "Catherine is the imaginary girl-friend I made up for you—a justice-seeking lobbyist for the vulnerable and disadvantaged. But I'm sure she probably smuggles Bibles into communist countries as a side hustle, too."

After several beats of silence, Silas said, "You are without a doubt the strangest woman I've ever known."

"I believe it." I watched the ceiling fan go round and round. "All I'm saying is that my old routine can't be my long-term goal anymore—I mean, I won't make any drastic changes until after that scholarship is deposited and we get through The Event without issue, but after that, I don't know. It just feels so shallow. Like why would eye creams and hair diffusers matter to God? Why does any of it matter at all?"

Silas was quiet for so long it caused me to lift my head. Not surprisingly, he was staring right at me. "It matters because *you* matter to Him. Molly, your enjoyment of makeup and fashion and every shade of sparkle was not some accident. You don't honor God with your life by changing your personality and tossing out everything that is unique about who you are. You honor Him by offering those very gifts back to Him." He tucked my crazy hair behind my ear. "What if God wants to work through the platforms you already have? Through the followers you already have influence with?"

Could God really have been part of Makeup Matters all along? "But how?" Yet even as I asked it, I could feel Silas's gaze rove over my self-cut hair.

I shook my head. "Oh no. Don't even think of it. I couldn't go on camera like this."

"Why not?"

"This . . ." I grabbed at the ends of my chopped mane. "Nobody would even believe it was me. Plus, what would I even say?"

"The truth. You'd say the truth."

"Silas." I closed my eyes, seeing Wren's face behind my eyelids, her sweet voice describing the kind of vulnerability she believed I possessed. The kind of bravery that would go on a livestream video without any of the pretty armor I usually hid behind. "It feels so much riskier to just . . . be myself. Especially on camera in front of thousands of people."

"I'm sure it does." I felt the warmth of his fingertips graze my cheek. "But I think you'll be surprised at how your viewers might respond to a heartfelt post from a woman they admire. I'm pretty partial to her myself."

Allowing the idea to take root, I captured his hand against my cheek and refused its release. "Then you do it, too."

He peered at me quizzically.

"I'll do a livestream if you call your brother's mentor. Two hard things for the price of one."

Our standoff lasted all of ten seconds before Silas said, "I have a stipulation to add."

"Shoot."

"Do the livestream from here."

"From Fir Crest Manor?" I nearly choked on the words.

"Yes. I'll even volunteer to be your cameraman."

I tilted my head as irony smacked me square in the chest. "But doesn't that break like every social media rule you have?"

"Some rules are worth amending." He stood, offered me his

hand, and pulled me up from the floor. "And I want to be a part of this."

I immediately wrapped my arms around him and pressed my cheek to his chest. I'd been wrong. It wasn't Silas's office that provided the much-needed respite I'd come to count on in the last couple months.

It was Silas.

◇◇◇

After taking a few moments to compose my thoughts and send up a silent prayer, asking God for strength and direction, I finger combed my cropped hair one last time, took a deep breath, and then nodded at Silas. With my phone in his right hand, he nodded back and then pointed at me as if he'd done this a thousand times before. A role reversal if there ever was one, as I felt like this was my first time ever on camera.

In a way, I supposed it was.

"Hello, friends. It's me, Molly, with Makeup Matters with Molly." I smiled, twisting my hands in my lap as I watched the tiny notification bubbles float across the screen in Silas's grip. "I know it's been a while since I've done a live on any of my platforms, but . . . " I swallowed, watching several comments and emojis slip up from the bottom of the screen, all mentioning my hair with exclamations. But I couldn't stop to reply to any of them. Instead, I focused my gaze near the top of the display, catching Silas's steady and reassuring gaze. "But I wanted to hop on tonight and say hello." Only, that wasn't exactly true. "Actually, I'd like to say a bit more than a hello. A tough habit to break for someone who's on camera often is the desire to want to polish up every word and make it sound as pretty as possible . . . but I'm realizing that some words are just meant to be spoken raw. And that's what tonight's video will be. A raw, unfiltered, unedited version of me, just Molly."

I chuckled a bit and glanced down at my hands, working to rein in my thoughts. "In the three years I've been recording and posting these videos, this is the first time I've done it without a plan or a script or a product to discuss." I tucked a short piece of hair behind my ear. "I'm not totally sure who this might be for tonight, but whether you've been following me for one or all two-hundred-plus videos, I want you to know that the Molly you've subscribed to on Makeup Matters is not nearly as authentic as she's led you to believe." I released a deep breath. "Or even as she led herself to believe.

"Though I've loved the fashion and makeup world since I was a teenager, and though I've had every intention of becoming a positive and honest voice in the beauty industry, there's been something missing for a while. A lot of somethings, actually." I pointed to the screen, at the image reflected there of this new self with the short hair and the natural face. "Over the last couple months, as I've worked with some pretty outstanding people at a transitional home to equip young adults for the future . . . I've learned a lot of hard lessons. Most of those lessons have cumulated into a complete rewrite of the old narratives I've believed about myself, my worth, and where my hope for the future comes from. I've had to face the truth about the ways I've isolated myself from the real world and from the real people who are in it." My heart pounded in my chest as I implored viewers on the other side of that phone screen.

"But what I want you to see, to know, and to hear tonight is that no matter how much you strive to make over the outside with the products I've endorsed, none of them holds the power to make over what's on the inside. And I'm realizing more and more just how much I've neglected the most vital parts of who I am, of who I'm meant to be. When I'm focused inward, I miss out on divine opportunities to bless others—to serve, to help, to protect, to befriend. To love beyond my own capacity and capability." I laid a hand to my chest, glancing for half a second to Silas's face. "This heart makeover is still a work in progress." I closed my mouth, rubbed my lips together. "But in the end, the condition of our heart is all that really matters. I pray that the same grace that's been extended to me as I've begun this heart work will be extended to you, as well. Until next time, good night and God bless."

I reached forward and tapped the screen to stop the video, and Silas placed the phone on the side table, his eyes a bit glassier than they were at the start. As were mine.

"A heart makeover," he said.

"Yeah," I said. "It was the only way I knew to describe it."

"It was the perfect way to describe it."

Though we were sitting three feet away from each other, his words were an embrace so real my lungs fought to take in a full breath. "Thank you, for everything you've done for me, Silas. I'm . . ." My throat closed around another swell of emotion. "I don't deserve someone like you."

"I was thinking the same about you."

No matter what came of this raw livestream tonight, I wouldn't second-guess it. Instead, I would fall asleep knowing that I took the next right step in a journey I was only just beginning. And tomorrow, I would take even more.

Starting with a long overdue phone call to a friend I wasn't willing to lose.

33

Molly

My alarm sounded different this morning. Not the usual crescendo of violins and piano, but a ringtone I hadn't heard in quite some time. *Too long.* I fumbled for my phone, glanced at the screen, and then shot straight up in bed, hastily brushing at the hair poking into my eyeballs.

Val.

I swiped right to answer the video call.

"Val!" I blurted, a mix of groggy morning voice and overzealous enthusiasm at seeing the face that topped today's personal to-do list, or rather, my *to-call* list. "Hi—how are you?" I barely knew how to start this conversation. It was as if the culmination of the last eight weeks was perched on the tip of my tongue, and I had no idea how to hold a single thing back, because all I wanted in this world was to keep her on the phone for as long as possible.

"I'm sorry if I woke you."

"No, no. I'm good. It's good. I'm totally awake now." I rubbed at my eyes, waiting for the blurriness to clear, but even as it did, the moisture I thought I'd seen on Val's cheeks was still there, still glistening in the recessed lighting above her kitchen table. The place she'd so often videoed me from.

"Molly." She released a sound similar to a laugh and then patted her face with the sleeve of her purple Alaskan Frontier sweatshirt. "I just watched it, your video. That was . . . I mean, I don't even have the right words yet. I just had to call you."

Tears blurred my vision again. "I've missed you so much."

"I've missed you, too." She peered into the phone, her eyes shiny and bright. "Your hair." She breathed. "I could hardly believe it was you at first. But it is. You really cut it off."

My haircut was the least of all that had happened over our time apart. I pinched a wonky piece tickling my earlobe, and reality set in afresh. My long, billowy hair that was a signature to my brand was no more. And I was okay. Better than okay. "Yes, I really did." Quite literally.

"What you said, about the heart makeover and about authenticity . . . it was beautiful. I'm not surprised at all to see what's happening with it. And don't worry about the naysayers . . . you know there are hateful people in every crowd."

"Wait, what are you talking about? What's happening with it?"

Val's shocked expression was almost comical. "Molly, your video's been shared over ten thousand times already. Even Felicity Fashion Fix posted it to her page! It was very inspiring. *I* was inspired."

Felicity? I fought an unexpected rush of emotion at that. I'd sent Felicity a one-sentence apology DM after what went down in Malibu, hoping she could read between the lines of everything I couldn't say, seeing as I was still contractually bound to her ex-talent manager and boyfriend. I honestly hadn't expected to hear from her again.

I opened my mouth to respond to Val's shocking pronouncement, but I had nothing to say. The very idea of a post featuring my naked face, my self-cut hair, and my unpolished words going viral on a platform that promoted just the opposite was . . . nothing short of mind-blowing. Maybe Silas had been right. Maybe last night had been the beginning of something new.

"I'm proud of you," she continued. "I just wanted you to know that. I'm not even sure what all is different about you, but it's clear that it's more than just your hair. It's deeper than that." Regret shadowed her delicate features. "I should have called you sooner. I wanted to so many times, I just . . . I didn't."

"No." I shook my head. "*I'm* the one who should have called *you*. You were absolutely right to make the decision you made. It's what was best for you and Tuck. I can see that now." Her face fell, and my stomach dropped several floors. "What? What's that look for?"

She tried to pull her smile up to her natural dimples again but couldn't quite make it. "Nothing. It's just so good to see you. It's made me nostalgic is all."

"Val, please. Tell me. Is everything okay at home?"

"Yes, Tucker is great." She pursed her lips, and I watched a silent battle wage behind the screen of her amber eyes. Val never wanted to be a burden; it was her Achilles' heel. "I'm just not sure I did make the right decision."

"To take the promotion at Cobalt?" I scooted to the edge of my bed. "Why?"

She gave a single nod. "I promise this isn't why I called you. I didn't want to dump my problems on you, I just—"

"We're friends, Val. We can share our struggles and our victories. I promise I care equally about both."

"Something's going on there," she said. "At Cobalt. I've been uninvited to several meetings in the last few days."

My eyebrows furrowed. "What kind of meetings?"

"That's what I've been trying to figure out. I'm not sure, but I think they might have something to do with Makeup Matters. Ethan doesn't trust me. He's made that clear by limiting my access to anything involving you or your team." She blew out a deep breath, an indication that there was more news to come, something unpleasant by the crease in the middle of her eyebrows. "And I've heard some rumors lately."

"About what?"

"That Ethan's been entertaining other talent. Other fashion

industry influencers, specifically. Courtney, one of the admins in his office, told me he took a big rising name to lunch the other day."

Heat fumed from my cheeks at the very idea that Ethan would try to replace me. Too bad for him we were still legally bound to each other by contract until December. "It doesn't really matter who he's trying to woo," I said. "Cobalt can't acquire two beauty endorsers at the same time. It's a conflict of interest. My legal team has already examined our contract thoroughly. Neither of us can break without severe penalty until our contract is up for renewal."

Her eyes grew wide. "You have a legal team?"

No, I had Silas Whittaker. And he was better than a team. But Silas was a conversation all on its own, one I'd be telling Val the details of shortly.

"Is Ethan paying you what he promised? Is your job still secure?" I asked, rerouting the conversation temporarily.

"Yes, but—"

"Good. That's what matters—that you're taken care of until something better comes your way." Which I certainly hoped I could be a part of in some capacity.

Val's frown melted into a smile. "I think I'm gonna pour a big mug of coffee so that you can tell me everything I've missed."

"Only if you agree to do the same with me."

"Deal," she said, pouring her vanilla creamer into a steaming mug. "But, Molly?"

"What?" I made my way to the kitchen, taking Val's suggestion of coffee to heart. Whatever was waiting for me in my email inbox, private messages, and comment notifications could wait. This morning was about my best friend.

"Let's agree to never not talk to each other again," Val said. "That was brutal."

"You might live to regret those words after I fill you in with the longest catch-up session in history."

She shook her head, tears glistening in her eyes again. "I promise, I could never regret you."

"Same here."

34

Silas

For twenty-one years, I'd been the older of two brothers in the Whittaker family. It was a role custom fit for me from the first day I walked through their front door as an emergency placement, carrying a trash bag over my shoulder with every earthly possession I owned. Four-year-old Jake's affinity for Tonka trucks and sliced apples that he chomped like a horse won me over within minutes, and I wore my new big-brother label with pride. The invisible name badge paved a clear and definitive path to other titles I'd collected over the years: Silas the Caretaker, Silas the Teacher, Silas the Protector. At six years my junior, Jake had accepted my authority and brotherly advice without hesitation or pushback. To him, our birth order was as concrete as our parents' signature on my adoption decree.

And yet the blood in my veins knew otherwise. *Remembered* otherwise.

That I'd once been the younger, the weaker, the needier of two brothers. That I'd once had someone I looked up to more than any person in the world.

Molly McKenzie

Are you there? What's happening?

I pulled into the warehouse lot and located the rusty blue truck Pastor Peter had described before I parked and sent her a reply.

> **Just pulled up**

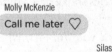

> **Is there a sentence for me to decipher in all that?**

Yes! It reads as follows: Yay! I'm so happy for you! And a little nervous, too! So I'm sending you prayers and kisses!

My chest expanded with the same intoxicating sensation I'd begun to identify with all things Molly.

> **Thank you**

Though I could just have easily texted *I love you*. In fact, it was becoming increasingly more difficult not to text that to her. Or to say it whenever she was near. But I didn't want to pressure her. Nor did I want to assume she felt the same way about me.

Call me later ♡

> **Of course**

And then before I sent it off, I scrolled through a keyboard entirely unfamiliar to me and found the same matching symbol to punctuate the end of my text.

After all, Molly had been the tipping point in this endeavor. The final prodding I'd needed to make the call to my brother's sponsor. To read the entire box of letters my mom had ferreted away with a hope I hadn't held until recently. To see my brother face-to-face for the first time since I saw him hauled away in handcuffs.

My brother's life was a revolving door of addiction, incarceration, and probation. A cycle he described in horrifying detail throughout the forty-two letters he wrote like an autobiography. And while I'd been cynical at best, unwilling to take him at his word, Peter had confirmed it all on the phone to me: the prison ministry Carlos had attended for two years, the halfway house he lived in now, the job he'd held for nearly three months without incident.

The echo of my pulse pounded in my jaw as I exited my car and walked through the lot with a heightened awareness of my surroundings. A dark memory of a parking lot not unlike this one called me a fool as I stepped past a row of empty delivery trucks and handcarts, all lined up at the front of an open storage warehouse. The place was nearly deserted, save for a driver who tipped his chin to me as he climbed into the cab of his semi and pulled off.

The instant the cloud of exhaust cleared from the opening, I saw him. *Mi hermano.* Only not as I remembered him at all. This version of Carlos wasn't wearing a buzz cut to his scalp like I'd seen during his arraignment. And his state-issued jumpsuit had been swapped for a blue vest with the words *May I Help You?* stitched on the back. But it was the tune he whistled that struck the loudest chord of surrealism—a melody Devon played often at the house during D&D nights. The arresting lyrics spoke of a Miracle Worker and His transformative power to bring the lost home.

"I was just as lost as your brother, and you didn't turn me away." Molly's words circled in my head as I listened to the chorus, my throat as tight as the pressure in my chest. Because I had turned Carlos away. With every letter I refused to open. With every collect call I refused to answer.

I'd withheld the same grace and hope I'd been shown without reservation. The same grace and hope I fought to offer every resident who entered The Bridge—the very program my brother's poor choices had inspired without him ever knowing it.

"Carlos," I called out with a strength not entirely my own, walking toward him with caution.

He tensed, turned, his mouth still shaped in a soundless whistle. The moment he registered my presence, he was in motion, his face lit by a sequence of emotions I'd never seen him wear—not rage or anger or resentment, but joy, peace, and maybe even . . . love.

At the sight of his focused, sober eyes, I could no longer swallow down the ache in my throat. The malicious countenance my memory had assigned to him for so many years had been replaced by a luminosity not even his most eloquent letter could have described.

"*Brother.*" A noun that spoke of so much more than name or blood.

His thick, tattooed neck depicted a history I'd only recently read, outlined on college-ruled paper. A life of choices and outcomes I could only relate to from afar. And yet, when those same inked arms crushed me into an embrace, my mind was far from our differences.

He pounded an open palm to my back. "I knew you would come. I told Peter you would. You just needed time." *To give me a chance* were likely the words he held back. Words imprisoned by a younger brother who had never once responded to his pleas and confessions.

"It's good to see you, Carlos," I said. "You look good, healthy." The fifty to sixty pounds he'd put on since I last saw him only added to the proof that his habits and lifestyle matched the change Peter had sworn to.

"Peter has us on a workout schedule. It's a part of the program."

Given the diameter of his biceps, I wondered if the program he spoke of took place in a weight room. "How is that going—the program?"

His eyes never strayed from my face, as if he, too, was having trouble seeing past the surreal factor of it all. "It's been eight hundred and forty-two days since I started a new life. A sober life. A better life."

Though I'd read about his last hit in his letters, after he'd traded two bags of Doritos for a bag of cocaine in the prison yard during the first year of his sentence, the number he spoke provoked a level of pride I didn't know I was capable of feeling toward him. "That's something to be proud of."

"Thank you," he said. "I used to hope I could make you proud of me one day."

Words that seemed to crush my diaphragm into my ribcage. "You are making me proud." I tried, and failed, to exhale the tension in my chest. But it was attached to a revelation of my own. "I didn't read your letters, Carlos. Not a single one, until two nights ago, when I read them all."

As if he was somehow expecting this, he nodded slowly. "Your mother told me to keep writing. Never to stop, not even if I never received one letter back from you. She said sometimes we need to write our story more than we need someone else to read it. She was right."

My mind skipped back a beat, and then another, where it stuck on his phrasing. On the only obvious conclusion I could make. "My mother wrote to you? For how long?"

Carlos stared back, unblinking, as if this was an interaction he hadn't expected. "Since my first letter to you after the trial. She sent me one letter for every letter I sent to you. You . . . didn't know that?"

"No." I shook my head, letting it soak in deep. For three years my mother wrote to my biological brother while he served time after an assault against her son. "But I'm glad she did." My mother had done what I couldn't. What I'd chosen not to do.

"She gave me hope when I couldn't find it for myself."

I swallowed the emotion rising in my throat. "She's good at that."

He nodded, his own throat bobbing. "I want to show you that I am what I say. That I'm changed. That my letters, they are all true."

"I want that, too." More than I ever believed possible. "I'm sorry it took me so long."

"No. No, Silas." His meaty grip was firm on my shoulders as

tears wet his face. He shook his head vehemently. "It's *your* name at the top of my amends list. I'm the one who messed up. Not you." He winced as his glance fell to the scar on my forearm. His expression was a mix of pain and hope, a sight that robbed me of my next breath. "I've never given you a reason to trust me."

"You have now." A statement that stripped the last of my protective armor bare. I wasn't here to be the savior my brother hadn't been to me. I was here because our Savior had been at work in us both.

"I hope, in time, you can forgive me for the pain I've caused you, your family."

"I have, Carlos. I've forgiven you."

It was a first step that felt more like a thousand, and yet it was the right place to start. Believing the worst was behind us, and that with time, accountability, counseling, boundaries, and trust . . . we could form a new kind of brotherhood.

Carlos tackled me into another embrace, and this time, I wasn't the first to let go. Because all that we'd lost—the years of trauma, the years of addiction, the years of anger, neglect, and silence, had finally come to an end.

My big brother had come home, and I wouldn't be the one to lock him out again.

35

Molly

If I had to choose a single month to relive for the rest of my life, these last four weeks would be a top contender. Between the hundreds of positive messages I'd received from followers responding to the livestream I did in Silas' office, to attending an adoption hearing for Wren's little brother, to rejoicing over the reunion of two estranged brothers and their subsequent meetups, to finalizing party preparations and talent selections with the residents and then convincing Val to take a week's vacation with her son to fly out to The Event next weekend . . . my cheek muscles felt as if they'd doubled in size from all the smiling.

And there truly had been *so* much smiling.

Especially when Silas's sexy shoulders were involved. *My goodness!* Who could have known how incredibly satisfying it was to watch a man work a pair of pruning shears in the sunshine?

"Earth to Molly," Miles said as he waved his hand in front of my face, leaning out the driver's-side window of his Chevy. "Maybe you could stop gawking long enough to give me some instructions on where you'd like this truckload of pea gravel."

Ignoring his comment, I scanned the perimeter of the manor

and pointed to an area not too far from where Silas pruned the apple trees. Sometimes I thought Miles had more sway than a celebrity in the area of asking for goods or services. Whatever he asked for—or didn't ask for!—people freely gave. Just like the pea gravel he'd been gifted for the grounds at Fir Crest Manor. "The tables will be placed near where the guys are building the stage out there, so if we could spread the gravel around the base of the trees and the paver walkways, that would be great."

"And by *we* I'm assuming you mean *me?*" Miles asked through a lighthearted grin.

I beamed up at my brother and patted him on the shoulder. "You've always been such a quick learner."

He rolled his eyes and tossed a dirty work glove out his window at me. I dodged it. "I think your short hair has made you even bossier."

"Hey, you have no room to complain. I paid you in hot apple fritters from Deb's Bakery."

Miles peered over the steering wheel to where Silas offered Diego a hand with a top-heavy wheelbarrow overloaded by tree limbs and weeds.

"Something tells me Silas is getting more out of this than hot apple fritters." He side-eyed me. "Come to think of it, I don't think I've ever seen Silas take orders from anybody like he took them from you today."

I picked the glove up off the gravel and slapped my brother's arm with it. "Perhaps he just recognizes my stellar event planning talents."

Miles made a disbelieving noise in his throat and continued to study me. "Anything you want to disclose?"

"As in . . . ?" I couldn't leave that one alone. My brother was never more uncomfortable than when talking about my love life.

"Come on, Molly." He cleared his throat. "It's obvious he cares for you. Anything with a pulse could pick up on that. Something is going on between you two." Miles arched an eyebrow.

"You're right. There is something going on between us."

He tipped his head back against the headrest, already in problem-solving mode. Already planning to fix his sister's poor judgment calls and impulsive behavior. Only, there wasn't a mess for him to clean up this time.

"But it's not . . ." How should I even word it? Silas wasn't like any of the men I'd ever dated. Least of all Ethan. "I mean, it's good, Miles. Silas is . . . well, Silas is the only man I've ever wanted to introduce Mom and Dad to."

Slowly, Miles twisted his neck to look at me. "You're serious?"

"Reverend." A sly smile tugged on my face as I turned my head to see Silas jogging toward Glo to unburden a tray of fresh sandwiches from her arms. I redirected my attention to Miles once again. "There is absolutely nothing you need to worry about. I promise you."

Miles's wide eyes looked from me to where Silas waved from across the property, gesturing to the sandwiches, chips, and water bottles. An invitation to join the troops for lunch. I nodded and held up a finger to indicate we'd be over in just a minute.

"You see a future with him?"

"I do." I'd never spent much time imagining myself as a bride or even as a wife. But I also couldn't imagine wanting to be married to anybody else.

"Then it really is too bad Mom and Dad couldn't rework their travel plans. I'm sure they'd want to meet him."

"Yeah, it's okay," I said, meaning it. "I knew it was a long shot since they're overseas."

"It meant a lot to Mom that you called to invite them to The Event, you know. She's mentioned it to me at least five times."

The call to my mom had been short and a bit awkward, but it had been the right next step to take with my parents. My family. We were different, yes, but those differences didn't have to divide us. Truth was, though I hadn't fit inside their full-time ministry box, I certainly hadn't made room for them in mine, either. "Sounds like they'll be stateside sometime in November to raise support again, so I'll make sure to plan some dinners with them so they can meet Silas and maybe come out here to the manor."

Miles smiled. "Good idea."

"Molly, will you eat with us?" Monica and Wren called out, looking up from their massive pile of printed programs under the picnic shelter. I gave them a thumbs-up, noting how adorable Wren's hair looked with a simple gold barrette pinned above her right ear. When I'd hired my stylist to come to the cottage to give all the girls a much-needed trim before our big day, she'd ended up donating her time for all our haircuts—including Glo's sassy new do!—asking me to call her again in the future. A beautiful gesture for a beautiful group of women.

"Come on, your next gravel load can wait. Your admirers are getting restless, and they want you to eat lunch with us as much as I do."

"They do, huh?" Miles placed his gearshift in park and smiled. "Good thing I'm always up for a free sandwich. And a chat with my future brother-in-law."

After taking a satisfying lunch break with Glo and Silas and all the residents—and laughing at all the ridiculous questions about "twin life" that Miles had been asked between bites of his ham and cheese sandwich—I hugged him good-bye and then popped into the house to retrieve my charging phone.

My hands began to shake the instant I picked it up off the desk and saw the three highlighted text notifications on my home screen. All from over three hours ago. All from Val.

My heart rate kicked up several notches as my eyes worked to focus on her messages.

Val

> Are you there? I really need you to call me.

> Molly? It's important. It's about Cobalt.

> Okay, I'm not sure what else to do. I didn't want to tell you over text, but I just quit my job. Call me as soon as you can.

"Molly?"

I jumped, nearly dropping my phone to the floor. It was Glo, her expression failing to put my nerves at ease.

"There's someone waiting downstairs for you. A real sharp-looking guy. I told him I'd need your approval before I buzzed him inside, though."

As if in slow motion, my mouth spoke a question I prayed I didn't know the answer to. Because it couldn't be him. He'd have no reason to be at The Bridge. "Who is it?"

"Says his name is Ethan Carrington."

A dizzying sensation washed over me as I stared at Glo and forced myself to nod, to breathe, to hear her next question over the swishing heartbeat in my ears.

"You know him?" she asked, her brows furrowing at whatever she saw in my face. "He made it sound like you two were old friends."

"I do know him, yes." And I was sure that was exactly how he'd made it sound to Glo. The man could sell any story to anyone. It's what made him a shark in the marketing industry. A quality I'd once admired. "He's my talent manager."

Strange how those words had lost their magic and pizzazz months ago.

"Oh, really? Wow. Well, that makes sense. He definitely looked New Yorkie to me in that tailored gray suit. Definitely don't see men around here wearing clothing like that."

I knew the exact suit she spoke of. His gray herringbone Solaro by Kiton. I'd been with him when he bought it. And I had no doubt he'd worn it today for a purpose. But what purpose? I hadn't a clue.

Drawing from a reserve of practiced smiles, I commanded myself to stay calm, to stay in control, even as I slipped my phone with Val's unanswered texts into my back pocket. "Did he happen to say what he was here for?"

"Hmm, no. He really didn't. Just that he was hoping to speak to you while he was in town."

While he was in town? Classic.

"Thanks, Glo," I said, trying not to tip her off in any way that opening the door to this part of my past was literally the last thing in the world I wanted to do. "I'll head down."

Robotically, I strode down the hall, down the stairs, through the lobby, and straight for the front door, where his shadow lurked on the other side of the fogged glass. The sight of his outline curdled whatever courage I'd felt in the safety of my upstairs office.

I'd dreaded this moment. Dreaded how it would feel to see him again after our last face-to-face confrontation in a Malibu driveway. After so much life had been lived apart from each other. I breathed a silent prayer, placed my hand on the doorknob, and yanked it open before I had time to pull the fire alarm and end this exchange before it could begin.

The slight swish in my ears morphed into crashing ocean waves at the sight of him. Neither of us spoke for several seconds, taking each other in. There was so much familiar about him—the same classically handsome face, the same classically athletic build, the same classically confident style. Yet the charm factor I'd once found so appealing about Ethan Carrington had faded to nonexistent.

In only a few months' time, he'd become nothing more to me than a familiar-looking stranger wearing seven-hundred-dollar loafers.

"Ethan," I said, as if I needed to further ground myself in the reality that he was, in fact, here. At Fir Crest Manor. I stepped onto the porch with him and pulled the door closed behind me, unwilling to let him inside this sacred part of my life. "I wasn't expecting you."

"Molly," he said, staring at me as if my name were explanation enough. "You look . . ."

But I didn't wait for him to finish that statement. It didn't matter how he thought I looked anymore. "Unfortunately," I said, both softer and kinder than I'd planned on, "this is a private establishment, and we can't have unregistered visitors on campus without permission—"

"I just flew twelve hundred miles to see you. Won't you give me just ten minutes?" When he looked up again, he made no effort to hide the way his gaze tracked my minimally made-up face and the outline of my freshly cropped hair. And for a moment, I wondered if Ethan hadn't come here in the name of business at all, but in the name of something far more personal in nature—*closure?* I fought the urge to fiddle with the ends of my hair or pin it back behind my ears. But I refused to show even the tiniest shred of remorse at my decision to start over. To move on. To be my own person apart from his expectations and control.

"This isn't what I wanted for us," he continued. "I never would have imagined you'd be avoiding communication with me at all costs. That's certainly not the Molly I signed or the Molly I believed in."

"You're right," I said, unwilling to be sucked back into his emotional tide. "I'm not the same Molly you signed. And I have no plans to be her ever again. That girl wasn't real."

Concern crimped his brow. "She was certainly real to me."

"Of course she was; you're the one who invented her." As irritation bloomed in my gut, I looked beyond him to the path that curved around the house, grateful that two dozen of my most cherished relationships were safe from his sight and schemes. There was no reason for him to be here. None. "Why did you come here, Ethan?"

He reached out his hand to me. I didn't take it. "You made it to the final round, babe."

My mind scrambled to make sense of his words, but I couldn't quite make the connection. "The final round of what?"

He flashed his most polished Hollywood grin at me. "*Project New You* auditions. I got a call from Al Richards and his team. He loved your video. And despite some of your professional hiccups as of late, he and his wife seem smitten with you. They've asked to fly you in for a final screening audition next week—said your empathetic attitude is exactly what they're looking for in a host." He touched the leather satchel he wore across his body. "I even brought their initial contract terms and negotiations with me to look over with you. I figured I could take you out for a drink, and we could talk everything through together, make sure you're completely comfortable before I give them the go-ahead to arrange your travel."

My eyes shot to his, my mouth opening and closing without sound.

"I know, I know." Ethan chuckled. "I was surprised, too—"

"I don't understand. I didn't think you sent in my original audition video, so how can I be a finalist?" Whatever hope I'd had of Ethan forwarding my audition video compilation to producers had died the second we'd broken up in Malibu.

"I didn't send one in." He blanched. "Al actually saw a recent video post from you on your channel. It's what edged out your competitors. He said it was exactly what he was looking for."

But since I could count the number of videos I'd posted this summer on one hand, there was only one that made any sense. Only one that . . . "Do you mean my last livestream?"

"Yes." He cleared his throat. "Turns out, I was right about you volunteering for such a needy place. Partnering with a cause might have won you the opportunity of a lifetime." He glanced at the building behind my back, as if he knew a thing about The Bridge other than its name. "Molly, Al's handing you a chance to go after everything you've ever wanted." His smile actually looked genuine this time. "All our dreams are about to come true."

Only, *my dreams* were already coming true, and strangely enough, none of them had to do with hosting a TV show in Hollywood for disadvantaged youth. Not now that I'd been given the chance to be part of the real thing, a real program that transformed real lives and offered real hope, support, and connection.

My dreams were here—with Silas and the kids and this program.

"I'm sorry, Ethan. But I have to turn it down. I'm needed here; it's where I want to be." Firm in my decision, I took a step back, only to have him advance two.

"Molly, I know you've been in a different headspace as of late. I get it, I do. You needed a break. But this whole *enlightenment* thing you've been experiencing, it's really just fame fatigue. It's what happens when you work in the spotlight for so long without taking a step back for self-care. I realize now that I should have been more attentive to you, but I promise everything will be different this time around. Better. Whatever you need, I'll make it happen for you."

My hands grew damp, sticky with a perspiration I only felt when trapped. "I can't go."

"Of course you can," he cooed. "I'll help you every step of the way. And don't worry about your hair. You'll have access to the best extensions and stylists Hollywood has to offer, as well as one of the most renowned celebrity therapists in the business. She's an expert in these issues, and she'll help you work through everything you're struggling with here."

"No, stop. You're not hearing me, Ethan. I don't want a Hollywood stylist or a therapist." How had this conversation taken a turn down this road? Confusion threatened to squeeze out all rational thought. "My life is here. It's the only place I want to be."

"You can have Val back, just like old times, but better." He pulled out his phone, held it between us like an olive branch. "I'll call her right now in front of you and double her pay, tell her she has a job working with you again if you're willing to leave all this behind and get your priorities straight again. Come back with me to Seattle tonight. We can talk everything out there before heading to LA next week. You're so much more than this, babe. Everyone at Cobalt knows it. It's why we've let so much slide. Your missed posts for our biggest sponsors, your lack of livestreams, your . . . poor judgment calls." His eyes lingered on my hair. "But your potential remains like nothing we've ever seen. That record-breaking reach you had last spring, those numbers we saw with your last sponsored campaign, your latest live—you're at nearly nine hundred thousand followers. We can triple that when you take on this show. Your net worth will be ten times what you made last year. *Ten times,* Molly! You just need a reset, some time away to clear your head and get back in the game." He tapped his phone screen with his finger and clicked into his contacts, scrolling down to Val's name. "Come on, Molly. Don't let some fame fatigue cost you your entire career. Or Val's happiness."

Vivid memories swarmed my thoughts, of the highs he spoke of, of the unprecedented paychecks and the VIP parties and the constant goal planning for bigger and bolder opportunities to be the best in my industry. . . .

I blinked, only to refocus on the phone screen in his hand, on Val's contact name.

My mind flipped back to her text. Her pronouncement.

"Val doesn't work for you anymore. She quit."

Ethan lowered his phone, a flicker of distress crossing his features momentarily. I didn't know the *why* behind her decision, of course, but for Val to quit a secure job as a single mother meant she'd had a darn good reason to jump ship.

And I was likely looking at him.

Ethan recovered quickly. "We both know she'd come back in a heartbeat if she knew she could work with you again."

"Molly? You all right?" At the sound of Silas's voice coming up the trail toward us, my insides became equal parts relief and dread. In a matter of seconds, my two worlds would collide into one, without proper warning or preparation.

Silas took each porch step with an authority I'd come to anticipate, his taut torso flexing under his black T-shirt. Despite the uncharacteristic dirt smudges on the knees of his blue jeans and the one swept across his right cheekbone, I'd never been more attracted to him than in this moment. He slipped off his grass-covered work gloves and extended a hand to Ethan. "Hello, I'm Silas Whittaker. And you are?"

Ethan looked from Silas to me, his eyebrow cocked, as if waiting for me to dismiss the intruder at my side. But that was never going to happen.

"This is a private business matter," Ethan said coldly.

But Silas shifted his stance and pressed a hand to my lower back, silently drawing my attention to his face, to his eyes that swore an oath of loyalty without ever speaking a word. "Would you like me to stay, Molly?"

"Yes, I would." I stepped closer to his side, grateful for the clarity his presence offered. "Silas, this is Ethan Carrington. My talent manager." *And the ex-boyfriend I'd hoped you'd never have to meet.*

As if I hadn't spoken, Ethan's gaze remained only on me, ignoring Silas completely.

"You're smarter than this, Molly. Think about your future for longer than a minute. You have a million-dollar career at stake here. Are you really willing to throw that away?"

His implication as to what—or whom—I was throwing my career away on was crystal clear.

"I've made my decision."

Silas's presence offered me strength as Ethan's neck flushed red. "That's a mistake. Likely the biggest one you'll ever make."

"I think it's time for you to leave, Mr. Carrington," Silas said in that same assured temperament.

"Actually, it's not. Not quite yet, anyway." Ethan reached into his satchel, and Silas immediately pushed me behind him.

"Whoa there, compadre." Ethan lifted his hands. "I'm just reaching for the paperwork I came to deliver to my former client." He thrust a manila envelope in my direction. "These were drawn up by Cobalt's legal team, to be served on the chance we couldn't reach an agreement."

A tremor of fear swept over me as I took the envelope and bent the gold brad at the back flap. The document on top of the crisp stack read *Cease and Desist.*

"What is this?"

"A cease and desist letter," he said through a thick fog of arrogance.

"But why? What's it for?" I skimmed the paragraphs referencing Makeup Matters with Molly, unclear at some of the jargon. It didn't make sense.

"It's an immediate stop order regarding use of my brand." He wore the cold, heartless gaze of a manager who was ready to cut his losses.

His brand?

"This letter isn't viable," Silas said, reading over my shoulder and addressing Ethan in his most lawyerly tone.

Ethan's offensive chuckle made it clear he thought Silas couldn't take him up on the challenge.

"Your company has delivered a C and D order for what is considered intellectual property. As an agency, you have no authority or jurisdiction over the handle of her social media platforms."

I smiled at Ethan's obvious surprise as Silas continued to flip through the paperwork. "Oh, I forgot to mention—Silas is also my legal representation."

"Well." Ethan's overconfident voice broke through my moment of victory. "As he'll see on page five, Makeup Matters with Molly is a registered Cobalt Group brand. And the followers, platforms, videos, photo shoot campaigns, and sponsored posts that bear that brand are, too. All of it belongs to us."

"No way. That's . . . that's absurd. Ridiculous," I said, shaking my head as I glanced up at Silas, who was studying the paperwork with an intensity I could feel. "That can't be true. I already had a growing platform when I signed with you."

"You did, but that platform wasn't under the name Makeup Matters with Molly, nor was it singularly focused on fashion and beauty. You were all over the place back then. I made you what you are—or I should say, what you were."

My mind scrolled back in time to memories of long conversations on expensive swivel chairs around oval tables, to dining in VIP lounges with Mr. Greggorio and Ethan, to brainstorming new and improved marketing techniques based on proven trends. To the day I went from *Made-Up with Molly* to *Makeup Matters with Molly.*

"Then I'll fight it. I'll take you to court. It's *my name* and *my face* on those posts and videos. You don't own me."

"You'd be surprised at what I own," Ethan said, as if he'd expected such an argument from me. "But I can assure you, court will be a waste of your time and money. You won't be taken seriously, as you've violated your contract multiple times over the past few months. The first, by contacting your sponsors directly and asking them to support a personal cause." He pointed to Silas. "You'll find that highlighted on page eight. There's a full rundown of the ways Molly has breached her contract with Cobalt and failed to meet multiple professional expectations." And then to me he said, "You won't have a chance, especially considering the cause you've invited my sponsors to fund is a youth home currently under investigation for assault and battery."

His words nearly plowed me over. "What? No. That's not even true! How do you even know anything about that?"

"Molly," Silas said in a resigned voice so low I almost didn't hear it through the pounding in my ears.

"But he's wrong—about everything." I pointed an accusatory finger in Ethan's face. "You've twisted everything. Silas, *tell* him!"

But Silas didn't tell him. Instead, he lowered the paperwork and gripped my arm at the elbow, as if there was nothing else to be discussed or done. As if this was over, all my failures bound inside a manila envelope.

Ethan closed the flap of his satchel and moved down the porch steps. "You should also note that by the time I pull out of this driveway, your access to any social media account associated with the brand *Makeup Matters with Molly* will be frozen. You'll have no further access to edit any past content or the ability to post new content. Our sponsors will be made aware of our partnership termination with you via email tomorrow morning, and all future communication regarding this matter to any of those sponsors will be subject to swift legal action." He clicked his fob to unlock his expensive rental car. "It likely goes without saying at this point, but as a terminated client of Cobalt Group, you are also no longer eligible to receive our corporate Dream Big Scholarship."

"*No.*" I darted after him, breaking Silas's hold on me. "You can't do that! These kids need that money, Ethan. *Please* don't punish them!"

Silas's arms were around me a half second later, holding my back tight to his chest as he spoke my name. But I was too broken to hear it. Too lost to a world I thought I could escape without consequences.

I couldn't have been more wrong.

Ethan looked at the two of us with disgust as he opened the driver's door of his shiny silver Mercedes. "I hope it was worth it, Molls."

36

Silas

As soon as Ethan's tires squealed out of the driveway, Molly pushed away from my chest and ran toward the house. For half a second, I debated my next move: to go after her or to hunt down her snake of an ex-boyfriend. The flare his haughty words had ignited in me burned hot, and if not for the close proximity of the two dozen residents working around the corner, Ethan would not have had the last word.

I would have seen to that.

I flexed and released the fists at my sides, forcing an exhale that did nothing to ease the growing pressure in my chest. Not only because I wanted to pin that pretentious jerk to a wall and use him for dart practice, but also because I had no solid solution to offer the woman I loved.

Ethan's legal team had covered all their bases. There were no loopholes to slip through this time. He'd annihilated Molly's entire career with one kill shot.

A short list of possibilities as to where Molly might have headed ticked through my mind. But as I threw open the door to Fir Crest, I didn't need to look far. She paced ten feet away from where I stood in the lobby. Her footsteps reverberated in the open space, her fingers pushing through the short locks of her hair.

"Talk to me, Molly," I said with a calm I didn't know I possessed. "Let me help you."

She glanced my way, her eyes unseeing, her face awash with the kind of devastation that cut to the core. "It can't be fixed, Silas. What he's done, it's . . . it's . . ." She stopped, stared straight ahead. "It ruins everything."

I positioned myself in front of her next pass, yet I wasn't stupid enough to restrict her movement. That would only upset her more. We were the same in that regard. Molly needed a physical outlet, a way to vent her building steam. It was the same reason I'd committed to running in the early mornings.

Moving meant processing.

"It might seem that way right now, but we can figure this out. Together. I'll make some calls and check on the validity of that C and D, and then I'll look into the appeal process to find out what it will take to unfreeze your accounts—"

"*Silas*." Her voice broke as she shook her head. "It's pointless. Even if we did request an appeal, the process to unfreeze flagged accounts can take weeks, especially when the claims involve a third party—which is exactly why he went the route he did. We don't have weeks until our event. We have *days*." She looked ill, the color draining from her cheeks as she worked through the tangled webs her ex had strung. "Making the offer in person was his last test. And when I failed, he knew exactly how to retaliate."

"What exactly did he offer you?" A question I'd been pondering since Glo told me an unregistered visitor was speaking to Molly.

With her back still to me, she exhaled slowly. "A final screening audition in LA. For *Project New You*." She twisted around to face me. "My livestream, the one we shot in your office together, it caught the producer's attention. I guess it was what he's been looking for . . . in a host."

My insides crystallized as a cold chokehold slipped around my neck. For several seconds I couldn't speak, couldn't utter a single word, much less a clarifying question. The idea of Molly leaving blindsided me. Yet, somehow the idea of her forfeiting her career, her dreams, her future was even more unbearable.

"Molly." I studied her, the rosy blotches on her cheeks, the tremble in her chin, the defeat of her slumped shoulders. "A decision this monumental has to be about you, what you want for your future, not about what anyone else wants." My words betrayed me, bucked against my chest like a caged animal, yet they were right. Painfully so.

"There is absolutely nothing Ethan could have offered that would have swayed me from what I decided weeks ago." Tears slipped to her jaw, marking her pink tank top as they dripped onto her chest. "From the moment you followed me out to the parking lot that night after D&D, I knew this was where I was supposed to be. For the first time in my adult life, I *want* to give my heart to something that really matters—something bigger than what I could have ever seen for myself or my future. So no, this decision isn't just about me at all. It's about this program, these residents . . . *you*."

She squeezed her eyes closed. "Only now I have nothing to offer in return for all you've given back to me. No platform to livestream The Event auction from, no voice to ask my followers for pledges, no brand to secure credibility and partnerships." She swiped at her cheeks. "By the time Ethan's email hits tomorrow morning, all the pledges I've secured from my sponsors will likely be revoked, and there's nothing I can do about it. Just like there's nothing I can do about the scholarship we've lost. If I had a month to regroup then maybe. But days?" She shook her head, more tears streaming down her cheeks. "We won't even have enough funds to cover the rental costs for The Event, much less bring in the five hundred thousand we need to be matched by the Murphey Grant."

I advanced, unwilling to stay frozen in place for another second. "That's what you're most worried about? The Event? The grant?" Certainly, they each held a spot on a long list of fallouts to be dealt with in short order, but they hardly took first place. In my mind, that spot belonged solely to Molly's career. Her reputation as a trusted voice in her industry had just been ransacked by a greedy manipulator.

"Of course that's what I'm worried about most." She reached for the envelope in my hand and tossed it to the couch as if it didn't represent hundreds of thousands of dollars and multiple years of network building and experience. "I can't change how I started my business or who I chose to partner with, but those aren't the decisions that will keep me awake at night. Breaking my promise to you and to our residents will. You counted on me and I . . . I failed you all."

No longer concerned about the uninvited eyes and ears that might be watching or hearing us, I wrapped her into an embrace. "You didn't fail us." I pressed my forehead to the side of her head, my lips skimming her cheek as I spoke. "This old manor would be as empty as I would be without you."

She lifted her head, her eyes unblinking as she took me in. "I wish I could fix this. For you as much as for the residents. I'm so, so sorry."

"I don't want you to be sorry. I only want you to understand . . ." I stopped, then realized I couldn't wait another day or even another minute to tell her the truth that had burned a hole in my chest for weeks. "I love you, Molly. Not for the promises you intended to keep or for the things your platform could have provided, but for you. For who you are right now."

She stared at me and then shook her head. "Silas, I just lost your chance at a million dollars."

"I love you." I spoke the words again, relief intermixed with conviction. There were so many solutions we didn't have, and yet, this was one answer I knew for certain.

Her pained features morphed into a look I couldn't quite identify. "But love shouldn't be forced to live in our disappointments and loss."

"It's not forced to live there—it chooses to." I framed her face in my hands. "Love lives in the hard places with us because that's what sets it apart. That's what makes it love."

"I love you, Silas." Tears slipped from the corners of her eyes. "I'll never be able to deserve you, but I love you just the same. So, so much." Her lips curved into a smile so sweet I had no choice but to press my lips to hers, if only for an instant. But as I drew back, she whispered, "And maybe that's exactly why this all hurts so deeply."

I nodded, pulling her close again, her meaning as clear as it was true. Even through the elation and hope we'd found in each other, our grief over what had been lost remained.

We stood there together, arms wrapped around each other, until our breaths became as quiet as our unspoken thoughts.

"How do I tell them?" she asked softly. "How do I tell the residents that everything we've worked so hard for this summer is canceled—the Dream Big Scholarship, The Event, the Murphey Grant, the expansion project. All of it lost."

"We'll tell them together." I ran my palm down the back of her head, her neck, her tensed shoulders. "Circumstances change, Molly. These kids know that better than most. There will be other years."

"Not for them."

Because none of them would be here in another five years for us to try again for the Murphey Grant.

"I know." I pulled her close as defeat pressed heavy against us both. "I know."

· 37 ·

Molly

Of the many times I'd been inside the fireside room this summer, listening to weekly highs and lows while eating gooey cookies made by Glo's bakers-in-training, last night's impromptu meeting was the first that had not been met with empathetic smiles and whoops of delight. Instead, it was as if the room's normal energy had been dialed back completely, leaving nothing but a lifeless tomb in its place.

Silas had insisted on taking the brunt of their questions, sparing me from the rising emotion I'd fought to choke down while he explained why The Event had to be canceled. Why their hard work on the grounds, in the kitchen, and in making and gathering auction items no longer had a purpose. How the expansion would now become a goal earmarked for an undetermined year in the future. For an undetermined group of residents who likely would have no connection to any of them.

As Silas had spoken to them in a patient tenor that could calm even the most chaotic of storms, I'd steadied my gaze on the framed blueprints above the unlit fireplace, the ones Jake had gifted the house out of hope for his brother's vision. A vision nearly as heartbreaking as the tears that had slid down Monica's rounded cheeks and the slumped shoulders Devon had tried to shrug off once he realized the songs he'd been rehearsing on his guitar had been for nothing.

After the meeting, Wren had been the one to jog after me, her voice as tender as the hug she offered. "Please don't feel bad, Molly. We all know how much work you put into this for us." I'd nearly buckled under her kindness. I didn't deserve it. Not when I'd been the one to lose the scholarship and the matching grant.

"You've all put in just as much work as I have . . . it deserved to be seen, to be shared and celebrated with the world. I hope you know that. I so wish . . ." I'd clamped my mouth closed, breathing through the warning tingle in my nose. "I wish I could have made it happen for you all."

Now, nearly twenty-four hours later, as I strolled through the east lawn alone, crunching over fresh pea gravel and taking in the beauty of yellow daffodils surrounding a stage that should have been the backdrop to a history-changing event for The Bridge . . . I allowed my heart to grieve in full. For what had almost been. And for all that had been lost.

While Silas had spent the better part of the morning making calls to the organizers of the Murphey Grant to ask for an extension on the August thirty-first deadline, I'd made some calls, too. Canceling the rental furniture, place settings, sound equipment, and catering. Every call ripped off another layer of failure, especially when I'd called Val.

She'd been horrified over everything that had transpired—not being able to stop Ethan from freezing my accounts when she'd gotten wind of it, the cease and desist order, the loss of the brand we'd built together. All things neither of us had any control over. Despite her adamant refusal, I'd sent her funds to reimburse the cost of her trip out here. There simply wasn't a good enough reason for her to spend the money or the time to fly out here now, not when The Event had been canceled, and not when I couldn't offer her a replacement job at Makeup Matters with Molly . . . seeing as there was no more Makeup Matters with Molly.

Disbelief clouded my mind as I looked to a sky swirling with muted pastels and streaks of sunlight. In a past life, I would have taken a selfie in this spot. I would have studied my phone screen, filtering the colors into the most eye-catching shades and then summarizing the moment with a vague inspirational quote no lengthier than 140 characters.

And by the time I'd finished, I would have missed it all. The regal bow of a lowering sun, the brilliance of an unfiltered horizon, the palpable depth of a sensation no single hashtag could ever describe.

A light breeze tickled the hair at the nape of my neck, and I turned my head toward the manor, feeling it again: the strangest desire to give up, to let go. Not only the dreams I'd once envisioned for my own life, but the dreams I'd had for this house, for this program, for a fundraiser that should have been a breeze given my platform and influence.

And yet . . . my efforts hadn't been enough.

Rarely did I sit in the tension between my plans and God's, between my wants and His, my way and His. Instead, I'd become an expert at throwing all my best efforts at problems bigger than myself and finding detours of escape without ever stopping to ask for guidance.

"I'm listening now, God." *Now that I have nothing left to give and nothing left to offer anyone.* My burdened shoulders sagged under the weight of that truth. "What do you want for this program? And what part am I supposed to play in it now?" I swallowed against the tightening in my throat, wishing I could go back in time and ask that of Him weeks ago.

Months ago.

Years ago.

Fresh humility fell over me as I rotated to view the entire property, silently pleading for God to intervene.

"Molly?"

I jumped at the sound of Glo's voice coming up behind me.

I whipped around and she put her hands up. "Sorry, hon.

Didn't mean to startle you, but we've been trying to track you down for nearly an hour. Finally had to resort to our security cameras."

"Have I really been out here for that long?" That didn't seem possible, and yet the sky was now a deep shade of violet, the grass shadowed in dusky gray and taupe.

"Not sure how long you've been out here." She smiled, something like mischief twinkling in her eyes. "But I do know your presence has been requested in the fireside room for a meeting with some very important people."

The levity of her tone and the hand she extended toward me came with a peace I'd been craving since the moment Ethan showed up at the front door. As I linked my arm through hers, I couldn't help but glance up at the darkened sky, begging God to tune my ears to whatever He was up to now.

◇◇◇

As I walked down the hallway toward the fireside room with Glo, Silas wasn't far behind us. Apparently, he'd received the same summons. He followed on the heels of a subdued Diego, his inquisitive expression much like my own.

Silas inclined his head to me. "You know anything about this?"

"Not a thing. Any luck on getting an extension on the Murphey Grant?"

He gave a resolved shake of his head, confirming what we both knew. We were out of time and out of options. Silas took my hand and lifted it to his mouth, sealing it with a kiss before letting it drop as our escorts walked ahead of us and entered the room. All sounds of shuffling feet ceased, and the hushed voices we could hear from the hallway dropped to a soft murmur.

The instant we cleared the doorway, we stopped, frozen in our tracks at the sight awaiting us.

Shoulder to shoulder, lining the entire back wall, were all twenty-two residents at The Bridge, each of them holding up a handwritten sign on white poster board. I read them one by one, from left to right, my heart pounding as their words drilled straight through my chest.

Devon: *Broke. No family.*

Monica: *High school dropout. Fear of homelessness.*

Amy: *Insecure. Bad relationships. No place to call home.*

Diego: *Addicted. No job. Sleeping in my car.*

Wren: *Grieving and afraid. No hope. No friends.*

As we neared the end of the line, reading and stepping our way down the row in silence, my hand hovered close to my heart, as if the action alone might soothe the ache. It didn't.

As we read the last sign, Monica gave a cue for everyone to flip their signs over, and I gasped, taking several steps back to read them all at once.

Wren: *No longer afraid. Enrolled in community college. Deep friendships.*

Diego: *Sober ten months. Mechanic school. Roommates like family.*

Amy: *Know my worth. Relationship with God. Thankful for my community.*

Monica: *Second year studying in PA program. Savings account. Security.*

Devon: *Part-time job. Full-time friends.*

Silas and I didn't move from our places on the carpet squares. But the way he cleared his throat and shifted his feet told me I hadn't been the only one affected by the powerful display of vulnerability and strength. Wren stepped forward, her shy smile as steady as her blue-eyed gaze. She focused on me.

"We understand why you say The Event has to be canceled. But you've also said our efforts deserve to be seen by the world. And that our voices deserve to be heard by people who could help our cause." She paused, looking at the others around her. "Each of us know kids our age who weren't fortunate enough to secure a home like this, or be in a program that helps them make a plan for their future. We think we can do something about that. Maybe it won't bring in as much as we could have raised with the fancy dinner, but we all have stories to tell about what our life was like before The Bridge and what it's like now. We want to ask you to help us share them—not some day in the future, but now, while we still have time."

Only, time was the one thing we didn't have. August thirty-first was only days away.

"Wow, this is . . . " I felt the weight of the room on my shoulders. On my heart. I studied each of their hope-filled faces, holding back a laugh-sob when Devon made pleading hands while he waggled his thick eyebrows in anticipation. But while I wanted nothing more than to say yes to them, and to create a special series post to promote each of their stories . . . I no longer had a platform to do so.

I looked at Silas, who seemed to be dealing with his own inner turmoil. No doubt he saw his oldest brother in each of these kids' signs. The Carlos who could have avoided much of his strife and addiction if only he'd been given a chance to thrive, a home that supported him the way The Bridge supported these twenty-two lives. But we both knew it couldn't happen like this. Not without a tried-and-true strategy, not without the use of a visible platform. Gaining any sort of traction on a single post would be next to impossible. It had taken me nearly three years to grow the kind of visibility these kids hoped to reach in days. Even for a glass-half-full thinker like me, I refused to be the one to fill them with false hope. Not again.

I swallowed and lifted my chin to address them all with the same courtesy and respect they'd addressed us with. This time I wouldn't let Silas be the deliverer of bad news. I was the one who had let them down, not him. I was the one who made promises I couldn't keep. "What you've done with these signs is powerful. A brilliant idea that should make you proud of your testimonies and of a program you've worked and succeeded in . . . but I'm afraid what you're asking can't be done. Not in so little time and not with so few resources. I don't have a platform I can access. I don't have hundreds of thousands of followers who can share your stories with the world and link to a donation account. Even if I had those things, the timing would still be tight to raise the funds we need by the deadline."

"I have five hundred followers," Monica said, stepping out and lowering her sign. "And I'm on a few study group pages for my classes at school. I can ask them all to share our posts, and they all have people who would share them, too. It's a great cause."

"And I have almost a thousand on my Instagram," Amy said. "And one of my old foster sisters has nearly four thousand. She's in a pop band."

"As of today," Devon said, glancing at his phone screen, "I have two hundred and thirty-six fans on TikTok. But that's only because I just signed up when I got my phone. I'm sure I can wrangle up more."

"See?" Wren pleaded. "We can do this if we all work together."

I glanced back at Silas, whose steadfast gaze was trained on the kids.

"I'm so sorry, I know how much this means to you all, but those numbers simply won't be enough to get us there."

"Would you say that to a waiting kid?" Diego asked, his voice tinged with tears. "Because if not for Silas going to bat for me after I failed my mechanic exam, I'd be back on that list. And I'd probably be living under a breezeway or in a friend's car. What's the harm in us trying? If not for The Bridge, every one of us could have been a statistic for homelessness, addiction . . . and worse."

My throat burned so badly I could barely speak. "I don't want to say no to you, Diego. I don't want to say no to any waiting teen on that list, but I . . . " And then, although I had no reason to pause, no reason to hesitate, I was suddenly out of words. Because my ears had heard it that time. The *I* in a sentence it had no right to be in. Because my answer wasn't only pointing to my lack of resources, it was pointing to my lack of faith. My lack of control. My lack of a calculated outcome.

These twenty-two kids who stood before me, these twenty-two kids who'd been beaten by life's hardships and trampled on by traumas I couldn't even imagine, were all willing to believe in the God who made the impossible possible. And why wouldn't they? Each of them was living it now. Each of them knew where they'd be without this house. Without this hope. Suddenly, their ask was so much bigger than a vision board or an off-the-page goal. Their ask was about lives being rescued and souls being saved from the prowling darkness of a world I'd only glimpsed from the safety of my cushy existence.

Not anymore.

"Molly?" Silas's tender voice drew my eyes up to his. "What do you think? Can you help them share their stories?"

The irony of the same man who'd once scolded me for posting a video from his lobby now asking me to link a video of his residents to an online fundraising campaign wasn't lost on me. Just like this moment. Just like this giant task before us.

And now, for an entirely different reason than when I'd first walked into this room, my heart began to pound and my palms began to sweat. I didn't know how it would all work out or if we'd even raise enough for a single mattress to be added to one of the cottages, but I did know what my answer had to be. Because I finally understood the question being asked. It wasn't about what I could give or what I could offer or what I could create in my own strength.

The real question, the bigger question, was about what God wanted to do with that waiting list of hurting kids—an answer, I realized, He'd never intended to come through my efforts alone.

Joy and determination rose within me. "I think I have no grounds to say no, especially since your online followers now outnumber mine by a hundred percent." Laughter bounced off the walls. "Let's do this."

Molly

If ever there was a need for a good under-eye concealer, it was today. Only there was no time for makeup routines or hair styling or any form of my usual Mandatory Recording Day Protocols. Filming had to begin within the next ninety minutes if we were going to be able to record, edit, post, and promote in time to get any kind of traction for our Bridge The Gap fundraising campaign. The night had been short and the morning had come early, and there were currently sixteen residents waiting for either me, Glo, or Clara to review their notes on what The Bridge had provided them during their time in the program.

While they had been preparing last night for their short on-camera testimonials today, I'd been researching with Val. She'd video chatted with me until the wee hours of the morning, propped on a soggy Chinese take-out box, providing moral support through my phone screen. What I wouldn't give to have her here with me in person today! Val was quite literally the savviest woman I knew. Even still, when you only had hours to research how to fundraise using social media . . . the results were limited at best. After we'd exhausted our efforts and our go-to resources on Google, the answer of how to pull this off had never been more clear: We needed a miracle sent on a two-day express from heaven.

"Molly?" Glo waved me over to the pretty garden area where she and Diego worked to set up the lights and tripod on the stage the way I'd instructed. "Can you explain about the angles again? Should the sun be in front of the interviewee or behind them?"

I opened my mouth to answer her, only to hear my name being called from somewhere behind me by Amy. The number of nervous tears that had already been shed this morning was at least five times greater than the cups of coffee I'd consumed.

Amy marched toward me, waving her notes in the air. "Monica and I have identical lines planned for our interviews—is that allowed? Does one of us need to change our testimony?"

"I'm sure there's a way we can tweak one of your lines to be a little diff—"

"Hey, Molly! I don't have a shirt without a logo on the front. Can you just, like, put one of those fuzzy stickers over my chest for the interview?" Devon strutted out of the guys' Bunkhouse, showing off his six-pack with what I was certain was a perfectly timed escapade, given the group of seven young women who stood not too far away from him.

I took a breath and held out my palms like a seven-year-old who still believed invisibility was a thing that could be achieved.

At that moment Silas stepped in front of me, gripping a to-go coffee cup with my name scrawled across the front. Goodness, how I loved this man.

"Okay, everyone," he said. "New rule. From this point on, if any of you has a question for Molly, you can run it past me first. We're on a tight production schedule today, and every delay costs us valuable time. Everyone understand?"

They answered with a unanimous "Yes, sir."

A mix of relief and renewed hope filled me as he offered me the coffee. "I thought you could use this."

I beamed up at him. Ever aware of our audience and their

prying eyes, I lowered my voice. "You make a strikingly handsome bouncer."

A slow smile crept over his face. "I aim to please."

Devon, who was standing just a few yards away, didn't let the moment go unnoticed. "Uh . . . is there some kind of purpling action going on here?" He waggled his finger between us.

I pursed my lips, heat flaring in my cheeks as Silas faced him and the rest of our curious onlookers. Truth be told, I was likely just as curious as they were to see how he planned to handle such a question.

"I think you all have more important matters to focus on today, Devon. Like putting on a shirt for starters."

"Is that your way of saying I'm right, then?" Devon tried, his eyes brightening as his gaze ping-ponged between me and Silas.

Monica and Wren shared a not-so-secret smile, while Glo did her best to hold in a laugh. A losing effort.

Silas glanced back at me, his eyebrow arching with a question meant only for me. I gave a single nod, trusting his judgment.

He backed up a step, took my free hand in his, and stared out at our rapt audience once again. "Like for many of you here, Molly has become an important person to me this summer—it's true." A sensation like feathers trailed down my neck and spine as Silas's pronouncement was met with obvious delight and excitement. "My hope in trusting you with this information is that you'd continue to show Molly the utmost respect as she continues to serve here at The Bridge."

A quiet chant trickled from the back, working its way up to the front, increasing in volume. "Kiss her! Kiss her! Kiss her!"

Silas gave a shake of his head as I bit my bottom lip. When he twisted around, I fully expected him to apologize for opening Pandora's box. But instead, he stepped in close, pulled me toward him, and planted a kiss square on my mouth, stunning the residents into near hyperventilation.

And me, too, for that matter.

"Now that we have that settled," Silas said through a smirk, "let's all get back to work. And, Devon," he said and pointed at the prankster, "*Shirt.* Now."

Devon whooped a reply as he jogged back to the guys' place.

I lifted my iced coffee to take a sip, but as I caught sight of Silas's devilish grin, I couldn't stop smiling long enough to complete the action. After mouthing the words *you're in big trouble*, I set the drink down and reached for the ten-pound binder of notes I'd taken with Val last night.

Just then the unmistakable sound of a young boy's voice at my back caused me to stop flipping pages and twist around. "Whoa! Is this place a castle or something? Does Harry Potter live here?"

The kid was so out of context, running through the east lawn at Fir Crest Manor and not telling jokes behind a screen, that I almost didn't recognize him. But I knew those freckles. And I knew that hair. And I knew that voice. "Tucker?"

He replied with a wild, toothy grin I'd seen a dozen times over the past three years. "Hey, Molly!"

If Tucker is here, then . . . I kept turning, my heart nearly bursting from my chest the second I spotted her closing the passenger door of an airport taxicab.

"Val?" But I was already sprinting toward her, already tossing my pink binder onto a mound of fresh mulch.

She pushed away from the cab, her balance a bit unsteady as she swung her purse over her shoulder and opened her arms for my incoming hug. A thousand emotions traveled through me at once. Val was here. *Here!* After three years of communicating long distance via every form of technology, we were both finally in the same place at the same time. In the flesh. And somehow, she was *tiny*—a miniature version of the woman I'd spoken to through a screen for so long. How did I not know she was so petite? The top of her head barely brushed the bottom of my chin. I loosened my bone-crushing embrace just long enough to squeal.

"You're here! You're actually here!"

She laughed that Tinker Bell laugh of hers. "Tucker was way too excited for his first plane ride for me to cancel, and his mommy had been looking forward to seeing her best friend in person for far too long."

I pulled her into another hug as Silas moved past me to retrieve her luggage from the trunk and tip the driver before Val even knew it had happened. Of course, I still wasn't sure how *any of it* had happened.

"Why didn't you ask us to pick you up?" I asked, trying to sound stern when instead I just sounded squeaky.

"We wanted to surprise you."

"Well, you succeeded! And it's the best surprise ever." I looped my arm through hers.

Miles couldn't call her Video Val any longer.

The sun reflected in her pale green eyes. "We're glad we can help. We know how important the next few days are—so please, put us to work however you need to. Tucker's a great help."

I laughed, because really, there were currently too many needs to name. After introducing her to Silas, whose arms were full of carry-on bags and checked luggage, I led her toward the campus, catching sight of Tucker breakdancing on the stage. He certainly wasn't shy.

"He'll fit in well here," Silas said with a chuckle as Val scrunched up her face.

"He's been awake since three this morning. I'm fully expecting him to crash hard by dinnertime."

As we maneuvered through the east lawn, I stopped to look at her, struck by a thought. "Val, we were on the phone last night till nearly one in the morning. I can't believe you caught such an early flight on so little sleep." It explained why she felt a bit shaky on my arm.

"I'm fine, just a bit stiff from all the traveling. Nothing caffeine and a few stretches won't fix. Oh—" She tugged on my sleeve, and I twisted to face her. "I think I found it, Molly. Last night. I found a strategy that might work for what we need to accomplish."

I narrowed my eyes at her. "After we hung up? Did you sleep at all before you boarded that plane?"

She waved away my concern. "It will take all of us working together at once, pushing and promoting from the new platform we create, but I think . . ." Val's eyes twinkled in that brilliant way of hers. "I think a collective launch is our best chance at gaining traction once we have a finished product and a live donation link."

I couldn't help but feel a giddy sense of awe. "I'm pretty sure you're the biggest answer to prayer we've had so far." I wasn't certain where Val stood on issues of faith, but her arrival wasn't coincidental. I knew that much for sure.

As a now shirt-wearing Devon strummed his guitar from under a nearby apple tree, and Monica and Amy squabbled about who would get to say the coveted line, and Diego and friends fiddled with the camera equipment and lighting props, I made a sweeping gesture with my arm for Val. "Welcome to The Bridge, where all your finest recording and editing dreams are about to come true."

◇◇◇

Turned out, Val had been right about two things: First, nine-year-old Tucker had crashed hard at approximately 6:00 p.m. after his third slice of cheese pizza. And second, the collective launch strategy she'd researched was not only our most viable option, it had quickly become our best option. If we were going to get this thing off the ground to attract mad cash from kindhearted donors by the cut-off date, we had just hours to do so.

And by *thing*, I meant the video clip currently under the editing knife of none other than my former assistant. Val had been on her laptop since the moment she arrived. Her fingers were numb, her eyes red-rimmed, and whatever stiffness she had tried to pass off as minor had certainly increased as the hours ticked on. Yet somehow, just past the stroke of midnight, while Tucker slept in my guest room, Silas worked on a spreadsheet, and I set up a brand-new platform entitled The Heart of The Matter, Val clicked the green button at the bottom of her edit screen: *Finalize*.

"It's ready," she said softly, tugging off her headphones and stifling a yawn. "Want to see it? I got the final cut down to four minutes, forty-seven seconds. And, of course, we'll have those five thirty-second teaser clips to share, too. I still have two more to finish up."

"You can finish those up tomorrow, Val," I said, stretching my neck side to side. "You need some sleep before the big day."

She twisted in my dining room chair and offered me a humble smile as if she knew she'd lose that argument if she tried. Silas and I set our laptops down and moved to the table where Val had set up camp. Her light chestnut hair was twisted in a topknot I'd seen a hundred times during our on-screen chats, and something about the sight of it caused nostalgia and gratitude to mist my eyes. Having her and Tucker here had brought an extra layer of fullness to my home, to my life, and I had no desire to let go of either of them any time soon.

I reached for Silas's strong hand as we stood behind Val's chair. Her pointer finger hovered over the play button as if she, too, knew how critical this moment was for us all. Because it was. This was our last chance at securing the Murphey Grant for The Bridge and for dozens of waiting young adults with nowhere to go.

Silas rubbed his thumb over my knuckles, his anticipation intertwining with mine.

The instant Val tapped the keyboard and those first three haunting piano notes trilled, emotion swelled inside me. I hadn't known the order Val would choose for the interview excerpts or even the stories she'd select for the main campaign video, but I trusted her creative instincts explicitly. This was her area to shine, her art, her brilliance. And it showed on every shot and on every perfectly captured expression. The way she played with time and focal points was astounding. Every spoken or typed word held impact for the viewer. I might have been the one to ask the questions and direct the residents while we recorded, but Val had woven all the random starts and stops into something profound and purposeful. We'd handed her a hope-filled idea, but she'd created a visual legacy.

Silent tears dripped off my chin as I listened to Diego retell his struggle with substance abuse and the months he'd spent in a cold car without a plan. And when Amy shared of running from her last group home, only to end up in a bad relationship with a man twice her age. And when Wren's unblinking gaze had stared into the eye of the camera lens as she described the day her brother was taken away from her after the death of their mother.

Silas tucked me into his side as we continued to watch the heart-wrenching montage. After Wren finished speaking, her face faded into a panoramic shot of Fir Crest Manor. The music morphed from the chilling solo notes of a lonely piano to the warmth and richness of a connected symphony. The footage we'd taken of the house, of the grounds and property, of the residents smiling and laughing outdoors while holding up their testimonial signs against a bright tangerine skyline, had been expertly spliced and arranged.

Silas had once described the moment he'd received the official approval to acquire Fir Crest Manor as the permanent location for The Bridge as *a miracle*. His word choice had stood out in my mind for weeks. Because Silas didn't inflate truth. He didn't speak in hyperbole. His vocabulary was as thoughtful as it was careful.

But now, seeing all the pieces come together in one place, enriched by color and sound and emotion, I understood. Each face represented a life transformed by a vision far bigger than anything Silas could have hoped for on his own. *Miracle* was the only word that could have described what had happened inside that old, dusty manor.

No, not just a manor, a home. One that equipped and supported, shepherded and loved. One that offered sanctuary in place of survival. And hope instead of heartache.

The current statistics that today's youth faced without a program like The Bridge faded in and out at the bottom of the screen. On the final slide, the donation link lingered long after the final sustained note of a cello played.

In the wake of an emotionally charged room, a reverent silence fell over us all.

Still nestled against Silas, I closed my eyes and prayed for tomorrow's collective efforts to succeed. For this four-minute, forty-seven-second video to have an impact. For the hurting, lost, and vulnerable to finally find a place to call home.

Do it again, God, my heart pleaded. *Give us a miracle.*

· 39 ·

Molly

It was incredible what happened when people banded together to fight for the good of others. Excitement pumped through me as I watched the fireside room overflow with volunteers of all ages and backgrounds to put their swiping fingers and devices to good use.

The premise for our Bridge The Gap Launch Day was simple enough: Anybody willing to give an hour of their time to share the campaign videos and donation links was welcome. As were their friends. And their friends of friends, too.

Naturally, Silas had worked out a schedule based on the research Val provided regarding the steady push we needed to build throughout the day and evening. And despite having a brand-new platform, The Heart of The Matter, I'd been surprised to find over two thousand followers waiting for me this morning—most of whom I recognized from an account formerly known as Makeup Matters with Molly. I could only hope their loyalty was stronger than my last five-star pick for ultra-hold hairspray.

While some of our participants today had committed to posting the campaign during their allotted time from home or carpool line or after-school study group, others had decided to join us here, in person, at Fir Crest Manor. It was a beautiful effort of solidarity for a cause worth far more than the ask.

Just before noon, Carlos showed up at the house with his mentor, Pastor Peter Rosario. And whether it was launch day nerves or the three shots of espresso I'd consumed before sunrise, the sight of Carlos standing next to Silas in a house built from the splinters of their childhood was enough to push me over the edge.

"Hi!" I said, sticking my hand out to him before Silas could even finish the introduction. "It's great to finally meet you, Carlos! Thank you both for coming, it means so much to us." I smiled at the line forming behind me: Jake, Clara, Glo. "Glo and a few of the residents baked muffins and cookies to share with our guests today, and there's coffee and juice, so please feel free to help yourselves."

"I've heard many good things about you, Molly." Carlos, who looked like a shorter version of The Rock, only with more hair and a more defined neck, had an accent that seemed to curl around each word he spoke. Most people here would likely suspect he and Pastor Rosario were hired as our security team, seeing as nobody in their right mind would try and get past them. Carlos arched a humorous eyebrow at Silas, then returned his attention to me. "My baby brother did not paint an adequate picture of your beauty. I think he could use less time at the dart board and more time studying poetry."

I blushed a thousand shades of flattered while Silas wrapped an arm around my waist.

"Thanks for that, Carlos," he deadpanned.

Peter laughed as Carlos slapped Silas on the back, putting the whole group at ease. While Wren and Devon waved me up to the stage for the big kickoff, Val gave me a thumbs-up as I reached the mic and looked out over the room. Incredibly, every round table was full. Friends, foster families, local clergy, past residents, teachers, and neighbors had all rallied to be here on such short notice, and the sight of them made my throat ache with gratitude.

I met Silas's eyes from across the room, wordlessly asking if he'd like to join me on stage as planned. But he simply dipped his chin for me to go ahead—a gesture of trust I'd never take for granted. "Welcome, everyone, to our Bridge The Gap Launch Day. We're thrilled you're here with us, and more than that, we're thrilled that you believe in a cause that's been near and dear to our hearts for . . ." I glanced at Silas, Carlos, and Jake, noting the unique trio of biological and adopted brothers they formed. "For years."

Reaching my arm out to the line-up of chairs filled by our residents at the side of the stage, I asked them to stand and introduce themselves. Each one of them had a part in the success of this day—whether keeping the refreshment trays filled, answering tech questions, or playing live music during the posting push.

I was just about to step down when Amy gestured to the projector screen over the fireplace. "Ah, yes, and as you can see, we've set up a place to monitor the donations as they come in throughout the day. This is a live counter, which is located at the bottom of the donation website."

A former foster mother from a neighboring town raised her hand. "What is the final goal?"

I did my best to keep my smile intact as I answered her. "We're hoping to raise five hundred thousand dollars to secure a matching grant for the expansion plan—" I took a breath but did not let my voice falter—"by tomorrow morning."

I couldn't decipher the chatter that hummed through the room at this announcement, but this wasn't a day for doubts. This was a day for miracles.

"I'm sure you'd all like to know a bit more about why we've asked you to come and what exactly we're asking you to share with your friends and followers to raise such an extravagant amount of money. . . . Well, I can make a pretty convincing case as to what The Bridge has done for our current twenty-two young adults in this room, and all the residents who've come before them, but I'd rather have them show you in their own words." I stepped off the stage and nodded at Val, who sat at the ready for this very moment.

As the lights dimmed and the video played, I held my breath and turned my gaze on the residents and volunteers instead of the screen. And even without the visual, emotion knocked against my ribs as I heard the sniffles and watched the tears being blotted from dozens of cheeks. I'd been confident it would have an effect, but this moment added even more fuel to the fire that burned inside us.

When the video was over, our residents hugged and fist-bumped and the volunteers applauded and stood as if the last four minutes and forty-seven seconds had been a Broadway production. The room buzzed with excitement and purpose.

Pride bloomed in my chest as Wren and Monica took their cue on stage, giving out Wi-Fi codes and the step-by-step instructions on the posting and sharing protocol we'd gone over early this morning. My eyes trailed to the screen above the fireplace, staring at the red train car on the donation tracker. As soon as it reached the destination, the color would change to black.

It was strange how different things felt on this side of things. I had a sudden image of the fundraising thermometer I'd seen a hundred times as a kid while my parents retold passionate stories of lost souls being saved in some of the poorest communities in America. Their testimonies had stirred the hearts of many, empowering a cause they believed in: opening church doors in economically challenged areas to reach underprivileged communities.

I placed a hand over my heart. Maybe I wasn't quite as different from them as I once believed.

"Hey, sorry I'm late." The familiar voice had me twisting to throw my arms around my brother. Like usual, his entrance had been perfectly timed.

"Hey, hey." Miles patted my back awkwardly. "Are you already emotional? I thought you'd be thrilled that you already have twenty grand showing up there. That's a great start. I need to hire you to do this for our missions teams. Of course, I can only pay you in apple fritters."

"I am thrilled." I beamed up at him and pushed away. "I'm just so happy you came."

"You know I'd never miss this."

I did know that.

A tap on my hip had me redirecting my attention from Miles to Tucker. He held up his iPad. "Look. My principal in Alaska just sent me this message after I sent her my mom's video."

Sure enough, there was a message waiting from a Mrs. Schultz with a donation of three hundred dollars. "Tucker, that's awesome. Good job sharing!"

Miles scrunched his eyebrows and inclined his head toward the nine-year-old in question.

"Oh, Tuck. This is my brother, Miles. He's my twin."

Tucker looked Miles up and down before reaching out his hand to shake. "Do you like baseball?"

"Not much. Do you?"

"Not at all."

Miles schooled his expression into focused concentration. "Do you like . . . basketball?"

"Still no," Tucker said matter-of-factly.

"Wall ball?"

"Never played it." Tucker's dry wit was intense.

"How about . . . the rodeo?"

Tucker's countenance brightened. "How'd you know?"

Miles shrugged, his eyes hovering on Tucker's cowboy hat. "Lucky guess."

I gave Tucker's hat a pat and pointed to the stage as Monica gave the all clear to start posting and Devon took the stage with his guitar and two buddies to provide ambiance as every participant in the room shared the campaign. "Hey, we're starting now, Tuck, so I need your help to watch and listen for questions, okay? Just like we talked about this morning."

He tipped his hat to me. "You got it."

Miles watched the boy march off with his iPad tucked up under his armpit. "Who is that kid?"

I narrowed my eyes at him, wondering how it could even be possible that I might have forgotten to mention the surprise arrival of my best friend. "Tucker is Val's son."

He rolled this news over in his brain. "Val, as in . . . *Video Val*?"

I swatted my brother's arm. "Yes, Video Val. And stop calling her that. She's real, and she's been an absolute saint since she arrived. I'm secretly hoping she forgets to go back home."

His eyes roved the room, and I grabbed his chin to redirect him to the petite woman sitting in the most Val-ish spot ever: a soundboard in the back corner of the room, surrounded by laptops and remote controls for various pieces of tech equipment I didn't even know the names of.

My brother said nothing as his gaze lingered on the target, yet something curious climbed into my subconscious at his silence. *What if . . .*

"Oh, I have something for you," he said, breaking my moment of wonder as he reached into his pocket and took out a piece of paper. "Here."

It was obviously a folded check. "Miles, is this—"

"It's not from me. Open it."

And when I did, I brought my hand to my mouth and squeezed my eyes closed, releasing a sob I had zero chance of concealing. It was a check written to The Bridge from John and Karen Mc-Kenzie. For $2,500.

"Stop that," Miles said. "You're gonna make my allergies start up."

I gawked at the figure, which to my parents was a sacrifice beyond my comprehension. "They can't afford this."

"They believe in what you're doing here—what you're all doing."

It was a sacrifice sown in faith . . . and in love. One I'd never, ever forget. "I'll call and thank them."

"I'm sure they'd like that." He smiled and looked around the room. "Now, where should I set up? I'll be posting the video to the church's platforms, as well."

"Seriously?"

"Yep. And hopefully a good amount of our members will share it, too."

As Miles found a place to work, following the directions the girls had written on the whiteboard, I took a moment to survey the room. Heads down, fingers tapping and typing, and lots and lots of happy faces.

Here we go, I thought, as I took out my own phone. Only four hundred seventy-seven thousand, two hundred dollars left to go.

◇◇◇

Nearly ten hours and 342 launch participants later, our race was nearing the thirty-five percent mark—a *huge* feat—and yet we still had a lot of ground to cover before morning. We'd cheered for every thousand-dollar mark our Little Engine That Could had passed and continued doing our best to blow up the internet with every new post and new share from our campaign launch page. Amazingly, The Heart of The Matter page had seen exponential growth—one hundred thousand new followers in a single day. I didn't even have time to wrap my mind around the wonder of that!

As the clock inched past 10:45 p.m., a handful of residents we'd deemed media admins for the event remained, scrolling through hundreds of online comments and answering pressing questions about the use of our funds, the matching grant, and our projected expansion timelines. Carlos and Peter had gone home for the night with a giant Ziploc bag of Glo's blueberry muffins, promising their assistance to us again whenever needed. And I had a feeling they'd be back soon. Given the lighthearted exchanges I'd observed throughout the day between Silas and Carlos, I was certain Silas hoped the same. Never would I have imagined that the very man who wrote those heartbreaking letters to his younger brother would have been such an important guest on this special day.

"Hey, Val? Where are we at on video views now? Over fifty thousand?"

When she didn't answer immediately, I popped my head up, blinking away the glare of my laptop screen. My friend wasn't in her little corner anymore but instead was crouched on the carpeted floor, where Tucker had curved his sleeping body into a C on an old beanbag chair. If he didn't look so pitifully uncomfortable, I would have laughed at the sight. I made my way over to her and watched as Val ran a hand over the side of his cheek.

"Hey," I said softly, touching her shoulder. "You guys should head out. It's late. Why don't you take my car back to my place?"

Val smiled up at me, looking just as exhausted as her son. We'd run them ragged from the moment they'd arrived. "Your car?" She huffed and tucked her hair away from her face. "I've never driven anything fancier than an early 2000s Honda. Besides, the international window is opening soon. We have another big push to start."

"I know, and I'll be fine holding down the fort so you can rest—look!" I gestured to the dozen-plus pajama-clad residents who'd decided to pull an all-nighter for the sake of the cause. "I have lots of fantastic helpers in here. Victory is in our grasp."

Val's smile wavered as Miles joined the conversation. "I'm actually about to call it a night myself. I'd be happy to drop you both off at Molly's, if you need a ride."

Val politely refused, but I didn't back down. "Come on, Val. He doesn't mind at all. My brother's favorite hobby is helping people." Something the two of them had in common. "Plus, Tuck deserves a real bed. He's been such a trooper all day."

Miles stared down at the boy with a curious expression. "He fixed my Wi-Fi connection issue earlier. He's a smart cookie."

"He is," Val said before tucking in her bottom lip, obviously debating her options.

"Why don't you plan to help us out remotely tonight, and that way Tuck can get a good night's sleep." And I hoped Val could get comfortable. I might have believed her stiff muscle excuse if I hadn't seen the way her balance seemed to come and go over the last twenty-four hours. But her quick deflection whenever I mentioned it made it obvious her limp wasn't a subject she wanted to discuss—not even with me.

She braced a hand on the chair seat next to her and pushed up, her arms straining under the effort as she worked herself to a standing position.

Val's gaze focused on my brother for the first time. "If it's really not a hassle for you, then we'd be grateful for a ride. Thank you."

"It's not," Miles and I said in tandem. He tilted his head and gave me a look that said *why are you being such a weirdo?*

While I helped pack up her laptop and supplies, Silas grabbed the tote near the soundboard and Miles bent down to collect the sleeping child.

Val immediately reached her arm out to stop him. "I can just wake him. You don't have to—"

But Miles had already lifted Tuck off the beanbag, the boy's head now resting on my brother's chest without disturbance. "I got him."

Val said nothing more as she followed the duo out to the parking lot.

Silas carried the tote of tech equipment to my brother's truck while Miles situated Tucker in the back seat. After a quick round of good-bye hugs, I leaned against the passenger side of my car and took a moment to breathe in the fresh air. Now that I didn't have a dozen residents looking to me as their cheerleader, I recalculated the reality of our funding needs. A sinking dread settled low in my belly as I worked the math over in my head. Twice.

We had less than ten hours and two hundred and eighty grand left to go. Even with the international push we planned to do overnight . . . that number was Goliath. We needed to do more. We needed to get creative.

I drummed my fingers against the cherry red paint of my car door, my thoughts going from zero to sixty in less than two-point-six seconds.

Much like my coveted Tesla.

Silas suddenly stepped right in front of me, his concerned eyes searching mine. "You realize that adrenaline and caffeine aren't a replacement strategy for sleep, right?"

"They'll have to be for tonight," I said as cheerily as possible. "We still have lots of ground to cover."

"Molly." He paused, exhaled. "Whatever happens tonight, I need you to know that I think you've done a—"

"No." I shook my head, cutting him off. "Please don't finish that. There will be no silver medals awarded for good participation. We're in this for gold, Silas. We're in this for the matching Murphey Grant and for the trustees' approval on a million-dollar expansion plan that will give a home to the kids who need it most. That's what we're fighting for, not a penny less. Please don't give up. Because I need you." It was hard enough to hide my fear from the kids, but I didn't want to hide from Silas. I needed him with me.

The doubt that lurked behind his beautiful dark eyes shifted into something far more pliable. Something I could work with. Because giving up wasn't an option.

"Do you know what time it is?" I asked.

"Eleven fifteen on the eve of August thirty-first," he said without missing a beat.

I swallowed back the creeping fear of a deadline that felt far too close. "Sounds like the perfect time for a miracle."

40

Silas

"Sounds like the perfect time for a miracle." Molly's words had been a shield against my doubts throughout the course of the night. Though I was a realist, she didn't need to be reminded of the deficit we fought as the hours ticked by. She needed a partner. She needed a hand to hold when her glass-full optimism sprung a leak.

Which, unfortunately, would be all too soon.

Sometime after six in the morning, as sunrise cut through the gaps in the blinds, my eyes cracked open for the first time in hours. Fifteen sleeping bodies were scattered in impossible positions around a room littered with pillows and blankets. My residents and staff who'd volunteered to hold an overnight campaign vigil in the fireside room—posting, commenting, sharing, and the like—had traded in the stiff metal chairs for sofas, recliners, and even the floor.

Though I hadn't slept soundly, or for longer than a few hours, my body was used to this time of day. It was used to the golden wash of a sun that had been commanded to rise no matter what had occurred the night before. Or, in our case, what hadn't occurred.

I didn't need to look at the final count to know the goal hadn't been reached, yet I did anyway. The red train had stalled out at three hundred twenty-two thousand, nine hundred and eight dollars. An incredible sum of money. A mountain in comparison to the molehill we'd started with. And yet . . . it wouldn't be enough to qualify for the Murphey Grant. Which meant it wasn't enough for the trustee board to approve a building project we couldn't afford.

I sighed, taking a moment to get my thoughts together. To be grateful for all the efforts made here yesterday and through the night. Even still, there was nothing I could do to prevent the dominoes from falling now.

We'd save every donation that came in by generous people, and we'd do everything we could to tighten our current budget . . . but without the matching grant, the possibility of an expansion plan would be years away.

I stood and stretched from my spot on the back wall, where I'd dozed on and off through the course of the night. Scanning the floor, I stepped over Devon and Tyler and the dueling guitars that had strummed song after song. My gaze stalled on the L-shaped sofa where Monica, Wren, and Amy had parked themselves for the night in odd angles. It was the same leather sofa that had been delivered to our lobby in early June without a name or a return address.

Donated by the same woman who was responsible for getting us sixty-two percent of the way to our funding goal.

Under a blanket, which looked as ragtag as the ottoman she used to prop her head on, slept the most tenacious woman I'd ever known. I'd been a fool to doubt the grit she possessed, because Molly McKenzie had grit. Enough to fight for a group of people who were rarely given the tools to fight for themselves.

Gingerly, I lowered myself to the floor and leaned my back against the ottoman beside her, closing the lid of her laptop to push it aside. The least I could do was protect her dreams while she slept. Though I knew exactly what she'd say if she were awake: "*We still have an hour left, Silas. You should have woken me!*"

But one hour or one day or even one week wouldn't matter if the timing wasn't right. And maybe that was the piece of the equation that had been off from the start. The timing. Had I rushed it? Had I heard wrong? Had I taken a leap when I'd only been meant to take a step?

"Hey, Duke of Fir Crest." Her sleepy voice shifted my eyes back to hers. She squinted against the light spilling over her delicate features. A sight I hoped to remember long after this moment passed. "You're awake?"

My laugh was no more than a rumble in my chest as I reached out to stroke her hair, her cheek. "It would appear you are, too."

She yawned and groggily rubbed at her eyes. The movement was slow and so unlike the hyperspeed she'd been operating at these last few days. She'd taken on my vision for this house, for these kids, for the brokenness in our world as if it had been her lifelong mission, as well. As if it were the only thing that ever mattered to her.

That thought, as well as so many others having to do with Molly, had me contemplating a timeline of an entirely different variety.

But first, I needed to address what she would be asking about as soon as—

With a sudden alertness, Molly snapped into action, digging into her pocket for her phone. "What's the time? How far are we now?"

"Molly."

My gut twisted the instant she saw it. The time. The dollar amount. The impossible gap that still remained.

I touched her arm, slid my hand down to her elbow. "Sweetheart, you've done an incredible job. I've never been prouder of anything or anyone in my life as I am of you and these kids."

She blinked as if she was still trying to sort something out, still trying to calculate an impossible victory.

"Wait. No, wait." She sat up straighter, tapping furiously on her screen to a site I didn't recognize. But her face broke into a smile that nearly cracked my heart in two. "There's more."

"More what?"

"Money. We have eighty-seven thousand dollars more than what our little train has accounted for."

I glanced up again at the projection screen that was still on, still live.

"How?" I asked with a skepticism I tried to tame. We only had one donation site advertised on the campaign link.

"Uh . . . it's from a private donor," she said almost as if it could have been a question and not a statement. Something wasn't adding up.

Before she could refuse, I swiped her phone from her grasp. A despicable move on my part, and yet her *uh* had been a red flag she couldn't unwave.

The second I flipped the screen around, all preconceived notions about what I might find were blotted out by the image of Molly's red Tesla, on an online auction, slashed by a digital SOLD sign. For $87,000.

I blinked down at her. "You sold your car."

"Yes." She lifted her chin slightly before launching into a monologue only Molly could produce on the spot. "I know it might seem crazy to you, Silas, but I couldn't have been talked out of it. It was the right thing to do. It's less than the Cobalt scholarship would have brought in, but it's still something. Something *I needed* to do. And I don't regret it. Not for a single second. Not even if . . ." She glanced up at the projector screen, her shoulders dropping as the math failed to add up to the end goal. "Not even if it didn't get us to the mark in time."

It hadn't, and yet, it wasn't the disappointment of an unmet goal that had captured my thoughts in this moment. It was the incredibly selfless woman in front of me.

I linked my hand in hers, rubbing my thumb along the soft skin of her wrist. "I love you," I said, studying the extravagance and depth of her eyes. "Even the crazy, impulsive parts of you that I don't always understand. Because those are the parts that have challenged me. That have changed me." I released the breath I'd been holding since before this campaign began. "I know there will be a lot of unknowns to come for us both in the future—in this program and in your career." Her gaze dipped to our joined hands. "But I don't want our relationship to be a part of those unknowns, Molly." I kissed the back of her hand. "I don't want you to doubt what I feel for you."

"And how do you feel?" she asked softly.

"Like I can't imagine a future that doesn't include you in it."

She moved her hands to the back of my neck. "Did Silas Whittaker just use the word *imagine*? Because I'm pretty sure he told me once that imagination wasn't his strong suit."

"That was the pre-Molly Silas."

"Ah, so then what does the post-Molly Silas imagine?"

I smiled down at her, more than willing to share that picture with her. "I imagine standing beside you as a partner. I imagine supporting you as a friend. I imagine encouraging you as a confidant. And I imagine loving you in all the ways a devoted husband would adore his wife." I kissed the tip of her nose. "How'd I do?"

Her breath came out shaky. "I'd definitely give you five stars."

I kissed her then, in a room where hope still remained in spite of uncertainty, challenges, and chances won and lost. Molly wrapped her arms around me, breaking our kiss to settle her head against my shoulder as we watched the rising sun together through the window. And even without her saying a word, I knew where her thoughts had traveled. It was impossible not to.

"It will be okay," I said, lowering my mouth to her ear and stroking her arm. "The kids will be okay. Everything we've raised so far, we'll invest it for the future. We can try for the Murphey Grant again." *In another five years* was what I didn't say.

She didn't reply for several minutes, though I knew her mind said much. "I really believed we would make it. I knew how big the number was, how impossible it seemed, but . . ."

"I know." I stretched out my legs, pressing her warmth even closer to me. "I know."

"It's hard not to question what we might have done differently. How much more we could have pushed."

I thought on her statement for some time, thinking back to the early days when Fir Crest Manor was being transformed into The Bridge. "I remember praying for the first kids in our program. Their needs felt so much bigger than what we were equipped for. The resources we had available in those early years were scarce."

Molly craned her neck to look at me. "How did you make it?"

I smiled, though at the time, I'd done anything but. "The only way we could—by taking one day at a time and continuing to trust God in the big and the small. This place has always been His. To grow and bless in His timing and in His way. It's a hard lesson, and one I've lived through repeatedly."

"But sometimes God's timing is brought through a miracle," Molly said in a way that called for a response.

"Yes, and I would never discount that. I've been the recipient of several miracles in my lifetime." I kissed her head. "You being one of them."

As Molly's lips angled for mine once again, a shrill scream cut through the silent room, jolting us both to our feet. Wren. Only whatever it was she was reacting to wasn't out of fear, not unless fear involved jumping up and down and waking up fourteen of her sleeping housemates.

"We did it! We did it!"

One by one, every pair of eyes in the room moved to the black train that had once been stalled out at sixty-four percent . . . which had somehow now registered at more than one hundred percent.

Molly clasped her hands over her mouth as disbelief settled over her face. She looked at me with a mix of shock and awe as the live donation site displayed nine minutes to spare.

"What?" she asked aloud to no one in particular. "But how . . . how can that be? We were short over ninety thousand dollars!"

A blurry-eyed Monica answered from across the room, tapping on her screen and holding it up as she read. "Looks like someone just donated a hundred thousand dollars seven minutes ago."

Molly twisted back to me, her expression far beyond overwhelmed.

"Silas . . ." was all she managed before she collapsed against me, her sob-laugh combo causing my own eyes to mist.

Holding her tight, I looked out at the awed, no-longer-sleepy faces of my residents and replied the only way I could. "Apparently, it was time for a miracle after all."

· 41 ·

Molly

A million questions pinged inside my skull at once as my phone vibrated from inside my back pocket. But it was impossible to concentrate, impossible to hold on to any one thought when the room was an explosion of cheers and joy in its rawest of forms. Someone had donated one hundred thousand dollars to our campaign in the last twenty minutes? But *who*?

I slid my phone out to investigate the name of the donor Monica had read from our campaign site—an A. S. R. Enterprises. Only the instant my screen brightened, the individual text boxes hovering from the top of my device stalled my swipe-happy fingers. Each sender's name blurred into the next as I read them through.

Val

Molly!!! Congratulations!!! I'm freaking out!!!

Oh my goodness! Did you see Felicity Fashion Fix donated 5K this morning?!?

Clara

Jake and I are totally crying right now! Thank you for everything you've done for the house! We love you!

Miles

Guess this means I'm buying the fritters . . .
😉 Proud of you.

Val

Tucker just asked if he can eat ice cream for
breakfast since we're all celebrating! 😋

Glo

I knew you'd do it, Kitten Heels!

Clicking out of the text messages and into my email inbox, my heart thudded in response to the question that hovered just beneath my fingertips. I gestured for Silas to follow me out of the happy chaos and into a place where we could focus.

Silas wasn't far behind me. "What is it?"

I held my phone out between us, showing him the subject line on an email that had just been sent to me via our mystery donor. I clicked into it.

To: Molly McKenzie
From: A. S. R. Enterprises
Subject: Bridge The Gap Campaign

Molly,

Congratulations on reaching your campaign goal this morning! What a moving and inspiring video. My husband, Al, and I have wanted to do more for this specific group of young adults for some time now. Four years ago, we opened a one-for-one model business called Basics First, which provided backpacks to teenage foster kids in need of personal supplies like toiletries and hygiene products mostly. But to be honest, we've done very little with it since then. Between raising our own family and the high demands of our careers, it's been a difficult vision to get any real traction on.

Your campaign jumpstarted some big conversations around our house last night, and we're wondering if you and your team would be open to a brainstorming session regarding an opportunity that might dovetail nicely with what you're already doing. Any chance you might have a few minutes for a video chat today?

XOXO,
Sophia (and Al) Richards

"Sophia Richards." I breathed her name as Silas continued to stare at the email in my inbox. "Sophia Richards just donated a hundred grand to our program."

Silas threaded his hands behind his neck, releasing a breath that reverberated in the empty lobby. "And it sounds like that's not all she has planned."

I bit my bottom lip in anticipation. "What do you think the opportunity is?"

"Molly," he laughed. "Whatever I thought I knew about the business world went to the wayside the minute you joined our ranks. There's no telling what she wants to brainstorm with you."

As I hit the reply tab, I gasped at the time. "Silas! You need to call the Murphey Grant Foundation."

"I already forwarded a screenshot of our final standing to my contact at the foundation, and another one to the trustee board for The Bridge." His lips curled into a lopsided grin. "We secured the match, Molly. The expansion is actually going to happen." He shook his head. "We did it."

We did it. Three words that didn't seem plausible, much less possible, even an hour ago. And yet . . . and yet here we were. We'd met our goal, secured the matching Murphey Grant, reached a total of a million dollars, and had finally received the green light to start the expansion Silas had dreamed of when he'd first acquired Fir Crest Manor five years ago.

"Just a little bit outrageous if you ask me," I teased.

Silas laughed. "Just a bit."

◇◇◇

Whatever church meeting had been on Miles's schedule for this morning must have ended early, because he was now standing in the lobby of Fir Crest Manor with Val, Tucker, and four dozen apple fritters from Deb's Bakery.

"We brought donuts," Tucker announced, looking as if he'd already consumed more sugar than his nine-year-old body could process. "Miles let me eat mine in his truck. Mom never lets me do that."

Val looked past her son and opened her arms to me. "Congratulations! I'm so happy for you all."

"We couldn't have done it without you, Val."

Silas stepped to my side. "Molly's right. You played a huge part in all this. We're very grateful you were here to help us." He placed his hand on my lower back, and I noted that the gesture was not lost on my brother.

I moseyed toward Miles and the stack of boxes in his arms. "Mind if I have one of these congratulatory fritters before you take them to the kitchen?"

Miles popped the lid off the top box and bent for me to take my pick.

I made a contemplative sound in the back of my throat and then looked at Tucker, who seemed as excited for me to pick a donut as he'd been about eating one in my brother's truck. "Tucker, I have a question for you. How many donuts do you think I should be allowed to choose if I have *three* super special things to celebrate today?"

"Three. Definitely three." Not even a second of hesitation. "Is today your birthday, Molly?"

"Nope," Miles and I answered at the same time.

Val looked between us. "So then what are the other two things?"

I smiled back at Silas, who was already shaking his head at my fun. "The first," I said, plucking out my favorite, a fritter with a dried pool of crackling white glaze around the edges, "is that Silas and I had a conference call with Sophia Richards and her husband this morning. And the four of us discussed a very intriguing opportunity."

"Sophia Richards," Val repeated slowly. "As in . . . *the* Sophia Richards?"

"Exactly."

"I don't understand. What kind of opportunity? Is she wanting to collaborate with you on The Heart of The Matter? I can't believe how quickly that platform is growing—you already have more than three hundred thousand followers. In just over thirty-six hours. That has to be some sort of new record."

I smiled at her enthusiasm. "I do believe she'll be involved in that after I spend a bit more time brainstorming the new vision, but that's not actually why she called." I'd need to set some significant time aside to think and pray on how best to approach my new platform, how to be true to the woman God made me to be and also give back to a community I'd grown to love. "But it turns out, the Richardses were our not-so-anonymous, eleventh-hour miracle donors this morning. Their generosity pushed us over the edge. And then some."

"Seriously?" Val's face was glowing, and I was glad I'd waited to share this information until I was face-to-face with her.

Silas cleared his throat and raised an eyebrow at me. "As did other generous last-minute donations."

But I refused to give in to his bait to reveal the Tesla sale and instead nodded again at Val. "The Sophia Richards and her husband have been sitting on a business idea they've had for some time, an idea that supports the one-for-one model we've seen in other successful companies with a humanitarian cause. This plan has a similar marketing strategy to Sophia's monthly subscription box for The Fit Glam Kit, but with an added benefit: For every new product box she sells, she wants to donate a box of basic supplies to kids who've aged out of group homes or foster families across the U.S. They're essentially starter kits containing towels, sheets, shampoo, conditioner, toiletries, and the like. And . . ." I had to bite back the emotion threatening to creep up. "They want their employees to be the same individuals these one-for-one packages are meant to help. Their vision is for their employees to pack and assemble each consumer box for shipping, possibly even personalize them somehow, to both educate and encourage our world about this huge need in our nation. In the meantime, they will be equipped with on-site job training skills." A point Silas had made during our call that had both Al and Sophia jazzed with excitement. "They have a ton in the works already . . . they were just missing a few key components."

"Not to interrupt your stellar storytelling abilities, sis," Miles said with his usual lick of humor, "but this tower of donuts is making it difficult to focus on all the details. Would anybody care to point me in the direction of the kitchen so I can drop these off?"

"Oh, perfect timing," Glo said, smiling ear-to-ear as she rounded the intersection of the hall and lobby. "I can take those from you. I was just on my way back to the kitchen. What a thoughtful gesture."

"Can I help?" Tucker asked his mom, his eyes focused on Glo.

"I could certainly use a helper with muscles as strong as yours."

Tucker flexed. "I do have strong muscles. See?" Miles passed two boxes to Glo and gave the other two to Tucker—after giving his tiny bump of a bicep a squeeze and then shaking his hand out, as if he was injured.

Tucker laughed and followed after Glo.

Val's gaze seemed to linger on my brother for an extra beat before she refocused. "That's all really incredible. What components are they still missing?"

I shared a glance with Silas. "A connection to a program like the one Silas has directed for the last five years. And a few dedicated team members they could trust to operate it."

Silas slipped his hand in mine. "That's about the time they asked if Molly would consider working as their Chief Marketing Officer." I smiled back at him, still in a daze at God's abundant faithfulness.

"Seriously?" Miles focused in on me. "Is that something you could do remotely?"

"Yes and no." I beamed. "While a lot of marketing can be done online, they'll have a physical location as well. A warehouse they'll want me to check in on and oversee."

I could see Miles speeding ahead and connecting the dots. "You're talking about here. Something in our area."

"They're calling their real estate agent now." A production

warehouse in Spokane would be far more affordable than one in Orange County. Plus, it would mean our residents at The Bridge would be the first benefactors of such a generous company. A plan that couldn't be more custom fit to the one Silas had dreamed of for graduating residents at the house.

"Sis, that's awesome." Miles pulled me into a hug.

"But," I said, breaking out of Miles's hold to deliver the kicker to Val. "I told them that I could only accept such a position if they offered me a package deal, with one Val Locklier."

The instant my words registered, Val shook her head. "But, Molly, I haven't worked as your assistant in months now—"

"Which is why I didn't tell them you were my assistant. I told them you were my business partner."

Her mouth hung open as she stared me down. "Molly . . . I don't even, I'm not sure what to even say."

"Say you'll think about it." I rushed to take her hands in mine. "I know your folks are still in Alaska, but you could make a good life here, Val. For you and Tucker. There are some great schools for Tuck, and you could live with me until we find you a place you love. I have every reason to believe Sophia would offer you a very reasonable wage."

"I was impressed by Sophia's attention to detail," Silas added generously. "She's very thorough."

"I'm sure I could ask around, too. As far as availability on local properties go," Miles said. "There are quite a few real estate brokers at the church."

Though Val looked absolutely flabbergasted, I didn't miss the glint of excitement in her eyes. Perhaps it was time for her to start a new adventure.

"Was that two out of three?" my brother asked. "Since you made your job offer a package deal with Val?"

"You've always been so good at math, Miles." I smiled at him, and he promptly rolled his eyes. "Which is going to come in quite handy, since we're going to be recruiting a lot of free help soon."

Val and Miles shared a questioning glance, then immediately looked away from each other.

I nudged Silas. After all, this should be his news to share, especially since he hadn't stopped smiling since the president of the trustee board had called to congratulate him. "If all the necessary permits get approved on time, it looks like we'll be breaking ground sometime next spring."

At the sight of their stunned faces, another round of hugs ensued, which quickly multiplied into a mob when several residents rushed in to join our celebration a few minutes later. And as I stood in their midst, enjoying the exuberance of so many people I loved sharing the same space, I couldn't help but think that this impromptu, spontaneous moment was a billion times better than the fancy black-tie event I'd spent months planning.

I felt a pressure at my back and then a familiar whisper in my ear. "Do you know what I never imagined?" Silas wrapped his arms around me and held me close. "That the woman who came into my office with all her sparkle and grit would be the same woman I'd want to write all my future off-the-page goals with."

I spun toward him and hooked my hands around the back of his neck, smiling as I recalled my words to Silas that spring day not so long ago. "That's good, because the only thing I like better than making goals is crushing them."

The End

Acknowledgments

God: Even in the midst of a global shutdown, your constant love and strength sustained me throughout the writing (and apple-fritter eating) of this book. Thank you for your many, many promises to me and to all your beloved children.

Tim, my self-proclaimed number one fan for eighteen years and counting: Thank you for destroying all records of the apple fritters I purchased and consumed during my 2020 writing deadline. "What happens in a global shutdown, stays in a global shutdown." And thank you, as always, for remaining a constant example of the kind of love I pray our children find with their spouses one day . . . but not a day before they turn twenty-five, of course. Haha! I love, love, love you.

Preston, Lincoln, Lucy: Mommy loves and appreciates you all. Thank you for yet another crazy deadline season where you've shown me patience and grace beyond your years. I adore each of you.

Connilyn Cossette and Tammy Gray: There are never enough words to explain just how much your support and love have meant to me through the years—and through the dozen or so full-length drafts we've shared and critiqued for one another so far. If not for you, my loyal writing sisters, I would have lost my joy of first chapters and happy endings long ago. Some may think I'm exaggerating (which I may be prone to do from time to time 😊), but as Molly and Miles would say, "Reverend."

Coast to Coast Plotting Society: A huge thank-you to my girls—Amy Matayo, Christy Barritt, Connilyn Cossette, and Tammy Gray. Our annual plotting retreat is my favorite week of the year (unless it's the year I finally get to go to Ireland . . . but you know what I mean). Each time we're together, my gratitude for your input in my books and in my life increases tenfold. Thank you for being my people.

Kristin Avila, a.k.a The Story Queen: Thank you for answering my panicked phone call that cold day in April when I needed your story expertise (and a swift kick in the behind) the most. I'm so very, very thankful for your friendship (though I still abhor the 1,824 miles between us). And thank you (and Dan) for guiding me in the ways of the Enneagram One hero. "Super Silas" is forever in your debt.

A special thanks to Sarah Loudin Thomas: Thank you so much for returning my call last summer when I was feeling a bit lost on how to solve a few logistical issues I'd created by hosting a privately run program (like The Bridge) at a co-ed campus (like Fir Crest Manor). Your professional insight, compassionate heart, and overall expertise in this field became the foundation blocks of my novel. Your helpful problem-solving that day (along with several pages of notes I took while you answered my many questions!) allowed me to write *All That Really Matters* with confidence. (And, naturally, any mistakes or oversights I may have made while drafting this fictional story are mine and mine alone.) You're awesome, Sarah!

Rel Mollet, my precious author assistant and friend: Our weekly (sometimes daily!) video chats with each other are some of my most special treasures. You are one of the most admirable and self-less people I know, and you truly make the world a better place by the grace and kindness you extend to all. Thank you for the many, MANY ways you've helped me promote, market, and launch my books over the years. And thank you, especially, for the legal jargon help you provided when it came to Silas and all the lawyer-y, contract-y stuff. Enneagram Ones keep us all in order!

Our Life Group (Real Life Ministries, Post Falls, Idaho): Santha Yinger, Jeff and Bobbi Deitz, and Jan and Joanie Schultz. Tim and I are so blessed to have you as our community and as our friends. We love you.

My Book Nook and Early Readers Friends: Thank you for ALL the ways you inspire me to keep writing by sharing your love of reading with the world. A special thanks to Kacy Gourley, Lara Arkin, Renee D'Anna, Jessica Wardell, Joanie Schultz, Kedron Annotti, and Rel Mollet.

Jessica Kirkland at Kirkland Media Management: For all the years we've walked this journey together, thank you. Your *grit* and determination would make Molly proud. I love you.

Bethany House Publishers: It's an honor to be a part of the BHP family. Thank you again for the G-O-R-G-E-O-U-S cover! I'm still trying to convince Tim to let me hang it above the mantel in a poster-size frame—guess we'll see who wins that one. Truly, though, it's my favorite cover yet. A special thanks to my editors Raela Schoenherr and Sarah Long. Your expertise, suggestions, and story insights ALWAYS serve to improve my craft as a writer and as a storyteller. I'm so grateful for you both.

Look for
Miles and Val's story
in Spring 2022!

Val Locklier has always struggled to keep her balance in life, but after agreeing to a cross-country move to be near her best friend, a solid foundation might finally be within her reach. Meanwhile, the ever-steady Miles McKenzie, the pastor who thrives on helping others to solid ground, can't seem to find his own footing when everything he stands for is shaken to the core.

Nicole Deese's nine humorous, heartfelt, and hope-filled novels include the 2017 Carol Award–winning *A Season to Love*. Her 2018 release, *A New Shade of Summer*, was a finalist in the RITA, Carol, and INSPY Awards. When she's not working on her next contemporary romance, she can usually be found reading one by a window overlooking the inspiring beauty of the Pacific Northwest. She lives in small-town Idaho with her happily-ever-after hubby, two rambunctious sons, and a princess daughter with the heart of a warrior. Find her online at www.nicoledeese.com.